Pirates

Swashbuckling Stories from the Seven Seas

Pirates

Swashbuckling Stories
from the Seven Seas

edited by Jennifer Schwamm Willis

Thunder's Mouth Press
New York

PIRATES: *Swashbuckling Stories from the Seven Seas*

Compilation copyright © 2004 by Jennifer Schwamm Willis
Introduction copyright © 2004 by Jennifer Schwamm Willis

Published by
Thunder's Mouth Press
An Imprint of Avalon Publishing Group Inc.
245 West 17th Street, 11th floor
New York, NY 10011

AVALON
publishing group incorporated

Library of Congress Cataloging-in-Publication Data is available.

ISBN: 1-56025-616-8

Book design: Michael Walters
Printed the United States of America
Distributed by Publishers Group West

For my beautiful son Harper
A graceful and intrepid voyager

Table of Contents

Introduction

I f you've opened this book, pirates intrigue you. You may not know much about them, or you may be intimately familiar with the literature inspired by those rogues and scoundrels who roved the sea in search of riches and adventure. Maybe when you were little you dressed up as a pirate at every opportunity. Maybe you get up when everyone else is asleep and dance around the house with a make believe sword in your hand, leaping from one piece of furniture to the next like a pirate boarding a Spanish galleon. As for me, at the age of 45 I got myself a little tattoo and a small gold nose ring.

Why do pirates and their stories enthrall us? What is it about these rakes that speaks to us, even though we know they often behaved very badly indeed? I think we love them because they lived outside convention, with no patience for the often restrictive and repressive social hierarchy of their times. They forsook security for risk, and social position for camaraderie. The sea was unpredictable, always changing and moving beneath them. They had to learn to live in the moment, to be keenly aware of what was actually happening at any given instant. They had to be adaptable—quick-witted and quick on their feet. In a world where birth determined social class, and class boundaries were utterly rigid, a pirate's life offered a man (and the occasional woman!) the chance to live as an equal among comrades. A pirate's life was a brutal and dangerous one, but it offered a measure of personal freedom denied to the common man.

Pirates spent much of their lives in pursuit of treasure, but I like to think their pursuit was about more than gold. It was about the excitement of not knowing what lay around the next island or across the wide expanse of the ocean; it was about not knowing what the next day would hold. This sense of possibility and mystery is what I love about pirate lore.

We don't have to be pirates to break free of the constraints that prevent us from listening to our hearts and giving reign to our imaginations. When we sense that freedom we will find that there is a bounty of joy and wisdom to be uncovered through our experiences in this vast and ever-changing world. When we open to the possibilities for freedom and adventure in our own lives we will find ourselves rich beyond Blackbeard's wildest dreams.

—*Jennifer Schwamm Willis*

from

The Coral Island

by R.M. Ballantyne (1825–1894)

Three boys—Jack, Peterkin and Ralph—are shipwrecked
on a coral reef in the South Seas. After many long months
they spy a schooner heading for the island, and rejoice in
their imminent rescue. But to their horror they discover as
it draws near that the ship flies the skull and crossbones.

One day we were all enjoying ourselves in the Water
Garden, preparatory to going on a fishing excursion; for Peterkin had
kept us in such constant supply of hogs that we had become quite tired
of pork, and desired a change. Peterkin was sunning himself on the
ledge of rock, while we were creeping among the rocks below. Happening to look up, I observed Peterkin cutting the most extraordinary
capers and making violent gesticulation for us to come up; so I gave
Jack a push, and rose immediately.

'A sail! a sail! Ralph, look! Jack, away on the horizon there, just
over the entrance to the lagoon!' cried Peterkin, as we scrambled up
the rocks.

'So it is, and a schooner, too!' said Jack, as he proceeded hastily to dress.

Our hearts were thrown into a terrible flutter by this discovery, for if it should touch at our island we had no doubt the captain would be happy to give us a passage to some of the civilized islands, where we could find a ship sailing for England, or some other part of Europe. Home, with all its associations, rushed in upon my heart like a flood, and, much though I loved the Coral Island and the bower which had now been our home so long, I felt that I could have quitted all at that moment without a sigh. With joyful antici- pations we hastened to the highest point of rock near our dwelling, and awaited the arrival of the vessel, for we now perceived that she was making straight for the island, under a steady breeze.

In less then an hour she was close to the reef, where she rounded to, and backed her topsails in order to survey the coast. Seeing this, and fearing that they might not perceive us, we all three waved pieces of coconut cloth in the air, and soon had the satisfaction of seeing them beginning to lower a boat and bustle about the decks as if they meant to land. Suddenly a flag was run up to the peak, a little cloud of white smoke rose from the schooner's side, and, before we could guess their intentions, a cannon shot came crashing through the bushes, carried away several coconut trees in its passage, and burst in atoms against the cliff a few yards below the spot on which we stood.

With feelings of terror we now observed that the flag at the schooner's peak was black, with a death's head and cross-bones upon it. As we gazed at each other in blank amazement, the word 'pirate' escaped our lips simultaneously.

'What is to be done?' cried Peterkin, as we observed a boat shoot from the vessel's side, and make for the entrance of the reef. 'If they take us off the island, it will either be to throw us overboard for sport, or to make pirates of us.'

I did not reply, but looked at Jack, as being our only resource in this emergency. He stood with folded arms, and his eyes fixed with a grave, anxious expression on the ground. 'There is but one hope,' said he, turning with sad expression of countenance to Peterkin; 'perhaps, after all, we may not have to resort to it. If these villains are anxious to take us, they will soon overrun the whole island. But come, follow me.'

Stopping abruptly in his speech, Jack bounded into the woods, and led us by a circuitous route to Spouting Cliff. Here he halted, and, advancing cautiously to the rocks, glanced over their edge. We were soon by his side, and saw the boat, which was crowded with armed men, just touching the shore. In an instant the crew landed, formed line, and rushed up to our bower.

In a few seconds we saw them hurrying back to the boat, one of them swinging the poor cat round his head by the tail. On reaching the water's edge, he tossed it far into the sea, and joined his companions, who appeared to be holding a hasty council.

'You see what we may expect,' said Jack, bitterly. 'The man who will wantonly kill a poor brute for sport will think little of murdering a fellow-creature. Now, boys, we have but one chance left—the Diamond Cave.'

'The Diamond Cave!' cried Peterkin; 'then my chance is a poor one, for I could not dive into it if all the pirates on the Pacific were at my heels.'

'Nay, but,' said I, 'we will take you down, Peterkin, if you will only trust us.'

As I spoke, we observed the pirates scatter over the beach, and radiate, as if from a centre, towards the woods and along the shore.

'Now, Peterkin,' said Jack, in a solemn tone, 'you must make up your mind to do it, or we must make up our minds to die in your company.'

'Oh, Jack, my dear friend,' cried Peterkin, turning pale, 'leave me; I don't believe they'll think it worth while to kill me. Go, you and Ralph, and dive into the cave.'

'That will not I,' answered Jack quietly, while he picked up a stout cudgel from the ground. 'So now, Ralph, we must prepare to meet these fellows. Their motto is, "No quarter". If we can manage to floor those coming in this direction, we may escape into the woods for a while.'

'There are five of them,' said I; 'we have no chance.'

'Come, then,' cried Peterkin, starting up, and grasping Jack convulsively by the arm, 'let us dive; I will go.'

Those who are not naturally expert in the water know well the feelings of horror that overwhelm them, when in it, at the bare idea of being held down, even for a few seconds—that spasmodic, involuntary recoil from compulsory immersion which has no connection whatever with cowardice; and they will understand the amount of resolution that it required in Peterkin to allow himself to be dragged down to a depth of ten feet, and then, through a narrow tunnel, into an almost pitch-dark cavern. But there was no alternative. The pirates had already caught sight of us, and were now within a short distance of the rocks.

Jack and I seized Peterkin by the arms.

'Now, keep quite still, no struggling,' said Jack, 'or we are lost.'

Peterkin made no reply, but the stern gravity of his marble features, and the tension of his muscles, satisfied us that he had fully made up his mind to go through with it. Just as the pirates gained the foot of the rocks, which hid us for a moment from their view, we bent over the sea, and plunged down together head foremost. Peterkin behaved like a hero. He floated passively between us like a log of wood, and we passed the tunnel and rose into the cave in a shorter space of time than I had ever done it before.

Peterkin drew a long, deep breath on reaching the surface; and in a few seconds we were all standing on the ledge of rock in safety. Jack now searched for the tinder and torch, which always lay in the cave. He soon found them, and, lighting the torch, revealed to Peterkin's wondering gaze the marvels of the place. But we were too wet to waste much time in looking about us. Our first care was to take off our clothes, and wring them as dry as we could. This done, we proceeded to examine into the state of our larder, for, as Jack truly remarked, there was no knowing how long the pirates might remain on the island.

'Perhaps,' said Peterkin, 'they may take it into their heads to stop here altogether, and so we shall be buried alive in this place.'

'Don't you think, Peterkin, that it's the nearest thing to being drowned alive that you ever felt?' said Jack with a smile. 'But I've no fear of that. These villains never stay long on shore. The sea is their home, so you may depend upon it that they won't stay more than a day or two at the furthest.'

We now began to make arrangements for spending the night in the cavern. At various periods Jack and I had conveyed coconuts and other fruits, besides rolls of coconut cloth, to this submarine cave, partly for amusement, and partly from a feeling that we might possibly be driven one day to take shelter here.

We found the coconuts in good condition, and the cooked yams, but the bread-fruits were spoiled. We also found the cloth where we had left it; and, on opening it out, there proved to be sufficient to make a bed; which was important as the rock was damp. Having collected it all together, we spread out our bed, placed our torch in the midst of us, and ate our supper. It was indeed a strange chamber to feast in; and we could not help remarking on the cold ghastly appearance of the walls, and the black water at our side, with the thick darkness beyond, and the sullen sound of the drops that fell at long intervals from the roof of the cavern into the still water; and the strong contrast between all this and our bed and supper, which, with our faces, were lit up with the deep red flame of the torch.

We sat long over our meal, talking together in subdued voices, for we did not like the dismal echoes that rang through the vault above when we happened to raise them. At last the faint light that came through the opening died away, warning us that it was night and time for rest. We therefore put out our torch and lay down to sleep.

On awaking, it was some time ere we could collect our faculties so as to remember where we were, and we were in much uncertainty as to whether it was early or late. We saw by the faint light that it was day, but could not guess at the hour; so Jack proposed that he should dive out and reconnoitre.

'No, Jack,' said I, 'do you rest here. You've had enough to do during the last few days. Rest yourself now, and take care of Peterkin, while I go out to see what the pirates are about. I'll be very careful not to expose myself, and I'll bring you word again in a short time.'

'Very well, Ralph,' answered Jack, 'please yourself, but don't be long;

and if you'll take my advice you'll go in your clothes, for I would like to have some fresh coconuts, and climbing trees without clothes is uncomfortable, to say the least of it.'

'The pirates will be sure to keep a sharp look-out,' said Peterkin, 'so, pray, be careful.'

'No fear,' said I; 'good-bye.'

'Good-bye,' answered my comrades.

And while the words were yet sounding in my ears, I plunged into the water, and in a few seconds found myself in the open air. On rising, I was careful to come up gently and to breathe softly, while I kept close in beside the rocks; but, as I observed no one near me, I crept slowly out, and ascended the cliff a step at a time, till I obtained a full view of the shore. No pirates were to be seen—even their boat was gone; but as it was possible they might have hidden themselves, I did not venture too boldly forward. Then it occurred to me to look out to sea, when, to my surprise, I saw the pirate schooner sailing away almost hull down on the horizon! On seeing this I uttered a shout of joy. Then my first impulse was to dive back to tell my companions the good news; but I checked myself, and ran to the top of the cliff, in order to make sure that the vessel I saw was indeed the pirate schooner. I looked long and anxiously at her, and giving vent to a deep sigh of relief, said aloud: 'Yes, there she goes; the villains have been baulked of their prey this time at least.'

'Not so sure of that!' said a deep voice at my side; while, at the same moment, a heavy hand grasped my shoulder, and held it as if in a vice.

My heart seemed to leap into my throat at the words; and, turning round, I beheld a man of immense stature and fierce aspect regarding me with a smile of contempt. He was a white man—that is to say, he was a man of European blood, though his face, from long exposure to the weather, was deeply bronzed. His dress was that of a common seaman, except that he had on a Greek skullcap, and wore a broad shawl of the richest silk round his waist. In this shawl were placed two pair of pistols and a heavy cutlass. He wore a beard and moustache, which, like the locks on his head, were short, curly, and sprinkled with grey hairs.

'So, youngster,' he said, with a sardonic smile, while I felt his grasp tighten on my shoulder, 'the villains have been baulked of their prey, have they? We shall see, we shall see. Now, you whelp, look yonder.' As he spoke, the pirate uttered a shrill whistle. In a second or two it was answered, and the pirate boat rowed round the point at the Water Garden, and came rapidly towards us. 'Now, go, make a fire on that point; and hark'ee, youngster, if you try to run away, I'll send a quick and sure messenger after you,' and he pointed significantly at his pistols.

I obeyed in silence, and as I happened to have the burning-glass in my pocket, a fire was speedily kindled, and a thick smoke ascended into the air. It had scarcely appeared for two minutes when the boom of a gun rolled over the sea, and, looking up, I saw that the schooner was making for the island again. It now flashed across me that this was a ruse on the part of the pirates, and that they had sent their vessel away, knowing that it would lead us to suppose that they had left altogether. But there was no use of regret now. I was completely in their power, so I stood helplessly beside the pirate watching the crew of the boat as they landed on the beach. For an instant I contemplated rushing over the cliff into the sea, but this I saw I could not now accomplish, as some of the men were already between me and the water.

There was a good deal of jesting at the success of their scheme, as the crew ascended the rocks and addressed the man who had captured me by the title of captain. They were a ferocious set of men, with shaggy beards and scowling brows. All of them were armed with cutlasses and pistols, and their costumes were, with trifling variations, similar to that of the captain. As I looked from one to the other, and observed the low scowling brows, that never unbent, even when the men laughed, and the mean, rascally expression that sat on each face, I felt that my life hung by a hair.

'But where are the other cubs?' cried one of the men, with an oath that made me shudder. "I'll swear to it there were three, at least, if not more.'

'You hear what he says, whelp; where are the other dogs?' said the captain.

'If you mean my companions,' said I, in a low voice, 'I won't tell you.'

A loud laugh burst from the crew at this answer.

The pirate captain looked at me in surprise. Then drawing a pistol from his belt, he cocked it and said: 'Now, youngster, listen to me. I've no time to waste here. If you don't tell me all you know, I'll blow your brains out! Where are your comrades?'

For an instant I hesitated, not knowing what to do in this extremity. Suddenly a thought occurred to me.

'Villain,' said I, shaking my clenched fist in his face, 'to blow my brains out would make short work of me, and be soon over. Death by drowning is as sure, and the agony prolonged, yet, I tell you to your face, if you were to toss me over yonder cliff into the sea, I would not tell you where my companions are, and I dare you to try me!'

The pirate captain grew white with rage as I spoke. 'Say you so?' cried he, uttering a fierce oath. 'Here lads, take him by the legs and heave him in—quick!'

The men, who were utterly silenced with surprise at my audacity, advanced and seized me, and, as they carried me towards the cliff, I congratulated myself not a little on the success of my scheme, for I knew that once in the water I should be safe, and could rejoin Jack and Peterkin in the cave. But my hopes were suddenly blasted by the captain crying out: 'Hold on, lads, hold on. We'll give him a taste of the thumb-screws before throwing him to the sharks. Away with him into the boat. Look alive! the breeze is freshening.'

The men instantly raised me shoulder high, and hurrying down the rocks, tossed me into the bottom of the boat, where I lay for some time stunned with the violence of my fall.

On recovering sufficiently to raise myself on my elbow, I perceived that we were already outside the coral reef, and close alongside the schooner, which was of small size and clipper built. I had only time to observe this much when I received a severe kick on the side from one of the men, who ordered me, in a rough voice, to jump aboard. Rising hastily I clambered up the side. In a few minutes the boat was hoisted on deck, the vessel's head put close to the wind, and the Coral Island dropped slowly astern as we beat up against a head sea.

Immediately after coming aboard, the crew were too busily engaged in working the ship and getting in the boat to attend to me, so I remained leaning against the bulwarks close to the gangway, watching their operations. I was surprised to find that there were no guns of any kind in the vessel, which had more of the appearance of a fast-sailing trader than a pirate. But I was struck with the neatness of everything. The brass work of the binnacle and about the tiller, as well as the copper belaying-pins, were as brightly polished as if they had just come from the foundry. The decks were pure white, and smooth. The masts were clean-scraped and varnished, except at the cross-trees and truck, which were painted black. The standing and running rigging was in the most perfect order, and the sails white as snow. In short, everything, from the single narrow red stripe on her low black hull to the trucks on her tapering masts, evinced an amount of care and strict discipline that would have done credit to a ship of the Royal Navy. There was nothing lumbering or unseemly about the vessel, excepting, perhaps, a boat, which lay on the deck with its keel up between the fore and mainmasts. It seemed disproportionately large for the schooner; but, when I saw that the crew amounted to between thirty and forty men, I concluded that this boat was held in reserve, in case of any accident compelling the crew to desert the vessel.

As I have before said, the costumes of the men were similar to that of the captain. But in head gear they differed not only from him but from each other, some wearing the ordinary straw hat of the merchant service, while others wore cloth caps and red worsted nightcaps. I observed that all their arms were sent below; the captain only retaining his cutlass and a single pistol in the folds of his shawl. Although the captain was the tallest and most powerful man in the ship, he did not strikingly excel many of his men in this respect, and the only difference that an ordinary observer would have noticed was, a certain degree of open candour, straightforward daring, in the bold, ferocious expression of his face, which rendered him less repulsive than his low-browed associates, but did not by any means induce the belief that he was a hero. This look was, however, the indication of that spirit which gave him the pre-eminence among the crew of despera-does who called him captain. He was a lion-like villain; totally devoid of personal fear, and utterly reckless of consequences, and, therefore, a terror to his men, who individually hated him, but unitedly felt it to be their advantage to have him at their head.

But my thoughts soon reverted to the dear companions whom I had left on shore, and as I turned towards the Coral Island, which was now far away to leeward, I sighed deeply, and the tears rolled slowly down my cheeks as I thought that I might never see them more.

'So you're blubbering, are you, you obstinate whelp?' said the deep voice of the captain, as he came up and gave me a box on the ear that nearly felled me to the deck. 'I don't allow any such weakness aboard o' this ship. So clap a stopper on your eyes or I'll give you something to cry for.'

I flushed with indignation at this rough and cruel treatment, but felt that giving way to anger would only make matters worse, so I made no reply, but took out my handkerchief and dried my eyes.

'I thought you were made of better stuff,' continued the captain, angrily; 'I'd rather have a mad bulldog aboard than a water-eyed puppy. But I'll cure you, lad, or introduce you to the sharks before long. Now go below, and stay there till I call you.'

As I walked forward to obey, my eye fell on a small keg standing by the side of the mainmast, on which the word gunpowder was written in pencil. It immediately flashed across me that, as we were beating up against the wind, anything floating in the sea would be driven on the reef encircling the Coral Island. I also recollected—for thought is more rapid than the lightning—that my old companions had a pistol. Without a moment's hesitation, therefore, I lifted the keg from the deck and tossed it into the sea! An exclamation of surprise burst from the captain and some of the men who witnessed this act of mine.

Striding up to me, and uttering fearful imprecations, the captain raised his hand to strike me, while he shouted: 'Boy! whelp! what mean you by that?'

'If you lower your hand,' said I, in a loud voice, while I felt the blood rush to my temples, 'I'll tell you. Until you do so I'm dumb!'

The captain stepped back and regarded me with a look of amazement.

'Now,' continued I, 'I threw that keg into the sea because the wind and waves will carry it to my friends on the Coral Island, who happen to have a pistol, but no powder. I hope that it will reach them soon, and my only regret is that the keg was not a bigger one. Moreover, pirate, you said just now that you thought I was made of better stuff! I don't know what stuff I am made of—I never thought much about that subject; but I'm quite certain of this, that I am made of such stuff as the like of you shall never tame, though you should do your worst.'

To my surprise the captain, instead of flying into a rage, smiled, and, thrusting his hand into the voluminous shawl that encircled his waist, turned on his heel and walked aft, while I went below.

Here, instead of being rudely handled, as I had expected, the men received me with a shout of laughter, and one of them, patting me on the back, said: 'Well done, lad! you're a brick, and I have no doubt will turn out a rare cove. Bloody Bill, there, was just such a fellow as you are, and he's now the biggest cutthroat of us all.'

'Take a can of beer, lad,' cried another, 'and wet your whistle after that speech o' your'n to the captain. If any one o' us had made it, youngster, he would have had no whistle to wet by this time.'

'Stop your clapper, Jack,' vociferated a third; 'give the boy a junk o' meat. Don't you see he's a'most goin' to kick the bucket?'

'And no wonder,' said the first speaker, with an oath, 'after the tumble you gave him into the boat. I guess it would have broke *your* neck if you had got it.'

I did indeed feel somewhat faint; which was owing, doubtless, to the combined effects of ill-usage and hunger; for it will be recollected that I had dived out of the cave that morning before breakfast, and it was now near midday. I therefore gladly accepted a plate of boiled pork and a yam, which were handed to me by one of the men from the locker on which some of the crew were seated eating their dinner. But I must add that the zest with which I ate my meal was much abated in consequence of the frightful oaths and the terrible language that flowed from the lips of these godless men, even in the midst of their hilarity and good humour. The man who had been alluded to as Bloody Bill was seated near me, and I could not help wondering at the moody silence he maintained among his comrades. He did indeed reply to their questions in a careless, offhand tone, but he never volunteered a remark. The only difference between him and the others was his taciturnity and his size, for he was nearly, if not quite, as large a man as the captain.

During the remainder of the afternoon I was left to my own reflections, which were anything but agreeable, for I could not banish from my mind the threat about the thumbscrews, of the nature and use of which I had a vague but terrible conception. I was still meditating on my unhappy fate when, just after nightfall, one of the watch on deck called down the hatchway:

'Hallo, there! one o' you, tumble up and light the cabin lamp, and send that boy aft to the captain—sharp!'

'Now then, do you hear, youngster? the captain wants you. Look alive,' said Bloody Bill, raising his huge frame from the locker on which he had been asleep for the last two hours. He sprang up the ladder and I instantly followed him, and, going aft, was shown into the cabin by one of the men, who closed the door after me.

A small silver lamp which hung from a beam threw a dim soft light over the cabin, which was a small apartment, and comfortably but plainly furnished. Seated on a camp-stool at the table, and busily engaged in examining a chart of the Pacific, was the captain, who looked up as I entered, and, in a quiet voice, bade me be seated, while he threw down his pencil, and, rising from the table, stretched himself on a sofa at the upper end of the cabin.

'Boy,' said he, looking me full in the face, 'what is your name?'

'Ralph Rover,' I replied.

'Where did you come from, and how came you to be on that island? How many companions had you on it? Answer me, now, and mind you tell no lies.'

'I never tell lies,' said I, firmly.

The captain received this reply with a cold sarcastic smile, and bade me answer his questions.

I then told him the history of myself and my companions from the time we sailed till the day of his visit to the island, taking care, however, to make no mention of the Diamond Cave. After I had concluded, he was silent for a few minutes; then, looking up, he said: 'Boy, I believe you.'

I was surprised at this remark, for I could not imagine why he should not believe me. However, I made no reply.

'And what,' continued the captain, 'makes you think that this schooner is a pirate?'

'The black flag,' said I, 'showed me what you are; and if any further proof were wanting I have had it in the brutal treatment I have received at your hands.'

The captain frowned as I spoke, but subduing his anger he continued: 'Boy, you are too bold. I admit that we treated you roughly, but that was because you made us lose time and gave us a good deal of trouble. As to the black flag, that is merely a joke that my fellows play off upon people sometimes in order to frighten them. It is their humour, and does no harm. I am no pirate, boy, but a lawful trader— a rough one, I grant you, but one can't help that in these seas, where there are so many pirates on the water and such murderous black- guards on the land. I carry on a trade in sandal-wood with the Feejee Islands; and if you choose, Ralph, to behave yourself and be a good boy, I'll take you along with me and give you a good share of the profits. You see, I'm in want of an honest boy like you, to look after the cabin and keep the log, and superintend the traffic on shore sometimes. What say you, Ralph, would you like to become a sandal- wood trader?'

I was much surprised by this explanation, and a good deal relieved to find that the vessel, after all, was not a pirate; but instead of replying I said: 'If it be as you state, then why did you take me from my island, and why do you not now take me back?'

The captain smiled as he replied: 'I took you off in anger, boy, and I'm sorry for it. I would even now take you back, but we are too far away from it. See, there it is,' he added, laying his finger on the chart, 'and we are here—fifty miles at least. It would not be fair to my men to put about now, for they have all an interest in the trade.'

I could make no reply to this; so, after a little more conversation, I agreed to become one of the crew, at least until we could reach some civilized island where I might be put ashore. The captain assented to this proposition, and after thanking him for the promise, I left the cabin and went on deck with feelings that ought to have been lighter, but which were, I could not tell why, marvellously heavy and uncomfortable still.

Three weeks after the conversation narrated in the last chapter, I was standing on the quarterdeck of the schooner watching the gambols of a shoal of porpoises that swam round us. It was dead calm. One of those still, hot, sweltering days, so common in the Pacific, when Nature seems to have gone to sleep, and the only thing in water or in air that proves her still alive, is her long, deep breathing, in the swell of the mighty sea. No cloud floated in the deep blue above; no ripple broke the reflected blue below.

No sound broke on our ears save the soft puff now and then of a porpoise, the slow creak of the masts, as we swayed gently on the swell, the patter of the reef-points, and the occasional flap of the hanging sails. An awning covered the fore and after parts of the schooner, under which the men composing the watch on deck lolled in sleepy indolence, overcome with excessive heat. Bloody Bill, as the men invariably called him, was standing at the tiller, but his post for the present was a sinecure, and he whiled away the time by alternately gazing in dreamy abstraction at the compass in the binnacle, and by walking to the taffrail in order to spit into the sea. In one of these turns he came near to where I was standing, and, leaning over the side, looked long and earnestly down into the blue wave.

This man, although he was always taciturn and often surly, was the only human being on board with whom I had the slightest desire to become better acquainted. The other men, seeing that I did not relish their company, and knowing that I was a protégé of the captain, treated me with total indifference. Bloody Bill, it is true, did the same; but as this was his conduct towards every one else, it was not peculiar in reference to me. Once or twice I tried to draw him into conversation, but he always turned away after a few cold monosyllables. As he now leaned over the taffrail close beside me, I said to him:

'Bill, why is it that you are so gloomy? Why do you never speak to anyone?'

Bill smiled slightly as he replied: 'Why, I s'pose it's because I haint got nothin' to say!'

'That's strange,' said I, musingly; 'you look like a man that could think, and such men usually speak.'

'So they can, youngster,' rejoined Bill, somewhat sternly; 'and I could speak too if I had a mind to, but what's the use o' speakin' here? The men only open their mouths to curse and swear, an' they seem to find it entertainin'; but I don't, so I hold my tongue.'

'Well, Bill, that's true, and I would rather not hear you speak at all than hear you speak like the other men; but I don't swear, Bill, so you might talk to me sometimes, I think. Besides, I'm weary of spending day after day in this way, without a single soul to say a pleasant word to. I've been used to friendly conversation, Bill, and I really would take it kind if you would talk with me a little now and then.'

Bill looked at me in surprise, and I thought I observed a sad expression pass across his sunburnt face.

'An' where have you been used to friendly conversation said Bill, looking down again into the sea; 'not on that Coral Island, I take it?'

'Yes, indeed,' said I, energetically: 'I have spent many of the happiest months in my life on that Coral Island'; and without waiting to be further questioned, I launched out into a glowing account of the happy life that Jack and Peterkin and I had spent together, and related minutely every circumstance that befell us while on the island.

'Boy, boy,' said Bill, in a voice so deep that it startled me, 'this is no place for you.'

'That's true,' said I; 'I'm of little use on board, and I don't like my comrades; but I can't help it, and at any rate I hope to be free again soon.'

'Free?' said Bill, looking at me in surprise.

'Yes, free,' returned I; 'the captain said he would put me ashore after this trip was over.'

'*This trip!* Hark'ee, boy,' said Bill, lowering his voice, 'what said the captain to you the day you came aboard?'

'He said that he was a trader in sandal-wood and no pirate, and told me that if I would join him for this trip he would give me a good share of the profits or put me on shore in some civilized island if I chose.'

Bill's brows lowered savagely as he muttered: 'Ay, he said truth when he told you he was a sandal-wood trader, but he lied when—'

'Sail ho!' shouted the look-out at the mast-head.

'Where away?' cried Bill, springing to the tiller; while the men, startled by the sudden cry, jumped up and gazed round the horizon.

'On the starboard quarter, hull down sir,' answered the look-out.

At this moment the captain came on deck, and mounting into the rigging, surveyed the sail through the glass. Then sweeping his eye round the horizon he gazed steadily at a particular point.

'Take in top-sails!' shouted the captain, swinging himself down on the deck by the main-back stay.

'Take in top-sails!' roared the first mate.

'Ay, ay, sir-r-r!' answered the men as they sprang into the rigging and went aloft like cats.

Instantly all was bustle on board the hitherto quiet schooner. The top-sails were taken in and stowed, the men stood by the sheets and halyards, and the captain gazed anxiously at the breeze which was now rushing towards us like a sheet of dark blue. In a few seconds it struck me. The schooner trembled as if in surprise at the sudden onset, while she fell away, then bending gracefully to the wind, as though in acknowledgement of her subjection, she cut through the waves with her sharp prow like a dolphin, while Bill directed her course towards the strange sail.

In half an hour we neared her sufficiently to make out that she was a schooner, and, from the clumsy appearance of her masts and sails we judged her to be a trader. She evidently did not like our appearance, for, the instant the breeze reached her, she crowded all sail and showed us her stern. As the breeze had moderated a little our top-sails were again shaken out, and it soon became evident that we doubled her speed and would overhaul her speedily. When within a mile we hoisted British colours, but receiving no acknowledgement, the captain ordered a shot to be fired across her bows. In a moment, to my surprise, a large portion of the bottom of the boat amidships was removed, and in the hole thus exposed appeared an immense brass gun. It worked on a swivel and was elevated by means of machinery. It was quickly loaded and fired. The heavy ball struck the water a few yards ahead of the chase, and, ricochetting into the air, plunged into the sea a mile beyond it.

This produced the desired effect. The strange vessel backed her top-sails and hove-to, while we ranged up and lay-to, about a hundred yards off.

'Lower the boat,' cried the captain.

In a second the boat was lowered and manned by a part of the crew, who were all armed with cutlasses and pistols. As the captain passed me to get into it, he said: 'Jump into the stern sheets, Ralph, I may want you.' I obeyed, and in ten minutes more we were standing on the stranger's deck. We were all much surprised at the sight that met our eyes. Instead of a crew of such sailors as we were accustomed to see, there were only fifteen blacks standing on the quarterdeck and regarding us with looks of undisguised alarm. They were totally unarmed and most of them unclothed; one or two, however, wore portions of European attire. One had a pair of duck trousers which were much too large for him and stuck out in a most ungainly manner. Another wore nothing but the common scanty native garment round the loins, and a black beaver hat. But the most ludicrous personage of all, and one who seemed to be chief, was a tall middle-aged man, of a mild, simple expression of countenance, who wore a white cotton shirt, a swallow-tailed coat, and a straw hat, while his black brawny legs were totally uncovered below the knees.

'Where's the commander of this ship?' inquired our captain, stepping up to this individual.

'I is capin,' he answered, taking off his straw hat and making a low bow.

'You!' said our captain, in surprise. 'Where do you come from, and where are you bound? What cargo have you aboard?'

'We is come,' answered the man with the swallowtail, 'from Aitutaki; we was go for Rarotonga. We is native miss'nary ship; our name is de *Olive Branch*; an' our cargo is two tons coconuts, seventy pigs, twenty cats, and de gosp'l.'

This announcement was received by the crew of our vessel with a shout of laughter, which, however, was peremptorily checked by the captain, whose expression instantly changed from one of severity to that of rank urbanity as he advanced towards the missionary and shook him warmly by the hand.

'I am very glad to have fallen in with you,' said he, 'and I wish you much success in your missionary labours. Pray take me to your cabin, as I wish to converse with you privately.'

The missionary immediately took him by the hand, and as he led him away I heard him saying: 'Me most glad to find you trader; we t'ought you be pirate. You very like one 'bout the masts.'

What conversation the captain had with this man I never heard, but he came on deck again in a quarter of an hour, and, shaking hands cordially with the missionary, ordered us into our boat and returned to the schooner, which was immediately put before the wind. In a few minutes the *Olive Branch* was left far behind us.

That afternoon, as I was down below at dinner, I heard the men talking about this curious ship.

'I wonder,' said one, 'why our captain looked so sweet on yon swallow-tailed super-cargo o' pigs and gospels. If it had been an ordinary trader, now, he would have taken as many o' the pigs as he required and sent the ship with all on board to the bottom.'

'Why, Dick, you must be new to these seas if you don't know that,' cried another. 'The captain cares as much for the gospel as you do (an' that's precious little), but he knows, and everybody knows, that the only place among the southern islands where a ship can put in and get what she wants in comfort, is where the gospel has been sent to. There are hundreds o' islands, at this blessed moment, where you might as well jump straight into a shark's maw as land without a band o' thirty comrades armed to the teeth to back you.'

'Ay,' said a man with a deep scar over his right eye, 'Dick's new to the work. But if the captain takes us for a cargo o' sandal-wood to the Feejees he'll get a taste o' these black gentry in their native condition. For my part I don't know, an' I don't care, what the gospel does to them; but I know that when any o' the islands chance to get it, trade goes all smooth an' easy; but where they ha'nt got it, Beelzebub himself could hardly desire better company.'

'Well, you ought to be a good judge,' cried another, laughing, 'for you've never kept any company but the worst all your life!'

'Ralph Rover!' shouted a voice down the hatchway. 'Captain wants you, aft.'

On coming again on deck I found Bloody Bill at the helm, and as we were alone together I tried to draw him into conversation. After repeating to him the conversation in the forecastle about the missionaries, I said:

'Tell me, Bill, is this schooner really a trader in sandal-wood?'

'Yes, Ralph, she is; but she's just as really a pirate. The black flag you saw flying at the peak was no deception.'

'Then how can you say she's a trader?' asked I.

'Why, as to that, she trades when she can't take by force, but she takes by force, when she can, in preference. Ralph,' he added, lowering his voice, 'if you had seen the bloody deeds that I have witnessed done on these decks you would not need to ask if we were pirates. But you'll find it out soon enough. As for the missionaries, the captain favours them because they are useful to him. The South Sea islanders are such incarnate fiends that they are the better of being tamed, and the missionaries are the only men who can do it.'

Our track after this lay through several clusters of small islets, among which we were becalmed more than once. During this part of our voyage the watch on deck and the look-out at the masthead were more than usually vigilant, as we were not only in danger of being attacked by the natives, who, I learned from the captain's remarks, were a bloody and deceitful tribe at this group, but we were also exposed to much risk from the multitudes of coral reefs that rose up in the channels between the islands, some of them just above the surface, others a few feet below it. Our precautions against the savages I found were indeed necessary.

One day we were becalmed among a group of small islands, most of which appeared to be uninhabited. As we were in want of fresh water the captain sent the boat ashore to bring off a cask or two. But we were mistaken in thinking there were no natives; for scarcely had we drawn near to the shore when a band of naked blacks rushed out of the bush and assembled on the beach, brandishing their clubs and spears in a threatening manner. Our men were well armed, but refrained from showing any signs of hostility, and rowed nearer in order to converse with the natives; and I now found that more than one of the crew could imperfectly speak dialects of the language peculiar to the South Sea islanders. When within forty yards of the shore, we ceased rowing, and the first mate stood up to address the multitude; but, instead of answering us, they replied with a shower of stones, some of which cut the men severely. Instantly our muskets were levelled, and a volley was about to be fired, when the captain hailed us in a loud voice from the schooner, which lay not more than five or six hundred yards off the shore.

'Don't fire!' he shouted angrily. 'Pull off to the point ahead of you.'

The men looked surprised at this order, and uttered deep curses as they prepared to obey, for their wrath was roused and they burned for revenge. Three or four of them hesitated, and seemed disposed to mutiny.

'Don't distress yourselves, lads,' said the mate, while a bitter smile curled his lip. 'Obey orders. The captain's not the man to take an insult tamely. If Long Tom does not speak presently I'll give myself to the sharks.'

The men smiled significantly as they pulled from the shore, which was now crowded with a dense mass of savages, amounting, probably, to five or six hundred. We had not rowed off above a couple of hundred yards when a loud roar thundered over the sea, and the big brass gun sent a withering shower of grape point-blank into the midst of the living mass, through which a wide lane was cut, while a yell, the like of which I could not have imagined, burst from the miserable survivors as they fled to the woods. Amongst the heaps of dead that lay on the sand, just where they had fallen, I could distinguish mutilated forms writhing in agony, while ever and anon one and another rose convulsively from out the mass, endeavoured to stagger towards the wood, and ere they had taken a few steps, fell and wallowed on the bloody sand. My blood curdled within me as I witnessed this frightful and wanton slaughter; but I had little time to think, for the captain's deep voice came again over the water towards us: 'Pull ashore, lads, and fill your water casks.' The men obeyed in silence, and it seemed to me as if even their hard hearts were shocked by the ruthless deed. On gaining the mouth of the rivulet at which we intended to take in water, we found it flowing with blood, for the greater part of those who were slain had been standing on the banks of the stream, a short way above its mouth. Many of the wretched creatures had fallen into it, and we found one body, which had been carried down, jammed between two rocks, with the staring eyeballs turned towards us and his black hair waving in the ripples of the blood-red stream. No one dared to oppose our landing now, so we carried our casks to the pool above the murdered group, and having filled them, returned on board. Fortunately a breeze sprang up soon afterwards and carried us away from the dreadful spot; but it could not waft me away from the memory of what I had seen.

'And this,' thought I, gazing in horror at the captain, who, with a quiet look of indifference, leaned upon the taffrail smoking a cigar and contemplating the fertile green islets as they passed like a lovely picture before our eyes—'this is the man who favours the missionaries because they are useful to him and can tame the savages better than anyone else can do it!' Then I wondered in my mind whether it were possible for any missionary to tame *him!*

from

Treasure Island

by Robert Louis Stevenson (1850-1894)

Robert Louis Stevenson and his 12-year-old stepson Lloyd drew a map and invented a tale of an imaginary Treasure Island to pass a rainy day. That story became Stevenson's most beloved novel. Here young Jim Hawkins, the innkeeper's son at the Admiral Benbow Inn, meets his first pirate.

I remember him as if it were yesterday, as he came plodding to the inn door, his sea-chest following behind him in a hand-barrow—a tall, strong, heavy, nut-brown man, his tarry pigtail falling over the shoulders of his soiled blue coat, his hands ragged and scarred, with black, broken nails, and the sabre cut across one cheek, a dirty, livid white. I remember him looking round the cove and whistling to himself as he did so, and then breaking out in that old sea-song that he sang so often afterwards:

Fifteen men on the dead man's chest—
Yo-ho-ho, and a bottle of rum!

in the high, old tottering voice that seemed to have been tuned and broken at the capstan bars. Then he rapped on the door with a bit of stick like a handspike that he carried, and when my father appeared, called roughly for a glass of rum. This, when it was brought to him, he drank slowly, like a connoisseur, lingering on the taste and still looking about him at the cliffs and up at our signboard.

"This is a handy cove," says he at length; "and a pleasant sittyated grog-shop. Much company, mate?"

My father told him no, very little company, the more was the pity. "Well, then," said he, "this is the berth for me. Here you, matey," he cried to the man who trundled the barrow; "bring up alongside and help up my chest. I'll stay here a bit," he continued. "I'm a plain man; rum and bacon and eggs is what I want, and that head up there for to watch ships off. What you mought call me? You mought call me captain. Oh, I see what you're at—there"; and he threw down three or four gold pieces on the threshold. "You can tell me when I've worked through that," says he, looking as fierce as a commander.

And indeed bad as his clothes were and coarsely as he spoke, he had none of the appearance of a man who sailed before the mast, but seemed like a mate or skipper accustomed to be obeyed or to strike. The man who came with the barrow told us the mail had set him down the morning before at the Royal George, that he had inquired what inns there were along the coast, and hearing ours well spoken of, I suppose, and described as lonely, had chosen it from the others for his place of residence. And that was all we could learn of our guest.

He was a very silent man by custom. All day he hung round the cove or upon the cliffs with a brass telescope; all evening he sat in a corner of the parlour next the fire and drank rum and water very strong. Mostly he would not speak when spoken to, only look up sudden and fierce and blow through his nose like a fog-horn; and we and the people who came about our house soon learned to let him be. Every day when he came back from his stroll he would ask if any seafaring men had gone by along the road. At first we thought it was the want of company of his own kind that made him ask this question, but at last we began to see he was desirous to avoid them. When a seaman put up at the Admiral Benbow (as now and then some did, making by the coast road for Bristol), he would look in at him through the curtained door before he entered the parlour; and he was always sure to be as silent as a mouse when any such was present. For me, at least, there was no secret about the matter, for I was, in a way, a sharer in his alarms. He had taken me aside one day and promised me a silver fourpenny on the first of every month if I would only keep my "weather-eye open for a seafaring man with one leg" and let him know the moment he appeared. Often enough when the first of the month came round and I applied to him for my wage, he would only blow through his nose at me and stare me down, but before the week was out he was sure to think better of it, bring me my fourpenny piece, and repeat his orders to look out for "the seafaring man with one leg."

How that personage haunted my dreams, I need scarcely tell you. On stormy nights, when the wind shook the four corners of the house and the surf roared along the cove and up the cliffs, I would see him in a thousand forms, and with a thousand diabolical expressions. Now the leg would be cut off at the knee, now at the hip; now he was a monstrous kind of a creature who had never had but the one leg, and that in the middle of his body. To see him leap and run and pursue me over hedge and ditch was the worst of nightmares. And altogether I paid pretty dear for my monthly fourpenny piece, in the shape of these abominable fancies.

But though I was so terrified by the idea of the seafaring man with one leg, I was far less afraid of the captain himself than anybody else who knew him. There were nights when he took a deal more rum and water than his head would carry; and then he would sometimes sit and sing his wicked, old, wild sea-songs, minding nobody; but sometimes he would call for glasses round and force all the trembling company to listen to his stories or bear a chorus to his singing. Often I have heard the house shaking with "Yo-ho-ho, and a bottle of rum," all the neighbours joining in for dear life, with the fear of death upon them, and each singing louder than the other to avoid remark. For in these fits he was the most overriding companion ever known; he would slap his hand on the table for silence all round; he would fly up in a passion of anger at a question, or sometimes because none was put, and so he judged the company was not following his story. Nor would he allow anyone to leave the inn till he had drunk himself sleepy and reeled off to bed.

His stories were what frightened people worst of all. Dreadful stories they were—about hanging, and walking the plank, and storms at sea, and the Dry Tortugas, and wild deeds and places on the Spanish Main. By his own account he must have lived his life among some of the wickedest men that God ever allowed upon the sea, and the language in which he told these stories shocked our plain country people almost as much as the crimes that he described. My father was always saying the inn would be ruined, for people would soon cease coming there to be tyrannized over and put down, and sent shivering to their beds; but I really believe his presence did us good. People were frightened at the time, but on looking back they rather liked it; it was a fine excitement in a quiet country life, and there was even a party of the younger men who pretended to admire him, calling him a "true seadog" and a "real old salt" and such like names, and saying there was the sort of man that made England terrible at sea.

In one way, indeed, he bade fair to ruin us, for he kept on staying week after week, and at last month after month, so that all the money had been long exhausted, and still my father never plucked up the heart to insist on having more. If ever he mentioned it, the captain blew through his nose so loudly that you might say he roared, and stared my poor father out of the room. I have seen him wringing his hands after such a rebuff, and I am sure the annoyance and the terror he lived in must have greatly hastened his early and unhappy death.

All the time he lived with us the captain made no change whatever in his dress but to buy some stockings from a hawker. One of the cocks of his hat having fallen down, he let it hang from that day forth, though it was a great annoyance when it blew. I remember the appearance of his coat, which he patched himself upstairs in his room, and which, before the end, was nothing but patches. He never wrote or received a letter, and he never spoke with any but the neighbours, and with these, for the most part, only when drunk on rum. The great sea-chest none of us had ever seen open.

He was only once crossed, and that was towards the end, when my poor father was far gone in a decline that took him off. Dr. Livesey came late one afternoon to see the patient, took a bit of dinner from my mother, and went into the parlour to smoke a pipe until his horse should come down from the hamlet, for we had no stabling at the old Benbow. I followed him in, and I remember observing the contrast the neat, bright doctor, with his powder as white as snow and his bright, black eyes and pleasant manners, made with the coltish country folk, and above all, with that filthy, heavy, bleared scarecrow of a pirate of ours, sitting, far gone in rum, with his arms on the table. Suddenly he—the captain, that is—began to pipe up his eternal song:

> *Fifteen men on the dead man's chest—*
> *Yo-ho-ho, and a bottle of rum!*
> *Drink and the devil had done for the rest—*
> *Yo-ho-ho, and a bottle of rum!*

At first I had supposed "the dead man's chest" to be that identical big box of his upstairs in the front room, and the thought had been mingled in my nightmares with that of the one-legged seafaring man. But by this time we had all long ceased to pay any particular notice to the song; it was new, that night, to nobody but Dr. Livesey, and on him I observed it did not produce an agreeable effect, for he looked up for a moment quite angrily before he went on with his talk to old Taylor, the gardener, on a new cure for the rheumatics. In the meantime, the captain gradually brightened up at his own music, and at last flapped his hand upon the table before him in a way we all knew to mean silence. The voices stopped at once, all but Dr. Livesey's; he went on as before, speaking dear and kind and drawing briskly at his pipe between every word or two. The captain glared at him for, a while, flapped his hand again, glared still harder, and at last broke out with a villainous, low oath, "Silence, there, between decks!"

"Were you addressing me, sir?" says the doctor; and when the ruffian had told him, with another oath, that this was so, "I have only one thing to say to you, sir," replies the doctor, "that if you keep on drinking rum, the world will soon be quit of a very dirty scoundrel!"

The old fellow's fury was awful. He sprang to his feet, drew and opened a sailor's clasp-knife, and balancing it open on the palm of his hand, threatened to pin the doctor to the wall.

The doctor never so much as moved. He spoke to him as before, over his shoulder and in the same tone of voice, rather high, so that all the room might hear, but perfectly calm and steady: "If you do not put that knife this instant in your pocket, I promise, upon my honour, you shall hang at the next assizes."

Then followed a battle of looks between them, but the captain soon knuckled under, put up his weapon, and resumed his seat, grumbling like a beaten dog.

"And now, sir," continued the doctor, "since I now know there's such a fellow in my district, you may count I'll have an eye upon you day and night. I'm not a doctor only; I'm a magistrate; and if I catch a breath of complaint against you, if it's only for a piece of incivility like tonight's, I'll take effectual means to have you hunted down and routed out of this. Let that suffice."

Soon after, Dr. Livesey's horse came to the door and he rode away, but the captain held his peace that evening, and for many evenings to come.

It was not very long after this that there occurred the first of the mysterious events that rid us at last of the captain, though not, as you will see, of his affairs. It was a bitter cold winter, with long, hard frosts and heavy gales; and it was plain from the first that my poor father was little likely to see the spring. He sank daily, and my mother and I had all the inn upon our hands, and were kept busy enough without paying much regard to our unpleasant guest.

It was one January morning, very early—a pinching, frosty morning—the cove all grey with hoar-frost, the ripple lapping softly on the stones, the sun still low and only touching the hilltops and shining far to seaward. The captain had risen earlier than usual and set out down the beach, his cutlass swinging under the broad skirts of the old blue coat, his brass telescope under his arm; his hat tilted back upon his head. I remember his breath hanging like smoke in his wake as he strode off, and the last sound I heard of him as he turned the big rock was a loud snort of indignation, as though his mind was still running upon Dr. Livesey.

Well, mother was upstairs with father and I was laying the breakfast-table against the captain's return when the parlour door opened and a man stepped in on whom I had never set my eyes before. He was a pale, tallowy creature, wanting two fingers of the left hand, and though he wore a cutlass, he did not look much like a fighter. I had always my eye open for seafaring men, with one leg or two, and I remember this one puzzled me. He was not sailorly, and yet he had a smack of the sea about him too.

I asked him what was for his service, and he said he would take rum; but as I was going out of the room to fetch it, he sat down upon a table and motioned me to draw near. I paused where I was, with my napkin in my hand.

"Come here, sonny," says he. "Come nearer here."

I took a step nearer.

"Is this here table for my mate Bill?" he asked with a kind of leer.

I told him I did not know his mate Bill, and this was for a person who stayed in our house whom we called the captain.

"Well," said he, "my mate Bill would be called the captain, as like as not. He has a cut on one cheek and a mighty pleasant way with him, particularly in drink, has my mate Bill. We'll put it, for argument like, that your captain has a cut on one cheek—and we'll put it, if you like, that that cheek's the right one. Ah, well! I told you. Now, is my mate Bill in this here house?"

I told him he was out walking.

"Which way, sonny? Which way is he gone?"

And when I had pointed out the rock and told him how the captain was likely to return, and how soon, and answered a few other questions, "Ah," said he, "this'll be as good as drink to my mate Bill."

The expression of his face as he said these words was not at all pleasant, and I had my own reasons for thinking that the stranger was mistaken, even supposing he meant what he said. But it was no affair of mine, I thought; and besides, it was difficult to know what to do. The stranger kept hanging about just inside the inn door, peering round the corner like a cat waiting for a mouse. Once I stepped out myself into the road, but he immediately called me back, and as I did not obey quick enough for his fancy, a most horrible change came over his tallowy face, and he ordered me in with an oath that made me jump. As soon as I was back again he returned to his former manner, half fawning, half sneering, patted me on the shoulder, told me I was a good boy and he had taken quite a fancy to me. "I have a son of my own," said he, "as like you as two blocks, and he's all the pride of my 'art. But the great thing for boys is discipline, sonny—discipline. Now, if you had sailed along of Bill, you wouldn't have stood there to be spoke to twice—not you. That was never Bill's way, nor the way of sich as sailed with him. And here, sure enough, is my mate Bill, with a spyglass under his arm, bless his old 'art, to be sure. You and me'll just go back into the parlour, sonny, and get behind the door, and we'll give Bill a little surprise—bless his 'art, I say again."

So saying, the stranger backed along with me into the parlour and put me behind him in the corner so that we were both hidden by the open door. I was very uneasy and alarmed, as you may fancy, and it rather added to my fears to observe that the stranger was certainly frightened himself. He cleared the hilt of his cutlass and loosened the blade in the sheath; and all the time we were waiting there he kept swallowing as if he felt what we used to call a lump in the throat.

At last in strode the captain, slammed the door behind him, without looking to the right or left, and marched straight across the room to where his breakfast awaited him.

"Bill," said the stranger in a voice that I thought he had tried to make bold and big.

The captain spun round on his heel and fronted us; all the brown had gone out of his face, and even his nose was blue; he had the look of a man who sees a ghost, or the evil one, or something worse, if anything can be; and upon my word, I felt sorry to see him in a moment turn so old and sick.

"Come, Bill, you know me; you know an old shipmate, Bill, surely," said the stranger.

The captain made a sort of gasp.

"And who else?" returned the other, getting more at his ease. "Black Dog as ever was, come for to see his old shipmate Billy, at the Admiral Benbow inn. Ah, Bill, Bill, we have seen a sight of times, us two, since I lost them two talons," holding up his mutilated hand.

"Now, look here," said the captain, "you've run me down; here I am; well, then, speak up; what is it?"

"That's you, Bill," returned Black Dog, "you're in the right of it, Billy. I'll have a glass of rum from this dear child here, as I've took such a liking to; and we'll sit down, if you please, and talk square, like old shipmates."

When I returned with the rum, they were already seated on either side of the captain's breakfast-table—Black Dog next to the door and sitting sideways so as to have one eye on his old shipmate and one, as I thought, on his retreat.

He bade me go and leave the door wide open. "None of your keyholes for me, sonny," he said; and I left them together and retired into the bar.

For a long time, though I certainly did my best to listen, I could hear nothing but a low gabbing; but at last the voices began to grow higher, and I could pick up a word or two, mostly oaths, from the captain.

"No, no, no, no; and an end of it!" he cried once. And again, "If it comes to swinging, swing all, say I."

Then all of a sudden there was a tremendous explosion of oaths and other noises—the chair and table went over in a lump, a clash of steel followed, and then a cry of pain, and the next instant I saw Black Dog in full flight, and the captain hotly pursuing, both with drawn cutlasses, and the former streaming blood from the left shoulder. Just at the door the captain aimed at the fugitive one last tremendous cut, which would certainly have split him to the chin had it not been intercepted by our big signboard of Admiral Benbow. You may see the notch on the lower side of the frame to this day.

That blow was the last of the battle. Once out upon the road, Black Dog, in spite of his wound, showed a wonderful clean pair of heels and disappeared over the edge of the hill in half a minute. The captain, for his part, stood staring at the signboard like a bewildered man. Then he passed his hand over his eyes several times and at last turned back into the house.

"Jim," says he, "rum"; and as he spoke, he reeled a little, and caught himself with one hand against the wall.

"Are you hurt?" cried I.

"Rum," he repeated. "I must get away from here. Rum! Rum!" I ran to fetch it, but I was quite unsteadied by all that had fallen out, and I broke one glass and fouled the tap, and while I was still getting in my own way, I heard a loud fall in the parlour, and running in, beheld the captain lying full length upon the floor. At the same instant my mother, alarmed by the cries and fighting, came running downstairs to help me. Between us we raised his head. He was breathing very loud and hard, but his eyes were closed and his face a horrible colour.

"Dear, deary me," cried my mother, "what a disgrace upon the house! And your poor father sick!"

In the meantime, we had no idea what to do to help the captain, nor any other thought but that he had got his death-hurt in the scuffle with the stranger. I got the rum, to be sure, and tried to put it down his throat, but his teeth were tightly shut and his jaws as strong as iron. It was a happy relief for us when the door opened and Dr. Livesey came in, on his visit to my father.

"Oh, doctor," we cried, "what shall we do? Where is he wounded?"

"Wounded? A fiddle-stick's end!" said the doctor. "No more

wounded than you or I. The man has had a stroke, as I warned him. Now, Mrs. Hawkins, just you run upstairs to your husband and tell him, if possible, nothing about it. For my part, I must do my best to save this fellow's trebly worthless life; Jim, you get me a basin."

When I got back with the basin, the doctor had already ripped up the captain's sleeve and exposed his great sinewy arm. It was tattooed in several places. "Here's luck," "A fair wind," and "Billy Bones his fancy," were very neatly and clearly executed on the forearm; and up near the shoulder there was a sketch of a gallows and a man hanging from it—done, as I thought, with great spirit.

"Prophetic," said the doctor, touching this picture with his finger. "And now, Master Billy Bones, if that be your name, we'll have a look at the colour of your blood. Jim," he said, "are you afraid of blood?"

"No, sir," said I.

"Well, then," said he, "you hold the basin"; and with that he took his lancet and opened a vein.

A great deal of blood was taken before the captain opened his eyes and looked mistily about him. First he recognized the doctor with an unmistakable frown; then his glance fell upon me, and he looked relieved. But suddenly his colour changed, and he tried to raise himself, crying, "Where's Black Dog?"

"There is no Black Dog here," said the doctor, "except what you have on your own back. You have been drinking rum; you have had a stroke, precisely as I told you; and I have just, very much against my own will, dragged you headforemost out of the grave. Now, Mr. Bones—"

"That's not my name," he interrupted.

"Much I care," returned the doctor. "It's the name of a buccaneer of my acquaintance; and I call you by it for the sake of shortness, and what I have to say to you is this: one glass of rum won't kill you, but if you take one you'll take another and another, and I stake my wig if you don't break off short, you'll die—do you understand that?—die, and go to your own place, like the man in the Bible. Come, now, make an effort. I'll help you to your bed for once."

Between us, with much trouble, we managed to hoist him upstairs, and laid him on his bed, where his head fell back on the pillow as if he were almost fainting.

"Now, mind you," said the doctor, "I clear my conscience—the name of rum for you is death."

And with that he went off to see my father, taking me with him by the arm.

"This is nothing," he said as soon as he had closed the door. "I have drawn blood enough to keep him quiet awhile; he should lie for a week where he is—that is the best thing for him and you; but another stroke would settle him."

About noon I stopped at the captain's door with some cooling drinks and medicines. He was lying very much as we had left him, only a little higher, and he seemed both weak and excited.

"Jim," he said, "you're the only one here that's worth anything, and you know I've been always good to you. Never a month but I've given you a silver fourpenny for yourself. And now you see, mate, I'm pretty low, and deserted by all; and Jim, you'll bring me one noggin of rum, now, won't you, matey?"

"The doctor—" I began.

But he broke in cursing the doctor, in a feeble voice but heartily. "Doctors is all swabs," he said; "and that doctor there, why, what do he know about seafaring men? I been in places hot as pitch, and mates dropping round with Yellow Jack, and the blessed land a-heaving like the sea with earthquakes—what do the doctor know of lands like that?—and I lived on rum, I tell you. It's been meat and drink, and man and wife, to me; and if I'm not to have my rum now I'm a poor old hulk on a lee shore, my blood'll be on you, Jim, and that doctor swab"; and he ran on again for a while with curses. "Look, Jim, how my fingers ridges," he continued in the pleading tone. "I can't keep 'em still, not I. I haven't had a drop this blessed day. That doctor's a fool, I tell you. If I don't have a drain o' rum, Jim, I'll have the horrors; I seen some on 'em already. I seen old Flint in the corner there, behind you; as plain as print, I seen him; and if I get the horrors, I'm a man that has lived rough, and I'll raise Cain. Your doctor hisself said one glass wouldn't hurt me. I'll give you a golden guinea for a noggin, Jim."

He was growing more and more excited, and this alarmed me for my father, who was very low that day and needed quiet; besides, I was reassured by the doctor's words, now quoted to me, and rather offended by the offer of a bribe.

"I want none of your money," said I, "but what you owe my father. I'll get you one glass, and no more."

When I brought it to him, he seized it greedily and drank it out.

"Aye, aye," said he, "that's some better, sure enough. And now, matey, did that doctor say how long I was to lie here in this old berth?"

"A week at least," said I.

"Thunder!" he cried. "A week! I can't do that; they'd have the black spot on me by then. The lubbers is going about to get the wind of me this blessed moment; lubbers as couldn't keep what they got, and want to nail what is another's. Is that seamanly behaviour, now, I want to know? But I'm a saving soul. I never wasted good money of mine, nor lost it neither; and I'll trick 'em again. I'm not afraid on 'em. I'll shake out another reef, matey, and daddle 'em again."

As he was thus speaking, he had risen from bed with great difficulty, holding to my shoulder with a grip that almost made me cry out, and moving his legs like so much dead weight. His words, spirited as they were in meaning, contrasted sadly with the weakness of the voice in which they were uttered. He paused when he had got into a sitting position on the edge.

"That doctor's done me," he murmured. "My ears is singing. Lay me back."

Before I could do much to help him he had fallen back again to his former place, where he lay for a while silent.

"Jim," he said at length, "you saw that seafaring man today?"

"Black Dog?" I asked.

"Ah! Black Dog," says he. "*He's* a bad un; but there's worse that put him on. Now, if I can't get away nohow, and they tip me the black spot, mind you, it's my old sea-chest they're after; you get on a horse—you can, can't you? Well, then, you get on a horse, and go to—well, yes, I will!—to that eternal doctor swab, and tell him to pipe all hands—magistrates and sich—and he'll lay 'em aboard at the Admiral Benbow—all old Flint's crew, man and boy, all on 'em that's left. I was first mate, I was, old Flint's first mate, and I'm the on'y one as knows the place. He gave it me at Savannah, when he lay a-dying, like as if I was to now, you see. But you won't peach unless they get the black spot on me, or unless you see that Black Dog again or a seafaring man with one leg, Jim—him above all."

"But what is the black spot, captain?" I asked.

"That's a summons, mate. I'll tell you if they get that. But you keep your weather-eye open, Jim, and I'll share with you equals, upon my honour."

He wandered a little longer, his voice growing weaker; but soon after I had given him his medicine, which he took like a child, with the remark, "If ever a seaman wanted drugs, it's me," he fell at last into a heavy, swoonlike sleep, in which I left him. What I should have done had all gone well I do not know. Probably I should have told the whole story to the doctor, for I was in mortal fear lest the captain should repent of his confessions and make an end of me. But as things fell out, my poor father died quite suddenly that evening, which put all other matters on one side. Our natural distress, the visits of the neighbours, the arranging of the funeral, and all the work of the inn to be carried on in the meanwhile kept me so busy that I had scarcely time to think of the captain, far less to be afraid of him.

He got downstairs next morning, to be sure, and had his meals as usual, though he ate little and had more, I am afraid, than his usual supply of rum, for he helped himself out of the bar, scowling and blowing through his nose, and no one dared to cross him. On the night before the funeral he was as drunk as ever; and it was shocking, in that house of mourning, to hear him singing away at his ugly old sea-song; but weak as he was, we were all in the fear of death for him, and the doctor was suddenly taken up with a case many miles away and was never near the house after my father's death. I have said the captain was weak, and indeed he seemed rather to grow weaker than regain his strength. He clambered up and down stairs, and went from the parlour to the bar and back again, and sometimes put his nose out of doors to smell the sea, holding on to the walls as he went for support and breathing hard and fast like a man on a steep mountain. He never particularly addressed me, and it is my belief he had as good as forgotten his confidences; but his temper was more flighty, and allowing for his bodily weakness, more violent than ever. He had an alarming way now when he was drunk of drawing his cutlass and laying it bare before him on the table. But with all that, he minded people less and seemed shut up in his own thoughts and rather wandering. Once, for instance, to our extreme wonder, he piped up to a different air, a kind of country love-song that he must have learned in his youth before he had begun to follow the sea.

So things passed until, the day after the funeral, and about three o'clock of a bitter, foggy, frosty afternoon, I was standing at the door for a moment, full of sad thoughts about my father, when I saw someone drawing slowly near along the road. He was plainly blind, for he tapped before him with a stick and wore a great green shade over his eyes and nose; and he was hunched, as if with age or weakness, and wore a huge old tattered sea-cloak with a hood that made him appear positively deformed. I never saw in my life a more dreadful-looking figure. He stopped a little from the inn, and raising his voice in an odd sing-song, addressed the air in front of him, "Will any kind friend inform a poor blind man, who has lost the precious sight of his eyes in the gracious defence of his native country, England—and God bless King George!—where or in what part of this country he may now be?"

"You are at the Admiral Benbow, Black Hill Cove, my good man," said I.

"I hear a voice," said he, "a young voice. Will you give me your hand, my kind young friend, and lead me in?"

I held out my hand, and the horrible, soft-spoken, eyeless creature gripped it in a moment like a vise. I was so much startled that I struggled to withdraw, but the blind man pulled me close up to him with a single action of his arm.

"Now, boy," he said, "take me in to the captain."

"Sir," said I, "upon my word I dare not."

"Oh," he sneered, "that's it! Take me in straight or I'll break your arm."

And he gave it, as he spoke, a wrench that made me cry out.

"Sir," said I, "it is for yourself I mean. The captain is not what he used to be. He sits with a drawn cutlass. Another gentleman—"

"Come, now, march," interrupted he; and I never heard a voice so cruel, and cold, and ugly as that blind man's. It cowed me more than the pain, and I began to obey him at once, walking straight in at the door and towards the parlour, where our sick old buccaneer was sitting, dazed with rum. The blind man clung close to me, holding me in one iron fist and leaning almost more of his weight on me than I could carry. "Lead me straight up to him, and when I'm in view, cry out, 'Here's a friend for you, Bill.' If you don't, I'll do this," and with that he gave me a twitch that I thought would have made me faint. Between this and that, I was so utterly terrified of the blind beggar that I forgot my terror of the captain, and as I opened the parlour door, cried out the words he had ordered in a trembling voice.

The poor captain raised his eyes, and at one look the rum went out of him and left him staring sober. The expression of his face was not so much of terror as of mortal sickness. He made a movement to rise, but I do not believe he had enough force left in his body.

"Now, Bill, sit where you are," said the beggar. "If I can't see, I can hear a finger stirring. Business is business. Hold out your left hand. Boy, take his left hand by the wrist and bring it near to my right."

We both obeyed him to the letter, and I saw him pass something from the hollow of the hand that held his stick into the palm of the captain's, which closed upon it instantly.

"And now that's done," said the blind man; and at the words he suddenly left hold of me, and with incredible accuracy and nimbleness, skipped out of the parlour and into the road, where, as I still stood motionless, I could hear his stick go tap-tap-tapping into the distance. It was some time before either I or the captain seemed to gather our senses, but at length, and about at the same moment, I released his wrist, which I was still holding, and he drew in his hand and looked sharply into the palm.

"Ten o'clock!" he cried. "Six hours. We'll do them yet," and he sprang to his feet.

Even as he did so, he reeled, put his hand to his throat, stood swaying for a moment, and then, with a peculiar sound, fell from his whole height face foremost to the floor.

I ran to him at once, calling to my mother. But haste was all in vain. The captain had been struck dead by thundering apoplexy. It is a curious thing to understand, for I had certainly never liked the man, though of late I had begun to pity him, but as soon as I saw that he was dead, I burst into a flood of tears. It was the second death I had known, and the sorrow of the first was still fresh in my heart.

I lost no time, of course, in telling my mother all that I knew, and perhaps should have told her long before, and we saw ourselves at once in a difficult and dangerous position. Some of the man's money—if he had any—was certainly due to us, but it was not likely that our captain's shipmates, above all the two specimens seen by me, Black Dog and the blind beggar, would be inclined to give up their booty in payment of the dead man's debts. The captain's order to mount at once and ride for Dr. Livesey would have left my mother alone and unprotected, which was not to be thought of. Indeed, it seemed impossible for either of us to remain much longer in the house; the fall of coals in the kitchen grate, the very ticking of the clock, filled us with alarms. The neighbourhood, to our ears, seemed haunted by approaching footsteps; and what between the dead body of the captain on the parlour floor and the thought of that detestable blind beggar hovering near at hand and ready to return, there were moments when, as the saying goes, I jumped in my skin for terror. Something must speedily be resolved upon, and it occurred to us at last to go forth together and seek help in the neighbouring hamlet. No sooner said than done. Bareheaded as we were, we ran out at once in the gathering evening and the frosty fog.

The hamlet lay not many hundred yards away, though out of view, on the other side of the next cove; and what greatly encouraged me, it was in an opposite direction from that whence the blind man had made his appearance and whither he had presumably returned. We were not many minutes on the road, though we sometimes stopped to lay hold of each other and hearken. But there was no unusual sound—nothing but the low wash of the ripple and the croaking of the inmates of the wood.

It was already candle-light when we reached the hamlet, and I shall never forget how much I was cheered to see the yellow shine in doors and windows; but that, as it proved, was the best of the help we were likely to get in that quarter. For—you would have thought men would have been ashamed of themselves—no soul would consent to return with us to the Admiral Benbow. The more we told of our troubles, the more—man, woman, and child—they clung to the shelter of their houses. The name of Captain Flint, though it was strange to me, was well enough known to some there and carried a great weight of terror. Some of the men who had been to field-work on the far side of the Admiral Benbow remembered, besides, to have seen several strangers on the road, and taking them to be smugglers, to have bolted away; and one at least had seen a little lugger in what we called Kitts Hole. For that matter, anyone who was a comrade of the captain's was enough to frighten them to death. And the short and the long of the matter was, that while we could get several who were willing enough to ride to Dr. Livesey's, which lay in another direction, not one would help us to defend the inn.

They say cowardice is infectious; but then argument is, on the other hand, a great emboldener; and so when each had said his say, my mother made them a speech. She would not, she declared, lose money that belonged to her fatherless boy; "If none of the rest of you dare," she said, "Jim and I dare. Back we will go, the way we came, and small thanks to you big, hulking, chicken-hearted men. We'll have that chest open, if we die for it. And I'll thank you for that bag, Mrs. Crossley, to bring back our lawful money in."

Of course I said I would go with my mother, and of course they all cried out at our foolhardiness, but even then not a man would go along with us. All they would do was to give me a loaded pistol lest we were attacked, and to promise to have horses ready saddled in case we were pursued on our return, while one lad was to ride forward to the doctor's in search of armed assistance.

My heart was beating finely when we two set forth in the cold night upon this dangerous venture. A full moon was beginning to rise and peered redly through the upper edges of the fog, and this increased our haste, for it was plain, before we came forth again, that all would be as bright as day, and our departure exposed to the eyes of any watchers. We slipped along the hedges, noiseless and swift, nor did we see or hear anything to increase our terrors, till, to our relief, the door of the Admiral Benbow had closed behind us.

I slipped the bolt at once, and we stood and panted for a moment in the dark, alone in the house with the dead captain's body. Then my mother got a candle in the bar, and holding each other's hand, we advanced into the parlour. He lay as we had left him, on his back, with his eyes open and one arm stretched out.

"Draw down the blind, Jim," whispered my mother; "they might come and watch outside. And now," said she when I had done so, "we have to get the key off *that*; and who's to touch it, I should like to know!" and she gave a kind of sob as she said the words.

I went down on my knees at once. On the floor close to his hand there was a little round of paper, blackened on the one side. I could not doubt that this was the *black spot*; and taking it up, I found written on the other side, in a very good, clear hand, this short message: "You have till ten tonight."

"He had till ten, mother," said I; and just as I said it, our old clock began striking. This sudden noise startled us shockingly; but the news was good, for it was only six. "Now, Jim," she said, "that key."

I felt in his pockets, one after another. A few small coins, a thimble, and some thread and big needles, a piece of pigtail tobacco bitten away at the end, his gully with the crooked handle, a pocket compass, and a tinder box were all that they contained, and I began to despair. "Perhaps it's round his neck," suggested my mother.

Overcoming a strong repugnance, I tore open his shirt at the neck, and there, sure enough, hanging to a bit of tarry string, which I cut with his own gully, we found the key. At this triumph we were filled with hope and hurried upstairs without delay to the little room where he had slept so long and where his box had stood since, the day of his arrival.

It was like any other seaman's chest on the outside, the initial "B" burned on the top of it with a hot iron and the corners somewhat smashed and broken as by long, rough usage.

"Give me the key," said my mother; and though the lock was very stiff, she had turned it and thrown back the lid in a twinkling.

A strong smell of tobacco and tar rose from the interior, but nothing was to be seen on the top except a suit of very good clothes, carefully brushed and folded. They had never been worn, my mother said. Under that, the miscellany began—a quadrant, a tin canikin, several sticks of tobacco, two brace of very handsome pistols, a piece of bar silver, an old Spanish watch and some other trinkets of little value and mostly of foreign make, a pair of compasses mounted with brass, and five or six curious West Indian shells. I have often wondered since why he should have carried about these shells with him in his wandering, guilty, and hunted life.

In the meantime, we had found nothing of any value but the silver and the trinkets, and neither of these were in our way. Underneath there was an old boat-cloak, whitened with sea-salt on many a harbour-bar. My mother pulled it up with impatience, and there lay before us, the last things in the chest, a bundle tied up in oilcloth, and looking like papers, and a canvas bag that gave forth, at a touch, the jingle of gold.

"I'll show these rogues that I'm an honest woman," said my mother. "I'll have my dues, and not a farthing over. Hold Mrs. Crossley's bag." And she began to count over the amount of the captain's score from the sailor's bag into the one that I was holding.

It was a long, difficult business, for the coins were of all countries and sizes—doubloons, and louis d'ors, and guineas, and pieces of eight, and I know not what besides, all shaken together at random. The guineas, too, were about the scarcest, and it was with these only that my mother knew how to make her count.

When we were about half-way through, I suddenly put my hand upon her arm, for I had heard in the silent frosty air a sound that brought my heart into my mouth—the tap-tapping of the blind man's stick upon the frozen road. It drew nearer and nearer, while we sat holding our breath. Then it struck sharp on the inn door, and then we could hear the handle being turned and the bolt rattling as the wretched being tried to enter; and then there was a long time of silence both within and without. At last the tapping recommenced, and, to our indescribable joy and gratitude, died slowly away again until it ceased to be heard.

"Mother," said I, "take the whole and let's be going," for I was sure the bolted door must have seemed suspicious and would bring the whole hornet's nest about our ears, though how thankful I was that I had bolted it, none could tell who had never met that terrible blind man.

But my mother, frightened as she was, would not consent to take a fraction more than was due to her and was obstinately unwilling to be content with less. It was not yet seven, she said, by a long way; she knew her rights and she would have them; and she was still arguing with me when a little low whistle sounded a good way off upon the hill. That was enough, and more than enough, for both of us. "I'll take what I have," she said, jumping to her feet. "And I'll take this to square the count," said I, picking up the oilskin packet.

Next moment we were both groping downstairs, leaving the candle by the empty chest; and the next we had opened the door and were in full retreat. We had not started a moment too soon. The fog was rapidly dispersing; already the moon shone quite clear on the high ground on either side; and it was only in the exact bottom of the dell and round the tavern door that a thin veil still hung unbroken to conceal the first steps of our escape. Far less than half-way to the hamlet, very little beyond the bottom of the hill, we must come forth into the moonlight.

Nor was this all, for the sound of several footsteps running came already to our ears, and as we looked back in their direction, a light tossing to and fro and still rapidly advancing showed that one of the newcomers carried a lantern.

"My dear," said my mother suddenly, "take the money and run on. I am going to faint."

This was certainly the end for both, of us, I thought. How I cursed the cowardice of the neighbours; how I blamed my poor mother for her honesty and her greed, for her past foolhardiness and present weakness! We were just at the little bridge, by good fortune; and I helped her, tottering as she was, to the edge of the bank, where, sure enough, she gave a sigh and fell on my shoulder. I do not know how I found the strength to do it at all, and I am afraid it was roughly done, but I managed to drag her down the bank and a little way under the arch. Farther I could not move her, for the bridge was too low to let me do more than crawl below it. So there we had to stay—my mother almost entirely exposed and both of us within earshot of the inn.

My curiosity, in a sense, was stronger than my fear, for I could not remain where I was, but crept back to the bank again, whence, sheltering my head behind a bush of broom, I might command the road before our door. I was scarcely in position ere my enemies began to arrive, seven or eight of them, running hard, their feet beating out of time along the road and the man with the lantern some paces in front. Three men ran together, hand in hand; and I made out, even through the mist, that the middle man of this trio was the blind beggar. The next moment his voice showed me that I was right.

"Down with the door!" he cried.

"Aye, aye, sir!" answered two or three; and a rush was made upon the Admiral Benbow, the lantern-bearer following; and then I could see them pause, and hear speeches passed in a lower key, as if they were surprised to find the door open. But the pause was brief, for the blind man again issued his commands. His voice sounded louder and higher, as if he were afire with eagerness and rage.

"In, in, in!" he shouted, and cursed them for their delay. Four or five of them obeyed at once, two remaining on the road with the formidable beggar. There was a pause, then a cry of surprise, and then a voice shouting from the house, "Bill's dead."

But the blind man swore at them again for their delay.

"Search him, some of you shirking lubbers, and the rest of you aloft and get the chest," he cried.

I could hear their feet rattling up our old stairs, so that the house must have shook with it. Promptly afterwards, fresh sounds of astonishment arose; the window of the captain's room was thrown open with a slam and a jingle of broken glass, and a man leaned out into the moonlight, head and shoulders, and addressed the blind beggar on the road below him.

"Pew," he cried, "they've been before us. Someone turned the chest out alow and aloft."

"Is it there?" roared Pew.

"The money's there."

The blind man cursed the money.

"Flint's fist, I mean," he cried.

"We don't see it here nohow," returned the man.

"Here, you below there, is it on Bill?" cried the blind man again.

At that another fellow, probably him who had remained below to search the captain's body, came to the door of the inn. "Bill's been overhauled a'ready," said he; "nothin' left."

"It's these people of the inn—it's that boy. I wish I had put his eyes out!" cried the blind man, Pew. "They were here no time ago—they had the door bolted when I tried it. Scatter, lads, and find 'em."

"Sure enough, they left their glim here," said the fellow from the window.

"Scatter and find 'em! Rout the house out!" reiterated Pew, striking with his stick upon the road.

Then there followed a great to-do through all our old inn, heavy feet pounding to and fro, furniture thrown over, doors kicked in, until the very rocks re-echoed and the men came out again, one after another, on the road, and declared that we were nowhere to be found. And just then the same whistle that had alarmed my mother and myself over the dead captain's money was once more clearly audible through the night, but this time twice repeated. I had thought it to be the blind man's trumpet, so to speak, summoning his crew to the assault, but I now found that it was a signal from the hillside towards the hamlet, and from its effect upon the buccaneers, a signal to warn them of approaching danger.

"There's Dirk again," said one. "Twice! We'll have to budge, mates."

"Budge, you skulk!" cried Pew. "Dirk was a fool and a coward from the first—you wouldn't mind him. They must be close by; they can't be far; you have your hands on it. Scatter and look for them, dogs! Oh, shiver my soul," he cried, "if I had eyes!"

This appeal seemed to produce some effect, for two of the fellows began to look here and there among the lumber, but half-heartedly, I thought, and with half an eye to their own danger all the time, while the rest stood irresolute on the road.

"You have your hands on thousands, you fools, and you hang a leg! You'd be as rich as kings if you could find it, and you know it's here, and you stand there skulking. There wasn't one of you dared face Bill, and I did it—a blind man! And I'm to lose my chance for you! I'm to be a poor, crawling beggar, sponging for rum, when I might be rolling in a coach! If you had the pluck of a weevil in a biscuit you would catch them still."

"Hang it, Pew, we've got the doubloons!" grumbled one. "They might have hid the blessed thing," said another. "Take the Georges, Pew, and don't stand here squalling."

Squalling was the word for it; Pew's anger rose so high at these objections till at last, his passion completely taking the upper hand, he struck at them right and left in his blindness and his stick sounded heavily on more than one

These, in their turn, cursed back at the blind miscreant, threatened him in horrid terms, and tried in vain to catch the stick and wrest it from his grasp.

This quarrel was the saving of us, for while it was still raging, another sound came from the top of the hill on the side of the hamlet—the tramp of horses galloping. Almost at the same time a pistol-shot, flash and report, came from the hedge side. And that was plainly the last signal of danger, for the buccaneers turned at once and ran, separating in every direction, one seaward along the cove, one slant across the hill, and so on, so that in half a minute not a sign of them remained but Pew. Him they had deserted, whether in sheer panic or out of revenge for his ill words and blows I know not; but there he remained behind, tapping up and down the road in a frenzy, and groping and calling for his comrades. Finally he took the wrong turn and ran a few steps past me, towards the hamlet, crying, "Johnny, Black Dog, Dirk," and other names, "you won't leave old Pew, mates— not old Pew!"

Just then the noise of horses topped the rise, and four or five riders came in sight in the moonlight and swept at full gallop down the slope. At this Pew saw his error, turned with a scream, and ran straight for the ditch, into which he rolled. But he was on his feet again in a second and made another dash, now utterly bewildered, right under the nearest of the coming horses.

The rider tried to save him, but in vain. Down went Pew with a cry that rang high into the night; and the four hoofs trampled and spurned him and passed by. He fell on his side, then gently collapsed upon his face and moved no more.

I leaped to my feet and hailed the riders. They were pulling up, at any rate, horrified at the accident; and I soon saw what they were. One, tailing out behind the rest, was a lad that had gone from the hamlet to Dr. Livesey's; the rest were revenue officers, whom he had met by the way, and with whom he had had the intelligence to return at once. Some news of the lugger in Kitt's Hole had found its way to Supervisor Dance and set him forth that night in our direction, and to that cir- cumstance my mother and I owed our preservation from death. Pew was dead, stone dead. As for my mother, when we had carried her up to the hamlet a little cold water and salts and that soon brought her back again, and she was none the worse for her terror, though she still continued to deplore the balance of the money. In the meantime the supervisor rode on, as fast as he could, to Kitt's Hole; but his men had to dismount and grope down the dingle, leading, and sometimes supporting, their horses, and in continual fear of ambushes; so it was no great matter for surprise that when they got down to the Hole the lugger was already under way, though still close in. He hailed her. A voice replied, telling him to keep out of the moonlight or he would get some lead in him, and at the same time a bullet whistled close by his arm. Soon after, the lugger doubled the point and disappeared. Mr. Dance stood there, as he said, "like a fish out of water," and all he could do was to dispatch a man to B— to warn the cutter. "And that," said he, "is just about as good as nothing. They've got off clean, and there's an end. Only," he added, "I'm glad I trod on Master Pew's corns," for by this time he had heard my story.

I went back with him to the Admiral Benbow, and you cannot imagine a house in such a state of smash; the very clock had been thrown down by these fellows in their furious hunt after my mother and myself; and though nothing had actually been taken away except the captain's money-bag and a little silver from the till, I could see at once that we were ruined. Mr. Dance could make nothing of the scene. "They got the money, you say? Well, then, Hawkins, what in fortune were they after? More money, I suppose?"

"No, sir; not money, I think," replied I. "In fact, sir, I believe I have the thing in my breast pocket; and to tell you the truth, I should like to get it put in safety."

"To be sure, boy; quite right," said he. "I'll take it, if you like."

"I thought perhaps Dr. Livesey—" I began.

"Perfectly right," he interrupted very cheerily, "perfectly right—a gentleman and a magistrate. And, now I come to think of it, I might as well ride round there myself and report to him or squire. Master Pew's dead, when all's done; not that I regret it, but he's dead, you see, and people will make it out against an officer of His Majesty's revenue, if make it out they can. Now, I'll tell you, Hawkins, if you like, I'll take you along."

I thanked him heartily for the offer, and we walked back to the hamlet where the horses were. By the time I had told mother of my purpose they were all in the saddle.

"Dogger," said Mr. Dance, "you have a good horse; take up this lad behind you."

As soon as I was mounted, holding on to Dogger's belt, the supervisor gave the word, and the party struck out at a bouncing trot on the road to Dr. Livesey's house.

We rode hard all the way till we drew up before Dr. Livesey's door. The house was all dark to the front.

Mr. Dance told me to jump down and knock, and Dogger gave me a stirrup to descend by. The door was opened almost at once by the maid. "Is Dr. Livesey in?" I asked.

No, she said, he had come home in the afternoon but had gone up to the hall to dine and pass the evening with the squire. "So there we go, boys," said Mr. Dance.

This time, as the distance was short, I did not mount, but ran with Dogger's stirrup-leather to the lodge gates and up the long, leafless, moonlit avenue to where the white line of the hall buildings looked on either hand on great old gardens. Here Mr. Dance dismounted, and taking me along with him, was admitted at a word into the house.

The servant led us down a matted passage and showed us at the end into a great library, all lined with bookcases and busts upon the top of them, where the squire and Dr. Livesey sat, pipe in hand, on either side of a bright fire.

I had never seen the squire so near at hand. He was a tall man, over six feet high, and broad in proportion, and he had a bluff, rough-and-ready face, all roughened and reddened and lined in his long travels. His eyebrows were very black, and moved readily, and this gave him a look of some temper, not bad, you would say, but quick and high.

"Come in, Mr. Dance," says he, very stately and condescending.

"Good evening, Dance," says the doctor with a nod. "And good evening to you, friend Jim. What good wind brings you here?"

The supervisor stood up straight and stiff and told his story like a lesson; and you should have seen how the two gentlemen leaned forward and looked at each other, and forgot to smoke in their surprise and interest. When they heard how my mother went back to the inn, Dr. Livesey fairly slapped his thigh, and the squire cried "Bravo!" and broke his long pipe against the grate. Long before it was done, Mr. Trelawney (that, you will remember, was the squire's name) had got up from his seat and was striding about the room, and the doctor, as if to hear the better, had taken off his powdered wig and sat there looking very strange indeed with his own close-cropped black poll.

At last Mr. Dance finished the story.

"Mr. Dance," said the squire, "you are a very noble fellow. And as for riding down that black, atrocious miscreant, I regard it as an act of virtue, sir, like stamping on a cockroach. This lad Hawkins is a trump, I perceive. Hawkins, will you ring that bell? Mr. Dance must have some ale."

"And so, Jim," said the doctor, "you have the thing that they were after, have you?"

"Here it is, sir," said I, and gave him the oilskin packet.

The doctor looked it all over, as if his fingers were itching to open it; but instead of doing that, he put it quietly in the pocket of his coat.

"Squire," said he, "when Dance has had his ale he must, of course, be off on His Majesty's service; but I mean to keep Jim Hawkins here to sleep at my house, and with your permission, I propose we should have up the cold pie and let him sup."

"As you will, Livesey," said the squire; "Hawkins has earned better than cold pie."

So a big pigeon pie was brought in and put on a side-table, and I made a hearty supper, for I was as hungry as a hawk, while Mr. Dance was further complimented and at last dismissed.

"And now, squire," said the doctor.

"And now, Livesey," said the squire in the same breath.

"One at a time, one at a time," laughed Dr. Livesey. "You have heard of this Flint, I suppose?"

"Heard of him!" cried the squire. "Heard of him, you say! He was the bloodthirstiest buccaneer that sailed. Blackbeard was a child to Flint. The Spaniards were so prodigiously afraid of him that, I tell you, sir, I was sometimes proud he was an Englishman. I've seen his top-sails with these eyes, off Trinidad, and the cowardly son of a rum-puncheon that I sailed with put back—put back, sir, into Port of Spain."

"Well, I've heard of him myself, in England," said the doctor. "But the point is, had he money?"

"Money!" cried the squire. "Have you heard the story? What were these villains after but money? What do they care for but money? For what would they risk their rascal carcasses but money?"

"That we shall soon know," replied the doctor. "But you are so confoundedly hot-headed and exclamatory that I cannot get a word in. What I want to know is this: Supposing that I have here in my pocket some clue to where Flint buried his treasure, will that treasure amount to much?"

"Amount, sir!" cried the squire. "It will amount to this: If we have the clue you talk about, I fit out a ship in Bristol dock, and take you and Hawkins here along, and I'll have that treasure if I search a year."

"Very well," said the doctor. "Now, then, if Jim is agreeable, we'll open the packet"; and he laid it before him on the table.

The bundle was sewn together, and the doctor had to get out his instrument case and cut the stitches with his medical scissors. It contained two things—a book and a sealed paper.

"First of all we'll try the book," observed the doctor. The squire and I were both peering over his shoulder as he opened it, for Dr. Livesey had kindly motioned me to come round from the side-table, where I had been eating, to enjoy the sport of the search. On the first page there were only some scraps of writing, such as a man with a pen in his hand might make for idleness or practice. One was the same as the tattoo mark, "Billy Bones his fancy"; then there was "Mr. W. Bones, mate,"

"No more rum," "Off Palm Key he got itt," and some other snatches, mostly single words and unintelligible. I could not help wondering who it was that had "got itt," and what "itt" was that he got. A knife in his back as like as not.

"Not much instruction there," said Dr. Livesey as he passed on. The next ten or twelve pages were filled with a curious series of entries. There was a date at one end of the line and at the other a sum of money, as in common account-books, but instead of explanatory writing, only a varying number of crosses between the two. On the 12th of June, 1745, for instance, a sum of seventy pounds had plainly become due to someone, and there was nothing but six crosses to explain the cause. In a few cases, to be sure, the name of a place would be added, as "Offe Caraccas," or a mere entry of latitude and longitude, as, "62° 17°, 20°, 19° 2° 40°."

The record lasted over nearly twenty years, the amount of the separate entries growing larger as time went on, and at the end a grand total had been made out after five or six wrong additions, and these words appended, "Bones, his pile."

"I can't make head or tail of this," said Dr. Livesey.

"The thing is as dear as noonday," cried the squire. "This is the blackhearted hound's account-book. These crosses stand for the names of ships or towns that they sank or plundered. The sums are the scoundrel's share, and where he feared an ambiguity, you see he added something dearer. 'Offe Caraccas' now; you see, here was some unhappy vessel boarded off that coast God help the poor souls that manned her—coral long ago."

"Right!" said the doctor. "See what it is to be a traveller. Right! And the amounts increase, you see, as he rose in rank."

There was little else in the volume but a few bearings of places noted in the blank leaves towards the end and a table for reducing French, English, and Spanish moneys to a common value.

"Thrifty man!" cried the doctor. "He wasn't the one to be cheated."

"And now," said the squire, "for the other."

The paper had been sealed in several places with a thimble by way of seal; the very thimble, perhaps, that I had found in the captain's pocket. The doctor opened the seals with great care, and there fell out the map of an island, with latitude and longitude, soundings, names of hills and bays and inlets, and every particular that would be needed to bring a ship to a safe anchorage upon its shores. It was about nine miles long and five across, shaped, you might say, like a fat dragon standing up, and had two fine land-locked harbours, and a hill in the centre part marked "The Spy-glass." There were several additions of a later date, but above all, three crosses of red ink—two on the north part of the island, one in the southwest—and beside this last, in the same red ink, and in a small, neat hand, very different from the captain's tottery characters, these words: "Bulk of treasure here."

Over on the back the same hand had written this further information:

Tall tree, Spy-glass shoulder, bearing a point to the N. of
N.N.E.
Skeleton Island E.S.E. and by E.
Ten feet.
The bar silver is in the north cache; you can find it by the
trend of the east hummock, ten fathoms south of the black
crag with the face on it.
The arms are easy found, in the sand-hill, N. point of north
inlet cape, bearing E. and a quarter N.

—J. F.

That was all; but brief as it was, and to me incomprehensible, it filled the squire and Dr. Livesey with delight.

"Livesey," said the squire, "you will give up this wretched practice at once. Tomorrow I start for Bristol. In three weeks' time—three weeks!— two weeks—ten days—we'll have the best ship, sir, and the choicest crew in England. Hawkins shall come as cabin-boy. You'll make a famous cabin-boy, Hawkins. You, Livesey, are ship's doctor; I am admiral. We'll take Redruth, Joyce, and Hunter. We'll have favourable winds, a quick passage, and not the least difficulty in finding the spot, and money to eat, to roll in, to play duck and drake with ever after."

"Trelawney," said the doctor, "I'll go with you; and I'll go bail for it, so will Jim, and be a credit to the undertaking. There's only one man I'm afraid of."

"And who's that?" cried the squire. "Name the dog, sir!"

"You," replied the doctor, "for you cannot hold your tongue. We are not the only men who know of this paper. These fellows who attacked the inn tonight—bold, desperate blades, for sure—and the rest who stayed aboard that lugger, and more, I dare say not far off, are one, and all, through thick and thin, bound that they'll get that money. We must none of us go alone till we get to sea. Jim and I shall stick together in the meanwhile you'll take Joyce and Hunter when you ride to Bristol, and from first to last, not one of us must breathe a word of what we've found."

"Livesey," returned the squire, "you are always in the right of it. I'll be as silent as the grave."

The Ghost of Captain Brand

by Howard Pyle (1853–1911)
from *Howard Pyle's Book of Pirates*

Howard Pyle was an influential author and illustrator of children's adventure literature. In this selection the ghost of an old pirate appears to his grandson.

I t is not so easy to tell why discredit should be cast upon a man because of something that his grandfather may have done amiss, but the world, which is never overnice in its discrimination as to where to lay the blame, is often pleased to make the innocent suffer in the place of the guilty.

Barnaby True was a good, honest, biddable lad, as boys go, but yet he was not ever allowed altogether to forget that his grandfather had been that very famous pirate, Capt. William Brand, who, after so many marvelous adventures (if one may believe the catchpenny stories and ballads that were written about him), was murdered in Jamaica by Capt. John Malyoe, the commander of his own consort, the *Adventure* galley.

It has never been denied, that ever I heard, that up to the time of Captain Brand's being commissioned against the South pirates he had always been esteemed as honest, reputable a captain as could be.

When he started out upon that adventure it was with a ship, the *Royal Sovereign*, fitted out by some of the most decent merchants of New York. The governor himself had subscribed to the adventure, and had himself signed Captain Brand's commission. So, if the unfortunate man went astray, he must have had great temptation to do so, many others behaving no better when the opportunity offered in those far-away seas where so many rich purchases might very easily be taken and no one the wiser.

To be sure, those stories and ballads made our captain to be a most wicked, profane wretch; and if he were, why, God knows he suffered and paid for it, for he laid his bones in Jamaica, and never saw his home or his wife and daughter again after he had sailed away on the *Royal Sovereign* on that long misfortunate voyage, leaving them in New York to the care of strangers.

At the time when he met his fate in Port Royal Harbor he had obtained two vessels under his command—the *Royal Sovereign*, which was the boat fitted out for him in New York, and the *Adventure* galley, which he was said to have taken somewhere in the South Seas. With these he lay in those waters of Jamaica for over a month after his return from the coasts of Africa, waiting for news from home, which, when it came, was of the very blackest; for the colonial authorities were at that time stirred up very hot against him to take him and hang him for a pirate, so as to clear their own skirts for having to do with such a fellow. So maybe it seemed better to our captain to hide his ill-gotten treasure there in those far-away parts, and afterward to try and bargain with it for his life when he should reach New York, rather than to sail straight for the Americas with what he had earned by his piracies, and so risk losing life and money both.

However that might be, the story was that Captain Brand and his gunner, and Captain Malyoe of the *Adventure* and the sailing master of the *Adventure* all went ashore together with a chest of money (no one of them choosing to trust the other three in so nice an affair), and buried the treasure somewhere on the beach of Port Royal Harbor. The story then has it that they fell a-quarreling about a future division of the money, and that, as a wind-up to the affair, Captain Malyoe shot Captain Brand through the head, while the sailing master of the *Adventure* served the gunner of the *Royal Sovereign* after the same fashion through the body, and that the murderers then went away, leaving the two stretched out in their own blood on the sand in the staring sun, with no one to know where the money was hid but they two who had served their comrades so.

It is a mighty great pity that anyone should have a grandfather who ended his days in such a sort as this, but it was no fault of Barnaby True's, nor could he have done anything to prevent it, seeing that he was not even born into the world at the time that his grandfather turned pirate, and was only one year old when he so met his tragical end. Nevertheless, the boys with whom he went to school never tired of calling him "Pirate," and would sometimes sing for his benefit that famous catchpenny song beginning thus:

> Oh, my name was Captain Brand,
>> A-sailing,
>> And a-sailing;
> Oh, my name was Captain Brand,
>> A-sailing free.
> Oh, my name was Captain Brand,
> And I sinned by sea and land,
> For I broke God's just command,
>> A-sailing free.

'Twas a vile thing to sing at the grandson of so misfortunate a man, and oftentimes little Barnaby True would double up his fists and would fight his tormentors at great odds, and would sometimes go back home with a bloody nose to have his poor mother cry over him and grieve for him.

Not that his days were all of teasing and torment, neither; for if his comrades did treat him so, why, then, there were other times when he and they were as great friends as could be, and would go in swimming together where there was a bit of sandy strand along the East River above Fort George, and that in the most amicable fashion. Or, maybe the very next day after he had fought so with his fellows, he would go a-rambling with them up the Bowerie Road, perhaps to help them steal cherries from some old Dutch farmer, forgetting in such adventure what a thief his own grandfather had been.

Well, when Barnaby True was between sixteen and seventeen years old he was taken into employment in the countinghouse of Mr. Roger Hartright, the well-known West India merchant, and Barnaby's own stepfather.

It was the kindness of this good man that not only found a place for Barnaby in the countinghouse, but advanced him so fast that against our hero was twenty-one years old he had made four voyages as supercargo to the West Indies in Mr. Hartright's ship, the *Belle Helen,* and soon after he was twenty-one undertook a fifth. Nor was it in any such subordinate position as mere supercargo that he acted, but rather as the confidential agent of Mr. Hartright, who, having no children of his own, was very jealous to advance our hero into a position of trust and responsibility in the countinghouse, as though he were indeed a son, so that even the captain of the ship had scarcely more consideration aboard than he, young as he was in years.

As for the agents and correspondents of Mr. Hartright throughout these parts, they also, knowing how the good man had adopted his interests, were very polite and obliging to Master Barnaby—especially, be it mentioned, Mr. Ambrose Greenfield, of Kingston, Jamaica, who, upon the occasions of his visits to those parts, did all that he could to make Barnaby's stay in that town agreeable and pleasant to him.

So much for the history of our hero to the time of the beginning of this story, without which you shall hardly be able to understand the purport of those most extraordinary adventures that befell him shortly after he came of age, nor the logic of their consequence after they had occurred.

For it was during his fifth voyage to the West Indies that the first of those extraordinary adventures happened of which I shall have presently to tell.

At that time he had been in Kingston for the best part of four weeks, lodging at the house of a very decent, respectable widow, by name Mrs. Anne Bolles, who, with three pleasant and agreeable daughters, kept a very clean and well-served lodging house in the outskirts of the town.

One morning, as our hero sat sipping his coffee, clad only in loose cotton drawers, a shirt, and a jacket, and with slippers upon his feet, as is the custom in that country, where everyone endeavors to keep as cool as may be—while he sat thus sipping his coffee Miss Eliza, the youngest of the three daughters, came and gave him a note, which, she said, a stranger had just handed in at the door, going away again without waiting for a reply. You may judge of Barnaby's surprise when he opened the note and read as follows:

> MR. BARNABY TRUE.
>
> Sir,—Though you don't know me, I know you, and I tell you this: if you will be at Pratt's Ordinary on Harbor Street on Friday next at eight o'clock of the evening, and will accompany the man who shall say to you, "The *Royal Sovereign* is come in," you shall learn something the most to your advantage that ever befell you. Sir, keep this note, and show it to him who shall address these words to you, so to certify that you are the man he seeks.

Such was the wording of the note, which was without address, and without any superscription whatever.

The first emotion that stirred Barnaby was one of extreme and profound amazement. Then the thought came into his mind that some witty fellow, of whom he knew a good many in that town—and wild, waggish pranks they were—was attempting to play off some smart jest upon him. But all that Miss Eliza could tell him when he questioned her concerning the messenger was that the bearer of the note was a tall, stout man, with a red neckerchief around his neck and copper buckles to his shoes, and that he had the appearance of a sailorman, having a great big queue hanging down his back. But, Lord! what was such a description as that in a busy seaport town, full of scores of men to fit such a likeness? Accordingly, our hero put away the note into his wallet, determining to show it to his good friend Mr. Greenfield that evening, and to ask his advice upon it. So he did show it, and that gentleman's opinion was the same as his—that some wag was minded to play off a hoax upon him, and that the matter of the letter was all nothing but Smoke.

Nevertheless, though Barnaby was thus confirmed in his opinion as to the nature of the communication he had received, he yet determined in his own mind that he would see the business through to the end, and would be at Pratt's Ordinary, as the note demanded, upon the day and at the time specified therein.

Pratt's Ordinary was at that time a very fine and well-known place of its sort, with good tobacco and the best rum that ever I tasted, and had a garden behind it that, sloping down to the harbor Front, was planted pretty thick with palms and ferns grouped into clusters with flowers and plants. Here were a number of little tables, some in little grottoes, like our Vauxhall in New York, and with red and blue and white paper lanterns hung among the foliage, whither gentlemen and ladies used sometimes to go of an evening to sit and drink lime juice and sugar and water (and sometimes a taste of something stronger), and to look out across the water at the shipping in the cool of the night.

Thither, accordingly, our hero went, a little before the time appointed in the note, and passing directly through the Ordinary and the garden beyond, chose a table at the lower end of the garden and close to the water's edge, where he would not be easily seen by anyone coming into the place. Then, ordering some rum and water and a pipe of tobacco, he composed himself to watch for the appearance of those witty fellows whom he suspected would presently come thither to see the end of their prank and to enjoy his confusion.

The spot was pleasant enough; for the land breeze, blowing strong and full, set the leaves of the palm tree above his head to rattling and clattering continually against the sky, where, the moon then being about full, they shone every now and then like blades of steel. The waves also were splashing up against the little landing place at the foot of the garden, sounding very cool in the night, and sparkling all over the harbor where the moon caught the edges of the water. A great many vessels were lying at anchor in their ridings, with the dark, prodigious form of a man-of-war looming up above them in the moonlight.

There our hero sat for the best part of an hour, smoking his pipe of tobacco and sipping his grog, and seeing not so much as a single thing that might concern the note he had received.

It was not far from half an hour after the time appointed in the note, when a rowboat came suddenly out of the night and pulled up to the landing place at the foot of the garden above mentioned, and three or four men came ashore in the darkness. Without saying a word among themselves they chose a near-by table and, sitting down, ordered rum and water, and began drinking their grog in silence. They might have sat there about five minutes, when, by and by, Barnaby True became aware that they were observing him very curiously; and then almost immediately one, who was plainly the leader of the party, called out to him:

"How now, messmate! Won't you come and drink a dram of rum with us?"

"Why, no," says Barnaby, answering very civilly; "I have drunk enough already, and more would only heat my blood."

"All the same," quoth the stranger, "I think you will come and drink with us; for, unless I am mistook, you are Mr. Barnaby True, and I am come here to tell you that the *Royal Sovereign is come in.*"

Now I may honestly say that Barnaby True was never more struck aback in all his life than he was at hearing these words uttered in so unexpected a manner. He had been looking to hear them under such different circumstances that, now that his ears heard them addressed to him, and that so seriously, by a perfect stranger, who, with others, had thus mysteriously come ashore out of the darkness, he could scarce believe that his ears heard aright. His heart suddenly began beating at a tremendous rate, and had he been an older and wiser man, I do believe he would have declined the adventure, instead of leaping blindly, as he did, into that of which he could see neither the beginning nor the ending. But being barely one-and-twenty years of age, and having an adventurous disposition that would have carried him into almost anything that possessed a smack of uncertainty or danger about it, he contrived to say, in a pretty easy tone (though God knows how it was put on for the occasion):

"Well, then, if that be so, and if the *Royal Sovereign* is indeed come in, why, I'll join you, since you are so kind as to ask me." And therewith he went across to the other table, carrying his pipe with him, and sat down and began smoking, with all the appearance of ease he could assume upon the occasion.

"Well, Mr. Barnaby True," said the man who had before addressed him, so soon as Barnaby had settled himself, speaking in a low tone of voice, so there would be no danger of any others hearing the words— "Well, Mr. Barnaby True—for I shall call you by your name, to show you that though I know you, you don't know me—I am glad to see that you are man enough to enter thus into an affair, though you can't see to the bottom of it. For it shows me that you are a man of mettle, and are deserving of the fortune that is to befall you to-night. Nevertheless, first of all, I am bid to say that you must show me a piece of paper that you have about you before we go a step farther."

"Very well," said Barnaby; "I have it here safe and sound, and see it you shall." And thereupon and without more ado he fetched out his wallet, opened it, and handed his interlocutor the mysterious note he had received the day or two before. Whereupon the other, drawing to him the candle, burning there for the convenience of those who would smoke tobacco, began immediately reading it.

This gave Barnaby True a moment or two to look at him. He was a tall, stout man, with a red handkerchief tied around his neck, and with copper buckles on his shoes, so that Barnaby True could not but wonder whether he was not the very same man who had given the note to Miss Eliza Bolles at the door of his lodging house.

" 'Tis all right and straight as it should be," the other said, after he had so glanced his eyes over the note. "And now that the paper is read" (suiting his action to his words), "I'll just burn it, for safety's sake."

And so he did, twisting it up and setting it to the flame of the candle.

"And now," he said, continuing his address, "I'll tell you what I am here for. I was sent to ask you if you're man enough to take your life in your own hands and to go with me in that boat down there? Say 'Yes,' and we'll start away without wasting more time, for the devil is ashore here at Jamaica—though you don't know what that means—and if he gets ahead of us, why, then we may whistle for what we are after. Say 'No,' and I go away again, and I promise you you shall never be troubled again in this sort. So now speak up plain, young gentleman, and tell us what is your mind in this business, and whether you will adventure any farther or not."

If our hero hesitated it was not for long. I cannot say that his courage did not waver for a moment; but if it did, it was, I say, not for long, and when he spoke up it was with a voice as steady as could be.

"To be sure I'm man enough to go with you," he said; "and if you mean me any harm I can look out for myself; and if I can't, why, here is something can look out for me," and therewith he lifted up the flap of his coat pocket and showed the butt of a pistol he had fetched with him when he had set out from his lodging house that evening.

At this the other burst out a-laughing. "Come," says he, "you are indeed of right mettle, and I like your spirit. All the same, no one in all the world means you less ill than I, and so, if you have to use that barker, 'twill not be upon us who are your friends, but only upon one who is more wicked than the devil himself. So come, and let us get away."

Thereupon he and the others, who had not spoken a single word for all this time, rose from the table, and he having paid the scores of all, they all went down together to the boat that still lay at the landing place at the bottom of the garden.

Thus coming to it, our hero could see that it was a large yawl boat manned with half a score of black men for rowers, and there were two lanterns in the stern sheets, and three or four iron shovels.

The man who had conducted the conversation with Barnaby True for all this time, and who was, as has been said, plainly the captain of the party, stepped immediately down into the boat; our hero followed, and the others followed after him; and instantly they were seated the boat was shoved off and the black men began pulling straight out into the harbor, and so, at some distance away, around under the stern of the man-of-war.

Not a word was spoken after they had thus left the shore, and presently they might all have been ghosts, for the silence of the party. Barnaby True was too full of his own thoughts to talk—and serious enough thoughts they were by this time, with crimps to trepan a man at every turn, and press gangs to carry a man off so that he might never be heard of again. As for the others, they did not seem to choose to say anything now that they had him fairly embarked upon their enterprise.

And so the crew pulled on in perfect silence for the best part of an hour, the leader of the expedition directing the course of the boat straight across the harbor, as though toward the mouth of the Rio Cobra River. Indeed, this was their destination, as Barnaby could after a while see, by the low point of land with a great long row of coconut palms upon it (the appearance of which he knew very well), which by and by began to loom up out of the milky dimness of the moonlight. As they approached the river they found the tide was running strong out of it, so that some distance away from the stream it gurgled and rippled along-side the boat as the crew of black men pulled strongly against it. Thus they came up under what was either a point of land or an islet covered with a thick growth of mangrove trees. But still no one spoke a single word as to their destination, or what was the business they had in hand.

The night, now that they were close to the shore, was loud with the noise of running tide-water, and the air was heavy with the smell of mud and marsh, and over all the whiteness of the moonlight, with a few stars pricking out here and there in the sky; and all so strange and silent and mysterious that Barnaby could not divest himself of the feeling that it was all a dream.

So, the rowers bending to the oars, the boat came slowly around from under the clump of mangrove bushes and out into the open water again.

Instantly it did so the leader of the expedition called out in a sharp voice, and the black men instantly lay on their oars.

Almost at the same instant Barnaby True became aware that there was another boat coming down the river toward where they now drifting with the strong tide out into the harbor again, and he knew that it was because of the approach of that boat that the other had called upon his men to cease rowing.

The other boat, as well as he could see in the distance, was full of men, some of whom appeared to be armed, for even in the dusk of the darkness the shine of the moonlight glimmered sharply now and then on the barrels of muskets or pistols, and in the silence that followed after their own rowing had ceased Barnaby True could hear the chug! chug! of the oars sounding louder and louder through the watery still-ness of the night as the boat drew nearer and nearer. But he knew nothing of what it all meant, nor whether these others were friends or enemies, or what was to happen next.

The oarsmen of the approaching boat did not for a moment cease their rowing, not till they had come pretty close to Barnaby and his companions. Then a man who sat in the stern ordered them to cease rowing, and as they lay on their oars he stood up. As they passed by, Barnaby True could see him very plain, the moonlight shining full upon him—a large, stout gentleman with a round red face, and clad in a fine laced coat of red cloth. Amidship of the boat was a box or chest about the bigness of a middle-sized traveling trunk, but covered all over with cakes of sand and dirt. In the act of passing, the gentleman, still standing, pointed at it with an elegant gold-headed cane which he held in his hand. "Are you come after this, Abraham Dawling?" says he, and thereat his countenance broke into as evil, malignant a grin as ever Barnaby True saw in all of his life.

The other did not immediately reply so much as a single word, but sat as still as any stone. Then, at last, the other boat having gone by, he suddenly appeared to regain his wits, for he bawled out after it, "Very well, Jack Malyoe! very well, Jack Malyoe! you've got ahead of us this time again, but next time is the third, and then it shall be our turn, even if William Brand must come back from hell to settle with you."

This he shouted out as the other boat passed farther and farther away, but to it my fine gentleman made no reply except to burst out into a great roaring fit of laughter.

There was another man among the armed men in the stern of the passing boat—a villainous, lean man with lantern jaws, and the top of his head as bald as the palm of my hand. As the boat went away into the night with the tide and the headway the oars had given it, he grinned so that the moonlight shone white on his big teeth. Then, flourishing a great big pistol, he said, and Barnaby could hear every word he spoke, "Do but give me the word, Your Honor, and I'll put another bullet through the son of a sea cook."

But the gentleman said some words to forbid him, and therewith the boat was gone away into the night, and presently Barnaby could hear that the men at the oars had begun rowing again, leaving them lying there, without a single word being said for a long time.

By and by one of those in Barnaby's boat spoke up. "Where shall you go now?" he said.

At this the leader of the expedition appeared suddenly to come back to himself, and to find his voice again. "Go?" he roared out. "Go to the devil! Go? Go where you choose! Go? Go back again—that's where we'll go!" and therewith he fell a-cursing and swearing until he foamed at the lips, as though he had gone clean crazy, while the black men began rowing back again across the harbor as fast as ever they could lay oars into the water.

They put Barnaby True ashore below the old custom house; but so bewildered and shaken was he by all that had happened, and by what he had seen, and by the names that he heard spoken, that he was scarcely conscious of any of the familiar things among which he found himself thus standing. And so he walked up the moonlit street toward his lodging like one drunk or bewildered; for "John Malyoe" was the name of the captain of the *Adventure* galley—he who had shot Barnaby's own grandfather—and "Abraham Dawling" was the name of the gunner of the *Royal Sovereign* who had been shot at the same time with the pirate captain, and who, with him, had been left stretched out in the staring sun by the murderers.

The whole business had occupied hardly two hours, but it was as though that time was no part of Barnaby's life, but all a part of some other life, so dark and strange and mysterious that it in no wise belonged to him.

As for that box covered all over with mud, he could only guess at that time what it contained and what the finding of it signified.

But of this our hero said nothing to anyone, nor did he tell a single living soul what he had seen that night, but nursed it in his own mind, where it lay so big for a while that he could think of little or nothing else for days after.

Mr. Greenfield, Mr. Hartright's correspondent and agent in these parts, lived in a fine brick house just out of the town, on the Mona Road, his family consisting of a wife and two daughters—brisk, lively young ladies with black hair and eyes, and very bright teeth that shone whenever they laughed, and with a plenty to say for themselves. Thither Barnaby True was often asked to a family dinner; and, indeed, it was a pleasant home to visit, and to sit upon the veranda and smoke a cigarro with the good old gentleman and look out toward the mountains, while the young ladies laughed and talked, or played upon the guitar and sang. And oftentimes so it was strongly upon Barnaby's mind to speak to the good gentleman and tell him what he had beheld that night out in the harbor; but always he would think better of it and hold his peace, falling to thinking, and smoking away upon his cigarro at a great rate.

A day or two before the *Belle Helen* sailed from Kingston Mr. Greenfield stopped Barnaby True as he was going through the office to bid him to come to dinner that night (for there within the tropics they breakfast at eleven o'clock and take dinner in the cool of the evening, because of the heat, and not at midday, as we do in more temperate latitudes). "I would have you meet," says Mr. Greenfield, "your chief passenger for New York, and his granddaughter, for whom the state cabin and the two staterooms are to be fitted as here ordered [showing a letter]—Sir John Malyoe and Miss Marjorie Malyoe. Did you ever hear tell of Capt. Jack Malyoe, Master Barnaby?"

Now I do believe that Mr. Greenfield had no notion at all that old Captain Brand was Barnaby True's own grandfather and Capt. John Malyoe his murderer, but when he so thrust at him the name of that man, what with that in itself and the late adventure through which he himself had just passed, and with his brooding upon it until it was so prodigiously big in his mind, it was like hitting him a blow to so fling the questions at him. Nevertheless, he was able to reply, with a pretty straight face, that he had heard of Captain Malyoe and who he was.

"Well," says Mr. Greenfield, "if Jack Malyoe was a desperate pirate and a wild, reckless blade twenty years ago, why, he is Sir John Malyoe now and the owner of a fine estate in Devonshire. Well, Master Barnaby, when one is a baronet and come into the inheritance of a fine estate (though I do hear it is vastly cumbered with debts), the world will wink its eye to much that he may have done twenty years ago. I do hear say, though, that his own kin still turn the cold shoulder to him."

To this address Barnaby answered nothing, but sat smoking away at his cigarro at a great rate.

And so that night Barnaby True came face to face for the first time with the man who murdered his own grandfather—the greatest beast of a man that ever he met in all of his life.

That time in the harbor he had seen Sir John Malyoe at a distance and in the darkness; now that he beheld him near by it seemed to him that he had never looked at a more evil face in all his life. Not that the man was altogether ugly, for he had a good nose and a fine double chin; but his eyes stood out like balls and were red and watery, and he winked them continually, as though they were always smarting; and his lips were thick and purple-red, and his fat, red cheeks were mottled here and there with little clots of purple veins; and when he spoke his voice rattled so in his throat that it made one wish to clear one's own throat to listen to him. So, what with a pair of fat, white hands, and that hoarse voice, and his swollen face, and his thick lips sticking out, it seemed to Barnaby True he had never seen a countenance so distasteful to him as that one into which he then looked.

But if Sir John Malyoe was so displeasing to our hero's taste, why, the granddaughter, even this first time he beheld her, seemed to him to be the most beautiful, lovely young lady that ever he saw. She had a thin, fair skin, red lips, and yellow hair—though it was then powdered pretty white for the occasion—and the bluest eyes that Barnaby beheld in all of his life. A sweet, timid creature, who seemed not to dare so much as to speak a word for herself without looking to Sir John for leave to do so, and would shrink and shudder whenever he would speak of a sudden to her or direct a sudden glance upon her. When she did speak, it was in so low a voice that one had to bend his head to hear her, and even if she smiled would catch herself and look up as though to see if she had leave to be cheerful.

As for Sir John, he sat at dinner like a pig, and gobbled and ate and drank, smacking his lips all the while, but with hardly a word to either her or Mrs. Greenfield or to Barnaby True; but with a sour, sullen air, as though he would say, "Your damned victuals and drink are no better than they should be, but I must eat 'em or nothing." A great bloated beast of a man!

Only after dinner was over and the young lady and the two misses sat off in a corner together did Barnaby hear her talk with any ease. Then, to be sure, her tongue became loose, and she prattled away at a great rate, though hardly above her breath, until of a sudden her grandfather called out, in his hoarse, rattling voice, that it was time to go. Whereupon she stopped short in what she was saying and jumped up from her chair, looking as frightened as though she had been caught in something amiss, and was to be punished for it.

Barnaby True and Mr. Greenfield both went out to see the two into their coach, where Sir John's man stood holding the lantern. And who should he be, to be sure, but that same lean villain with bald head who had offered to shoot the leader of our hero's expedition out on the harbor that night! For, one of the circles of light from the lantern shining up into his face, Barnaby True knew him the moment he clapped eyes upon him. Though he could not have recognized our hero, he grinned at him in the most impudent, familiar fashion, and never so much as touched his hat either to him or to Mr. Greenfield; but as soon as his master and his young mistress had entered the coach, banged to the door and scrambled up on the seat alongside the driver, and so away without a word, but with another impudent grin, this time favoring both Barnaby and the old gentleman.

Such were these two, master and man, and what Barnaby saw of them then was only confirmed by further observation—the most hateful couple he ever knew; though, God knows, what they afterward suffered should wipe out all complaint against them.

The next day Sir John Malyoe's belongings began to come aboard the *Belle Helen,* and in the afternoon that same lean, villainous manservant comes skipping across the gangplank as nimble as a goat, with two black men behind him lugging a great sea chest. "What!" he cried out, "and so you is the supercargo, is you? Why, I thought you was more account when I saw you last night a-sitting talking with His Honor like his equal. Well, no matter; 'tis something to have a brisk, genteel young fellow for a supercargo. So come, my hearty, lend a hand, will you, and help me set His Honor's cabin to rights."

What a speech was this to endure from such a fellow, to be sure! and Barnaby so high in his own esteem, and holding himself a gentleman! Well, what with his distaste for the villain, and what with such odious familiarity, you can guess into what temper so impudent an address must have cast him. "You'll find the steward in yonder," he said "and he'll show you the cabin," and therewith turned and walked away with prodigious dignity, leaving the other standing where he was.

As he entered his own cabin he could not but see, out of the tail of his eye, that the fellow was still standing where he had left him, regarding him with a most evil, malevolent countenance, so that he had the satisfaction of knowing that he had made one enemy during that voyage who was not very likely to forgive or forget what he must regard as a slight put upon him.

The next day Sir John Malyoe himself came aboard, accompanied by his granddaughter, and followed by this man, and he followed again by four black men, who carried among them two trunks, not large in size, but prodigious heavy in weight, and toward which Sir John and his follower devoted the utmost solicitude and care to see that they were properly carried into the state cabin he was to occupy. Barnaby True was standing in the great cabin as they passed close by him; but though Sir John Malyoe looked hard at him and straight in the face, he never so much as spoke a single word, or showed by a look or a sign that he knew who our hero was. At this the serving man, who saw it all with eyes as quick as a cat's, fell to grinning and chuckling to see Barnaby in his turn so slighted.

The young lady, who also saw it all, flushed up red, then in the instant of passing looked straight at our hero, and bowed and smiled at him with a most sweet and gracious affability, then the next moment recovering herself, as though mightily frightened at what she had done.

The same day the *Belle Helen* sailed, with as beautiful, sweet weather as ever a body could wish for.

There were only two other passengers aboard, the Rev. Simon Styles, the master of a flourishing academy in Spanish Town, and his wife, a good, worthy old couple, but very quiet, and would sit in the great cabin by the hour together reading, so that, what with Sir John Malyoe staying all the time in his own cabin with those two trunks he held so precious, it fell upon Barnaby True in great part to show attention to the young lady; and glad enough he was of the opportunity, as anyone may guess. For when you consider a brisk, lively young man of one-and-twenty and a sweet, beautiful miss of seventeen so thrown together day after day for two weeks, the weather being very fair, as I have said, and the ship tossing and bowling along before a fine humming breeze that sent white caps all over the sea, and with nothing to do but sit and look at that blue sea and the bright sky overhead, it is not hard to suppose what was to befall, and what pleasure it was to Barnaby True to show attention to her.

But, oh! those days when a man is young, and, whether wisely or no, fallen in love! How often during that voyage did our hero lie awake in his berth at night, tossing this way and that without sleep—not that he wanted to sleep if he could, but would rather lie so awake thinking about her and staring into the darkness!

Poor fool! He might have known that the end must come to such a fool's paradise before very long. For who was he to look up to Sir John Malyoe's granddaughter, he, the supercargo of a merchant ship, and she the granddaughter of a baronet.

Nevertheless, things went along very smooth and pleasant, until one evening, when all came of a sudden to an end. At that time he and the young lady had been standing for a long while together, leaning over the rail and looking out across the water through the dusk toward the westward, where the sky was still of a lingering brightness. She had been mightily quiet and dull all that evening, but now of a sudden she began, without any preface whatever, to tell Barnaby about herself and her affairs. She said that she and her grandfather were going to New York that they might take passage thence to Boston town, there to meet her cousin Captain Malyoe, who was stationed in garrison at that place. Then she went on to say that Captain Malyoe was the next heir to the Devonshire estate, and that she and he were to be married in the fall.

But, poor Barnaby! what a fool was he, to be sure! Me-thinks when she first began to speak about Captain Malyoe he knew what was coming. But now that she had told him, he could say nothing, but stood there staring across the ocean, his breath coming hot and dry as ashes in his throat. She, poor thing, went on to say, in a very low voice, that she had liked him from the very first moment she had seen him, and had been very happy for these days, and would always think of him as a dear friend who had been very kind to her, who had so little pleasure in life, and so would always remember him.

Then they were both silent, until at last Barnaby made shift to say, though in a hoarse and croaking voice, that Captain Malyoe must be a very happy man, and that if he were in Captain Malyoe's place he would be the happiest man in the world. Thus, having spoken, and so found his tongue, he went on to tell her, with his head all in a whirl, that he, too, loved her, and that what she had told him struck him to the heart, and made him the most miserable, unhappy wretch in the whole world.

She was not angry at what he said, nor did she turn to look at him, but only said, in a low voice, he should not talk so, for that it could only be a pain to them both to speak of such things, and that whether she would or no, she must do everything as her grandfather bade her, for that he was indeed a terrible man.

To this poor Barnaby could only repeat that he loved her with all his heart, that he had hoped for nothing in his love, but that he was now the most miserable man in the world.

It was at this moment, so tragic for him, that some one who had been hiding nigh them all the while suddenly moved away, and Barnaby True could see in the gathering darkness that it was that villain manservant of Sir John Malyoe's and knew that he must have overheard all that had been said.

The man went straight to the great cabin, and poor Barnaby, his brain all a tingle, stood looking after him, feeling that now indeed the last drop of bitterness had been added to his trouble to have such a wretch overhear what he had said.

The young lady could not have seen the fellow, for she continued leaning over the rail, and Barnaby True, standing at her side, not moving, but in such a tumult of many passions that he was like one bewildered, and his heart beating as though to smother him.

So they stood for I know not how long when, of a sudden, Sir John Malyoe comes running out of the cabin, without his hat, but carrying his gold-headed cane, and so straight across the deck to where Barnaby and the young lady stood, that spying wretch close at his heels, grinning like an imp.

"You hussy!" bawled out Sir John, so soon as he had come pretty near them, and in so loud a voice that all on deck might have heard the words; and as he spoke he waved his cane back and forth as though he would have struck the young lady, who, shrinking back almost upon the deck, crouched as though to escape such a blow. "You hussy!" he bawled out with vile oaths, too horrible here to be set down. "What do you do here with this Yankee supercargo, not fit for a gentlewoman to wipe her feet upon? Get to your cabin, you hussy" (only it was something worse he called her this time), "before I lay this cane across your shoulders!"

What with the whirling of Barnaby's brains and the passion into which he was already melted, what with his despair and his love, and his anger at this address, a man gone mad could scarcely be less accountable for his actions than was he at that moment. Hardly knowing what he did, he put his hand against Sir John Malyoe's breast and thrust him violently back, crying out upon him in a great, loud, hoarse voice for threatening a young lady, and saying that for a farthing he would wrench the stick out of his hand and throw it overboard.

Sir John went staggering back with the push Barnaby gave him, and then caught himself up again. Then, with a great bellow, ran roaring at our hero, whirling his cane about, and I do believe would have struck him (and God knows then what might have happened) had not his manservant caught him and held him back. "Keep back!" cried out our hero, still mighty hoarse. "Keep back! If you strike me with that stick I'll fling you overboard!"

By this time, what with the sound of loud voices and the stamping of feet, some of the crew and others aboard were hurrying up, and the next moment Captain Manly and the first mate, Mr. Freesden, came running out of the cabin. But Barnaby, who was by this fairly set agoing, could not now stop himself.

"And who are you, anyhow," he cried out, "to threaten to strike me and to insult me, who am as good as you? You dare not strike me! You may shoot a man from behind, as you shot poor Captain Brand on the Rio Cobra River, but you won't dare strike me face to face. I know who you are and what you are!"

By this time Sir John Malyoe had ceased to endeavor to strike him, but stood stock-still, his great bulging eyes staring as though they would pop out of his head.

"What's all this?" cries Captain Manly, bustling up to them with Mr. Freesden. "What does all this mean?"

But, as I have said, our hero was too far gone now to contain himself until all that he had to say was out.

"The damned villain insulted me and insulted the young lady," he cried out, panting in the extremity of his passion, "and then he threatened to strike me with his cane. But I know who he is and what he is. I know what he's got in his cabin in those two trunks, and where he found it, and whom it belongs to. He found it on the shores of the Rio Cobra River, and I have only to open my mouth and tell what I know about it."

At this Captain Manly clapped his hand upon our hero's shoulder and fell to shaking him so that he could scarcely stand, calling out to him the while to be silent. "What do you mean?" he cried. "An officer of this ship to quarrel with a passenger of mine! Go straight to your cabin, and stay there till I give you leave to come out again."

At this Master Barnaby came somewhat back to himself and into his wits again with a jump. "But he threatened to strike me with his cane, Captain," he cried out, "and that I won't stand from any man!"

"No matter what he did," said Captain Manly, very sternly. "Go to your cabin, as I bid you, and stay there till I tell you to come out again, and when we get to New York I'll take pains to tell your stepfather of how you have behaved. I'll have no such rioting as this aboard my ship."

Barnaby True looked around him, but the young lady was gone. Nor, in the blindness of his frenzy, had he seen when she had gone nor whither she went. As for Sir John Malyoe, he stood in the light of a lantern, his face gone as white as ashes, and I do believe if a look could kill, the dreadful malevolent stare he fixed upon Barnaby True would have slain him where he stood.

After Captain Manly had so shaken some wits into poor Barnaby he, unhappy wretch, went to his cabin, as he was bidden to do, and there, shutting the door upon himself, and flinging himself down, all dressed as he was, upon his berth, yielded himself over to the profoundest passion of humiliation and despair.

There he lay for I know not how long, staring into the darkness, until by and by, in spite of his suffering and his despair, he dozed off into a loose sleep, that was more like waking than sleep, being possessed continually by the most vivid and distasteful dreams, from which he would awaken only to doze off and to dream again.

It was from the midst of one of these extravagant dreams that he was suddenly aroused by the noise of a pistol shot, and then the noise of another and another, and then a great bump and a grinding jar, and then the sound of many footsteps running across the deck and down into the great cabin. Then came a tremendous uproar of voices in the great cabin, the struggling as of men's bodies being tossed about, striking violently against the partitions and bulkheads. At the same instant arose a screaming of women's voices, and one voice, and that Sir John Malyoe's, crying out as in the greatest extremity: "You villains! You damned villains!" and with the sudden detonation of a pistol fired into the close space of the great cabin.

Barnaby was out in the middle of his cabin in a moment, and taking only time enough to snatch down one of the pistols that hung at the head of his berth, flung out into the great cabin, to find it as black as night, the lantern slung there having been either blown out or dashed out into darkness. The prodigiously dark space was full of uproar, the hubbub and confusion pierced through and through by that keen sound of women's voices screaming, one in the cabin and the other in the stateroom beyond. Almost immediately Barnaby pitched headlong over two or three struggling men scuffling together upon the deck, falling with a great clatter and the loss of his pistol, which, however, he regained almost immediately.

What all the uproar meant he could not tell, but he presently heard Captain Manly's voice from somewhere suddenly calling out, "You bloody pirate, would you choke me to death?" wherewith some notion of what had happened came to him like a flash, and that they had been attacked in the night by pirates.

Looking toward the companionway, he saw, outlined against the darkness of the night without, the blacker form of a man's figure, standing still and motionless as a statue in the midst of all this hubbub, and so by some instinct he knew in a moment that that must be the master maker of all this devil's brew. Therewith, still kneeling upon the deck, he covered the bosom of that shadowy figure point-blank, as he thought, with his pistol, and instantly pulled the trigger.

In the flash of red light, and in the instant stunning report of the pistol shot, Barnaby saw, as stamped upon the blackness, a broad, flat face with fishy eyes, a lean, bony forehead with what appeared to be a great blotch of blood upon the side, a cocked hat trimmed with gold lace, a red scarf across the breast, and the gleam of brass buttons. Then the darkness, very thick and black, swallowed everything again.

But in the instant Sir John Malyoe called out, in a great loud voice: "My God! 'Tis William Brand!" Therewith came the sound of some one falling heavily down.

The next moment, Barnaby's sight coming back to him again in the darkness, he beheld that dark and motionless figure still standing exactly where it had stood before, and so knew either that he had missed it or else that it was of so supernatural a sort that a leaden bullet might do it no harm. Though if it was indeed an apparition that Barnaby beheld in that moment, there is this to say, that he saw it as plain as ever he saw a living man in all of his life.

This was the last our hero knew, for the next moment somebody— whether by accident or design he never knew—struck him such a terrible violent blow upon the side of the head that he saw forty thousand stars flash before his eyeballs, and then, with a great humming in his head, swooned dead away.

When Barnaby True came back to his senses again it was to find himself being cared for with great skill and nicety, his head bathed with cold water, and a bandage being bound about it as carefully as though a chirurgeon was attending to him.

He could not immediately recall what had happened to him, nor until he had opened his eyes to find himself in a strange cabin,

extremely well fitted and painted with white and gold, the light of a
lantern shining in his eyes, together with the gray of the early daylight
through the dead-eye. Two men were bending over him—one, a negro
in a striped shirt, with a yellow handkerchief around his head and
silver earrings in his ears; the other, a white man, clad in a strange outlandish dress of a foreign make, and with great mustachios hanging
down, and with gold earrings in his ears.

It was the latter who was attending to Barnaby's hurt with such
extreme care and gentleness.

All this Barnaby saw with his first clear consciousness after his
swoon. Then remembering what had befallen him, and his head
beating as though it would split asunder, he shut his eyes again, con-
triving with great effort to keep himself from groaning aloud, and wondering as to what sort of pirates these could be who would first knock
a man in the head so terrible a blow as that which he had suffered, and
then take such care to fetch him back to life again, and to make him
easy and comfortable.

Nor did he open his eyes again, but lay there gathering his wits
together and wondering thus until the bandage was properly tied
about his head and sewed together. Then once more he opened his
eyes, and looked up to ask where he was.

Either they who were attending to him did not choose to reply, or
else they could not speak English, for they made no answer, excepting
by signs; for the white man, seeing that he was now able to speak, and
so was come back into his senses again, nodded his head three or four
times, and smiled with a grin of his white teeth, and then pointed, as
though toward a saloon beyond. At the same time the negro held up
our hero's coat and beckoned for him to put it on, so that Barnaby,
seeing that it was required of him to meet some one without, arose,
though with a good deal of effort, and permitted the negro to help him
on with his coat, still feeling mightily dizzy and uncertain upon his
legs, his head beating fit to split, and the vessel rolling and pitching at
a great rate, as though upon a heavy ground swell.

So, still sick and dizzy, he went out into what was indeed a fine saloon beyond, painted in white and gilt like the cabin he had just quitted, and fitted in the nicest fashion, a mahogany table, polished very bright, extending the length of the room, and a quantity of bottles, together with glasses of clear crystal, arranged in a hanging rack above.

Here at the table a man was sitting with his back to our hero, clad in a rough pea-jacket, and with a red handkerchief tied around his throat, his feet stretched out before him, and he smoking a pipe of tobacco with all the ease and comfort in the world.

As Barnaby came in he turned round, and, to the profound astonishment of our hero, presented toward him in the light of the lantern, the dawn shining pretty strong through the skylight, the face of that very man who had conducted the mysterious expedition that night across Kingston Harbor to the Rio Cobra River.

This man looked steadily at Barnaby True for a moment or two, and then burst out laughing; and, indeed, Barnaby, standing there with the bandage about his head, must have looked a very droll picture of that astonishment he felt so profoundly at finding who was this pirate into whose hands he had fallen.

"Well," says the other, "and so you be up at last, and no great harm done, I'll be bound. And how does your head feel by now, my young master?"

To this Barnaby made no reply, but, what with wonder and the dizziness of his head, seated himself at the table over against the speaker, who pushed a bottle of rum toward him, together with a glass from the swinging shelf above.

He watched Barnaby fill his glass, and so soon as he had done so began immediately by saying: "I do suppose you think you were treated mightily ill to be so handled last night. Well, so you were treated ill enough—though who hit you that crack upon the head I know no more than a child unborn. Well, I am sorry for the way you were handled, but there is this much to say, and of that you may believe me, that nothing was meant to you but kindness, and before you are through with us all you will believe that well enough."

Here he helped himself to a taste of grog, and sucking in his lips, went on again with what he had to say. "Do you remember," said he, "that expedition of ours in Kingston Harbor, and how we were all of us balked that night?"

"Why, yes," said Barnaby True, "nor am I likely to forget it."

"And do you remember what I said to that villain, Jack Malyoe, that night as his boat went by us?"

"As to that," said Barnaby True, "I do not know that I can say yes or no, but if you will tell me, I will maybe answer you in kind."

"Why, I mean this," said the other. "I said that the villain had got the better of us once again, but that next time it would be our turn, even if William Brand himself had to come back from hell to put the business through."

"I remember something of the sort," said Barnaby, "now that you speak of it, but still I am all in the dark as to what you are driving at."

The other looked at him very cunningly for a little while, his head on one side, and his eyes half shut. Then, as if satisfied, suddenly burst out laughing. "Look hither," said he, "and I'll show you something," and therewith, moving to one side, disclosed a couple of traveling cases or small trunks with brass studs, so exactly like those that Sir John Malyoe had fetched aboard at Jamaica that Barnaby, putting this and that together, knew that they must be the same.

Our hero had a strong enough suspicion as to what those two cases contained, and his suspicions had become a certainty when he saw Sir John Malyoe struck all white at being threatened about them, and his face lowering so malevolently as to look murder had he dared do it. But, Lord! what were suspicions or even certainty to what Barnaby True's two eyes beheld when that man lifted the lids of the two cases—the locks thereof having already been forced—and, flinging back first one lid and then the other, displayed to Barnaby's astonished sight a great treasure of gold and silver! Most of it tied up in leathern bags, to be sure, but many of the coins, big and little, yellow and white, lying loose and scattered about like so many beans, brimming the cases to the very top.

Barnaby sat dumb-struck at what he beheld; as to whether he breathed or no, I cannot tell; but this I know, that he sat staring at that marvelous treasure like a man in a trance, until, after a few seconds of this golden display, the other banged down the lids again and burst out laughing, whereupon he came back to himself with a jump.

"Well, and what do you think of that?" said the other. "Is it not enough for a man to turn pirate for? But," he continued, "it is not for the sake of showing you this that I have been waiting for you here so long a while, but to tell you that you are not the only passenger aboard, but that there is another, whom I am to confide to your care and attention, according to orders I have received; so, if you are ready, Master Barnaby, I'll fetch her in directly." He waited for a moment, as though for Barnaby to speak, but our hero not replying, he arose and, putting away the bottle of rum and the glasses, crossed the saloon to a door like that from which Barnaby had come a little while before. This he opened, and after a moment's delay and a few words spoken to some one within, ushered thence a young lady, who came out very slowly into the saloon where Barnaby still sat at the table.

It was Miss Marjorie Malyoe, very white, and looking as though stunned or bewildered by all that had befallen her.

Barnaby True could never tell whether the amazing strange voyage that followed was of long or of short duration; whether it occupied three days or ten days. For conceive, if you choose, two people of flesh and blood moving and living continually in all the circumstances and surroundings as of a nightmare dream, yet they two so happy together that all the universe beside was of no moment to them! How was anyone to tell whether in such circumstances any time appeared to be long or short? Does a dream appear to be long or to be short?

The vessel in which they sailed was a brigantine of good size and build, but manned by a considerable crew, the most strange and outlandish in their appearance that Barnaby had ever beheld—some white, some yellow, some black, and all tricked out with gay colors, and gold earrings in their ears, and some with great long mustachios, and others with handkerchiefs tied around their heads, and all talking a language together of which Barnaby True could understand not a single word, but which might have been Portuguese from one or two phrases he caught. Nor did this strange, mysterious crew, of God knows what sort of men, seem to pay any attention whatever to Barnaby or to the young lady. They might now and then have looked at him and her out of the corners of their yellow eyes, but that was all; otherwise they were indeed like the creatures of a nightmare dream. Only he who was the captain of this outlandish crew would maybe speak to Barnaby a few words as to the weather or what not when he would come down into the saloon to mix a glass of grog or to light a pipe of tobacco, and then to go on deck again about his business. Otherwise our hero and the young lady were left to themselves, to do as they pleased, with no one to interfere with them.

As for her, she at no time showed any great sign of terror or of fear, only for a little while was singularly numb and quiet, as though dazed with what had happened to her. Indeed, methinks that wild beast, her grandfather, had so crushed her spirit by his tyranny and his violence that nothing that happened to her might seem sharp and keen, as it does to others of an ordinary sort.

But this was only at first, for afterward her face began to grow singularly clear, as with a white light, and she would sit quite still, permitting Barnaby to gaze, I know not how long, into her eyes, her face so transfigured and her lips smiling, and they, as it were, neither of them breathing, but hearing, as in another far-distant place, the outlandish jargon of the crew talking together in the warm, bright sunlight, or the sound of creaking block and tackle as they hauled upon the sheets.

Is it, then, any wonder that Barnaby True could never remember whether such a voyage as this was long or short?

It was as though they might have sailed so upon that wonderful voyage forever. You may guess how amazed was Barnaby True when, coming upon deck one morning, he found the brigantine riding upon an even keel, at anchor off Staten Island, a small village on the shore, and the well-known roofs and chimneys of New York town in plain sight across the water.

'Twas the last place in the world he had expected to see.

And, indeed, it did seem strange to lie there alongside Staten Island all that day, with New York town so nigh at hand and yet so impossible to reach. For whether he desired to escape or no, Barnaby True could not but observe that both he and the young lady were so closely watched that they might as well have been prisoners, tied hand and foot and laid in the hold, so far as any hope of getting away was concerned.

All that day there was a deal of mysterious coming and going aboard the brigantine, and in the afternoon a sailboat went up to the town, carrying the captain, and a great load covered over with a tarpaulin in the stern. What was so taken up to the town Barnaby did not then guess, but the boat did not return again till about sundown.

For the sun was just dropping below the water when the captain came aboard once more and, finding Barnaby on deck, bade him come down into the saloon, where they found the young lady sitting, the broad light of the evening shining in through the skylight, and making it all pretty bright within.

The captain commanded Barnaby to be seated, for he had something of moment to say to him; whereupon, as soon as Barnaby had taken his place alongside the young lady, he began very seriously, with a preface somewhat thus: "Though you may think me the captain of this brigantine, young gentleman, I am not really so, but am under orders, and so have only carried out those orders of a superior in all these things that I have done." Having so begun, he went on to say that there was one thing yet remaining for him to do, and that the greatest thing of all. He said that Barnaby and the young lady had not been fetched away from the *Belle Helen* as they were by any mere chance of accident, but that 'twas all a plan laid by a head wiser than his, and carried out by one whom he must obey in all things. He said that he hoped that both Barnaby and the young lady would perform willingly what they would be now called upon to do, but that whether they did it willingly or no, they must, for that those were the orders of one who was not to be disobeyed.

You may guess how our hero held his breath at all this; but whatever might have been his expectations, the very wildest of them all did not reach to that which was demanded of him. "My orders are these," said the other, continuing: "I am to take you and the young lady ashore, and to see that you are married before I quit you; and to that end a very good, decent, honest minister who lives ashore yonder in the village was chosen and hath been spoken to and is now, no doubt, waiting for you to come. Such are my orders, and this is the last thing I am set to do; so now I will leave you alone together for five minutes to talk it over, but be quick about it, for whether willing or not, this thing must be done."

Thereupon he went away, as he had promised, leaving those two alone together, Barnaby like one turned into stone, and the young lady, her face turned away, flaming as red as fire in the fading light.

Nor can I tell what Barnaby said to her, nor what words he used, but only, all in a tumult, with neither beginning nor end he told her that God knew he loved her, and that with all his heart and soul, and that there was nothing in all the world for him but her; but, nevertheless, if she would not have it as had been ordered, and if she were not willing to marry him as she was bidden to do, he would rather die than lend himself to forcing her to do such a thing against her will. Nevertheless, he told her she must speak up and tell him yes or no, and that God knew he would give all the world if she would say "yes."

All this and more he said in such a tumult of words that there was no order in their speaking, and she sitting there, her bosom rising and falling as though her breath stifled her. Nor may I tell what she replied to him, only this, that she said she would marry him. At this he took her into his arms and set his lips to hers, his heart all melting away in his bosom.

So presently came the captain back into the saloon again, to find Barnaby sitting there holding her hand, she with her face turned away, and his heart beating like a trip hammer, and so saw that all was settled as he would have it. Wherewith he wished them both joy, and gave Barnaby his hand.

The yawlboat belonging to the brigantine was ready and waiting alongside when they came upon deck, and immediately they descended to it and took their seats. So they landed, and in a little while were walking up the village street in the darkness, she clinging to his arm as though she would swoon, and the captain of the brigantine and two other men from aboard following after them. And so to the minister's house, finding him waiting for them, smoking his pipe in the warm evening, and walking up and down in front of his own door. He immediately conducted them into the house, where, his wife having fetched a candle, and two others of the village folk being present, the good man having asked several questions as to their names and their age and where they were from, the ceremony was performed, and the certificate duly signed by those present—excepting the men who had come ashore from the brigantine, and who refused to set their hands to any paper.

The same sailboat that had taken the captain up to the town in the afternoon was waiting for them at the landing place, whence, the captain, having wished them Godspeed, and having shaken Barnaby very heartily by the hand, they pushed off, and, coming about, ran away with the slant of the wind, dropping the shore and those strange beings alike behind them into the night.

As they sped away through the darkness they could hear the creaking of the sails being hoisted aboard of the brigantine, and so knew that she was about to put to sea once more. Nor did Barnaby True ever set eyes upon those beings again, nor did anyone else that I ever heard tell of.

It was nigh midnight when they made Mr. Hartright's wharf at the foot of Wall Street, and so the streets were all dark and silent and deserted as they walked up to Barnaby's home.

You may conceive of the wonder and amazement of Barnaby's dear stepfather when, clad in a dressing gown and carrying a lighted candle in his hand, he unlocked and unbarred the door, and so saw who it was had aroused him at such an hour of the night, and the young and beautiful lady whom Barnaby had fetched with him.

The first thought of the good man was that the *Belle Helen* had come into port; nor did Barnaby undeceive him as he led the way into the house, but waited until they were all safe and sound in privity together before he should unfold his strange and wonderful story.

"This was left for you by two foreign sailors this afternoon, Barnaby," the good old man said, as he led the way through the hall, holding up the candle at the same time, so that Barnaby might see an object that stood against the wainscoting by the door of the dining room.

Nor could Barnaby refrain from crying out with amazement when he saw that it was one of the two chests of treasure that Sir John Malyoe had fetched from Jamaica, and which the pirates had taken from the *Belle Helen.* As for Mr. Hartright, he guessed no more what was in it than the man in the moon.

The next day but one brought the *Belle Helen* herself into port, with the terrible news not only of having been attacked at night by pirates, but also that Sir John Malyoe was dead. For whether it was the sudden shock of the sight of his old captain's face—whom he himself had murdered and thought dead and buried—flashing so out against the darkness, or whether it was the strain of passion that overset his brains, certain it is that when the pirates left the *Belle Helen,* carrying with them the young lady and Barnaby and the traveling trunks, those left aboard the *Belle Helen* found Sir John Malyoe lying in a fit upon the floor, frothing at the mouth and black in the face, as though he had been choked, and so took him away to his berth, where, the next morning about ten o'clock, he died, without once having opened his eyes or spoken a single word.

As for the villain manservant, no one ever saw him afterward; though whether he jumped overboard, or whether the pirates who so attacked the ship had carried him away bodily, who shall say?

Mr. Hartright, after he had heard Barnaby's story, had been very uncertain as to the ownership of the chest of treasure that had been left by those men for Barnaby, but the news of the death of Sir John Malyoe made the matter very easy for him to decide. For surely if that treasure did not belong to Barnaby, there could be no doubt that it must belong to his wife, she being Sir John Malyoe's legal heir. And so it was that that great fortune (in actual computation amounting to upward of sixty-three thousand pounds) came to Barnaby True, the grandson of that famous pirate, William Brand; the English estate in Devonshire, in default of male issue of Sir John Malyoe, descended to Captain Malyoe, whom the young lady was to have married.

As for the other case of treasure, it was never heard of again, nor could Barnaby ever guess whether it was divided as booty among the pirates, or whether they had carried it away with them to some strange and foreign land, there to share it among themselves.

And so the ending of the story, with only this to observe, that whether that strange appearance of Captain Brand's face by the light of the pistol was a ghostly and spiritual appearance, or whether he was present in flesh and blood, there is only to say that he was never heard of again; nor had he ever been heard of till that time since the day he was so shot from behind by Capt. John Malyoe on the banks of the Rio Cobra River in the year 1733.

from

Peter Duck:
A Treasure Hunt in the Caribbees

by Arthur Ransome (1884–1967)

Arthur Ransome's classic series "Swallow and Amazons" relates the ongoing adventures of six engaging young sailing enthusiasts. In this volume the children, together with Captain Flint and an old sailor named Peter Duck, race the nasty pirate Black Jake for buried treasure.

T hat night, after supper, the whole ship's company were on deck enjoying the quiet of the evening after the busy day. During the afternoon, they had filled up the tanks with fresh drinking-water, so that they had enough for a long cruise. "With all the water ballast we've got under the flooring we could sail round the world," said Captain Flint proudly. They had taken aboard a lot of fresh meat, butter, eggs, vegetables and bread. There was no point in using the tinned things if they did not need to. They had bought a grand lot of fresh fruit and half a dozen of those big Dutch cheeses, red as giant cherries, because they happened to see them in a window. Everybody knew that tomorrow they were going to set sail in earnest and now, with the ship so well provisioned, feeling that they could go anywhere, and were already no longer dependent on the land, they were all gathered together up in the bows of the ship talking of places to visit.

Polly, the ship's parrot, was singing out "Pieces of eight" and reminding people that he was a Pretty Polly, and crawling beak over claw up the forestay and down to the bowsprit and along the top of the rail. Gibber alone was below decks. He had been given a bag of monkey nuts that Captain Flint had bought in the town, by way of a little extra for him, and as he did not quite trust the others, he had taken the bag down below and was eating the nuts in his bunk. Captain Flint was sitting on the capstan smoking his pipe. Peter Duck was smoking his, and putting a whipping on the end of a new warp. The others were hanging about and dropping in a word or two now and then and mostly all at the same time. Captain Flint had a chart of the Channel with him and he was showing them how they would be going across the mouth of the Thames and between the Goodwins and the coast, and past Dover, and within sight maybe of Cape Gris Nez. It grew dusk, and hard to see the names on the chart, and, as nobody seemed to want to go in, he sent Peggy to the deckhouse to bring the hanging lantern. Far away, beyond the bridge, from one of the boats in the Trawler Basin, came the noise of an accordion. Someone over there was playing "Amsterdam." Everybody in the *Wild Cat* was so much interested in the chart and in Captain Flint's plans for visiting the Channel ports and then perhaps crossing to Brest and going down across the Bay to Cape Villano and Vigo, and perhaps even to Madeira if they got a spell of fine weather, that nobody was thinking about the *Viper* and Black Jake, though there had been some talk a little earlier about the oddness of her returning to port.

At the other side of the narrow inner harbour lay the *Viper* in her old berth, and Black Jake was sitting on a hatch, looking across at the *Wild Cat* in the gathering dusk. He was alone on deck. Bill, the red-haired boy, was curled up on some sacking in the forecastle, forgetting in sleep the aching of his bones. Black Jake had taken it out of Bill that morning when he had come on deck and found the *Wild Cat's* berth empty and the *Wild Cat* nowhere to be seen. He had been surly with his crew, too, when he had got them together in a hurry from their lairs in the town. And they had all turned furiously against him when, after all the work of hoisting sail and warping the ship out, they had met the *Wild Cat*, with Peter Duck at her wheel, coming back to Lowestoft, and Black Jake had turned about and brought the *Viper* in again. They had tied up to the quay once more, but then had stumped off back to their taverns leaving the whole ship in disorder, with sails lowered and not stowed. And Black Jake sat there alone on deck, biting his nails, and staring over the water at the *Wild Cat*.

What were they talking about, over there, on the foredeck of the little green schooner? Could he be mistaken, when he himself had seen Peter Duck bring his dunnage aboard? What else could it mean when Peter Duck, after sticking to his wherry for so many years, had made up his mind to go to sea again? "Three captains aboard and two mates." That fool of a boy had learnt that much anyhow, and what could it mean but the one thing. It was no ordinary voyage when so many officers were shipping together. That a voyage was planned he was sure enough. He had seen the stores going aboard steadily, day by day, and such masses of them. As much as he had thought necessary for the *Viper*. No wonder, if they were bound for the same place. And then he thought of Peter Duck again. Black Jake bit his nails and scowled. The beauty of the evening meant nothing to him. He did not hear the old tunes played on the accordion in the Trawler Basin. He did not hear when the accordion-player rested, and some Irishman with a fiddle set sea-boots dancing on the decks of the trawlers. There was no room in his mind for anything but the one question: What was it that was being planned between old Peter Duck and that fat man who owned the little green schooner? Was Peter Duck after all these years going to tell that fat man over there what he had always refused to tell to Black Jake, or indeed to anyone else? What was that chart they were looking at? If he could get a sight of that it might be the answer to his question. If he could only hear what was being said as they crowded round the capstan head and peered into the chart. And then the great anchor caught his eye, hanging from the bows of the *Wild Cat*, its chain disappearing into a hawse-hole on the level of the deck. Black Jake stopped biting his nails. He stood up and walked to the stern of the *Viper*. Below him the *Viper's* dinghy was lying. He looked up and down the deserted quays. He took one more glance across the harbour to the little group in the twilight on the foredeck of the *Wild Cat*, looking at the chart by the glimmer of a lantern. Then he swung himself over the side, lowered himself down the warp into the dinghy, cast off, leaving the warp dangling in the water, and rowed noiselessly away.

He did not row straight across to the *Wild Cat*. Someone might have seen him. He rowed up the inner harbour as if to visit one of the moored ketches. No one saw that dark figure in the dark boat slipping silently along in the shadow of the quay. No one saw him work his way across to the other side among the anchored vessels. No one saw him paddling slowly, idly, as if for no purpose at all, under the quay where the *Wild Cat* was moored. He passed close under the bows of a rusty black trawler, waiting her turn on the slip. Above him in the twilight was the square green stern of the *Wild Cat*. He shipped his oars and, more quietly than ever, clawed his way along her steep, green side. The anchor was above him at last. He took his dinghy's painter, made a loop in it and hooked it over a fluke of the anchor. The tide was flowing in and the slight current kept the dinghy steady where he needed it. He took a hold of the anchor, as high as he could reach. Quietly, quietly, he pulled himself up. A knee was on the anchor. He took a higher grip. A foot was on the anchor. He gripped the chain above. Slowly he raised himself. His head, at last, was level with the hawse-hole. What was that they were saying? Under his breath he cursed the chattering parrot.

Something like four fathom of anchor chain had been ranged on deck. The anchor had not been used after all, but it had not seemed worth while to stow the chain again as it was likely to be wanted in the morning if it seemed best to anchor while making sail. Nothing makes more noise than getting chain up from below, and perhaps Captain Flint, knowing how early he would have to be to catch a helping tide down the coast, had already made up his mind not to wake the younger part of his crew before he could help it. Anyhow, there was the chain on deck ranged forward of the capstan. Two turns and a half hitch had been taken round the samson-post[*], and besides, a small belaying-pin had been stuck through a link of the chain when it ran between small bollards on deck on its way to the hawse-hole. There was no danger of the anchor slipping before this pin had been taken out and the chain unfastened. Some very small noise made Peter Duck look down at the chain. It may have been that a link shifted and clanked against another as Black Jake hoisted himself up. It may have been, as Titty still believes, that Black Jake's ear-rings jingled. Anyhow, something did catch the attention of Peter Duck and made him look at the chain. And something did catch the attention of Titty, so that she noticed that something was wrong with the parrot. The parrot was on the rail along the top of the bulwarks, flapping his wings and chattering and looking down. He had stopped saying "Pieces of eight." He was not even saying "Pretty Polly." He was just chattering, as if he were afraid or angry.

"What's the matter with . . . ?"

But Titty never finished her sentence. She caught the eye of Peter Duck. That was enough. The others went on talking.

"Yo, ho, ho for the Canaries," said Nancy.

"Or the Azores," said John.

Titty, with her mouth open and her sentence unfinished, saw Peter Duck bend quietly and unfasten the chain from the samson-post. She saw him pick up a mallet. And still the parrot chattered and napped its wings.

She saw Peter Duck swing the mallet and strike the belaying-pin out of the link. Four fathom of chain flew with a roar through the hawse-hole. There was a crash of breaking wood and a tremendous splash, as the anchor, with Black Jake upon it, dropped, smashed the dinghy and plunged to the bottom of the harbour.

---

[*] The samson-post is a very strong post that goes right through the deck and down to the keel.—NANCY.

Everybody rushed to the side and looked down. Bits of broken dinghy showed in the dusk. And then a dark head came to the surface.

"Black Jake again!" cried Titty.

"Who else?" said Peter Duck.

They watched him swim across to the *Viper*. They saw the dark figure, dim in the dusk, swarm up the warp over the *Viper*'s stern.

"Gosh!" said Nancy.

Captain Flint spoke as quietly and calmly as if someone had dropped a teaspoon. "What happened, Mr Duck?" he said.

"Anchor went with a run, sir," said Peter Duck. "It just seemed to me it could do with a bit of washing. So I knocked the pin out and let it go. Black Jake was on it."

"On it?" said Captain Flint, looking, for the first time, a little astonished.

"He was listening through the hawse-hole," said Peter Duck.

"There's something very funny about all this," said Captain Flint.

"You may well say that," said Peter Duck. "Worse than funny, you might say."

The others were staring first at Captain Flint and then at the old sailor.

No one else in the harbour seemed to have noticed that anything had happened. The fiddler was still scraping out a jig tune in one of the vessels over by the market. Foot passengers were crossing the swing bridge. A light showed for a moment on the *Viper* and then vanished.

"He'll have to change everything he's got on," said Susan.

"And then he'll come charging round with a policeman or two because of our anchor smashing his dinghy," said Peggy.

"What a galoot you are," said Captain Nancy to her mate. "How can he go to the police? He'd have to explain how he happened to be on our anchor and squinting through our hawse-hole . . ."

"Then he'll do something else," said John.

"It's as if he'd got something against us," said Susan.

"Well, he has now, even if he hadn't before," said Nancy cheerfully. "He must have got a nasty shock when he went down with the anchor."

"But, but, but . . ." said Roger, but got no further.

"What's the fellow after?" said Captain Flint.

"It's a long yarn, is that," said Peter Duck.

"Let's have it," said Captain Flint.

Peter Duck looked up at the quay above them, dark in the gathering dusk.

"You never know who might be listening," he said.

"Come along to the deckhouse," said Captain Flint. "We can take a look out now and again to see that no one's near enough to listen."

"Better so," said Peter Duck.

"Come on," said Titty eagerly. There was almost a stampede along the decks, as Captain Flint, taking the lantern with him, walked aft with Peter Duck.

"What about your bedtime, Roger?" said Susan.

"Oh, I say," said Roger. "Just this once . . ."

And so it happened that the whole ship's company were crowded into the deckhouse when Peter Duck, sitting on edge of his bunk, began to spin his yarn.

Everyone had grown accustomed to Peter Duck. He seemed, somehow, to be part of the ship, and they themselves seemed to have lived in the *Wild Cat* for a long time. They would have been startled if anyone had suddenly reminded them that the Swallows had come aboard for the first time only three days before, and the Amazons less than a week before them. But now, as they waited for the old sailor to begin, and he sat there on the edge of his bunk, pushing the dottle of tobacco into his pipe with a horny thumb, he seemed different. The light of the lantern hanging under the beam fell on the same old kindly wrinkled face, but it was as if those shrewd old eyes of his were looking at them out of another world. This, perhaps, was because he was remembering things that had happened a very long time ago.

"By my thinking," he said at last, "there's nothing there to make much of a do about. A little money maybe, and if any man were to have it in his own pocket he'd find it burning a hole there, and he'd spend it likely on what he'd be sorry for, and in the end he'd be worse off than if he'd never had the handling of it. By my thinking that's what it is, and I've been sorry enough that ever I tell that yarn to my wife that's dead now, and my three daughters when they was little girls, thirty years ago maybe or more. It's been a plague to me ever since, not but what most folk know by now that I'm not going to do a thing about it . . ."

"About what?" said Roger.

"Treasure?" said Captain Flint.

"About whatever it is," said Peter Duck. "Whatever it is I saw buried down at the foot of a coconut palm, fifty, sixty or maybe seventy years ago."

"But where were you?" asked Roger.

"In the coconut tree, of course," said Peter Duck, "in the coconut tree, just waking out of my night's sleep."

Another idea struck Roger. "Did you snore then, too?" he asked.

"Roger," said Susan severely.

"He does now," said Roger. "Beautifully."

"I reckon I didn't then," said Peter Duck slowly, "or they'd have heard me and buried it in some other place. And maybe they'd have buried me too," he added after a pause.

"Who?"

"Shut up, Roger," said Captain Flint. "You'll hear if you keep your ears open and your mouth shut."

"I'd better begin at the beginning," said Peter Duck, "and tell you how it all come about. You see I'd slipped my cable out of Lowestoft, and gone to London in a coaster. And I'd run away from her at Greenhithe, and then in the docks I shipped aboard a fine vessel trading to the Brazils, shipped as cabin-boy I had, when I was no bigger than this ship's boy that keeps wanting me to crowd on topsails before my anchor's fair out of the ground. We'd a fair passage across the Western Ocean but it ended over soon. Struck a pampero or a Sugar Coast hurricane or one of them other big winds she did, and lost both her sticks and broke her back, and we took to the boats and she smashed one of them, and the other one, the one that I was in, didn't last long, but a seaman in her lashed me to a spar, and the next I knew was that I was washed up, beached good and proper on a bit of an island. There was a big surf roaring along that shore, and if I'd chosen any other place I'd have had the life pounded out of me at once, but I'd had no choosing in it, being lashed to the spar and half drowned anyways, and I was washed up between some rocks into a narrow little hole of a place where the surf didn't run though the spray was spouting over from the swell that was rolling in against the rocks outside. I never see any of the others again off that ship. The first thing I did see was crabs."

"Big ones?" asked Roger, and Titty nudged him with her elbow.

"All sizes," said Peter Duck, "but mostly small. And these crabs they wasn't the sort of crabs you know. They look at me greedy-like, and come on, waving them clippers of theirs and opening and shutting them. It wasn't above a minute or so before one of them crabs was taking a hold of the calf of my leg. Well, you may lay to it, I wasted no more time than I could help in getting free from that spar, and then I fetched that crab a kick and threw a stone at the others. I got one, too, and he fell over. And his friends was on him in a minute, and their clippers clacking like a watermill, and waving over him, and then they had him to pieces and into their mouths and crunch, crunch . . . horrible sight it was . . . and them crabs looking greedy at me all the time.

"And then when I walk up that beach to have a look about me and to see if there was any others of us saved, I might have been a drum-major, the way that regiment of crabs come following after, running sideways, and lifting themselves, and clapping their clippers, and gog-gling at me with them eyes of theirs, set on their faces like them martello towers you see along the south coast. I hadn't the tonnage of Roger there, and I didn't like the look of them crabs.

"But in the end I was glad of them. I couldn't find a thing to eat, not at first. And then, after I'd killed a few more of them crabs, I was lis-tening to the others cracking them and crunching them, and I didn't see why I shouldn't have a share. So the next one of them crabs that come too close to me, I killed him with a stone and grabbed him up before them others could get at him, and pulled his clippers off, and smashed his shell with the stone, and found him pretty good eating, particularly the handle end of them clippers of his. The stuff I sucked out of them was good and tasty and there was a bit in there that was decent chewing too. I was hungry, of course, to begin, but the taste of them crabs was a long ways better than what you might think it might be. I ate three or four of them right away.

"And my eating them crabs seemed to do me a bit of good with the others, for pretty soon they'd slither away in a hurry if I stepped sharply, and I had only to pick up a stone to send them scuttling all ways at once. But the worst as you might say was to come. For them crabs that was running about in the daytime was as harmless as lambs beside them that showed up at night. Just as night come down these other crabs come up, and they was the sort that if I threw a stone at one of them he'd just think nothing of catching it in them clippers of his and heaving it back. That was the sort of crabs these was, and they seemed to think as I was just what they was wanting. They was tired of eating them small crabs and I reckon they think I was something new, with a softer kind of shell.

"I legged it just in time, and the biggest of them had a clipper full of the starn of my breeches and I hope it choked him. Them breeches was no good after, no protection at all. But, as I was saying, I legged it, and swarmed up one of them young coconut palms as was growing along that shore a bit above high-water mark. And up in the top of that tree there was some young coconuts, and I cut a hole in one with my knife, and the milk came trickling out, and I found just a little meat in it too. And I slept up in the tree all that night and come down in the morning and took it out of them smaller crabs, and did well enough what with them and the coconuts. But when night come there was them bigger crabs again, and I knew enough now not to let one get a hold of me. I was shinning up that tree with time and to spare.

"And so it went on, day after day and night after night, and I got into a regular way of living, always shinning up that tree at fall of night

and coming down again when I felt hungry and the sun was up. It was
a lazy kind of life, and the winds used to rock them coconut palms. It
was like sleeping in a cradle, or a hammock, an easy kind of motion.
It wasn't no kind of blame to me that I come to sleep long hours.
There wasn't no bells striking, and there wasn't no bosun after me with
a rope's end. It all come as a kind of a holiday. And then one day when
I'd slept maybe longer than usual, I waked up in a hurry with the
sound of folk talking under my tree."

"Who was it?" asked Titty breathlessly, and Roger might have
nudged her with his elbow, but he didn't think of it.

"Lucky for me I looked to see before shouting out," said Peter Duck.
"I looked down through them palm leaves, and there was two men at
the foot of my tree, digging a hole in the ground with a long knife."

"Pirates?" said Titty.

"They looked all that to me," said Peter Duck. "And they sounded
all that, the way they was talking. One of them was crouching and digging, while t'other one of them was looking round. And then that one
would dig away and the one that had been digging before would
stretch his arms and take a turn at looking round.

" 'I'd be sorry for the one that sees us at this,' says one of them.

" 'There's not one will have thought of following us, not with that
keg I let them take ashore,' says the other.

"No boy gets brought up at a rope's end, as you might say, without
knowing when to keep his mouth shut, and I see quick enough this
was no time for talking. So I kept still up there among the leaves at the
top of that palm and looking down on them and watching what they
was doing. Pretty soon one says he reckons the hole's deep enough,
and the other one says there's none likely to come seeking for it on this
side of the island where there's no shelter for ships. 'And it isn't as if we
was going to leave it for long,' says the other. And with that they takes
a sort of a square bag they had from right under the tree where I hadn't
seed it before . . . Square all ways that bag was . . ."

"Couldn't it have been a box that they'd put in the bag for easy carrying?" asked Captain Flint. He dropped a match that had burnt all the

way to his fingers. He had lit it meaning to light his pipe but had somehow forgotten about it.

"That's just what it likely was," said Peter Duck. "You could see the corners of it sticking through the canvas. Well, they took this square bag and lowered it down into their hole, and then they scraped the sand and earth in again with their knives and their hands and stamped it down and smoothed it over till they was satisfied, and with that they slapped each other on the back and went walking off again among the trees.

"I was down out of my bedroom quick enough after that. You see, it come to me clear that pirates was humans, which crabs is not, and that them two had a ship somewheres, and that maybe I'd see Lowestoft again, which I'd given up all thought of. So I went legging it away through the trees after them two. And they went clean across the island, with me not so far from them among the trees, over the shoulder of the big hill there is there, and sure enough, looking down the other side, I see a smart brig lying to her anchor. So I hurried me on down on that side of the island, and there was a boat drawn up there by a stream I'd known nothing of, me not daring to go in among the trees before. And there was a fire burning, and half a dozen men singing and laughing round a keg they had there chocked up between a couple of stones. I had sense enough to slip away through the trees till I could come at the men from along the shore, and then I set up yelling and shouting till they see me."

"What happened then?" said Peggy.

"Shut up, you galoot," said Nancy. "He's just going to tell you."

"They ask me how I come there, and I told them about the shipwreck and how I'd been eating crabs and drinking coconut milk, and one of them give me a hunk of bread and another give me the first swig of rum that ever I had in my life, which near took the skin off my gullet. 'You're all right now,' says one. 'Captain's luck holds. You'll be welcome. It's as if you knowed we was short of a cabin-boy since the old man threw the last one overboard to teach him swimming one day when he was playful like.' I can tell you I begin to think I'd have done better to stay by them crabs.

"But just then them other two come, the two that buried that square bag under my bedroom. That's what I used to call that tree of mine. They was the captain and the mate. They asked me sharp enough where I'd come from, and I told them I didn't know, but I'd been wrecked out of a London ship and wanted to get home to Lowestoft where I belonged. They took me aboard in the end. Sailing for London they was, and a rare passage they made of it. All the way home across the Western Ocean they kept me on the run fetching tots of rum for them to the state-room aft. I've often wondered since how we got as far as we did. And all the time while they was drinking they'd be talking one t'other and t'other back again, secret-like, about something they'd left, which I took to be that square bag. But likely it wasn't . . ."

"It couldn't have been anything else," said Captain Flint.

" 'Let 'em lie,' they'd say, 'let 'em lie. And then when all's clear, and they've no line on us about the ship, we'll call for 'em and bring 'em home and sell 'em gradual, and ride in carriages we will and nod to princes when they lifts their hats to us.

"What was the name of the ship?" asked Captain Flint suddenly.

"The *Mary Cahoun*," said Peter Duck. "But that wasn't the vessel they were talking of. They'd but new got the *Mary* and they'd come up from round the Horn in some other ship. I knew that from their talk, for when they was meaning this other ship they'd call her 'the old packet,' and they called the *Mary* by her name. And from what I heard, the captain and the mate of that other ship had died something sudden, and it's come to me since that this precious pair I was with had taken their papers and their names at the same time. Captain Jonas Fielder they called one of them, the one that was skipper, but he'd R. C. B. tattooed on his forearm. Many's the time I see it when he was sitting there in his shirt-sleeves lifting his glass of grog. There was something wrong most ways, it seem to me. They knew it too. The nearer we come to England the more they'd drink. They kept on lifting their glasses and swilling their grog and choking with it, and banging each other on the back as if they was afraid of something and wanted to think of something else. And then other times they would pull out a chart and look at it, and wore a hole in it they did, marking one of the islands with pencil and then rubbing the marks out. And when they'd swigged an extra lot of rum they'd just sit and wink at each other and show each other bits of paper where they'd written down some figures. And then in the morning when they was sober, more or less, they would go hunting round the cabin floor for them scraps of paper and wondering how many they'd left there, and if the crew had found them. And if they found one of them scraps of paper they'd lay into me with a rope's end for not tidying it overboard. And if they didn't find one they'd lay into me and say I'd picked it up for myself. Well naturally in the end I come to know those scraps of paper pretty well, and I see they all had the same figures, and I sewed up one of them in the inside of my jacket thinking whatever it was I'd paid for it in rope's-ending anyways."

"And those were the bearings of the island?" Captain Flint dropped another burnt but unused match on the floor and put his foot on it.

"Longitude and latitude they was. No more. Them two reckoned to find that island again, and needed no more to help them find their square bag, for they'd buried it themselves, and I dare say they'd taken all the bearings they needed. They knew those figures by heart, did them two, and before we come to the end of the voyage I knew them too, with seeing them so often. Anyhow the figures was no good to either of them chaps, for they come home with a westerly gale and full skin of rum apiece, and they piled the *Mary Cahoun* on Ushant rocks. There was nobody saved out of her but the bosun and me, and the bosun had his ribs stove in and his skull cracked, and he was dead when some of them French fishermen come by and take us off the rock we was on just before the tide rose high enough to sweep us off. Another ten minutes and they'd have been too late for me. They was too late for the bosun anyway.

"That's the yarn. That's all there was to it, and you never would have thought it'd have sent half the young lads of Lowestoft crazy when I come to tell it thirty years after, and maybe more than that."

"But I don't see what all this has to do with Black Jake," said Captain Flint.

"I'm coming to that," said Peter Duck.

There was a short breathless pause. Everybody stirred a little and looked round at the others. This story of wrecks and pirates and distant islands had taken them all a long way from the snug little deckhouse of the *Wild Cat* lying comfortably against the quay in Lowestoft inner harbour. Peter Duck lit his pipe, took a puff or two, and then once more rammed his thumb into the bowl.

Titty leaned forward and looked eagerly up at him.

"What happened when you got home?" she asked.

"I didn't get home," said Peter Duck. "Not that year nor many a year after. I worked for my keep with them French fishermen, and then one day off Ushant there was a fine clipper becalmed near where they was fishing and they rowed up to her and put me aboard in exchange for a bag of negro head . . ."

"What's that?" asked Roger.

"Tobacco," said Captain Flint. "But let Mr Duck go on."

"I reckon they sold me cheap," said Mr Duck. "That clipper was short-handed and they could have got more if they'd asked for it. As much as two bags, maybe. Anyways they put me aboard her and I was further than ever from getting home to Lowestoft. She was a Yankee clipper, the *Louisiana Belle*, and she carried skysails above her royals when other folk was taking in to'gallants. Hard driving there was in that ship. Round the Horn westaways I sailed in her, and left her in 'Frisco, and stowed away in a tea ship bound for the Canton River. And after that I was in one ship and another, here today and gone tomorrow, as you might say. There's not many ports about the world but what I've been into in my time. And I copied out them figures from that bit of paper I was telling you about, one time, and I learned that way whereabout that island was, out of curiosity, mind you for I never had a mind to go there. And I learnt what its name was too, for it had a name. 'Crab Island'* they call it, and a shipmate of mine pointed it out to me once, when we was up on the fo'c'sle head together, two hills showing but the island itself hull down, and he told me he'd watered there from a spring on the western side. That'd be where I found them with the boat that day when I was taken off."

"But did you never find a way of going back there?" asked Captain Flint.

"I'd a horror of them crabs," said Peter Duck. "And more than that I'd a horror of them drowned men of the *Mary Cahoun*. What had they done, them two, that they was afraid to take that bag with them but buried it out there with none but them crabs to watch it? It brought them no good. And what did I want with it either? The sea was enough for me. It wasn't cluttered up with screw steamships. There was great sailing in them days, and whenever I did come ashore paid off, I couldn't so much as see a vessel going down river outward bound without wishing I was aboard her. Money? I'd all I wanted and spent it quick enough so as not to waste time ashore. But I did keep that scrap of paper with the longitude and latitude of that island written on it, though I knew them figures well enough by heart. Couldn't forget them if I tried. But I cut out that bit of jacket when I threwed the jacket away, that bit where I had the paper sewed, and I kept it and the paper in it, until the day come when I wished I hadn't.

"You see the years was passing and I'd brought to in Lowestoft at last, paying off in London River, and going down to Norfolk in the railway train, thinking I'd like to see the old place now I was a man, and not so young neither. There was a good few remembered me, but none of my own folk. They was all gone, but no matter. It's no good looking for the dead. And I met a young woman there, clipper built, you might say, with a fine figurehead to her, well found, too, and her dad kept a marine store, no, not the one where you was fitting out, but another, cleared away long since from where the new market is. And we got married, and I put to sea again, coming home when I could, and

---

* Not to be confounded with the much larger Crab Island east of Porto Rico.

she went on living along with her old dad in the marine store, and we had three daughters. And then one day when I was home from sea, she was turning things out of this and that, and she come on that bit of old pea-jacket sewed up square with tarred twine, and she asked me what it was. And I told her the yarn that I've been telling to you, and my three daughters sitting there listening with their mouths open. That was the beginning of it. They couldn't be tired of hearing that yarn. And they told it to others, and them others told it to some more, and it come so in the end that I could never put my foot ashore in Lowestoft without some fancy man or other getting at me to tell the yarn again and to give him that bit of paper and set him up rich for life. That square bag I told you about was growed into cases of gold dollars and casks of silver ingots from the mines. They was at me all the time to sail across there with them to fetch the treasure, as they call it, when I'd talked of no treasure but only of a square bag with something in it that likely didn't belong to the two that buried it, and they buried, too, now, forty years back in a hundred fathom of blue water."

Captain Flint opened his mouth to speak, but said nothing. Peter Duck went on.

"My three daughters grow up, proper young clippers like their mother, and folk was beginning to leave me alone about that scrap of paper that I wished I'd lost off Ushant all them years before, and then Black Jake come along. My old wife she was dead then, and I was away from the sea, sailing my wherry between Norwich and Lowestoft, me and my three daughters. Knitting needles and quants* was all the same to them. They was good at both. It was a pretty sight to see them taking that old boat upstream against the wind by themselves with me sitting on the hatch, smoking my pipe and drinking my pot like any admiral.

"Well, Black Jake come along with his long hair and them ear-rings of his, and always plenty of money in his pockets that nobody knows how he come by. He'd heard that yarn in the taverns in Lowestoft and

---

* A quant is a long pole for poling ("quanting") a wherry along when there is no wind to help her or where the channel is too narrow for sailing against the wind.

he waited his chance to get at me. I could never be quit of him. No matter where I tied up, there he'd be, and talking always of the one thing. Nothing else would suit him. I must draw him a picture of that island, a chart, to show him just where my tree was and where I see that bag buried, and then I must give him the sailing directions to find the island and he would be off there to make my fortune as well as his own. You've seen Black Jake. He don't look the sort of man it's safe to share a fortune with, now does he? And I wasn't wanting a fortune anyway. Well, naturally, I wouldn't tell him nothing at all.

"And then he tried to marry my daughters, thinking he'd get one of them to wheedle what he wanted out of me. He had a try at one and then at another. But my daughters has more sense than to be marrying Black Jakes, and they married farmers, one at Beccles, one at Acle, and one at Potter Heigham. And that's just right for me. Gives me three ports of call, where I can tie up my old wherry, and have a pipe by the fireside."

"And which of them do you like the best?" asked Roger.

"Depends which way the wind is," said Peter Duck. "A south wind takes me up the Thurne River, and then I always think most of Rose, that's the gal that lives at Potter Heigham. An east wind blows fair for Beccles, and my daughter there has a good little farm and a sheltered mooring just above the bridge. And if there comes on a south wind while I'm there, or a north wind while I'm at Potter Heigham, why it's a right wind for Acle, and when it comes so, why, I just naturally think that Annie's the best of the lot and I take my chance of the tide to go and have a look at her."

"I see," said Roger, and he really did a little later when Peggy had explained it to him.

"But their marrying didn't stop him," said Peter Duck. "When he knew he couldn't get what he wanted that way, Black Jake started hanging round my wherry whenever he come home from sea. Again and again I found my cabin rummaged when I'd been ashore. And in the end I found that bit of paper sewed up in the square of old pea-jacket was missing. Missing it was, that bit of cloth with the paper with them figures on it sewed up inside. I searched for it high and low, not but what I knew them figures. It wasn't that. But I didn't like letting Black Jake get it after all. And the next thing I hear was that Black Jake was missing and two others with him. That was the first time I'd had a kind thought for them crabs. I knowed where he'd gone, of course, and I hoped they'd make a meal of him.

"Best part of a year he was gone, and I'd begun to hope we'd seen the last of him, when he come back alone, and I knowed he'd found nothing. How could he, without he'd dug the whole island. Then two that went with him died of fever, he said, and as they was the same sort as himself nobody minded. He come back raging mad, worse than before. For Lowestoft folk knew how I'd missed that square of old pea-jacket, and what was in it, and they knew the old yarn and there wasn't a boy that met Black Jake in the street, and had a door handy to bolt into, that didn't ask him how much treasure them crabs had left him. Raging mad he was, and folk did tell me I should keep a watch for flying knives at night. But ever since then he could never see me down at the harbour without thinking I was shipping foreign to go to the island and he's sworn that what I wouldn't tell him I should tell no man else . . . Five year ago it is now since he come back, and these last four months he's been fitting out the *Viper* for sea, and some rare bad lots he's taking with him. He's likely going to have another look. And then when he see me come aboard here, shipping along with you . . ."

"That was why he was spying round in the dark," said Captain Flint. He laughed aloud. "And I told that red-haired boy we were carrying three captains and a couple of mates. That was why he hurried out after us, and turned sharp round and came in again when he met us in the harbour mouth."

"He thinks you're bound for Crab Island sure enough," said Peter Duck.

Captain Flint for a moment seemed hardly to see Peter Duck or the others, crowded together in the little deckhouse. Sitting on the edge of the chart-table, his head bent under the roof, he was seeing things very far away. "It stands to reason," he said at last, "there's something in that bag, and if no one's been there and picked it up, it's the safest, surest thing in buried treasure that ever I heard of. I crossed the Andes, travelling day and night, on much less of a hint than that."

The old sailor looked up at Captain Flint, leaning forward to look at him without being dazzled by the lantern.

"I don't care who digs up that bag so long as Black Jake don't," he said. "But whatever it is it's best let lie. You don't want it, not with a tidy little schooner like this fit to take you anywheres. I don't want it, not with my old wherry that'll last my time and a bit more."

Captain Flint looked away, and tapped the tobacco out of his pipe.

"I can't help thinking it's wasted on those crabs," he said. "I don't wonder Black Jake wants to go and have a look for it."

"He don't want to go looking for it," said Peter Duck. "He wants to walk straight to it on that island, and pick it up. He can't do that without me. He'll stick at nothing, will Black Jake. You've seen enough to know that. And if you want to have no more trouble, you'd best put me ashore and get another able-seaman for your trip down Channel, and you'll find Black Jake won't be bothering you at all."

"No, no! Oh, I say! What!" There was a sudden startled chorus of protest. Captain Flint hit the top of his head on a beam under the deckhouse roof. He took no notice of the bump but spoke at once.

"I thought you said you wanted another voyage?"

"And so I do," said Peter Duck.

"And the ship and the crew suit you?"

"Couldn't ask for better."

"Then stow this talk of leaving us. If we suit you, you suit us. And if you think I'm the sort to leave you ashore because of a scowling, crook-eyed son of a sea-cook with a fancy for gold ear-rings, you're mistaken."

"That's the stuff, Captain Flint," said Nancy delightedly.

"Of course you mustn't go," said Roger.

"Mr Duck!" said Titty.

"We'll sail tomorrow, Mr Duck," said Captain Flint, "and if your Black Jake is fool enough to follow us, we'll lead him a bit of a dance."

"He'll follow, sure enough," said Peter Duck.

"Let him," said Captain Flint. "Anyway, we'll sail. And you'll sail with us. Below decks, you others! Below decks and into your bunks and sharp about it. We're sailing first thing."

"But what about the anchor?" asked John.

"It'll be clean enough by now," said Peter Duck.

"Man the capstan then," said Captain Flint. "Man the capstan and heave it up, and then below decks without waiting another minute."

He took the lantern, and the whole ship's company went forward along the dark deck. There was silence in the harbour. They peered across at the *Viper*, but all was dark, where she lay. The capstan bars were ranged handy along the bulwarks, and in a minute the Swallows and Amazons, all six of them, had fitted their bars into the slots in the capstan head, and, walking steadily round and round, were walking the anchor up as if it were a feather. It is astonishing what six people, even small ones, can lift with a capstan, all working together.

Captain Flint flashed a pocket torch over the side. The anchor had come up clean. The dinghy's painter must have slipped off it before.

There was a sudden squawk of annoyance in the darkness.

"I'd forgotten all about him," said Titty, rather ashamed.

The parrot had fallen asleep, perched on the bulwarks, and was not pleased to be waked. Titty picked him up and took him down with her into the saloon and put him into his cage for the night. Roger was nearly as sleepy as the parrot. But the others were for some time too full of talk to sleep. They undressed, talking. And, when they were in their bunks, they talked still from one cabin to another. Treasure. Black Jake. Crabs. Peter Duck. That red-haired boy who was sailing with Black Jake. They had enough to talk about.

And then, long after they had stopped getting answers from each other when they spoke, long after they had stopped talking and fallen asleep, they woke again, listening to steps going to and fro overhead, along the *Wild Cat*'s decks.

"It's Mr Duck," said Susan quietly.

"Yes," said Titty. "It was Captain Flint before. I heard him tapping his pipe."

"They must think Black Jake may come again in the night," said John.

"Keeping watch," said Titty.

"Who?" A voice came now from the Amazons' cabin.

"Mr Duck and Captain Flint," whispered Susan. "Listen."

"Let's all go up and help," said Nancy.

"No, no," said Peggy. "Stop here."

"What's happening now?" This was Roger's squeak in the dark.

"Nothing. Go to sleep," said Susan. "We all ought to," she added. "If they want help they'll thump on the deck for us, or call down through the skylight."

They slept again.

But all night long, watch and watch about, Captain Flint and Peter Duck walked up and down above their sleeping crew.

from

The Dark Frigate

by Charles Boardman Hawes (1889–1923)

Phil Marsham is boatswain aboard *The Rose of Devon* under the command of Captain Candle. After a terrible storm at sea *The Rose* rescues some shipwrecked sailors and their captain, Thomas Jordan. Phil recognizes this Captain Jordan as "The Old One," a devilishly shrewd pirate, and knows no good can come from this villainous guest.

A sail! A sail!"

The seas had somewhat abated and the *Rose of Devon* was standing on her course under reefed mainsail when the cry sounded.

The vessel they sighted lay low in the water; and since she had one tall mast forward and what appeared to be a lesser mast aft they thought her a ketch. But while they debated the matter the faint sound of guns fired in distress came over the sea; and loosing the reef of their mainsail and standing directly toward the stranger, the men in the *Rose of Devon* soon made her out to be, instead, a ship which had lost her mainmast and mizzenmast and was wallowing like a log. While the *Rose of Devon* was still far off her men saw that some of the strange crew were aloft in the rigging and that others were huddled on the quarter-deck; and when, in the late afternoon, she came up under the stranger's stern, the unknown master and his men got down on their knees on the deck and stretched their arms above their bare heads.

"Save us," they cried in a doleful voice, "for the Lord Jesus' sake! For our ship hath six-foot water in the hold and we can no longer keep her afloat."

In all the *Rose of Devon* there was not a heart but relented at their lamentable cry, not a man but would do his utmost to lend them aid.

"Hoist out thy boat and we will stand by to succour thee," Captain Candle called. "We can do no more, for we ha' lost our own boat in the storm."

It appeared they had but one boat, which was small, so they must needs divide the crew to leave their vessel, part at one time and part at another; and the seas still ran so high, though wind and wave had moderated, that it seemed impossible they could make the passage. With men at both her pumps the *Rose of Devon* lay by the wind, wallowing and plunging, and her own plight seemed a hard one. But the poor stranger, though ever and again she rose on the seas so that the water drained from her scupper-holes, lay for the most part with her waist a-wash and a greater sea than its fellows would rise high on the stumps of mainmast and mizzenmast. Her ropes dragged over the side and her sails were a snarl of canvas torn to shreds, and a very sad sight she presented.

Three times they tried to hoist out their boat and failed; but the fourth time they got clear, and with four men rowing and one steering and seven with hats and caps heaving out the water, they came in the twilight slowly down the wind past the *Rose of Devon* and up into her lee.

The men at the waist of the ship saw more clearly, now, the features of those in the boat, and the one in the stern who handled the great steering oar had in the eyes of Philip Marsham an oddly familiar look. Phil gazed at the man, then he turned to Martin and knew he was not mistaken, for Martin's mouth was agape and he was on the very point of crying out.

"Holla!" Martin yelled.

The man in the stern of the boat looked up and let his eyes range along the waist of the ship. Not one of all those in sight on board the

Rose of Devon escaped his scrutiny, which was quick and sure; but he looked Martin coldly in the face without so much as a nod of recognition; and though his brief glance met Phil's gaze squarely and seemed for the moment to linger and search the lad's thoughts, it then passed to the one at Phil's side.

It was the thin man who had been Martin's companion on the road—it was Tom Jordan—it was the Old One.

Martin's face flamed, but he held his tongue.

A line thrown to the boat went out through the air in coils that straightened and sagged down between the foremost thwarts. A sailor in the boat, seizing the line, hauled upon it with might and main. The Old One hotly cursed him and bellowed, "Fend off, fend off, thou slubbering clown! Thy greed to get into the ship will be the means of drowning us all."

Some thrust out oars to fend away from the side of the ship and some held back; but two or three, hungering for safety, gave him no heed and hauled on the rope and struggled to escape out of their little boat, which was already half full of water. The Old One then rose with a look of the Fiend in his eyes and casting the steering oar at the foremost of them, knocked the man over into the sea, where he sank, leaving a blotch of red on the surface, which was a terrible sight and brought the others to observe the Old One's commands.

Some cried "Save him!" but the Old One roared, "Let the mutinous dog go!"

Perhaps he was right, for there are times when it takes death to maintain the discipline that will save many lives. At all events it was then too late to save either the man or the boat, for although they strove thereafter to do as the Old One bade them, the boat had already thumped against the side of the ship and it was each man for himself and the Devil take the last. The men above threw other ropes and bent over to give a hand to the poor fellows below, and all but the man who had sunk came scrambling safe on board.

The Old One leaned out and looked down at the boat, which lay full of water, with a great hole in her side.

"I would have given my life sooner than let this happen," he said. "There are seven men left on board our ship, who trusted me to save them. Indeed, I had not come away but these feared lest without the master you should refuse to take them. What say ye, my bawcocks, shall we venture back for our shipmates?"

Looking down at the boat and at the gaping holes the sea had stove by throwing her against the *Rose of Devon*, the men made no reply.

"Not one will venture back? Is there no one of ye?"

" 'Twere madness," one began. "We should—"

"See! She hath gone adrift!"

And in truth, her gunwales under water, the boat was already drifting astern. At the end of the painter, which a *Rose of Devon's* man still held, there dangled a piece of broken board.

"Let us bring thy ship nigh under the lee of mine," the Old One cried to Captain Candle. "It may be that by passing a line we can yet save them."

"It grieves me sorely to refuse them aid, but to approach nearer, with the darkness now drawing upon us, were an act of folly that might well cost the lives of us all. Mine own ship is leaking perilously and in this sea, were the two to meet, both would most certainly go down."

The Old One looked about and nodded. "True," said he. "There is no recovering the boat and darkness is upon us. Let us go as near to the ship as we may and bid them have courage till morning, when, God willing, we shall try to get aboard and save them."

"That we will. And I myself will con the ship."

Leaning over the rail, Tom Jordan, the Old One, called out, "Holla, my hearts! The boat hath gone adrift with her sides stove; but do you make a raft and keep abroad a light until morning, when God helping us, we will endeavor to get you aboard."

Perceiving for the first time that the boat was gone and there was no recovering her, those left on board the wreck gave a cry so sad that it pierced the hearts of all in the *Rose of Devon*, whose men saw them through the dusk doing what they could to save themselves; and presently their light appeared.

Working the *Rose of Devon* to windward of the wreck, Captain Candle lay by, but all his endeavours could not avail to help them, for about ten o'clock at night, three hours after the Old One and his ten men had got on board the *Rose of Devon*, their ship sank and their light went out and seven men lost their lives.

The Old One, standing beside Captain Candle, had watched the light to the last. "It is a bitter grief to bear," he said, "for they were seven brave men. A master could desire no better mariners. 'Tis the end of the *Blue Friggat* from Virginia, bound for Portsmouth, wanting seven weeks."

"A man can go many years to sea without meeting such a storm."

"Yea! Three days ago when the wind was increasing all night we kept only our two courses abroad. At daybreak we handed our main course, but before we had secured it the storm burst upon us so violently that I ordered the foreyard lowered away; but not with all their strength could the men get it down, and of them all not one had a knife to cut away the sail, for they wore only their drawers without pockets; so the gale drove us head into the sea and stopped our way and a mighty sea pooped us and filled us and we lay with only our masts and forecastle out of the water. I myself, being fastened to the mizzenmast with a rope, had only my head out of water. Yea, we expected to go straight down to the bottom, but God of his infinite goodness was pleased to draw us from the deep and another sea lifted up our ship. We got down our foresail and stowed it and bored holes between the decks to let the water into the hold and by dint of much pumping we kept her afloat until now. In all we have lost eight lives this day and a sad day it is."

"From Virginia, wanting seven weeks," Captain Candle mused.

Captain Jordan stole a swift glance at him but saw no suspicion in his face.

"Yea, from Virginia."

"You shall share mine own cabin but I fear you have come only from one wreck to another."

The two captains sat late that night at the table in the great cabin, one on each side, and ate and drank. There was fine linen on the table, and bread of wheat flour with butter less than two weeks from the dairy, and a fine old cheese, and a mutton stew, and canary and sack and aqua vitæ. At midnight they were still lingering over the suckets and almonds and comfits that the boy had set before them; and the boy, nodding in uncontrollable drowsiness as he stood behind his master's chair, strove to keep awake.

The murmuring voices of the men at the helm came faintly through the bulkhead, and up from below the deck came the creak of whipstaff and tiller. The moon, shining through the cabin window, added its wan light to the yellow radiance from the swinging lanthorns, and stars were to be seen. So completely had wind and weather changed in a night and a day that, save for the long rolling swell, the great gap where waist and boat and capstan had gone, the hole stuffed with blankets and rugs and hammocks, the stump of a mizzenmast, and the rescued men on board—save for these, a man might have forgotten storms and wrecks.

"You are well found," said Captain Thomas Jordan, tilting his glass and watching the wine roll toward the brim; "yea, and we are in good fortune." His thin face, as he lifted his brows and slightly smiled at his host, settled into the furrowed wrinkles that had won him the name of the Old One.

"We can give such entertainment as is set before you," his host drily replied. Francis Candle was too shrewd a man to miss his guest's searching appraisal of the cabin and its furnishings. In his heart he already distrusted the fellow.

Through the main deck to the gun-room and up into the forecastle there drifted smoke from the cookroom in the hold, which was the way of those old ships. At times it set choking the men at the pumps; it eddied about the water cask before the mainmast and about the riding butts by the heel of the bowsprit, and went curling out of the hawse pipes. It crept insidiously into the forecastle, and the men cursed fluently when their eyes began to smart and their noses to sting.

There were seven men in the forecastle and Martin Barwick was one of the seven, although his watch was on deck and he had no right to be there. Philip Marsham, whose watch was below, had stayed because he suspected there was some strange thing in the wind and was determined to learn if possible what it was. Two of the others were younkers of the *Rose of Devon*, who suspected nothing, and the remaining three were of the rescued men.

There was a step above and a round head appeared in the hatch. The dim smoky light gave a strange appearance to the familiar features.

"Ho, cook!" Martin cried, and thumped on the table. "Come thou down and bring us what tidings the boy hath brought thee in the cookroom. Yea, though the cook labour in the very bowels of the ship, is it not a proverb that he alone knows all that goes on?"

Slipping through the hatch, the cook drew a great breath and sat him down by the table. "She was the *Blue Friggat*, I hear, and seven weeks from Virginia—God rest the souls of them who went down in her!"

"From Virginia!" quoth Martin. "Either th'art gulled, in truth, or th'art the very prince of liars. From Virginia! Ho ho!" And Martin laughed loud and long.

Now it was for such a moment that Philip Marsham was waiting, nor had he doubted the moment would come. For although Martin had gone apart with the men who had come from the foundered ship, the fellow's head, which was larger than most heads, could never keep three ideas in flourish at the same time. To learn what game was in the wind there was need only to keep close at Martin's heels until his blunders should disclose his secrets.

"The Devil take thee, thou alehouse dog!" the cook cried in a thick, wheezy voice. "Did not the boy bring me word straight when he came down for a can of boiling water with which this Captain Jordan would prepare a wondrous drink for Captain Candle?"

"And did not I part with this Captain Jordan not—Wow-ouch!" With a yell Martin tipped back in his chair and went over. Crawling on his feet, he put on a long face and rubbed his head and hurled a flood of oaths at the sailor beside him, a small man and round like an apple, who went among his fellows—for he was one of those the *Rose of Devon* had rescued—by the name of Harry Malcolm.

"Nay," the little round man very quietly replied, "I fear you not, for all your bluster. Put your hand on your tongue, fellow, and see if you cannot hold it. I had not intended to tip you over. It was done casually."

"And why, perdy, did'st thou jam thy foot on mine till the bones crunched? I'll have they heart's blood."

"Nay," the man replied, so quietly, so calmly that he might have been a clerk sitting on his stool, "you have a way of talking overmuch, fellow, and I have a misliking of speech that babbles like a brook. It can make trouble." Martin stopped as if he had lost his voice, but continued to glare at the stranger, who still regarded him with no concern.

"It is thy weakness, fellow," he said, "and—" he looked very hard at Martin—"it may yet be the occasion of thine untimely end."

For a moment Martin stood still, then, swallowing once or twice, he went out of the dimly lighted forecastle into the darkness of the deck.

"He appears," the little man said, addressing the others, "to be an excitable fellow. Alas, what trouble a brisk tongue can bring upon a man!"

The little man, Harry Malcolm, looked from one to another and longest at Phil.

Now Phil could not say there had been a hidden meaning in the hard look the little man had given Martin or in the long look the little man had given Phil himself. But he knew that whether this was so or not, there was no more to be got that night from Martin, and he in turn, further bepuzzled by the little man's words and after all not much enlightened by Martin's blunder, left the forecastle to seek the main deck.

Passing the great cannon lashed in their places, and leaving behind him the high forecastle, he came into the shadow of the towering poop on which the lantern glowed yellow in the blue moonlight, and continued aft to the hatch ladder. Already it was long past midnight.

He imagined he heard voices in the great cabin, and although he well enough knew that it was probably only imagination—for the cabin door was closed fast—the presence of the Old One on board the *Rose of Devon* was enough to make a man imagine things, who had sat in Mother Taylor's cottage and listened to talk of the gentlemen who sailed from Bideford. He paused at the head of the ladder and listened, but heard nothing more.

An hour passed. There were fewer sounds to break the silence. There is no time like the very early morning for subtle and mysterious deeds.

Boatswain Marsham was asleep below and Captain Candle was asleep aft, when Captain Jordan arose and stretched himself, and in a voice that would have been audible to Captain Candle if he had been awake but that was so low it did not disturb his sleep, vowed he must breathe fresh air ere he could bury his head in a blanket for the night.

Emerging from the great cabin, Captain Jordan climbed first to the poop, whence he looked down on the brave old ship and the wide space of sky and darkly heaving sea within the circle of the horizon. To look thus at the sea is enough to make a philosopher of a thinking man, and this Captain Thomas Jordan was by no means devoid of thought.

But whereas many a one who stands under the bright stars in the small morning hours feels himself a brother with the most trifling creatures that live and is filled with humility to consider in relation to the immeasurable powers of the universe his weakness during even his brief space of life—whereas such a one perceives himself to be, like the prophets of ancient times, in a Divine Presence, the Old One, his face strangely youthful in its repose, threw back his head and softly laughed, as if there high on the poop he were a god of the heathen, who could blot out with his thumb the ship and all the souls that sailed in her. His face had again a haunting likeness to the devils in the old wood-cuts; and indeed there is something of the devil in the very egotism of a man who can thus assert his vain notions at such an hour.

Presently descending from the poop and with a nod passing on the quarter-deck the officer of the watch, he paced for a time the maintop-deck. He pretended to absorb himself in the sea and the damage the storm had done to the waist; but he missed nothing that happened and he observed the whereabouts of every man in the watch.

Edging slowly forward, he stood at last beside a big man who was leaning in the shadow of the forecastle.

"We meet sooner than you thought," he said in a low voice.

"Yea, for we were long on the road and entangled ourselves wonderfully among those byways and highways which cross the country in a manner perplexing beyond belief."

"Saw you your brother?"

"In all truth I saw him—and the Devil take him!" The Old One laughed softly.

"It is plain thy brother hath little love for a shipwrecked mariner," quoth he, "yet there is a most memorable antiquity about the use of ships, and even greater gluttons than thy brother have supped light that worthy seamen might not go hungry to bed. We will speak of him another time. What think you of this pretty pup we have met by the way?—Ah, thine eye darkens! Me thinks thou hast more than once felt the rough side of his tongue."

"He bears himself somewhat struttingly—" Martin hesitated, but added perforce, since he had received a friendly turn he could not soon forget, "yet he hath his good points."

"He was one too many for thee! Nay, confess it!"

"Th'art a filthy rascal!" Martin's face burned with anger.

"I knew he would be too cunning for thy woolgathering wits. Truly I believe he is a lad after my own heart. I have marked him well."

"But hast thou plumbed his inclination with thy sounding lead?"

"Why, no. At worst, he can disappear. It has happened to taller men than he, and in a land where there are men at arms to come asking questions."

"Hgh!"

"This for thy whining, though: we shall play upon him lightly. Some are not worth troubling over, but this lad is a cunning rogue and hath book learning."

"Came you in search of this ship?"

"It was chance alone that brought us across her course. Chance alone, Martin, that brought your old captain back to you."

Watching Martin, as he spoke, the Old One again laughed softly.

"Yea, Martin, it touches the heart of your old captain to see with what pleasure you receive him."

"Th'art a cunning devil," Martin mutered, and babbled opaths and curses.

"We must sleep, Martin—sleep and eat, for we are spent with much labour and many hardships, and it is well for them to sail our ship for us a while longer. But the hour will come, and do you then stand by."

The Old One went aft. The ship rolled drowsily and the watch nodded. Surveying her aloft and alow, as a man does who is used to command, and not as a guest on board might do, the Old One left the deck.

"Lacking the mizzen she labours by the wind, which hath veered sadly during the night," quoth Captain Jordan in a sleepy voice, as with his host he came upon deck betimes.

"I like it little," the master replied.

"It would be well to lay a new course and sail on a new voyage. There is small gain to be got from these fisheries. A southern voyage, now, promises returns worth the labour."

To this Captain Candle made no reply. He studied the sore damage done to the ship, upon which already the carpenter was at work.

"With a breadth of canvas and hoops to batten the edges fast, and over all a coating of tar, a man might make her as tight and dry as you please," said the Old One. He smiled when he spoke and his manner galled his host.

"It was in my own mind," Captain Candle replied, with an angry lift of his head. There are few things more grievously harassing than the importunity and easy assurance of a guest of whom there is no riddance. It puts a man where he is peculiarly helpless to defend himself, and already Captain Candle's patience had ebbed far. "Bid the boatswain overhaul his canvas, mate, and the carpenter prepare such material as be needful. Aye, and bid the 'liar' stand ready to go over the side. 'Twill cool his hot pride, of which it seems he hath full measure."

"Yea, yea!"

As the master paced the deck, back and forth and back and forth, the Old One walked at his side—for he was a shrewd schemer and had calculated his part well—until the master's gorge rose. "I must return to the cabin," he said at last, "and overhaul my journal."

"I will bear you company."

"No, no!"

The Old One smiled as if in deprecation; but as the master turned away, the smile broadened to a grin.

Boatswain Marsham and the one-eyed carpenter who wore a beard like a goat's were on their way to the fore-hold. The cook and his mate were far down in the cook-room. Ten men in the watch below were sound asleep—but Martin Barwick, the eleventh man in the watch, was on deck, *and of the eleven rescued men not one was below.* With Captain Candle safe in his cabin and busied over his journal, there were left from the company of the *Rose of Devon* eight men and the mate, and one man of the eight was at the helm. These the Old One counted as he took a turn on the quarter-deck.

The Old One and his men were refreshed by a night of sleep and restored by good food. To all appearances, without care or thought to trouble them, they ruffled about the deck. One was standing just behind the mate; two were straying toward the steerage.

"Thy boatswain is a brave lad," the Old One said to the mate, and stepping in front of him, he spread his legs and folded his arms.

The mate nodded. He had less liking for their guest, if it were possible, than the captain.

"A brave lad," the Old One repeated. "I can use him."

"You?"

"Yea, I."

The mate drew back a step, as a man does when another puts his face too near. He was on the point of speaking; but before his lips had phrased a word the Old One raised his hand and the man behind the mate drove six inches of blue steel into the mate's back, between his ribs and through his heart.

He died in the Old One's arms, for the Old One caught him before he fell, and held him thus.

"Well done," the Old One said to his man. "Not so well as one could wish," the man replied, wiping his knife on the mate's coat. "He perished quietly enough, but the knife bit into a rib and the feeling of a sharp knife dragging upon bone sets my teeth on edge."

The Old One laughed. "Thy stomach is exceeding queasy," he said. "Come, let us heave him over the side."

All this, remember, had happened quickly and very quietly. There were the three men standing by the quarter-deck ladder—the Old One and his man and the mate—and by all appearances the Old One merely put out his hands in a friendly manner to the other, for the knife thrust was hidden by a cloak. But now the mate's head fell forward in a queer, lackadaisical way and four of the Old One's men, perceiving what they looked for, slipped past him through the door to the steerage room, where they clapped down the hatch to the main deck. One stood on the hatch; two stood by the door of the great cabin; and the fourth, stepping up to the man at the helm, flashed a knife from his sleeve and cut the fellow down.

It was a deft blow, but not so sure as the thrust that had killed the mate. The helmsman dropped the whip-staff and, falling, gave forth a yell and struck at his assailant, who again let drive at him with the knife and finished the work, so that the fellow lay with bloody froth at his lips and with fingers that twitched a little and then were still.

The man who had killed him took the whipstaff and called softly, "Holla, master! We hold the helm!" then from his place he heard a sailor cry out, "The mate is falling! Lend him aid!"

Then the Old One's voice, rising to a yell, called, "Stand back! Stand off! Now, my hearts!"

There came a quick tempest of voices, a shrill cry, the pounding of many feet, then a splash, then a cry wilder and more shrill than any before, "Nay, I yield—quarter! Quarter, I say! Mercy! God's mercy, I beg of you! Help—O God!"

There was at the same time a rumble of hoarse voices and a sound of great struggling, then a shriek and a second splash.

The man at the helm kicked the dead helmsman to one side and listened. In the great cabin, behind the bulkhead at his back, he heard a sudden stir. As between the mainmast and the forecastle the yells rose louder, the great cabin door burst open and out rushed Captain Francis Candle in a rich waist with broad cuffs at his wrists, his hair new oiled with jessamine butter, and gallant bows at his knees, for he was a fine gentleman who had first gone to sea as a lieutenant in the King's service. As he rushed out the door the man lying in wait on the left struck a fierce blow to stab him, but the knife point broke on a steel plate which it seemed Captain Candle wore concealed to foil just such dastardly work.

Thereupon, turning like a flash, Captain Candle spitted the scoundrel with his sword. But the man lying in wait on the right of the door saw his fellow's blow fail and perceived the reason, and leaping on the captain from behind, he seized his oiled hair with one hand and hauled back his head, and reaching forward with the other hand, drove a knife into the captain's bare throat.

Dark blood from a severed vein streamed out over Captain Candle's collar and his gay waist. He coughed and his eyes grew dull. He let go his sword, which remained stuck through the body of the man who had first struck at him, clapped his hand to his neck, and went down in a heap.

The yells on deck had ceased and the man who had killed Francis Candle, after glancing into the great cabin where the captain's cloak lay spread over the chair from which he rose to step out of his door and die—where the captain's pen lay across the pages of the open journal and a bottle of the captain's wine, which he had that morning shared with his guest, Captain Thomas Jordan, stood beside the unstoppered bottle of ink—walked forth upon the deck and nodded to the Old One, who stood with his hand on the after swivel gun.

There were a few splotches of blood on the deck and three men of the *Rose of Devon's* crew lay huddled in a heap; there were left standing three other men of the *Rose of Devon*, and sick enough they looked; Martin Barwick was stationed by the ladder to the forecastle, where he stood like a pigeon cock with his head haughtily in the air and his chest thrust out; and the little round apple of a man, Harry Malcolm, who had broken in upon Martin the night before, bearing now a new and bloody gash across his forehead, was prowling among the guns and tapping the breech rings with a knowing air.

The Old One from the quarter-deck looked down at the newcomer.

"Rab took the steel," the fellow said.

"Rab!" the Old One cried. "Not Rab, you say?"

"Yea, he struck first but the master wore an iron shirt which turned the point and he was then at him with his sword."

"We have lost nine good men by this devil-begotten storm, but of them all Rab is the one I am most loath to see go to the sharks." The Old One paced the deck a while and the others talked in undertones. "Yea, Martin," he called at last, "nine good men. But we have got us a ship and I have great hopes of our boatswain, who may yet make us two of Rab. At all events, my bullies, we must lay us a new course, for I have no liking of these northern fisheries. Hark! They are pounding on the hatch."

The sound of knocking and a muffled calling came from the main hatch, whereat the men on deck looked at one another and some of them smiled.

"It were well—" the little round man began. He glanced at the huddled bodies and shrugged.

"True, true!" the Old One replied, for he needed no words to complete the meaning. "You men of the *Rose of Devon*, heave them into the sea."

The three looked at one another and hesitated, and the youngest of the three turned away his face and put his hand on his belly, and sick enough he looked, at which a great laugh went up.

"Go, Harry," the Old One cried to the little round man, "and tell them at the hatch to be still, for that we shall presently have them on deck. We must learn our brave recruits a lesson."

Again a roar of laughter rose, and as the little man went in to the hatch, the others drew about the three who cowered against the forecastle ladder, as well they might.

"Come, silly dogs," said the Old One, "in faith, you must earn your foolish lives. Lay hands on those carcasses and heave them to the fishes."

They looked into the faces of the men about them, but got small comfort as they edged toward their unwelcome task.

"It is hard to use thus a shipmate of three voyages," the oldest of them muttered.

"True," replied the Old One, "but so shall you buy your way into a goodlier company of shipmates, who traffic in richer cargoes than pickled codfish and New England herrings."

The three picked up the bodies, one at a time, each with its arms and legs dragging, and carried them to the waist and pushed them over. But the youngest of the three was trembling like a dead weed in November when they had finished, and the Old One chuckled to see the fellow's white face.

"Have courage, bawcock," the Old One cried; "there shall soon be a round of aqua vitæ to warm thy shaking limbs and send the blood coursing through thy veins. Now, Mate Harry, lift off the hatch and summon our good boatswain and carpenter."

"As you please, as you please," came the quick, gentle voice of the little round man. "But there are two of 'em left still—Rab and the captain—and there's a deal of blood hereabouts."

They heard the hatch creak as the little man pried it off. They heard his quick sentences pattering out one after another; "Hasten out on deck—nay, linger not. The master would have speech of thee. Nay, linger not. Ask me no questions! There's no time for lingering."

Then out burst Phil Marsham with the older carpenter puffing at his heels.

"What's afoot?" cried Phil. "Where's the master?—what—where—"

So speedily had they hurried from the hatch (and so cleverly had the little round man interposed himself between the hatch and the two bodies at the cabin door) that in the dim light of the steerage room the two had perceived nothing amiss. But now, looking about for the source of the fierce cries and yells they had heard, they saw red stains on the deck, and men with scared white faces.

All looked toward the Old One as if awaiting his reply; and when Phil Marsham, too, looked toward him, he met such another quizzing, searching, understanding gaze as he had long ago met when he had taken the words from Martin's lips on the little hill beside the road.

"Why, I am master now, good boatswain."

"But Captain Candle—"

"His flame is out."

The lad glanced about him at the circle of hard old sea dogs—for they were all of them that, were their years few or many—and drew away till he stood with the waist at his back. Laying hands on his dirk, he said in a voice that slightly trembled, "And now?"

"Why," quoth the Old One, "you have sat in Mother Taylor's kitchen and heard talk of the gentlemen. You know too many secrets. Unless you are one of us—" He finished with a shrug.

"You ask me, then, to join you?"

"Yea."

"I refuse." He looked the Old One in the eye.

"Why, then," said the Old One, "you are the greater fool."

The circle drew closer.

"What then?"

" 'Tis but another candle to be snuffed."

With hand on dirk and with back against the waist, the boatswain looked one and another and then another in the eye. "Why, then," said he, "I must even join you, as you say. But I call upon you all to witness I am a forced man." And he looked longest and hardest at the three men from the old crew of the *Rose of Devon*.

The Old One looked back at the lad and there was, for the first time, doubt in his glance. He stood for a while pondering in silence all that had taken place and studying the face of his boatswain; but his liking of the lad's spirit outweighed his doubts, for such bold independence, whether in friend or foe, was the one sure key to Tom Jordan's heart. "So be it," he said at last. "But remember, my fine young fellow, that many a cockerel hath got his neck wrung by crowing out of season." He turned to the carpenter. "And what say you? We can use a man of your craft."

"I am thy man!" the fellow cried. The stains on the deck had made him surpassingly eager, and his one eye winked and his beard wagged, so eager was he to declare his allegiance.

"Well said!" the Old One responded. "And now, Master Harry, have them up from below—the sleepers, and the cook and his mate, and all! We have taken a fine ship—a fine ship she will be, at all events, once our good carpenter has done his work—and well found. We needs must sign a crew to sail and fight her."

They heard the little round man calling down the hatch and at a great distance in the ship they heard the voices of men grumbling at being summoned out of sleep. But the grumbling was stilled when one by one the men came out on deck; and of them all, not a man refused to cast his lot with the Old One and the rest. The mere sight of a little blood and of the hard faces that greeted them was enough for most. And two or three, of whom Will Canty was one, must fain perceive how futile would be present resistance. Indeed, in the years since the old Queen had died, and the navy had gone to the dogs, and merchantmen had come to sail from the Downs knowing they were likely enough to meet a squadron of galleys lying in wait fifty leagues off the Lizard, many a sailor had taken his fling at buccaneering; and those that had not, had heard such great tales of galleons laden with treasures of the Indies and with beautiful dames of Spain that their palates were whetted for a taste of the life.

The cook smiled broadly and clapped the boy on the back and cried out that as a little lad he had sailed with John Jennings that time John Jennings's wench had turned his luck, and that having begun life in such brave company, he would gladly end it in a proper voyage if it was written that his time was near. They all laughed to see the boy turn white and tremble, and they huzzaed the cook for his gallant words. But Will Canty met Phil's eyes and there passed between them a look that made the Old One frown, for he was a man who saw everything.

The *Rose of Devon*, although close-hauled by the wind, rolled heavily, which was the way of those old tall ships; but the adverse winds and high seas she had encountered were of fancy as well as of fact. The sun was shining brightly and sky and sea were a clear blue; but despite sun and sky and sea no weatherwise man could have believed the dark days of the *Rose of Devon* were at an end. Like so many iron bars the shadows of the ropes fell blue on the sails, and the red blotches on the deck matched the dull red paint of the stanchions and the waist. The carpenter, who had come up with his plane in his hand, fingered the steel blade. The boy turned his back on the bloody deck and looked away at the sea, for he was a little fellow and not hardened by experience of the world.

"Come, my hearts," cried the Old One, and gaily enough he spoke. "We are banded together for the good of all. There is no company of merchants to profit by our labour and our blood. God hath placed in our keeping this brave ship, which will be staunch and seaworthy when our carpenter hath done his work. Harry Malcolm is our mate and master gunner as of old, and Phil Marsham shall continue as our boatswain—nay, grumble not! He came with Martin Barwick and he hath sat in Mother Taylor's kitchen, where may we all sit soon and raise our cans and drink thanks for a rich voyage. There is work to be done, for all must be made clean and tight—yea, and Rab is to be buried."

The little round man was still wandering from gun to gun and smiling because the guns pleased him. They were demiculverins of brass, bored for a twelve-pound ball and fit to fight the King's battles; but alas! they had shown themselves powerless against a foe from within the ship. And as the *Rose of Devon* rolled along in the bright sun alone in a blue sea, the body of Francis Candle lay forgotten in the steerage room.

from

Pirates In Oz

by Ruth Plumly Thompson (1891–1923)

After L. Frank Baum died in 1919 Ruth Plumly Thompson
took over authorship of his hugely popular series about
the wonderful world of Oz. She wrote 19 books for the
series—including *Pirates in Oz*. In this selection the old
pirate Captain Salt tells the tale of how he has been abandoned by his treacherous crew.

N o Boat!" cried the pirate hoarsely. "How do you
suppose I reached this island, old Eighty Pate? Look yonder! There lies
my ship, the *Crescent Moon,* as fine a boat as ever rammed a sloop or
sank a merchantman. My ship—and not a man, mouse or biscuit
aboard her," he finished, in a depressed whisper.

"You mean you're alone?" piped the Read Bird, sticking out the end
of his bill. The pirate nodded gloomily, at which Roger scurried from
beneath the throne and hopped up on Ato's shoulder.

"You give him a clout in the middle while I drop this book on his
head," urged the Read Bird under his breath. "Come on now, all together!"

"No, wait!" begged Ato, who had been eyeing the pirate with more
interest than alarm. "I believe he's going to tell us his story."

"Story!" hissed Roger furiously. "Can't you think of anything but stories? Better do as I say or it will be the last story Your Majesty will ever hear." The pirate, lost in thought, seemed not to notice this whispered conversation, but as Roger, extremely displeased and ruffled, began to fan himself vigorously with his tail, Samuel Salt looked up.

"It happened on a Wednesday," he began moodily. "We had just put in at Elbow Island. That's where I hide my treasure and rest between voyages. I was in the green cavern studying over a map of Ozamaland, which I meant to explore, when Peggo the Red, Binx the Bad, and all the rest of the band crowded in on me and said they were leaving."

"Leaving?" Ato leaned forward, his eyes snapping with interest and sympathy. "How curious. And did they really leave you?"

"Flat!" said the pirate glumly. "I think it was Binx who banged me with the oar. But when I waked up they were gone, all the treasure was gone, all the food and supplies were gone and my second best ship, the *Sea Lion* was gone. Now, Elbow Island, mates, is a barren reef where nothing grows but rocks, and there being nought to eat and little water in the casks, I boarded the *Crescent Moon* and sailed east by nor'east till I sighted this island. Here I meant to help myself to what I needed, seize enough men to man my ship and go after those thieving rascals and bring 'em back in irons."

"Well," questioned Ato breathlessly, for he was more interested in the pirate's story than in his own safety, "why didn't you?" The pirate gazed at the King for a full moment in a stunned silence and then burst into a hearty roar.

"Hah, hah!" boomed Samuel Salt hilariously, "You're a fine King, asking me why I don't steal your treasure and enslave your men. Besides didn't you just tell me your subjects had gone off with everything of value? That's why I said we were in the same boat, old fellow. You've been robbed and deserted. I've been robbed and deserted. So, you see, we're shipmates and I couldn't treat you rough if I wanted to, could I, now?"

"No," Ato put his fingertips together and regarded his visitor thoughtfully, "I suppose not. But I suspect you of having a kind heart, Captain Salt." The pirate winced and turned red as an August moon.

"Hah, hah! You're a fine pirate!" teased the Read Bird, rocking back and forth on his perch.

"Why did your men leave you?" queried the King, shaking his finger reprovingly at Roger.

"Well," admitted Samuel Salt, shuffling his feet uncomfortably, "to tell the truth, they claimed I wasn't rough enough either in my talk or actions. Come to think of it, they only made me chief because I was clever at navigating. Now, I hold that once you've taken a ship and stowed her valuables, you should let the passengers and crew go. But Binx was all for planking 'em. And I wouldn't stand for it."

"Planking 'em?" Ato shuddered in spite of himself. "You mean shoving them into the sea, Captain Salt?" Samuel nodded ruefully and the Read Bird rolled up his eyes in horror.

"Then," continued the pirate in a grieved voice, "as we'd been pirating a long time and had accumulated considerable gold and treasure, I was planning to do a little exploring on my next voyage, a little exploring, honest discovery, and collecting of specimens. That's what I really like," he informed them earnestly.

"And they hit you with an oar just for that," mused the King, rubbing his chin reflectively. "Just because you like exploring and didn't talk rough enough. Dear, dear and dear, how dreadfully unreasonable."

"It seems to me you talked pretty rough when you stepped in here," sniffed Roger, ruffling up his neck feathers. "How about that, Mr. Pirate?"

"I was practicing," admitted Samuel Salt, clearing his throat apologetically. "If I am to win back my crew I must be rough, bluff and relentless, mates."

"And you wish to win them back?" asked Ato wonderingly.

"Of course, don't you?" Stepping a bit closer, the pirate looked earnestly at the King. "By the way, why did your subjects leave?"

"Because he likes stories better than people," chirped Roger, closing one eye. "Because he hasn't done any law-making, conquering or exploring. He's just too kind and easy-going, if you ask me, Mr. Salt. A King has to be hard, haughty and something of a rascal to get himself appreciated these days."

"I believe you're right," mused the pirate thoughtfully. "You'll have to practice being hard, mate. We'll both have to practice," blustered Samuel, tightening his belt and glaring around savagely.

"Well, you needn't practice on me," grumbled the Read Bird as Ato, following the pirate's example drew his face into a fierce and unaccustomed scowl. "How are you going to get your men back? What are you going to do and when are you going to do it?" demanded Roger, shutting his fan tail with a snap and pointing his claw severely at his master. Ato looked a trifle dashed, but the pirate, giving his belt another hitch, answered for him.

"We'll take the *Crescent Moon*, we'll pirate around a bit till we've enough supplies and men to man her, and then we'll sail after these rebels and bring them back by the necks, heels, ears and whiskers. Shiver my bones if we'll not! But first we must eat. *Hah!*" Expelling his breath in a mighty blast through his nose, the pirate patted his belt and looked inquiringly at Ato. "I'm hollow as a drum amidships!" The King, who had been listening in round-eyed admiration to the pirate, now brought his fist down with a tremendous thump on the arm of the throne.

"Vassals, bring the meat!" commanded Ato in a thunderous voice. "Varlets, fetch the fruit! Bring the bread and the pudding!"

"And make it lively or I'll give ye a taste of my belt!" bellowed Samuel Salt, rattling his blunderbuss threateningly. Then the King and the pirate exchanged pleased glances. "I guess that's telling 'em," rumbled Samuel Salt, rubbing his hands complacently together and striding up and down before the throne.

"Them?" coughed Roger, rocking backward and forward on his perch. "Ha, ha! What a waste of hard language. There's nobody below and you very well know it."

"That's so!" Completely crestfallen the King looked up at the Read Bird. "What are we to do, Roger?" he asked mournfully.

"Fetch it ourselves," answered Roger, flopping off his perch and making a bird line for the kitchen. But the kitchen, when they reached it, was in utmost confusion. Unwashed dishes were heaped on every table and chair, even spilling on to the floor, and though they searched in every chest and cupboard, they could find nothing but a small measure of flour, a pat of butter, half a pitcher of milk and three broken eggs in a bowl. The cook had taken everything else eatable, even the mouse trap cheese, As the three stared dismally at the unappetizing collection, the kitchen door gave a sudden creak and slowly began to open.

"Hi-sst!" warned the pirate, giving the King's cloak a warning tug. "Some of your men returning. Now brace up, mate! Rough, bluff and relentless is the game and under the hatches with all hands and villains! *Hah!*" Carried away by the pirate's example, Ato caught up a bread knife and faced about, just as a small boy stepped through the doorway. Water ran in riivulets from his hair and clothing and he had evidently been through some exciting and exhausting experiences. His face was freckled and inquiring, but as he caught a glimpse of the threatening figures on the other side of the kitchen table, he sprang back in dismay and would have taken to his heels had Roger not called out to him.

"Don't go!" twittered Roger, terribly relieved to find the enemy so small. "Don't go! They're only practicing!"

"Well, bless my buckles!" The pirate dropped his scimitar with a crash. "It's a boy! What ship spilled you, little lubber? You've had a taste of the sea, I see. Ha, ha! A joke!" Giving Ato a good-natured shove the pirate grinned so broadly that the boy stopped short and looked curiously from one to the other. "He's had a taste of the sea and for the sea. Nay, doubtless he ran off to sea to see what he could see. Ha, ha, ha!" finished Samuel Salt, laughing uproariously.

"Ha, ha!" echoed the King, putting down the bread knife, secretly delighted that the rough, bluff and relentless stuff was for the time being unnecessary.

"Shall I announce him in the usual fashion?" inquired Roger, leaning over to have a better look at the newcomer. "Name, young gentleman, and present business and past place of residence, if any?"

"My name is Peter Brown. I come from Philadelphia, in the United States. I'd like to dry off and have something to eat, if you don't mind," answered the boy, coming a step closer.

"We don't mind at all," said Ato pleasantly, "but unfortunately there's nothing to eat." He waved sorrowfully and apologetically around the disordered kitchen. "We've just been robbed and deserted," explained the King.

"Let me present His Majesty, Ato the Eighth, King of this island, and Samuel Salt the pirate, who came to capture but stayed to defend us," put in Roger, sweeping back his head feathers with a practiced claw. "I myself am the Royal Read Bird. And now would you mind telling me what you have under your arm, Master Peterdelphia, or whatever you call yourself?"

"Just Peter," corrected the boy, with a quick smile at Roger. "I found this flask in the water when I was washed up on your beach. I don't know what's in it," he added, obligingly holding up the wicker covered bottle he had under his arm.

"Do—not—open!" puffed the pirate, leaning forward to read the water-soaked label on the strange flask. "Do—not—open! Well, what may that mean?"

"Do not open." The Read Bird and the pirate repeated the phrase several more times and could not take their eyes from the mysterious bottle, but the King was much more interested in Peter.

"Tell me, boy," wheezed the fat monarch, easing himself slowly into a kitchen chair, "tell me how you happened to reach this island. Was it a shipwreck?" At the prospect of hearing another story Ato's eyes sparkled with pleasure and anticipation. Setting the flask on the table, Peter nodded so vigorously that drops of water flew in every direction.

"Hah!" The pirate looked up, his attention momentarily diverted from the flask. "A shipwreck you say? Were you rammed and sunk or blown on the rocks? Tell me that, young one."

"Yes," begged Ato, folding his hands on his stomach and benevolently regarding Peter, "start at the beginning and tell us everything about yourself."

"Well," began Peter thoughtfully, "there isn't much to tell. I live in Philadelphia with my grandfather. I'm eleven years old and go to the Blaine School and am captain of the baseball team." Ato pursed his lips and nodded understandingly, though he had no idea at all what a baseball team might be. Samuel Salt, whittling at the handle of a wooden spoon with his dagger, decided it must be a small ship. "Well, a friend of my grandfather's," went on Peter earnestly, "has a yacht and he invited us to go on a cruise, so of course we did. When we got off Cape Hatteras we struck a hurricane and the captain ordered all hands below, but I sneaked up to see what was going on and—"

"Were blown off!" chuckled the pirate, shaking the wooden spoon reprovingly at the boy.

"Yes," admitted Peter with a little shudder, "I was, and with almost all the stuff on deck. There was a big table that floated pretty well, so I climbed aboard. It was raining in torrents and thundering awfully. The waves were forty feet, I guess, and the wind so high I couldn't half breathe. I don't remember all that happened; I just went slamming ahead of the wind, crashing through one wave and then another so fast I couldn't think, and when the hurricane finally died down it was night and I couldn't see. I must have slept awhile, though, for when I waked up it was morning and I saw land. So I paddled with my feet and arms till I was close enough to swim ashore. Floating on the water I found this cask, so I brought it along. And say, am I anywhere near the Land of Oz? I've been to Oz a couple of times and it's the only country I know where birds can talk, and everything is sort of—er—sort of—"

"What?" demanded Roger stiffly.

"Well—different," concluded Peter, with a long, interested look at Ato and the pirate. Then, sobering quickly, he sighed. "Golly! I wish I knew what has happened to grandfather."

"Your grandfather, having obeyed orders, is probably safe aboard ship. I wouldn't worry about him," advised Samuel Salt slowly. "As to latitude and longitude, you are at present on Ato's Island and there's a lot of geozify between here and the Land of Oz: the Nonestic Ocean, Ev, and the Deadly Desert. I've never been to Oz myself, not caring much for inland places, but I've heard enough about it. We could set you down on the coast of Ev, though, and then you might find some way to reach Oz by yourself."

"Oh, could you, would you?" breathed Peter, glancing eagerly from the pirate to the King. "Gee, that would be great! Have you a ship? Are you sailing soon?"

"We're going to do a bit of pirating," explained Roger importantly. "Then we're going to find his crew," the Read Bird waved his claw at Samuel Salt, "his crew and our men, and bring 'em back in irons." In quick jerky sentences, Roger told how Ato and the pirate had been robbed and deserted, how Samuel, sailing from Elbow Island to find himself a new crew, had come to the Octagon Isle and finding the King in the same plight as himself, had decided to help him.

"You see, Peter," finished the Read Bird mournfully, "both these fellows were deserted because they were kind and easy-going, which should be a terrible example to you, my boy. Never be kind and easy-going!"

"He's only just come, so he won't be going easy or any other way, at least not until we find something to eat," observed the pirate cheerfully. "Food, mates! What we require most and foremost is food!"

Peter had been so interested in Roger's story that he had almost forgotten how wet and famished he was. Now suddenly reminded of the fact, he glanced hungrily around the kitchen, his quick eyes coming to rest on the pitcher of milk, the flour, the butter, and the bowl of eggs.

"Why, there's food," cried Peter, licking the salt water from him lips. "We'll make us some pancakes."

"P-pancakes?" exclaimed the pirate, his whiskers quivering with eagerness. "What are p-pancakes?"

"You mean to stand there and tell me you've never eaten pancakes?"

cried Peter incredulously. "Why, pancakes are flapjacks, and any scout can make flapjacks."

"You mustn't expect much assistance from these two," put in the Read Bird slyly. "They've never done a stroke of work in their lives, I fancy."

"There, there, Roger," muttered the King, as Peter began mixing the milk and flour and beating up the eggs. "It *will* be a bit awkward without the cook and bodyguards, and how I shall dress without some help I cannot imagine!"

"Oh, you'll get used to it," sniffed Peter in a matter-of-fact voice. "It's more fun doing things for yourself anyway."

"I believe you're right!" boomed the pirate, sweeping all the clutter of dishes from one end of the table with his scimitar. "And how do we eat these pot cakes, boy, with fist, fork or fingers?"

"Forks," grinned Peter, tasting the batter critically. "They're hot, you know." Darting over to the stove, Peter gave the fire a poke and soon the kitchen was full of the nose-tickling fragrance of griddle cakes. Samuel Salt, with surprising quickness, set the table; Roger after a long search in the pantry found a can of maple syrup, and presently they all sat down to as satisfying and merry a meal as had ever been eaten in the castle.

"You're going to be a great help to us, Peter," sighed Samuel, spearing another pancake with his scimitar. "Stick with me, little lubber, and I'll make an able-bodied seaman and an honest pirate of you yet. How would you like to ship as cabin boy and mate of the *Crescent Moon*?"

"Fine!" beamed Peter. "Just fine!" He smiled up at the burly pirate.

"And what will you make of *him*?" inquired Roger, pointing a claw at Ato.

"Cook and coxswain!" answered the pirate promptly. "And you, my bully bird, shall be lookout and take your turn with the watches."

"All that?" marvelled the Read Bird, preening his feathers self-consciously. Ato looked rather thoughtful as Samuel continued to enlarge upon their duties at sea, but Roger, settling on his shoulder, assured him that there was a cook book in the pantry, and that he himself would read off the recipes and help with the vegetables, and thus encouraged, Ato became not only resigned but positively excited over his new position aboard the *Crescent Moon*. Much refreshed and heartened they all jumped up and began to make immediate plans for leaving the island.

Peter, having nothing of his own to pack, helped Ato select the royal garbs best suited to a sea voyage. Roger flew back and forth between the castle and the ship with the fat volumes from the King's library. Samuel Salt, finding an old fishing rod behind the door set out for the beach to catch, as he jocularly put it, some supper and breakfast for the crew. In the excitement of getting off, the cask Peter had brought ashore was almost forgotten. On his final trip through the kitchen, the boy caught sight of it standing on the table, and tucking it hurriedly under one arm ran down to join the others in the jollyboat. They had made several trips between the island and the *Crescent Moon*, but this was the last.

"Hah!" chuckled the pirate, as Peter hoisted himself into the boat. "I see you've brought the mysterious bottle. Let's open it before we start, just to try our luck."

"Maybe it'll explode," objected Peter, shaking the cask dubiously, "or let something out that we'd rather not see. Besides, it says: 'Do not open.'"

"That's so," pondered the pirate, pulling vigorously at the oars, "but the question is, who says it?" The Read Bird, from his perch on Ato's shoulder, stared long and curiously at the cask, then opening *Maxims for Monarch* perused it for a few moments in silence.

"Nobody shall say 'No' to the King," mumbled Roger presently. "Let Ato open the bottle."

"Ah, no!" begged Peter, hugging the cask to his chest. "Let's wait!" He could not bear the thought of anything that would delay their sailing. The *Crescent Moon*, lying at anchor with her high forward deck, her gleaming masts and great pirate figurehead, seemed to Peter the grandest boat a boy ever shipped in, and he could scarcely wait to get aboard and under way. The King, for his part, was not at all anxious to open the cask, so nothing more was said of the matter and soon they were all climbing the rope ladder dangling down the side of the *Crescent Moon*— all except Roger, who flew easily aboard. In an astonishingly short time, Samuel Salt with such help as Peter, Roger and Ato could give him, had hoisted sail and anchor and pointed his ship into the wind. Peter, hanging eagerly over the rail as the *Crescent Moon* plunged her nose into the first wave and rose grandly to meet the second, took a long trembling breath. *Away!* They were off and away and the voyage really begun. Who knew what strange places and people they would be seeing— conquering for that matter, for had he not shipped as a pirate? A pirate, by ginger! What would his grandfather say to that? Feeling in his pocket he drew out his scout knife, the only weapon he possessed, and looked at it rather doubtfully. Samuel Salt, whistling light-heartedly at the wheel, seemed to read Peter's thoughts.

"There's an extra scimitar and some other gear in the cabin," he called gaily. "Help yourself, young one, and then come back and I'll show you how to take a turn here at the wheel." Without waiting for a second invitation, Peter rushed down to the pirate's cabin, and when he returned he sported Samuel Salt's second best scimitar and sword and a dashing red bandana. The slap of the scimitar against his knee gave him great confidence and courage, and feeling ready for anything and bold enough to capture a whole ship single handed, Peter presented himself for inspection.

"Hah!" exclaimed Samuel Salt, eyeing him approvingly. "You're a better pirate than I am, my boy. But a good pirate never gets anywhere," he continued, giving the wheel several quick turns as Peter dropped on a coil of rope beside him. "We must be rough, bluff and relentless. *Hah!*"

"Do you think we'll overtake a vessel soon, Captain Salt?" asked Peter, squinting happily out toward the sky line.

"Maybe, yes, maybe, no! Can't tell! That's what makes the sea what it is—exciting." Taking a pipe and some tobacco from his pocket, the pirate lighted it briskly and grinned sociably down at Peter. Peter nodded understandingly, for flying under that great cloud of canvas straight toward the setting sun anything seemed possible, and was possible. Roger had gone below to arrange his books. Ato was investigating his new quarters and presently an excited voice came floating up from the galley.

"Sam, Sam-u-e-l! How do you get the feathers off these fish?" bellowed Ato.

"Sam?" blustered the Pirate, puffing out his cheeks and turning quite red. "Wha'd'ye think of that, lad? Plain Sam to the captain! Plain Sam-u-e-l! *Hah!* Ah, well!" His expression grew milder. "After all, he's a King and if a King can't call a pirate 'Sam,' what good is a crown?"

"And he's never been a cook before," Peter reminded him, as Ato came lumbering cautiously across the deck, a slippery fish held high in each hand.

"What do you do to these?" panted Ato, facing the pirate in frank bewilderment.

"Maybe you pare them," sighed Samuel Salt in a dreamy voice, "or singe them, like fowl. Oh, just boil them in their jackets," he finished, with a careless wave of his hand.

"Ho! Ho!" roared Peter, bending nearly double. "It's plain to be seen you've never cleaned a fish in your lives. Ho! Ho! It's lucky I'm with you on this voyage. Come along, King, I'll fix 'em for you!" And remembering he was cabin boy as well as mate, Peter went below to help Ato prepare the pirates' supper.

from

Peter Pan

by J. M. Barrie (1860–1937)

There is perhaps no pirate we love to hate more than
Captain Hook—a devious and cowardly pirate whose enemies include a headstrong girl, a group of wayward boys
and a ticking crocodile.

O ne green light squinting over Kidd's Creek,
which is near the mouth of the pirate river, marked where the brig, the
Jolly Roger, lay, low in the water; a rakish-looking craft foul to the hull,
every beam in her detestable like ground strewn with mangled feathers.
She was the cannibal of the seas, and scarce needed that watchful eye,
for she floated immune in the horror of her name.

She was wrapped in the blanket of night, through which no sound
from her could have reached the shore. There was little sound, and
none agreeable save the whir of the ship's sewing machine at which
Smee sat, ever industrious and obliging, the essence of the common-
place, pathetic Smee. I know not why he was so infinitely pathetic,
unless it were because he was so pathetically unaware of it; but even

strong men had to turn hastily from looking at him, and more than once on summer evenings he had touched the fount of Hook's tears and made it flow. Of this, as of almost everything else, Smee was quite unconscious.

A few of the pirates leant over the bulwarks, drinking in the miasma of the night; others sprawled by barrels over games of dice and cards; and the exhausted four who had carried the little house lay prone on the deck, where even in their sleep they rolled skilfully to this side or that out of Hook's reach, lest he should claw them mechanically in passing.

Hook trod the deck in thought. O man unfathomable. It was his hour of triumph. Peter had been removed forever from his path, and all the other boys were on the brig, about to walk the plank. It was his grimmest deed since the days when he had brought Barbecue to heel; and knowing as we do how vain a tabernacle is man, could we be surprised had he now paced the deck unsteadily, bellied out by the winds of his success?

But there was no elation in his gait, which kept pace with the action of his sombre mind. Hook was profoundly dejected.

He was often thus when communing with himself on board ship in the quietude of the night. It was because he was so terribly alone. This inscrutable man never felt more alone than when surrounded by his dogs. They were socially so inferior to him.

Hook was not his true name. To reveal who he really was would even at this date set the country in a blaze; but as those who read between the lines must already have guessed, he had been at a famous public school; and its traditions still clung to him like garments, with which indeed they are largely concerned. Thus it was offensive to him even now to board a ship in the same dress in which he grappled her, and he still adhered in his walk to the school's distinguished slouch. But above all he retained the passion for good form.

Good form! However much he may have degenerated, he still knew that this is all that really matters.

From far within him he heard a creaking as of rusty portals, and through them came a stern tap-tap-tap, like hammering in the night when one cannot sleep. "Have you been good form to-day?" was their eternal question.

"Fame, fame, that glittering bauble, it is mine!" he cried.

"Is it quite good form to be distinguished at anything?" the tap-tap from his school replied.

"I am the only man whom Barbecue feared," he urged, "and Flint himself feared Barbecue."

"Barbecue, Flint—what house?" came the cutting retort.

Most disquieting reflection of all, was it not bad form to think about good form?

His vitals were tortured by this problem. It was a claw within him sharper than the iron one; and as it tore him, the perspiration dripped down his tallow countenance and streaked his doublet. Oftimes he drew his sleeve across his face, but there was no damming that trickle.

Ah, envy not Hook.

There came to him a presentiment of his early dissolution. It was as if Peter's terrible oath had boarded the ship. Hook felt a gloomy desire to make his dying speech, lest presently there should be no time for it.

"Better for Hook," he cried, "if he had had less ambition!" It was in his darkest hours only that he referred to himself in the third person.

"No little children love me!"

Strange that he should think of this, which had never troubled him before; perhaps the sewing machine brought it to his mind. For long he muttered to himself, staring at Smee, who was hemming placidly, under the conviction that all children feared him.

Feared him! Feared Smee! There was not a child on board the brig that night who did not already love him. He had said horrid things to them and hit them with the palm of his hand, because he could not hit with his fist, but they had only clung to him the more. Michael had tried on his spectacles.

To tell poor Smee that they thought him lovable! Hook itched to do it, but it seemed too brutal. Instead, he revolved this mystery in his mind: why do they find Smee lovable? He pursued the problem like the sleuth-hound that he was. If Smee was lovable, what was it that made him so? A terrible answer suddenly presented itself—"Good form?"

Had the bo'sun good form without knowing it, which is the best form of all?

He remembered that you have to prove you don't know you have it before you are eligible for Pop.

With a cry of rage he raised his iron hand over Smee's head; but he did not tear. What arrested him was this reflection:

"To claw a man because he is good form, what would that be?"

"Bad form!"

The unhappy Hook was as impotent as he was damp, and he fell forward like a cut flower.

His dogs thinking him out of the way for a time, discipline instantly relaxed; and they broke into a bacchanalian dance, which brought him to his feet at once, all traces of human weakness gone, as if a bucket of water had passed over him.

"Quiet, you scugs," he cried, "or I'll cast anchor in you"; and at once the din was hushed. "Are all the children chained, so that they cannot fly away?"

"Ay, ay."

"Then hoist them up."

The wretched prisoners were dragged from the hold, all except Wendy, and ranged in line in front of him. For a time he seemed unconscious of their presence. He lolled at his ease, humming, not unmelodiously, snatches of a rude song, fingering a pack of cards. Ever and anon the light from his cigar gave a touch of colour to his face.

"Not then, bullies," he said briskly, "six of you walk the plank to-night, but I have room for two cabin boys. Which of you is it to be?"

"Don't irritate him unnecessarily" had been Wendy's instructions in the hold; so Tootles stepped forward politely. Tootles hated the idea of signing under such a man, but an instinct told him that it would be prudent to lay the responsibility on an absent person; and though a somewhat silly boy, he knew that mothers alone are always willing to be the buffer. All children know this about mothers, and despise them for it, but make constant use of it.

So Tootles explained prudently, "You see, sir, I don't think my mother would like me to be a pirate. Would your mother like you to be a pirate, Slightly?"

He winked at Slightly, who said mournfully, "I don't think so," as if he wished things had been otherwise. "Would your mother like you to be a pirate, Twin?"

"I don't think so," said the first twin, as clever as the others. "Nibs, would—"

"Stow this gab," roared Hook, and the spokesmen were dragged back. "You, boy," he said, addressing John, "you look as if you had a little pluck in you. Didst never want to be a pirate, my hearty?"

Now John had sometimes experienced this hankering during maths; and he was struck by Hook's picking him out.

"I once thought of calling myself Red-handed Jack," he said diffidently.

"And a good name too. We'll call you that here, bully, if you join."

"What do you think, Michael?" asked John.

"What would you call me if I join?" Michael demanded.

"Blackbeard Joe."

Michael was naturally impressed. "What do you think, John?" He wanted John to decide, and John wanted him to decide.

"Shall we still be respectful subjects of the King?" John inquired.

Through Hook's teeth came the answer: "You would have to swear, 'Down with the King.'"

Perhaps John had not behaved very well so far, but he shone out now.

"Then I refuse!" he cried, banging the barrel in front of Hook.

"And I refuse," cried Michael.

"Rule Britannia!" squeaked Curly.

The infuriated pirates buffeted them in the mouth; and Hook roared out, "That seals your doom. Bring up their mother. Get the plank ready."

They were only boys, and they went white as they saw Jukes and Cecco preparing the fatal plank. But they tried to look brave when Wendy was brought up.

No words of mine can tell you how Wendy despised those pirates. To the boys there was at least some glamour in the pirate calling; but all that she saw was that the ship had not been tidied for years. There was not a porthole on the grimy glass of which you might not have written with your finger "Dirty pig"; and she had already written it on several. But as the boys gathered round her she had no thought, of course, save for them.

"So, my beauty," said Hook, as if he spoke in syrup, "you are to see your children walk the plank."

Fine gentleman though he was, the intensity of his communings had soiled his ruff, and suddenly he knew that she was gazing at it. With a hasty gesture he tried to hide it, but he was too late.

"Are they to die?" asked Wendy, with a look of such frightful contempt that he nearly fainted.

"They are," he snarled. "Silence all," he called gloatingly, "for a mother's last words to her children.

At this moment Wendy was grand. "These are my last words, dear boys," she said firmly. "I feel that I have a message to you from your real mothers, and it is this: 'We hope our sons will die like English gentlemen.' "

Even the pirates were awed, and Tootles cried out hysterically, "I am going to do what my mother hopes. What are you to do, Nibs?"

"What my mother hopes. What are you to do, Twin?"

"What my mother hopes. John, what are—"

But Hook had found his voice again.

"Tie her up!" he shouted.

It was Smee who tied her to the mast. "See here, honey," he whispered, "I'll save you if you promise to be my mother."

But not even for Smee would she make such a promise. "I would almost rather have no children at all," she said disdainfully.

It is sad to know that not a boy was looking at her as Smee tied her to the mast; the eyes of all were on the plank: that last little walk they were about to take. They were no longer able to hope that they would walk it manfully, for the capacity to think had gone from them; they could stare and shiver only.

Hook smiled on them with his teeth closed, and took a step toward Wendy. His intention was to turn her face so that she should see the boys walking the plank one by one. But he never reached her, he never heard the cry of anguish he hoped to wring from her. He heard something else instead.

It was the terrible tick-tick of the crocodile.

They all heard it—pirates, boys, Wendy—and immediately every head was blown in one direction; not to the water whence the sound proceeded, but toward Hook. All knew that what was about to happen concerned him alone, and that from being actors they were suddenly become spectators.

Very frightful was it to see the change that came over him. It was as if he had been clipped at every joint. He fell in a little heap.

The sound came steadily nearer; and in advance of it came this ghastly thought; "The crocodile is about to board the ship!"

Even the iron claw hung inactive; as if knowing that it was no intrinsic part of what the attacking force wanted. Left so fearfully alone, any other man would have lain with his eyes shut where he fell: but the gigantic brain of Hook was still working, and under its guidance he crawled on his knees along the deck as far from the sound as he could go. The pirates respectfully cleared a passage for him, and it was only when he brought up against the bulwarks that he spoke.

"Hide me!" he cried hoarsely.

They gathered round him, all eyes averted from the thing that was coming aboard. They had no thought of fighting it. It was Fate.

Only when Hook was hidden from them did curiosity loosen the limbs of the boys so that they could rush to the ship's side to see the crocodile climbing it. Then they got the strangest surprise of this Night of Nights; for it was no crocodile that was coming to their aid. It was Peter.

He signed to them not to give vent to any cry of admiration that might rouse suspicion. Then he went on ticking.

Odd things happen to all of us on our way through life without our noticing for a time that they have happened. Thus, to take an instance, we suddenly discover that we have been deaf in one ear for we don't know how long, but, say, half an hour. Now such an experience had come that night to Peter. When last we saw him he was stealing across the island with one finger to his lips and his dagger at the ready. He had seen the crocodile pass by without noticing anything peculiar about it, but by and by he remembered that it had not been ticking. At first he thought this eerie, but soon he concluded rightly that the clock had run down.

Without giving a thought to what might be the feelings of a fellow-creature thus abruptly deprived of its closest companion, Peter began to consider how he could turn the catastrophe to his own use; and he decided to tick, so that wild beasts should believe he was the crocodile and let him pass unmolested. He ticked superbly, but with one unforeseen result. The crocodile was among those who heard the sound, and it followed him, though whether with the purpose of regaining what it had lost, or merely as a friend under the belief that it was again ticking itself, will never be certainly known, for, like all slaves to a fixed idea, it was a stupid beast.

Peter reached the shore without mishap, and went straight on, his legs encountering the water as if quite unaware that they had entered a new element. Thus many animals pass from land to water, but no other human of whom I know. As he swam he had but one thought: "Hook or me this time." He had ticked so long that he now went on ticking without knowing that he was doing it. Had he known he would have stopped, for to board the brig by the help of the tick, though an ingenious idea, had not occurred to him.

On the contrary, he thought he had scaled her side as noiseless as a mouse; and he was amazed to see the pirates cowering from him, with Hook in their midst as abject as if he had heard the crocodile.

The crocodile! No sooner did Peter remember it than he heard the ticking. At first he thought the sound did come from the crocodile, and he looked behind him swiftly. Then he realised that he was doing it himself, and in a flash he understood the situation. "How clever of me!" he thought at once, and signed to the boys not to burst into applause.

It was at this moment that Ed Teynte, the quartermaster, emerged from the forecastle and came along the deck. Now, reader, time what happened by your watch. Peter struck true and deep. John clapped his hands on the ill-fated pirate's mouth to stifle the dying groan. He fell forward. Four boys caught him to prevent the thud. Peter gave the signal, and the carrion was cast overboard. There was a splash, and then silence. How long has it taken?

"One!" (Slightly had begun to count.)

None too soon, Peter, every inch of him on tiptoe, vanished into the cabin; for more than one pirate was screwing up his courage to look around. They could hear each other's distressed breathing now, which showed them that the more terrible sound had passed.

"It's gone, Captain," Smee said, wiping his spectacles. "All's still again."

Slowly Hook let his head emerge from his ruff, and listened so intently that he could have caught the echo of the tick. There was not a sound, and he drew himself up firmly to his full height.

"Then here's to Johnny Plank!" he cried brazenly, hating the boys more than ever because they had seen him unbend. He broke into the villainous ditty:

> Yo ho, yo ho, the frisky plank,
> > You walks along it so,
> Till it goes down and you goes down
> > To Davy Jones below!

To terrorise the prisoners the more, though with a certain loss of dignity, he danced along an imaginary plank, grimacing at them as he sang; and when he finished he cried, "Do you want a touch of the cat before you walk the plank?"

At that they fell on their knees. "No, no!" they cried so piteously that every pirate smiled.

"Fetch the cat, Jukes," said Hook. "It's in the cabin."

The cabin! Peter was in the cabin! The children gazed at each other.

"Ay, ay," said Jukes blithely, and he strode into the cabin. They followed him with their eyes; they scarece knew that Hook has resumed his song, his dogs joining in with him:

> Yo ho, yo ho, the scratching cat
>   Its tails are nine, you know,
> And when they're writ upon your back—

What was the last line will never be known, for of a sudden the song was stayed by a dreadful screech from the cabin. It wailed through the ship, and died away. Then was heard a crowing sound which was well understood by the boys, but to the pirates was almost more eerie than the screech.

"What was that?" cried Hook.

"Two," said Slightly solemnly.

The Italian Cecco hesitated for a moment and then swung into the cabin. He tottered out, haggard.

"What's the matter with Bill Jukes, you dog?" hissed Hook, towering over him.

"The matter wi' him is he's dead, stabbed," replied Cecco in a hollow voice.

"Bill Jukes dead!" cried the startled pirates.

"The cabin's as black as a pit," Cecco said, almost gibbering, "but there is something terrible in there: the thing you heard crowing."

The exultation of the boys, the lowering looks of the pirates, both were seen by Hook.

"Cecco," he said in his most steely voice, "go back and fetch me out that doodle-doo."

Cecco, bravest of the brave, cowered before his captain, crying, "No, no"; but Hook was purring to his claw.

"Did you say you would go, Cecco?" he said musingly.

Cecco went, first flinging up his arms despairingly. There was no more singing, all listened now; and again came a death-screech and again a crow.

No one spoke except Slightly. "Three," he said.

Hook rallied his dogs with a gesture. "S'death and odds fish," he thundered, "who is to bring me that doodle-doo?"

"Wait till Cecco comes out," growled Starkey, and the others took up the cry.

"I think I heard you volunteer, Starkey," said Hook, purring again.

"No, by thunder!" Starkey cried.

"My hook thinks you did," said Hook, crossing to him. "I wonder if it would not be advisable, Starkey, to humour the hook?"

"I'll swing before I go in there," replied Starkey doggedly, and again he had the support of the crew.

"Is it mutiny?" asked Hook more pleasantly than ever, "Starkey's ringleader!"

"Captain, mercy!" Starkey whimpered, all of a tremble now.

"Shake hands, Starkey," said Hook, proffering his claw.

Starkey looked round for help, but all deserted him. As he backed, Hook advanced, and now the red spark was in his eye. With a despairing scream the pirate leapt upon Long Tom and precipitated himself into the sea.

"Four," said Slightly.

"And now," Hook asked courteously, "did any other gentleman say mutiny?" Seizing a lantern and raising his claw with a menacing gesture, "I'll bring out that doodle-doo myself," he said, and sped into the cabin.

"Five." How Slightly longed to say it. He wetted his lips to be ready, but Hook came staggering out, without his lantern.

"Something blew out the light," he said a little unsteadily.

"Something!" echoed Mullins.

"What of Cecco?" demanded Noodler.

"He's as dead as Jukes," said Hook shortly.

His reluctance to return to the cabin impressed them all unfavourably, and the mutinous sounds again broke forth. All pirates are superstitious, and Cookson cried, "They do say the surest sign a ship's accurst is when there's one on board more than can be accounted for."

"I've heard," muttered Mullins, "he always boards the pirate craft at last. Had he a tail, Captain?"

"They say," said another, looking viciously at Hook, "that when he comes it's in the likeness of the wickedest man aboard."

"Had he a hook, Captain?" asked Cookson insolently; and one after another took up the cry, "The ship's doomed!" At this the children could not resist raising a cheer. Hook had well-nigh forgotten his prisoners, but as he swung round on them now his face lit up again.

"Lads," he cried to his crew, "here's a notion. Open the cabin door and drive them in. Let them fight the doodle-doo for their lives. If they kill him, we're so much the better; if he kills them, we're none the worse."

For the last time his dogs admired Hook, and devotedly they did his bidding. The boys, pretending to struggle, were pushed into the cabin and the door was closed on them.

"Now, listen!" cried Hook, and all listened. But not one dared to face the door. Yes, one, Wendy, who all this time had been bound to the mast. It was for neither a scream nor a crow that she was watching, it was for the reappearance of Peter.

She had not long to wait. In the cabin he had found the thing for which he had gone in search: the key that would free the children of their manacles, and now they all stole forth, armed with such weapons as they could find. First signing to them to hide, Peter cut Wendy's bonds, and then nothing could have been easier than for them all to fly off together; but one thing barred the way, an oath, "Hook or me this time." So when he had freed Wendy, he whispered to her to conceal herself with the others, and himself took her place by the mast, her cloak around him so that he should pass for her. Then he took a great breath and crowed.

To the pirates it was a voice crying that all the boys lay slain in the cabin; and they were panic-stricken. Hook tried to hearten them, but like the dogs he had made them they showed him their fangs, and he knew that if he took his eyes off them now they would leap at him.

"Lads," he said, ready to cajole or strike as need be, but never quailing for an instant, "I've thought it out. There's a Jonah aboard."

"Ay," they snarled, "a man wi' a hook."

"No, lads, no, it's the girl. Never was luck on a pirate ship wi' a woman on board. We'll right the ship when she's gone."

Some of them remembered that this had been a saying of Flint's. "It's worth trying," they said doubtfully.

"Fling the girl overboard," cried Hook; and they made a rush at the figure in the cloak.

"There's none can save you now, missy," Mullins hissed jeeringly.

"There's one," replied the figure.

"Who's that?"

"Peter Pan the avenger!" came the terrible answer; and as he spoke Peter flung off his cloak. Then they all knew who 'twas that had been undoing them in the cabin, and twice Hook essayed to speak and twice he failed. In that frightful moment I think his fierce heart broke.

At last he cried, "Cleave him to the brisket!" but without conviction.

"Down, boys, and at them!" Peter's voice rang out; and in another moment the clash of arms was resounding through the ship. Had the pirates kept together it is certain that they would have won; but the onset came when they were all unstrung, and they ran hither and thither, striking wildly, each thinking himself the last survivor of the crew. Man to man they were the stronger; but they fought on the defensive only, which enabled the boys to hunt in pairs and choose their quarry. Some of the miscreants leapt into the sea, others hid in dark recesses, where they were found by Slightly, who did not fight, but ran about with a lantern which he flashed in their faces, so that they were half blinded and fell an easy prey to the reeking swords of the other boys. There was little sound to be heard but the clang of weapons, an occasional screech or splash, and Slightly monotonously counting— five—six—seven—eight—nine—ten—eleven.

I think all were gone when a group of savage boys surrounded Hook, who seemed to have a charmed life, as he kept them at bay in that circle of fire. They had done for his dogs, but this man alone seemed to be a match for them all. Again and again they closed upon him, and again and again he hewed a clear space. He had lifted up one boy with his hook, and was using him as a buckler, when another, who had just passed his sword through Mullins, sprang into the fray.

"Put up your swords, boys," cried the newcomer, "this man is mine."

Thus suddenly Hook found himself face to face with Peter. The others drew back and formed a ring round them.

For long the two enemies looked at one another, Hook shuddering slightly, and Peter with the strange smile upon his face.

"So, Pan," said Hook at last, "this is all your doing."

"Ay, James Hook," came the stern answer, "it is all my doing."

"Proud and insolent youth," said Hook, "prepare to meet thy doom."

"Dark and sinister man," Peter answered, "have at thee."

Without more words they fell to, and for a space there was no advantage to either blade. Peter was a superb swordsman, and parried with dazzling rapidity; ever and anon he followed up a feint with a lunge that got past his foe's defence, but his shorter reach stood him in ill stead, and he could not drive the steel home. Hook, scarcely his inferior in brilliancy, but not quite so nimble in wrist play, forced him back by the weight of his onset, hoping suddenly to end all with a favourite thrust, taught him long ago by Barbecue at Rio; but to his astonishment he found this thrust turned aside again and again. Then he sought to close and give the quietus with his iron hook, which all this time had been pawing the air; but Peter doubled under it and, lunging fiercely, pierced him in the ribs. At sight of his own blood, whose peculiar colour, you remember, was offensive to him, the sword fell from Hook's hand, and he was at Peter's mercy.

"Now!" cried all the boys, but with a magnificent gesture Peter invited his opponent to pick up his sword. Hook did so instantly, but with a tragic feeling that Peter was showing good form.

Hitherto he had thought it was some fiend fighting him, but darker suspicions assailed him now.

"Pan, who and what art thou?" he cried huskily.

"I'm youth, I'm joy," Peter answered at a venture, "I'm a little bird that has broken out of the egg."

This, of course, was nonsense; but it was proof to the unhappy Hook that "Peter did not know in the least who or what he was, which is the very pinnacle of good form.

"To 't again," he cried despairingly.

He fought now like a human flail, and every sweep of that terrible sword would have severed in twain any man or boy who obstructed it; but Peter fluttered round him as if the very wind it made blew him out of the danger zone. And again and again he darted in and pricked.

Hook was fighting now without hope. That passionate breast no longer asked for life; but for one boon it craved: to see Peter in bad form before it was cold forever.

Abandoning the fight, he rushed into the powder magazine and fired it.

"In two minutes," he cried, "the ship will be blown to pieces."

Now, now, he thought, true form will show.

But Peter issued from the powder magazine with the shell in his hands, and calmly flung it overboard.

What sort of form was Hook himself showing? Misguided man though he was, we may be glad, without sympathising with him, that in the end he was true to the traditions of his race. The other boys were flying around him now, flouting, scornful; and as he staggered about the deck striking up at them impotently, his mind was no longer with them; it was slouching in the playing fields of long ago, or being sent up for good, or watching the wall-game from a famous wall. And his shoes were right, and his waistcoat was right, and his tie was right, and his socks were right.

James Hook, thou not wholly unheroic figure, farewell.

For we have come to his last moment.

Seeing Peter slowly advancing upon him through the air with dagger poised, he sprang upon the bulwarks to cast himself into the sea. He did not know that the crocodile was waiting for him; for we purposely stopped the clock that this knowledge might be spared him: a little mark of respect from us at the end.

He had one last triumph, which I think we need not grudge him. As he stood on the bulwark looking over his shoulder at Peter gliding through the air, he invited him with a gesture to use his foot. It made Peter kick instead of stab.

At last Hook had got the boon for which he craved.

"Bad form," he cried jeeringly, and went content to the crocodile.

Thus perished James Hook.

"Seventeen," Slightly sang out; but he was not quite correct in his figures. Fifteen paid the penalty for their crimes that night; but two reached the shore: Starkey to be captured by the redskins, who made him nurse for all their papooses, a melancholy come-down for a pirate; and Smee, who henceforth wandered about the world in his spectacles, making a precarious living by saying he was the only man that James Hook had feared.

Wendy, of course, had stood by, taking no part in the fight, though watching Peter with glistening eyes; but now that all was over she became prominent again. She praised them equally, and shuddered delightfully when Michael showed her the place where he had killed one; and then she took them into Hook's cabin and pointed to his watch which was hanging on a nail. It said half-past one!

The lateness of the hour was almost the biggest thing of all. She got them to bed in the pirates' bunks pretty quickly, you may be sure; all but Peter, who strutted up and down on deck, until at last he fell asleep by the side of Long Tom. He had one of his dreams that night, and cried in his sleep for a long time, and Wendy held him tight.

from

The King of Pirates

by Daniel Defoe (1660–1731)

Best known for his classic novel about the castaway Robinson Crusoe, Defoe later wrote this tale of Captain Avery—a lovable rogue and pirate who gives a detailed description of his adventures on the high seas in the form of two letters home. Here Avery tells of his encounter with a mogul's granddaughter.

In this time I pursued my voyage, coasted the whole Malabar shore, and met with no purchase but a great Portugal East India ship, which I chased into Goa, where she got out of my reach. I took several small vessels and barks, but little of value in them, till I entered the great Bay of Bengal, when I began to look about me with more expectation of success, though without prospect of what happened.

I cruised here about two months, finding nothing worth while; so I stood away to a port on the north point of the isle of Sumatra, where I made no stay; for here I got news that two large ships belonging to the Great Mogul were expected to cross the bay from Hoogly, in the Ganges, to the country of the King of Pegu, being to carry the granddaughter of the Great Mogul to Pegu, who was to be married to the king of that country, with all her retinue, jewels, and wealth.

This was a booty worth watching for, though it had been some months longer; so I resolved that we would go and cruise off Point Negaris, on the east side of the bay, near Diamond Isle; and here we plied off and on for three weeks, and began to despair of success; but the knowledge of the booty we expected spurred us on, and we waited with great patience, for we knew the prize would be immensely rich.

At length we spied three ships coming right up to us with the wind. We could easily see they were not Europeans by their sails, and began to prepare ourselves for a prize, not for a fight; but were a little disappointed when we found the first ship full of guns and full of soldiers, and in condition, had she been managed by English sailors, to have fought two such ships as ours were. However, we resolved to attack her if she had been full of devils as she was full of men.

Accordingly, when we came near them, we fired a gun with shot as a challenge. They fired again immediately three or four guns, but fired them so confusedly that we could easily see they did not understand their business; when we considered how to lay them on board, and so to come thwart them, if we could; but falling, for want of wind, open to them, we gave them a fair broadside. We could easily see, by the confusion that was on board, that they were frightened out of their wits; they fired here a gun and there a gun, and some on that side that was from us, as well as those that were next to us. The next thing we did was to lay them on board, which we did presently, and then gave them a volley of our small shot, which, as they stood so thick a great many of them, and made all the down under their hatches, crying out like creatures bewitched. In a word, we presently took the ship and having secured her men, we chased the other two. One was chiefly filled with women, other with lumber. Upon the whole, as the daughter of the Great Mogul was our prize in the first ship, so in the second was her women, or, in a word, her household, her eunuchs, all the necessaries of her wardrobe, of her stables, and of her kitchen; and in the last, great quantities of household stuff, and things less costly, though not less useful. But the first was the

main prize. When my men had entered and mastered the ship, one of
our lieutenants called for me, and accordingly I jumped on board. He
told me he thought nobody but I to go into the great cabin, or, at least,
nobody should go there before me; for that the lady herself and all her
attendance was there, and he feared the men were so heated they would
murder them all, or do worse.

I immediately went to the great cabin door, taking the lieutenant
that called me along with me, and caused the cabin door to be opened.
But such a sight of glory and misery was never seen by buccaneer
before. The queen (for such she was to have been) was all in gold and
silver, but frightened and crying, and, at the sight of me, she appeared
trembling, and just as if she was going to die. She sat on the side of a
kind of a bed like a couch, with no canopy over it, or any covering; only
made to lie down upon. She was, in a manner, covered with diamonds,
and I, like a true pirate, soon let her see that I had more mind to the
jewels than to the lady.

However, before I touched her, I ordered the lieutenant to place a
guard at the cabin door, and fastening the door, shut us both in, which
he did. The lady was young, and, I suppose, in their country esteem,
very handsome, but she was not very much so in my thoughts. At first,
her fright, and the danger she thought she was in of being killed,
taught her to do everything that she thought might interpose between
her and danger, and that was to take off her jewels as fast as she could,
and give them to me; and I, without any great compliment, took them
as fast as she gave me them, and put them into my pocket, taking no
great notice of them or of her, which frighted her worse than all the
rest, and she said something which I could not understand. However,
two of the other ladies came, all crying, and kneeled down to me with
their hands lifted up. What they meant, I knew not at first; but by their
gestures and pointings I found at last it was to beg the young queen's
life, and that I would not kill her.

When the three ladies kneeled down to me, and as soon as I understood what it was for, I let them know I would not hurt the queen, nor
let any one else hurt her, but that she must give me all her jewels and

money. Upon this they acquainted her that I would save her life; and no sooner had they assured her of that but she got up smiling, and went to a fine Indian cabinet, and opened a private drawer, from whence she took another little thing full of little square drawers and holes. This she brings to me in her hand, and offered to kneel down to give it me. This innocent usage began to rouse some good-nature in me (though I never had much), and I would not let her kneel; but sitting down myself on the side of her couch or bed, made a motion to her to sit down too. But here she was frightened again, it seems, at what I had no thought of. But as I did not offer anything of that kind, only made her sit down by me, they began all to be easier after some time, and she gave me the little box or casket, I know not what to call it, but it was full of invaluable jewels. I have them still in my keeping, and wish they were safe in England; for I doubt not but some of them are fit to be placed on the king's crown.

Being master of this treasure, I was very willing to be good-humored to the persons; so I went out of the cabin, and caused the women to be left alone, causing the guard to be kept still, that they might receive no more injury than I would do them myself. After I had been out of the cabin some time, a slave of the women's came to me, and made sign to me that the queen would speak with me again. I made signs back that I would come and dine with her majesty; and accordingly I ordered that her servants should prepare her dinner, and carry it in, and then call me. They provided her repast after the usual manner, and when she saw it brought in she appeared pleased, and more when she saw me come in after it; for she was exceedingly pleased that I had caused a guard to keep the rest of my men from her; and she had, it seems, been told how rude they had been to some of the women that belonged to her.

When I came in, she rose up, and paid me such respect as I did not well know how to receive, and not in the least how to return. If she had understood English, I could have said plainly, and in good rough words, "Madam, be easy; we are rude, rough-hewn fellows, but none of our men should hurt you, or touch you; I will be your guard and pro- tection; we are for money indeed, and we shall take what you have, but we will do you no other harm." But as I could not talk thus to her, I scarce knew what to say; but I sat down, and made signs to have her sit down and eat, which she did, but with so much ceremony that I did not know well what to do with it.

After we had eaten, she rose up again, and drinking some water out of a china cup, sat her down on the side of the couch as before. When she saw I had done eating, she went then to another cabinet, and pulling out a drawer, she brought it to me; it was full of small pieces of gold coin of Pegu, about as big as an English half-guinea, and I think there were three thousand of them. She opened several other drawers, and showed me the wealth that was in them, and then gave me the key of the whole.

We had revelled thus all day, and part of the next day, in a bottomless sea of riches, when my lieutenant began to tell me, we must consider what to do with our prisoners and the ships, for that there was no subsisting in that manner. Upon this we called a short council, and concluded to carry the great ship away with us, but to put all the prisoners—queen, ladies, and all the rest—into the lesser vessels, and let them go; and so far was I from ravishing this lady, as I hear is reported of me, that though I might rifle her of everything else, yet, I assure you, I let her go untouched for me, or, as I am satisfied, for any one of my men; nay, when we dismissed them, we gave her leave to take a great many things of value with her, which she would have been plundered of if I had not been so careful of her.

We had now wealth enough not only to make us rich, but almost to have made a nation rich; and to tell you the truth, considering the costly things we took here, which we did not know the value of, and besides gold and silver and jewels,—I say, we never knew how rich we were; besides which we had a great quantity of bales of goods, as well calicoes as wrought silks, which, being for sale, were perhaps as a cargo of goods to answer the bills which might be drawn upon them for the account of the bride's portion; all which fell into our hands, with a great sum in silver coin, too big to talk of among Englishmen, especially while I am living, for reasons which I may give you hereafter.

The Life of Benito de Soto

by The Marine Research Society
from *The Pirates Own Book*

Drawn from information about the actual trial of the infamous pirate Benito de Soto, the following account— published by The Marine Research Society of Salem, Massachusetts in 1924—tells the story of his life.

T he following narrative of the career of a desperate pirate who was executed in Gibraltar in the month of January, 1830, is one of two letters from the pen of the author of "the Military Sketch-Book." The writer says Benito de Soto "had been a prisoner in the garrison for nineteen months, during which time the British Government spared neither the pains not expense to establish a full train of evidence against him. The affair had caused the greatest excitement here, as well as at Cadiz, owing to the development of the atrocities which marked the character of this man, and the diabolical gang of which he was the leader. Nothing else is talked of; and a thousand horrors are added to his guilt, which, although he was guilty enough, he has no right to bear. The following is all the authentic information I could collect concerning him. I have drawn it from his trial, from the confession of his accomplices, from the keeper of his prison, and not a little from his own lips. It will be found more interesting than all the tales and sketches furnished in the 'Annuals,' magazines, and other vehicles of invention, from the simple fact—that it is truth and not fiction."

Benito de Soto was a native of a small village near Courna; he was bred a mariner, and was in the guiltless exercise of his calling at Buenos Ayres, in the year 1827. A vessel was there being fitted out for a voyage to the coast of Africa, for the smuggling of slaves; and as she required a strong crew, a great number of sailors were engaged, amongst whom was Soto. The Portuguese of South America have yet a privilege of dealing in slaves on a certain part of the African coast, but it was the intention of the captain of this vessel to exceed the limits of his trade, and to run farther down, so as to take his cargo of human beings from a part of the country which was proscribed, in the certainty of being there enabled to purchase slaves at a much lower rate than he could in the regular way; or, perhaps, to take away by force as many as he could stow away into his ship. He therefore required a considerable number of hands for the enterprise; and in such a traffic, it may be easily conceived, that the morals of the crew could not be a subject of much consideration with the employer. French, Spanish, Portuguese, and others, were entered on board, most of them renegadoes, and they set sail on their evil voyage, with every hope of infamous success.

Those who deal in evil carry along with them the springs of their own destruction, upon which they will tread, in spite of every caution, and their imagined security is but the brink of the pit into which they are to fall. It was so with the captain of this slave-ship. He arrived in Africa, took in a considerable number of slaves, and in order to complete his cargo, went on shore, leaving his mate in charge of the vessel. This mate was a bold, wicked, reckless and ungovernable spirit, and perceiving in Benito de Soto a mind congenial with his own, he fixed on him as a fit person to join in a design he had conceived, of running away with the vessel, and becoming a pirate. Accordingly the mate proposed his plan to Soto, who not only agreed to join in it, but declared that he himself had been contemplating a similar enterprise during the voyage. They both were at once of a mind, and they lost no time in maturing their plot.

Their first step was to break the matter to the other members of the crew. In this they proceeded cautiously, and succeeded so far as to gain over twenty-two of the whole, leaving eighteen who remained faithful to their trust. Every means were used to corrupt the well disposed; both persuasion and threats were resorted to, but without effect, and the leader of the conspiracy, the mate, began to despair of obtaining the desired object. Soto, however, was not so easily depressed. He at once decided on seizing the ship upon the strength of his party: and without consulting the mate, he collected all the arms of the vessel, called the conspirators together, put into each of their possession a cutlass and a brace of pistols, and arming himself in like manner, advanced at the head of the gang, drew his sword, and declared the mate to be the commander of the ship, and the men who joined him part owners. Still, those who had rejected the evil offer remained unmoved; on which Soto ordered out the boats, and pointing to the land, cried out, "There is the African coast; this is our ship—one or the other must be chosen by every man on board within five minutes."

This declaration, although it had the effect of preventing any resistance that might have been offered by the well disposed, to the taking of the vessel, did not change them from their purpose; they still refused to join in the robbery, and entered one by one into the boat, at the orders of Soto, and with but one pair of oars (all that was allowed to them) put off for the shore, from which they were then ten miles distant. Had the weather continued calm, as it was when the boat left the ship, she would have made the shore by dusk; but unhappily a strong gale of wind set in shortly after her departure, and she was seen by Soto and his gang struggling with the billows and approaching night, at such a distance from the land as she could not possibly accomplish while the gale lasted. All on board the ship agreed in opinion that the boat could not live, as they flew away from her at the rate of ten knots an hour, under close reefed topsails, leaving their unhappy messmates to their inevitable fate. Those of the pirates who were lately executed at Cadiz, declared that every soul in the boat perished.

The drunken uproar which that night reigned in the pirate ship was in horrid unison with the raging elements around her; contention and quarrelling followed the brutal ebriety of the pirates; each evil spirit sought the mastery of the others, and Soto's, which was the fiend of all, began to grasp and grapple for its proper place—the head of such a diabolical community.

The mate (now the chief) at once gave the reins to his ruffian tyranny; and the keen eye of Soto saw that he who had fawned with him the day before, would next day rule him with an iron rod. Prompt in his actions as he was penetrating in his judgment, he had no sooner conceived a jealousy of the leader than he determined to put him aside; and as his rival lay in his drunken sleep, Soto put a pistol to his head, and deliberately shot him. For this act he excused himself to the crew, by stating to them that it was in *their* protection he did the act; that *their* interest was the other's death; and concluded by declaring himself their leader, and promising a golden harvest to their future labors, provided they obeyed him. Soto succeeded to the height of his wishes, and was unanimously hailed by the crew as their captain.

On board the vessel, as I before stated, were a number of slaves, and these the pirates had well secured under hatches. They now turned their attention to those half starved, half suffocated creatures;—some were for throwing them overboard, while others, not less cruel, but more desirous of gain, proposed to take them to some port in one of those countries that deal in human beings, and there sell them. The latter recommendation was adopted, and Soto steered for the West Indies, where he received a good price for his slaves. One of those wretched creatures, a boy, he reserved as a servant for himself; and this boy was destined by Providence to be the witness of the punishment of those white men who tore away from their homes himself and his brethren. He alone will carry back to his country the truth of Heaven's retribution, and heal the wounded feelings of broken kindred with the recital of it.

The pirates now entered freely into their villianous pursuit, and plundered many vessels; amongst others was an American brig, the treatment of which forms the *chef d'œuvre* of their atrocity. Having taken out of this brig all the valuables they could find, they hatched down all hands to the hold, except a black man, who was allowed to remain on deck for the special purpose of affording in his torture an amusing exhibition to Soto and his gang. They set fire to the brig, then lay to, to observe the progress of the flames; and as the miserable African bounded from rope to rope, now climbing to the mast head—now clinging to the shrouds—now leaping to one part of the vessel, and now to another,—their enjoyment seemed raised to its heighest pitch. At length the hatches opened to the devouring element, the tortured victim of their fiendish cruelty fell exhausted into the flames, and the horrid and revolting scene closed amidst the shouts of the miscreants who had caused it.

Of their other exploits, that which ranks next in turpitude, and which led to their overthrow, was the piracy of the Morning Star. They fell in with that vessel near the island Ascension, in the year 1828, as she was on her voyage from Ceylon to England. This vessel, besides a valuable cargo, had on board several passengers, consisting of a major and his wife, an assistant surgeon, two civilians, about five and twenty invalid soldiers, and three or four of their wives. As soon as Benito de Soto perceived the ship, which was at day-light on the 21st of February, he called up all hands, and prepared for attacking her; he was at the time steering on an opposite course to that of the Morning Star. On reconnoitring her, he at first supposed she was a French vessel; but Barbazan, one of his crew, who was himself a Frenchman, assured him the ship was British. "So much the better," exclaimed Soto, in English (for he could speak that language), "we shall find the more booty." He then ordered the sails to be squared, and ran before the wind in chase of his plunder, from which he was about two leagues distant.

The Defensor de Pedro, the name of the pirate ship, was a fast sailer, but owing to the press of canvas which the Morning Star hoisted soon after the pirate had commenced the chase, he did not come up with her so quickly as he had expected: the delay caused great uneasiness to Soto, which he manifested by muttering curses, and restlessness of manner. Sounds of savage satisfaction were to be heard from every mouth but his at the prospect; he alone expressed his anticipated pleasure by oaths, menaces, and mental inquietude. While Barbazan was employed in superintending the clearing of the decks, the arming and breakfasting of the men, he walked rapidly up and down, revolving in his mind the plan of the approaching attack, and when interrupted by any of the crew, he would run into a volley of imprecations. In one instance, he struck his black boy a violent blow with a telescope, because he asked him if he would have his morning cup of chocolate; as soon, however, as he set his studding sails, and perceived that he was gaining on the Morning Star, he became somewhat tranquil, began to eat heartily of cold beef, drank his chocolate at a draught, and coolly sat down on the deck to smoke a cigar.

In less than a quarter of an hour, the pirate had gained considerable on the other vessel. Soto now, without rising from where he sat, ordered a gun, with blank cartridge, to be fired, and the British colors to be hoisted: but finding this measure had not the effect of bringing the Morning Star to, he cried out, "Shot the long gun and give it her point blank." The order was obeyed, but the shot fell short of the intention, on which he jumped up and cursed the fellows for bunglers who had fired the gun. He then ordered them to load with canister shot, and took the match in his own hand. He did not, however, fire immediately, but waited until he was nearly abreast of his victim; then directing the aim himself, and ordering a man to stand by the flag to haul it down, fired with an air that showed he was sure of his mark. He then ran to haul up the Colombian colors, and having done so, cried out through the speaking trumpet, "Lower your boat down this moment, and let your captain come on board with his papers."

During this fearful chase the people on board the Morning Star were in the greatest alarm; but however their apprehensions might have been excited, that courage, which is so characteristic of a British sailor, never for a moment forsook the captain. He boldly carried on sail, and although one of the men fell from a wound, and the ravages of the shot were every where around him, he determined not to strike. But unhappily he had not a single gun on board, and no small arms that could render his courage availing. The tears of the women, and the prudent advice of the passengers overcoming his resolution, he permitted himself to be guided by the general opinion. One of the passengers volunteered himself to go on board the pirate, and a boat was lowered for the purpose. Both vessels now lay to within fifty yards of each other, and a strong hope arose in those on board the Morning Star, that the gentleman who had volunteered to go to the pirate, might, through his exertions, avert, at least, the worst of the dreaded calamity. Some people here, in their quiet security, have made no scruple of declaring, that the commanding officer of the soldiers on board should not have so tamely yielded to the pirate, particularly as he had his wife along with him, and consequently a misfortune to dread, that might be thought even worse than death: but all who knew the true state of the circumstances, and reflect upon it, will allow that he adopted the only chance of escaping that, which was to be most feared by a husband. The long gun, which was on a pivot in the centre of the pirate ship, could in a few shots sink the Morning Star; and even had resistance been made to the pirates as they boarded her—had they been killed or made prisoners—the result would not be much better. It was evident that the Defensor de Pedro was the best sailer, consequently the Morning Star could not hope to escape; in fact, submission or total destruction was the only choice. The commanding officer, therefore, acted for the best when he recommended the former. There was some slight hope of escaping with life, and without personal abuse, by surrendering, but to contend must be inevitable death.

The gentleman who had gone in a boat to the pirate returned in a short time, exhibiting every proof of the ill treatment he had received from Soto and his crew. It appears that when the villains learned that he was not the captain, they fell upon and beat him, as well as the sailors along with him, in a most brutal manner, and with the most horrid imprecations told him, that if the captain did not instantly come, on his return to the vessel, they would blow the ship out of the water. This report as once decided the captain in the way he was to act. Without hesitation he stepped into the boat, taking with him his second mate, three soldiers and a sailor boy, and proceeded to the pirate. On going on board that vessel, along with the mate, Soto, who stood near the mainmast, with his drawn cutlass in his hand, desired him to approach, while the mate was ordered, by Barbazan, to go to the fore-castle. Both these unfortunate individuals obeyed, and were instantly slaughtered.

Soto now ordered six picked men to descend into the boat, amongst whom was Barbazan. To him the leader addressed his orders, the last of which was, to take care to put all in the prize to death, and then sink her.

The six pirates, who proceeded to execute his savage demand, were all armed alike,—they each carried a brace of pistols, a cutlass and a long knife. Their dress was composed of a sort of coarse cotton chequered jacket and trowsers, shirts that were open at the collar, red woollen caps, and broad canvas waistbelts, in which were the pistols and the knives. They were all athletic men, and seemed such as might well be trusted with the sanguinary errand on which they were despatched. While the boat was conveying them, Soto held in his hand a cutlass, reddened with the blood of the murdered captain, and stood scowling on them with silence: while another ruffian, with a lighted match, stood by the long gun, ready to support the boarding, if necessary, with a shot that would sweep the deck.

As the boarders approached the Morning Star, the terror of the females became excessive; they clung to their husbands in despair, who endeavored to allay their fears by their own vain hopes, assuring them that a quiet submission nothing more than the plunder of the vessel was to be apprehended. But a few minutes miserably undeceived them. The pirates rapidly mounted the side, and as they jumped on deck, commenced to cut right and left at all within their reach, uttering at the same time the most dreadful oaths. The females, screaming, hurried to hide themselves below as well as they were able, and the men fell or fled before the pirates, leaving them entire masters of the decks.

When the pirates had succeeded in effectually prostrating all the people on deck, they drove most of them below and reserved the remainder to assist in their operations. Unless the circumstances be closely examined, it may be wondered how six men could have so easily overcome a crew of English seamen supported by about twenty soldiers with a major at their head:—but it will not appear so surprising, when it is considered that the sailors were altogether unarmed, the soldiers were worn out invalids, and more particularly, that the pirate carried a heavy long gun, ready to sink her victim at a shot. Major Logic was fully impressed with the folly of opposing so powerful and desperate an enemy, and therefore advised submission as the only course for the safety of those under his charge; presuming no doubt that something like humanity might be found in the breasts even of the worst of men. But alas! he was woefully deceived in his estimate of the villains' nature, and felt, when too late, that even death would have been preferable to the barbarous treatment he was forced to endure.

Beaten, bleeding, terrified, the men lay huddled together in the hold, while the pirates proceeded in their work of pillage and brutality. Every trunk was hauled forth, every portable article of value heaped for the plunder; money, plate, charts, nautical instruments, and seven parcels of valuable jewels, which formed part of the cargo; these were carried from below on the backs of those men whom the pirates selected to assist them, and for two hours they were thus employed, during which time Soto stood upon his own deck directing the operations; for the vessels were within a hundred yards of each other. The scene which took place in the cabin exhibited a licentious brutality. The sick officer, Mr. Gibson, was dragged from his berth; the clothes of the other passengers stripped from their backs, and the whole of the cabin passengers driven on deck, except the females, whom they locked up in the roundhouse on deck, and the steward, who was detained to serve the pirates with wine and eatables. This treatment, no doubt hastened the death of Gibson; the unfortunate gentleman did not long survive it. As the passengers were forced up the cabin ladder, the feelings of Major Logic, it may be imagined, were of the most heart-rending description. In vain did he entreat to be allowed to remain; he was hurried away from even the chance of protecting his defenceless wife, and battened down with the rest in the hold, there to be racked with the fearful apprehensions of their almost certain doom.

The labors of the robbers being now concluded, they sat down to regale themselves, preparatory to the *chef d'œuvre* of their diabolical enterprise; and a more terrible group of demi-devils, the steward declares, could not be well imagined than commanded his attention at the cabin table. However, as he was a Frenchman, and naturally polite, he acquitted himself of the office of cup-bearer, if not as gracefully, at least as anxiously, as ever did Ganymede herself. Yet, notwithstanding this readiness to serve the visitors in their gastronomic desires, the poor steward felt ill-requited; he was twice frightened into an icicle, and twice thawed back into conscious horror, by the rudeness of those he entertained. In one instance, when he had filled out a sparkling glass for a ruffian, and believed he had quite won the heart of the drinker by the act, he found himself grasped roughly and tightly by the throat, and the point of a knife staring him in the face. It seems the fellow who thus seized him, had felt between his teeth a sharp bit of broken glass, and fancying that something had been put in the wine to poison him, he determined to prove his suspicions by making the steward swallow what remained in the bottle from which the liquor had been drawn, and thus unceremoniously prefaced his command; however, ready and implicit obedience averted further bad consequences. The other instance of the steward's jeopardy was this; when the repast was ended, one of the gentlemen coolly requested him to waive all delicacy, and point out the place in which the captain's money was concealed. He might as well have asked him to produce the philosopher's stone. However, pleading the truth was of no use; his determined requisitor seconded the demand by snapping a pistol at his breast; having missed fire, he recocked, and again presented; but the fatal weapon was struck aside by Barbazan, who reproved the rashness with a threat, and thus averted the steward's impending fate. It was then with feelings of satisfaction he heard himself ordered to go down to the hold, and in a moment he was bolted in among his fellow sufferers.

The ruffians indulged in the pleasures of the bottle for some time longer, and then having ordered down the females, treated them with even less humanity than characterised their conduct towards the others. The screams of the helpless females were heard in the hold by those who were unable to render them assistance, and agonizing, indeed, must those screams have been to their incarcerated hearers! How far the brutality of the pirates was carried in this stage of the horrid proceeding, we can only surmise; fortunately, their lives were spared, although, as it afterwards appeared, the orders of Soto were to butcher every being on board; and it is thought that these orders were not put into action, in consequence of the villains having wasted so much time in drinking, and otherwise indulging themselves; for it was not until the loud voice of their chief was heard to recall them, that they prepared to leave the ship; they therefore contented themselves with fastening the women within the cabin, heaping heavy lumber on the hatches of the hold, and boring holes in the planks of the vessel below the surface of the water, so that in destroying the unhappy people at one swoop, they might make up for the lost time. They then left the ship, sinking fast to her apparently certain fate.

It may be reasonably supposed, bad as their conduct was towards the females, and pitiable as was the suffering it produced, that the lives of the whole left to perish were preserved through it; for the ship must have gone down if the women had been either taken out of her or murdered, and those in the hold inevitably have gone with her to the bottom. But by good fortune, the females succeeded in forcing their way out of the cabin, and became the means of liberating the men confined in the hold. When they came on deck, it was nearly dark, yet they could see the pirate ship at a considerable distance, with all her sails set and bearing away from them. They prudently waited, concealed from the possibility of being seen by the enemy, and when the night fell, they crept to the hatchway, and called out to the men below to endeavor to effect their liberation, informing them that the pirate was away and out of sight. They then united their efforts, and the lumber being removed, the hatches gave way to the force below, so that the released captives breathed of hope again. The delightful draught, however, was checked, when the ship was found to contain six feet of water! A momentary collapse took possession of all their newly excited expectations; cries and groans of despair burst forth, but the sailors' energy quickly returned, and was followed by that of the others; they set to work at the pumps, and by dint of labor succeeded in keeping the vessel afloat. Yet to direct her course was impossible; the pirates having completely disabled her, by cutting away her rigging and sawing the masts all the way through. The eye of Providence, however, was not averted from the hapless people, for they fell in with a vessel next day that relieved them from their distressing situation, and brought them to England in safety.

We will now return to Soto, and show how the hand of that Providence that secured his intended victims, fell upon himself and his wicked associates. Intoxicated with their infamous success, the night had far advanced before Soto learned that the people in the Morning Star, instead of being slaughtered, were only left to be drowned. The information excited his utmost rage. He reproached Barbazan, and those who had accompanied them in the boarding, with disobeying his orders, and declared that now there could be no security for their lives. Late as the hour was, and long as he had been steering away from the Morning Star, he determined to put back, in the hope of effectually preventing the escape of those in the devoted vessel, by seeing them destroyed before his eyes. Soto was a follower of the principle inculcated by the old maxim, "Dead men tell no tales;" and in pursuance of his doctrine, lost not a moment in putting about and running back. But it was too late; he could find no trace of the vessel, and so consoled himself with the belief that she was at the bottom of the sea, many fathoms below the ken and cognizance of Admiralty Courts.

Soto, thus satisfied, bent his course to Europe. On his voyage he fell in with a small brig, boarded, plundered, sunk her, and, that he might not again run the hazard of encountering living witnesses of his guilt, murdered the crew, with the exception of one individual, whom he took along with him, on account of his knowledge of the course to Corunna, whither he intended to proceed. But, faithful to his principles of self-protection, as soon as he had made full use of the unfortunate sailor, and found himself in sight of the destined port, he came up to him at the helm, which he held in his hand, "My friend," said he "is that the harbor of Corunna?"—"Yes," was the reply. "Then," rejoined Soto, "You have done your duty well, and I am obliged to you for your services." On the instant he drew a pistol and shot the man; then coolly flung his body overboard, took the helm himself, and steered into his native harbor as little concerned as if he had returned from an honest voyage. At this port he obtained papers in a false name, disposed of a great part of his booty, and after a short stay set out for Cadiz, where he expected a market for the remainder. He had a fair wind until he came within sight of the coast near that city. It was coming on dark and he lay to, expecting to go into his anchorage next morning, but the wind shifted to the westward, and suddenly began to blow a heavy gale; it was right on the land. He luffed his ship as close to the wind as possible, in order to clear a point that stretched outward, and beat off to windward, but his lee-way carried him towards the land, and he was caught when he least expected the trap. The gale increased—the night grew pitchy dark—the roaring breakers were on his lee-beam—the drifting vessel strikes, rebounds, and strikes again—the cry of horror rings through the flapping cordage, and despair is in the eyes of the demon-crew. Helpless they lie amid the wrath of the storm, and the darkened face of Heaven, for the first time, strikes terror on their guilty hearts. Death is before them, but not with a merciful quickness does he approach; hour after hour the frightful vision glares upon them, and at length disappears only to come upon them again in a more dreadful form. The tempest abates, and the sinners were spared for the time.

As the daylight broke they took to their boats, and abandoned the vessel to preserve their lives. But there was no repentance in the pirates; along with the night and the winds went the voice of conscience, and they thought no more of what had passed. They stood upon the beach gazing at the wreck, and the first thought of Soto, was to sell it, and purchase another vessel for the renewal of his atrocious pursuits. With the marked decision of his character, he proposed his intention to his followers, and received their full approbation. The plan was instantly arranged; they were to present themselves as honest, shipwrecked mariners to the authorities at Cadiz; Soto was to take upon himself the office of mate, or *contra maestra* to an imaginary captain, and thus obtain their sanction in disposing of the vessel. In their assumed character, the whole proceeded to Cadiz, and presented themselves before the proper officers of the marine. Their story was listened to with sympathy, and for a few days every thing went on to their satisfaction. Soto had succeeded so well as to conclude the sale of the wreck with a broker, for the sum of one thousand seven hundred and fifty dollars; the contract was signed, but fortunately the money was not yet paid, when suspicion arose, from some inconsistencies in the pirates' account of themselves, and six of them were arrested by the authorities. Soto and one of his crew instantly disappeared from Cadiz, and succeeded in arriving at the neutral ground before Gibralter, and six more made their escape to the Carraccas.

None are permitted to enter the fortress of Gibralter, without permission from the governor, or a passport. Soto and his companion, therefore, took up their quarters at a Posade on the neutral ground, and resided there in security for several days. The busy and daring mind of the former could not long remain inactive; he proposed to his companion to attempt to enter the garrison in disguise and by stealth, but could not prevail upon him to consent. He therefore resolved to go in alone; and his object in doing so was to procure a supply of money by a letter of credit which he brought with him from Cadiz. His companion, more wise than he, chose the safer course; he knew that the neutral ground was not much controllable by the laws either of the Spanish or the English, and although there was not much probability of being discovered, he resolved not to trust to chance in so great a stake as his life; and he proved to have been right in his judgment, for had he gone to Gibralter, he would have shared the same fate of his chief. This man is the only one of the whole gang, who has not met with the punishment of his crimes, for he succeeded in effecting his escape on board some vessel. It is not even suspected to what country he is gone; but his description, no doubt, is registered. The steward of the Morning Star informed me, that he is a tall, stout man, with fair hair, and fresh complexion, of a mild and gentle countenance, but that he was one of the worst villains of the whole piratical crew. I believe he is stated to be a Frenchman.

Soto secured his admission into the garrison by a false pass, and took up his residence at an inferior tavern in a narrow lane, which runs off the main street of Gibralter, and is kept by a man of the name of Basso. The appearance of this house suits well with the associations of the worthy Benito's life. I have occasion to pass the door frequently at night, for our barrack, (the Casement,) is but a few yards from it. I never look at the place without feeling an involuntary sensation of horror—the smoky and dirty nooks—the distant groups of dark Spaniards, Moors, and Jews, their sallow countenances made yellow by the light of dim oil lamps—the unceiled rafters of the rooms above, seen through unshuttered windows and the consciousness of their having covered the atrocious Soto, combine this effect upon me.

In this den the villain remained for a few weeks, and during this time seemed to enjoy himself as if he had never committed a murder. The story he told Basso of his circumstances was, that he had come to Gibralter on his way to Cadiz from Malaga, and was merely awaiting the arrival of a friend. He dressed expensively—generally wore a white hat of the best English quality, silk stockings, white trowsers, and blue frock coat. His whiskers were large and bushy, and his hair, which was very black, profuse, long and naturally curled, was much in the style of a London preacher of prophetic and anti-poetic notoriety. He was deeply browned with the sun, and had an air and gait expressive of his bold, enterprising, and desperate mind. Indeed, when I saw him in his cell and at his trial, although his frame was attenuated almost to a skeleton, the color of his face a pale yellow, his eyes sunken, and hair closely shorn; he still exhibited strong traces of what he had been, still retained his erect and fearless carriage, his quick, fiery, and malevolent eye, his hurried and concise speech, and his close and pertinent style of remark. He appeared to me such a man as would have made a hero in the ranks of his country, had circumstances placed him in the proper road to fame; but ignorance and poverty turned into the most ferocious robber, one who might have rendered service and been an honor to his sunken country. I should like to hear what the phrenologists say of his head; it appeared to me to be the most peculiar I had ever seen, and certainly, as far as the bump of *destructiveness* went, bore the theory fully out. It is rumored here that the skull has been sent to the *savans* of Edinburg; if this be the case, we shall no doubt be made acquainted with their sage opinions upon the subject, and great conquerors will receive a farther assurance of how much they resemble in their physical natures the greatest murderers.

When I visited the pirate in the Moorish castle where he was confined, he was sitting in his cold, narrow, and miserable cell, upon a pallet of straw, eating his coarse meal from a tin plate. I thought him more an object of pity than vengeance; he looked so worn with disease, so crushed with suffering, yet so affable, frank, and kind in his address; for he happened to be in a communicative mood, a thing that was by no means common with him. He spoke of his long confinement, till I thought the tears were about to start from his eyes, and alluded to his approaching trial with satisfaction; but his predominant characteristic, ferocity, appeared in his small piercing black eyes before I left him, as he alluded to his keeper, the Provost, in such a way that made me suspect his desire for blood was not yet extinguished. When he appeared in court on his trial, his demeanor was quite altered; he seemed to me to have suddenly risen out of the wretch he was in his cell, to all the qualities I had heard of him; he stood erect and unembarrassed; he spoke with a strong voice, attended closely to the proceedings, occasionally examined the witnesses, and at the conclusion protested against the justice of his trial. He sometimes spoke to the guards around him, and sometimes affected an air of carelessness of his awful situation, which, however, did not sit easy upon him. Even here the

leading trait of his mind broke forth; for when the interpreter commenced his office, the language which he made use of being pedantic
and affected, Soto interrupted him thus, while a scowl sat upon his
brow that terrified the man of words: "I don't understand you, man;
speak Spanish like others, and I'll listen to you." When the dirk that
belonged to Mr. Robertson, the trunk and clothes taken from Mr.
Gibson, and the pocket book containing the ill-fated captain's hand-
writing were placed before him, and proved to have been found in his
room, and when the maid servant of the tavern proved that she found
the dirk under his pillow every morning on arranging his bed; and
when he was confronted with his own black slave, between two wax
lights, the countenance of the villain appeared in its true nature, not
depressed nor sorrowful, but vivid and ferocious; and when the patient
and dignified governor, Sir George Don, passed the just sentence of the
law upon him, he looked daggers at his heart, and assumed a horrid
silence, more eloquent than words.

The criminal persisted up to the day before his execution in
asserting his innocence, and inveighing against the injustice of his trial,
but the certainty of his fate, and the awful voice of religion, at length
subdued him. He made an unreserved confession of his guilt, and
became truly penitent; gave up to the keeper the blade of a razor which
he had secreted between the soles of his shoes for the acknowledged
purpose of adding suicide to his crimes, and seemed to wish for the
moment that was to send him before his Creator.

I witnessed his execution, and I believe there never was a more con-
trite man than he appeared to be; yet there were no drivelling fears
upon him—he walked firmly at the tail of the fatal cart, gazing sometimes at his coffin, sometimes at the crucifix which he held in his hand.
The symbol of divinity he frequently pressed to his lips, repeated the
prayers spoken in his ear by the attendant clergyman, and seemed
regardless of every thing but the world to come. The gallows was
erected beside the water, and fronting the neutral ground. He mounted
the cart as firmly as he had walked behind it, and held up his face to
Heaven and the beating rain, calm, resigned, but unshaken; and

finding the halter too high for his neck, he boldly stepped upon his coffin, and placed his head in the noose, then watching the first turn of the wheels, he murmured *"adios todos,"*[*] and leaned forward to facilitate his fall.

The black slave of the pirate stood upon the battery trembling before his dying master to behold the awful termination of a series of events, the recital of which to his African countrymen, when he shall return to his home, will give them no doubt, a dreadful picture of European civilization. The black boy was acquitted at Cadiz, but the men who had fled to the Carraccas, as well as those arrested after the wreck, were convicted, executed, their limbs severed, and hung on tenter hooks, as a warning to all pirates.

[*] "Farewell, all."

from

The Black Buccaneer

by Stephen W. Meader (1892–1977)

Left alone for the night by his father on a remote island off the coast of Maine in 1718, 14-year-old shepherd Jeremy Swan witnesses a battle at sea between two ships. Much to his surprise, the victorious ship makes for the island.

O n the morning of the 15th of July, 1718, anyone who had been standing on the low rocks of the Penobscot bay shore might have seen a large, clumsy boat of hewn planking making its way out against the tide that set strongly up into the river month. She was loaded deep with a shifting, noisy cargo that lifted white noses and huddled broad, woolly backs—in fact, nothing less extraordinary than fifteen fat Southdown sheep and a sober-faced collie-dog. The crew of this remarkable craft consisted of a sinewy, bearded man of forty-five who minded sheet and tiller in the stern, and a boy of fourteen, tall and broad for his age, who was constantly employed in soothing and restraining the bleating flock.

No one was present to witness the spectacle because, in those remote days, there were scarcely a thousand white men on the whole coast of Maine from Kittery to Louisberg, while at this season of the year the Indians were following the migrating game along the northern rivers. The nearest settlement was a tiny log hamlet ten miles up the bay, which the two voyagers had left that morning.

The boy's keen face, under its shock of sandy hair, was turned toward the sea and the dim outline of land that smudged the southern horizon.

"Father," he suddenly asked, "how big is the Island!"

"You'll see soon enough, Jeremy. Stop your questioning," answered the man. "We'll be there before night and I'll leave you with the sheep. You'll be lonesome, too, if I mistake not."

"Huh!" snorted Jeremy to himself.

Indeed it was not very likely that this lad, raised on the wildest of frontiers, would mind the prospect of a night alone on an island ten miles out at sea. He had seen Indian raids before he was old enough to know what frightened him; had tried his best with his fists to save his mother in the Amesbury massacre, six years before; and in a little settlement on the Saco River, when he was twelve, he had done a man's work at the blockhouse loophole, loading nearly as fast and firing as true as any woodsman in the company. Danger and strife had given the lad an alert self-confidence far beyond his years.

Amos Swan, his father, was one of those iron spirits that fought out the struggle with the New England wilderness in the early days. He had followed the advancing line of colonization into the Northeast, hewing his way with the other pioneers. What he sought was a place to raise sheep. Instead of increasing, however, his flock had dwindled—wolves here—lynxes there—dogs in the larger settlements. After the last onslaught he had determined to move with his possessions and his two boys—Tom, nineteen years old, and the smaller Jeremy—to an island too remote for the attacks of any wild animal.

So he had set out in a canoe, chosen his place of habitation and built a temporary shelter on it for family and flock, while at home the boys, with the help of a few settlers, had laid the keel and fashioned the hull of a rude but seaworthy boat, such as the coast fishermen used.

Preparations had been completed the evening before, and now, while Tom cared for half the flock on the mainland, the father and younger son were convoying the first load to their new home.

In the day when these events took place, the hundreds of rocky bits of land that line the Maine coast stood out against the gray sea as bleak and desolate as at the world's beginning. Some were merely huge up-ended rocks that rose sheer out of the Atlantic a hundred feet high, and on whose tops the sea-birds nested by the million. The larger ones, however, had, through countless ages, accumulated a layer of earth that covered their gaunt sides except where an occasional naked rib of gray granite was thrust out. Sparse grass struggled with the junipers for a foothold along the slopes, and low black firs, whose seed had been wind-blown or bird-carried from the mainland, climbed the rugged crest of each island. Few men visited them, and almost none inhabited them. Since the first long Norse galley swung by to the tune of the singing rowers, the number of passing ships had increased and their character had changed, but the isles were rarely touched at except by mishap—a shipwreck—or a crew in need of water. The Indians, too, left the outer ones alone, for there was no game to be killed there and the fishing was no better than in the sheltered inlets.

It was to one of the larger of these islands, twenty miles south of the Penobscot Settlement and a little to the southwest of Mount Desert, that a still-favoring wind brought the cumbersome craft near mid-afternoon. In a long bay that cut deep into the landward shore Amos Swan had found a pebbly beach a score of yards in length, where a boat could be run in at any tide. As it was just past the flood, the man and boy had little difficulty in beaching their vessel far up toward high water-mark. Next, one by one, the frightened sheep were hoisted over the gunwale into the shallow water. The old ram, chosen for the first to disembark, quickly waded out upon dry land, and the others followed as fast as they were freed, while the collie barked at their heels. The lightened boat was run higher up the beach, and the man and boy carried load after load of tools, equipment and provisions up the slope to the small log shack, some two hundred yards away.

Jeremy's father helped him drive the sheep into a rude fenced pen beside the hut, then hurried back to launch his boat and make the return trip. As he started to climb in, he patted the boy's shoulder. "Good-by, lad," said he gently. "Take care of the sheep. Eat your supper and go to bed. I'll be back before this time tomorrow."

"Aye, Father," answered Jeremy. He tried to look cheerful and unconcerned, but as the sail filled and the boat drew out of the cove he had to swallow hard to keep up appearances. For some reason he could not explain, he felt homesick. Only old Jock, the collie, who shouldered up to him and gave his hand a companionable lick, kept the boy from shedding a few unmanly tears.

The shelter that Amos Swan had built stood on a small bare knoll, at an elevation of fifty or sixty feet above the sea. Behind it and sheltering it from easterly and southerly winds rose the island in sharp and rugged ridges to a high hilltop perhaps a mile away. Between lay ascending stretches of dark fir woods, rough outcroppings of stone and patches of hardy grass and bushes. The crown of the hill was a bare granite ledge, as round and nearly as smooth as an inverted bowl.

Jeremy, scrambling through the last bit of clinging undergrowth in the late afternoon, came up against the steep side of this rocky summit and paused for breath. He had left Jock with the sheep, which comfortably chewed the cud in their pen, and, slipping a sort pistol, heavy and brass-mounted, into his belt, had started to explore a bit.

He must have worked halfway round the granite hillock before he found a place that offered foothold for a climb. A crevice in the side of the rock in which small stones had become wedged gave him the chance he wanted, and it took him only a minute to reach the rounded surface near the top. The ledge on which he found himself was reasonably flat, nearly circular, and perhaps twenty yards across.

Its height above the sea must have been several hundred feet, for in the clear light Jeremy could see not only the whole outline of the island but most of the bay as well, and far to the west the blue masses of the Camden Mountains. He was surprised at the size of the new domain spread out at his feet. The island seemed to be about seven miles in length by five at its widest part. Two deep bays cut into its otherwise rounded outline. It was near the shore of the northern one that the hut and sheep-pen were built. Southwesterly from the hill and farther away, Jeremy could see the head of the second and larger inlet. Between the bays the distance could hardly have been more than two miles, but a high ridge, the backbone of the island, which ran westward from the hilltop, divided them by its rugged barrier.

Jeremy looked away up the bay where he could still see the speck of white sail that showed his father hurrying landward on a long tack with the west wind abeam. The boy's loneliness was gone. He felt himself the lord of a great maritime province, which, from his high watch-tower, he seemed to hold in undisputed sovereignty.

Beneath him and off to the southward lay a little island or two, and then the cold blue of the Atlantic stretching away and away to the world's rim.

Even as he glowed with this feeling of dominion, he suddenly became aware of a gray spot to the southwest, a tiny spot that nevertheless interrupted his musing. It was a ship, apparently of good size, bound up the coast, and bowling smartly nearer before the breeze. The boy's dream of empire was shattered. He was no longer alone in his universe.

The sun was setting, and he turned with a yawn to descend. Ships were interesting, but just now he was hungry. At the edge of the crevice he looked back once more, and was surprised to see a second sail behind the first—a smaller vessel, it seemed, but shortening the distance between them rapidly. He was surprised and somewhat disgusted that so much traffic should pass the doors of this kingdom which he had thought to be at the world's end. So he clambered down the cliff and made his way homeward, this time following the summit of the ridge till he came opposite the northern inlet.

It was growing dark already in the dense fir growth that covered the hillside, and when Jeremy suddenly stepped upon the moss at the brink of a deep spring, he had to catch a branch to keep from falling in. There was an opening in the trees above and enough light came through for him to see the white sand bubbling at the bottom.

At one edge the water lapped softly over the moss and trickled down the northern slope of the hill in a little rivulet, which had in the course of time shaped itself a deep, well-defined bed a yard or two across. Following this, the boy soon came out upon the grassy slope beside the sheep-pen. He looked in at the placid flock, brought a bucket of water from the little stream, and, not caring to light a lantern, ate his supper of bread and cheese outside the hut on the slope facing the bay. The night settled chill but without fog. The boy wrapped his heavy homespun cloak round him, snuggled close to Jock's hairy side, and in his lonesomeness fell back on counting the stars as they came out. First the great yellow planet in the west, then, high overhead, the sparkling white of what, had he known it, was Vega; and in a moment a dozen others were in view before he could number them—Regulus, Altair, Spica, and, low in the south, the angry fire of Antares.

For him they were unnamed, save for the peculiarities he discovered in each. In common with most boys he could trace the dipper and find the North Star, but he regrouped most of the constellations to suit himself, and was able to see the outline of a wolf or the head of an Indian that covered half the sky whenever he chose. He wondered what had become of Orion, whose brilliant galaxy of stars appeals to every boy's fancy. It had vanished since the spring. In it he had always recognized the form of a brig he had seen hove-to in Portsmouth Harbor— high poop, skyward-sticking bowsprit and ominous, even row of gun-ports where she carried her carronades—three on a side. How those black cannon-mouths had gaped at the small boy on the dock! He wondered—

"Boom . . . !" came a hollow sound that seemed to hang like mist in a long echo over the island. Before Jeremy could jump to his feet he heard the rumbling report a second time. He was all alert now, and thought rapidly. Those sounds—there came another oven as he stood there—must be cannon-shots—nothing less. The ships he had seen from the hilltop were men-of-war, then. Could the French have sent a fleet? He did not know of any recent fighting. What could it mean?

Deep night had settled over the island, and the fir-woods looked very black and uninviting to Jeremy when he started up the hill once more.

As their shadow engulfed him, he was tempted to turn back—how he was to wish he had done so in the days that followed—but the hardy strain of adventure in his spirit kept his jaw set and his legs working steadily forward into the pitch-black undergrowth. Once or twice he stumbled over fallen logs or tripped in the rocks, but he held on upward till the trees thinned and he felt that the looming shape of the ledge was just in front. His heart seemed to beat almost as loudly as the cannonade while he felt his way up the broken stones.

Panting with excitement, he struggled to the top and threw himself forward to the southern edge.

A dull-gray, quiet sea met the dim line of the sky in the south. Halfway between land and horizon, perhaps a league distant, Jeremy saw two vague splotches of darkness. Then a sudden flame shot out from the smaller one, on the right. Seconds elapsed before his waiting ear heard the booming roar of the report. He looked for the larger ship to answer in kind, but the next flash came from the right as before. This time he saw a bright sheet of fire go up from the vessel on the left, illuminating her spars and topsails. The sound of the cannon was drowned in an instant by a terrific explosion. Jeremy trembled on his rock. The ships were in darkness for a moment after that first great flare, and then, before another shot could be fired, little tongues of flame began to spread along the hull and rigging of the larger craft. Little by little the fire gained headway till the whole upper works were a single great torch. By its light the victorious vessel was plainly visible. She was a schooner-rigged sloop-of-war, of eighty or ninety tons burden, tall-masted and with a great sweep of mainsail. Below her deck the muzzles of brass guns gleamed in the black ports. As the blazing ship drifted helplessly off to the east, the sloop came about, and, to Jeremy's amazement, made straight for the southern bay of the island. He lay as if glued to his rock, watching the stranger hold her course up the inlet and come head to wind within a dozen boat-lengths of the shore.

One of the first things a backwoods boy learns is that it pays to mind your own business, *after* you know what the other fellow is going to do. Jeremy had been threshing his brain for a solution to the scene he had just witnessed. Whether the crew of the strange sloop, just then effecting a landing in small boats, were friends or enemies it was impossible to guess. Jeremy feared for the sheep. Fresh meat would be welcome to any average ship's crew, and the lad had no doubt that they would use no scruple in dealing with a youngster of his age. He must know who they were and whether they intended crossing the island. There was no feeling of mere adventure in his heart now. It was purely sense of duty that drove his trembling legs down the hillside. He shivered miserably in the night air and felt for his pistol-butt, which gave him scant comfort.

The ridge, which has already been described, bore in a southerly direction from the base of the ledge, and sloped steeply to the head of the southern inlet. High above the arm of the bay, where the sloop was now moored, and scarcely a quarter of a mile from the shore, the ridge projected in rough granite crag like a bent knee. Jeremy had a very fair plan of all this in his mind, for his trained woodsman's eye had that afternoon noted every landmark and photographed it. He followed this mental map as he stumbled through the trees. It seemed a long time, perhaps twenty or thirty minutes, before he came out, stifling the sound of his gasping breath, and crouched for a minute on the bare stone to get his wind. Then he crawled forward along thorough cliff top, feeling his way with his hands. Soon he heard a distant shout. A faint glow of light shone over the edge of the crag. As he drew near, he saw, on the beach below, a great fire of driftwood and some score or more of men gathered in the circle of light. The distance was too great for him to tell much about their faces, but Jeremy was sure that no English or Colonial sloop-of-war would be manned by such a motley company. Their clothes varied from the sea-boots and sailor's jerkin of the average mariner to slashed leather breeches of antique cut and red cloth skirts reaching from the girdle to the knees. Some of the group wore three-cornered hats, others seamen's caps of rough wool, and here and there a face grimaced from beneath a twisted rag rakishly askew. Everywhere about them the fire gleamed on small-arms of one kind or another. Nearly every man carried a wicked-looking hanger at his side and most had one or two pistols tucked into waistband or holster.

This desperate gang was in a constant commotion. Even as Jeremy watched, a half dozen men were rolling a barrel up the beach. Wild howls greeted its appearance and as it was hustled into the circle of bright light, those who had been dancing, quarreling and throwing dice on the other side of the fire fell over each other to join the mob that surrounded it. The leaping flames threw a weird, uncertain brilliance upon the scene that made Jeremy blink his eyes to be sure that it was real. With every moment he had become more certain what manner of men these were.

His lips moved to shape a single terrible word—"Pirates!"

The buccaneers were much talked of in those days, and though the New England ports were less troubled, because better guarded, than those farther south, there had been many sea-rovers hanged in Boston within Jeremy's memory.

As if to clinch the argument a dozen of the ruffians swung their cannikins of rum in the air and began to shout a song at the top of their lungs. All the words that reached Jeremy were oaths except one phrase at the end of the refrain, repeated so often that he began to make out the sense of it. "Walk the bloody beggars all below!" it seemed to be— or "overboard"—he could not tell which. Either seemed bad enough to the boy just then and he turned to crawl homeward, with a sick feeling at the pit of his stomach.

His way led straight back across the ridge to the spring and thence down to the shelter on the north shore. He made the best speed he was able through the woods until he reached the height of land near the middle of the island. He had crashed along caring only to reach the sheep-pen and home, but as he stood for a moment to get his breath and his bearings, the westerly breeze brought him a sound of voices on the ridge close by. He prayed fervently that the wind which had warned him had served also to carry away the sound of his progress. Cowering against a tree, he stood perfectly still while the voices—there seemed to be two—came nearer and nearer. One was a very deep, rough bass that laughed hoarsely between speeches. The other voice was of a totally different sort, with a cool, even tone and a rather precise way of clipping the words.

"See here, David," Jeremy understood the latter to say, "It's for you to remember those bearings, not me. You're the sailor here. Give them again now!"

"Huh!" grunted Big Voice, "two hunder' an' ten north to a sharp rock; three-score an' five northeast by east to an oak tree in a gully; two an' thirty north to a fir tree blazed on the south; five north *an'* there you are!" He ended in a chuckle as if pleased by the accuracy of his figures.

"Ay, well enough," the other responded, "but it must be wrong, for here's the blazed tree and no spring by it."

Close below, Jeremy saw their lantern flash and a moment later the two men were in full view striding among the trees. As he had almost expected from their voices, one was a tremendous, bearded fellow in sea-boots and jerkin and with a villainous turban over one eye, while his companion was a lean, smooth-shaven man, dressed in a fine buff coat, well-fitting breeches and hose, and shoes with gleaming buckles.

They must have passed within ten feet of the terrified Jeremy while the tossing lantern, swung from the hairy fist of the man called David, shone all too distinctly upon the boy's huddled shape. When they were gone by he allowed himself a sigh of relief, and shifted his weight from one foot to the other. A twig broke loudly and both men stopped and listened. " 'Twas nought!" growled David. The other man paid no attention to him other than to say, "Hold you the lantern here!" and advanced straight toward Jeremy's tree. The boy froze against it, immovable, but it was of no avail.

"Aha," said the lean man, quietly, and gripped the lad's arm with his hand. As he dragged him into the light, his companion came up, staring with astonishment. A moment he was speechless, then began ripping out oath after oath under his breath. "How," he asked at length, "did the blarsted whelp come here?" The smaller man, who had been looking keenly into Jeremy's face, suddenly addressed him: "Here you, speak up! Do you live here?" he cried. "Ay," said the boy, beginning to get a grip on his thoughts.

"How long has there been a settlement here? There was none last Autumn," continued the well-dressed man. Jeremy had recovered his wits and reasoned quickly. He had little chance of escape for the present, while he must at all costs keep the sheep safe. So he lied manfully, praying the while to be forgiven.

" 'Tis a new colony," he mumbled, "a great new colony from Boston town. There be three ships of forty guns each in the north harbor, and they be watching for pirates in these parts," he finished.

"Boy!" growled the bearded man, seizing Jeremy's wrist and twisting it horribly. "Boy! Are you telling the truth?" With face white and set and knees trembling from the pain, the lad nodded and kept his voice steady as he groaned an "Ay!"

The two men looked at each other, scowling. The giant broke silence. "We'd best haul out now, Cap'n," he said.

"And so I believe," the other replied, "But the water-casks are empty. Here!" as he turned to Jeremy, "show us the spring." It was not far away and the boy found it without trouble.

"Now, Dave Herriot," said the Captain, "stay you here with the light, that we may return hither the easier. Boy, come with me. Make no fuss, either, or 'twill be the worse for you." And so saying he walked quickly back toward the southern shore, holding the stumbling Jeremy's wrist in a grip of iron.

Crashing down the hill through the brush, the lad had scant time or will for observing things about him, but as they crossed a gully he saw, or fancied he saw, on the knee-shaped crag above, the slouched figure of a buccaneer silhouetted against the sky. It was not the bearded giant called Herriot, but another, Jeremy was sure. He had no time for conjectures, for they plunged into the thicket and birch limbs whipped him across the face.

The events of that night made a terribly clear impression on the mind of the young New Englander. Years afterward he would wake with a shiver, imagining that the relentless hand of the pirate captain was again dragging him toward an unknown fate. It must have been the darkness and the sudden unexpectedness of it all that frightened him, for as soon as they came down the rocks into the flaring firelight he was able to control himself once more. The wild carouse was still in progress among the crew. Fierce faces, with unkempt beards and cruel lips, leered redly from above hairy, naked chests. Eyes, lit from within by liquor and from without by the dancing flames, gleamed below black brows. Many of the men wore earrings and metal bands about the knots of their pig-tails, while silver pistol-butts flashed everywhere.

As the Captain strode into the center of this group, the swinging chorus fell away to a single drunken voice which kept on uncertainly from behind the rum-barrel.

"Silence!" said the Captain sharply. The voice dwindled and ceased. All was quiet about the fire. "Men," went on Jeremy's captor, "clear heads, all, for this is no time for drinking. We have found this boy upon the hill, who tells of a fleet of armed ships not above a league from here. We must set sail within an hour and be out of reach before dawn. Every man now take a water-keg and follow me. You, Job Howland, keep the boy and the watch here on the beach."

Fresh commotion broke out as he finished. "Ay, ay, Captain Bonnet!" came in a broken chorus, as the crew, partially sobered by the words, hurried to the long-boat, where a line of small kegs lay in the sand. A moment later they were gone, plowing the hillside. Jeremy stood where he had been left. A tall, slack-jointed pirate in the most picturesque attire strolled over to the boy's side and looked him up and down with a roguish grin. Under his cloak Jeremy had on fringed leather breeches and tunic such as most of the northern colonists wore. The pirate, seeing the rough moccasins and deerskin trousers, burst into a roar. "Ho, ho, young woodcock, and how do ye like the company of Major Stede Bonnet's rovers?"

The lad said nothing, shut his jaw hard and looked the big buccaneer squarely in the face. There was no fear in his expression. The man nodded and chuckled approvingly. "That's pluck, boy, that's pluck," said he. "We'll clip the young cock's shank-feathers, and maybe make a pirate of him yet." He stooped over to feel the buckskin fringe on Jeremy's leg. The boy's hand went into his shirt like a flash. He had pulled out the pistol and cocked it, when he felt both legs snatched from under him.

His head hit the ground hard and he lay dazed for a second or two. When he regained his senses, Job Howland stood astride of him coolly tucking the pistol into his own waist-band. "Ay," said Job, "ye'll be a fine buccaneer, only ye should have struck with the butt. I heard the click." The pirate seemed to hold no grudge for what had occurred and sat down beside Jeremy in a friendly fashion.

"Free tradin' ain't what it was," he confided. "When Billy Kidd cleared for the southern seas twenty years agone, they say he had papers from the king himself, and no man-of-war dared come anigh him." He swore gently and reminiscently as he went on to detail the recent severities of the Massachusetts government and the insecurity of buccaneers about the Virginia capes. "They do say, tho', as Cap'n

Edward Teach, that they call Blackbeard, is plumb thick with all the magistrates and planters in Carolina, an' sails the seas as safe as if he had a fleet of twenty ships," said Job. "We sailed along with him for a spell last year, but him an' the old man couldn't make shift to agree. Ye see this Blackboard is so used to havin' his own way he wanted to run Stede Bonnet, too. That made Stede boilin', but we was under-manned just then and had to bide our time to cut loose.

"Cap'n Bonnet, ye see, is short on seamanship but long in his sword arm. Don't ye never anger him. He's terrible to watch when he's raised. Dave Herriot sails the ship mostly, but when we sight a big mer-chantman with maybe a long nine or two aboard, then's when Stede Bonnet comes on deck. That Frenchman we sunk tonight, blast her bloody spars"—here the lank pirate interrupted himself to curse his luck, and continued—"probably loaded with sugar and Jamaica rum from Martinique and headed up for the French provinces. Well, we'll never know—that's sure!" He paused, bit off the end of a rope of black tobacco and meditatively surveyed the boy. "I'm from New England myself," said he after a time. "Sailed honest out of Providence Port when I was a bit bigger nor you. Then when I was growed and an able seaman on a Virginia bark in the African trade, along comes Cap'n Ben Hornygold, the great rover of those days and picks us up. Twelve of the likeliest he takes on his ship, the rest he maroons somewhere south of the Cubas, and sends our bark into Charles Town under a prize crew. So I took to buccaneering, and I must own I've always found it a fine occupation—not to say that it's made me rich—maybe it might if I'd kept all my sharin's."

This life-history, delivered almost in one breath, had caused How-land an immense amount of trouble with his quid of tobacco, which nearly choked him as he finished. Except for the sound of his vast expectorations, the pair on the beach were quiet for what seemed to Jeremy a long while. Then on the rocks above was heard the clatter of shoes and the bumping of kegs. Job rose, grasping the hand of his charge, and they went to meet the returning sailors.

To the young woodsman, utterly unused to the ways of the sea, the next half-hour was a bewildering melee of hurrying, sweating toil, with low-spoken orders and half-caught oaths and the glimmer of a dying fire over all the scene. He was rowed to the sloop with the first boatload and there Job Howland set him to work passing water-kegs into the hold. He had had no rest in over twenty hours and his whole body ached as the last barrel bumped through the hatch. All the crew were aboard and a knot of swaying bodies turned the windlass to the rhythm of a muttered chanty. The chain creaked and rattled over the bits till the dripping anchor came out of water and was swung inboard. The mainsail and foresail went up with a bang, as a dozen stalwart pirates manned the halyards.

Dave Herriot stood at the helm, abaft the cabin companion, and his bull voice roared the orders as he swung her head over and the breeze steadied in the tall sails.

"Look alive there, mates!" he bellowed. "Stand by now to set the main jib!" Like most of the pirate sloops-of-war, Stede Bonnet's *Revenge* was schooner-rigged. She carried fore and main top-sails of the old, square style, and her long main boom and immense spread of jib gave her a tremendous sail area for her tonnage. The breeze had held steadily since sundown and was, if anything, rising a little. Short seas slapped and gurgled at the forefoot with a pleasant sound. Jeremy, desperately tired, had dropped by the mast, scarcely caring what happened to him. The sloop slid out past the dark headlands, and heeled to leeward with a satisfied grunt of her cordage that came gently to the boy's ears. His head sank to the deck and he slept dreamlessly.

from

Doubloons:
The Story of Buried Treasure
by Charles B. Driscoll (1885–1951)

Edward Teach—known as Blackbeard, the Terror of the Seas—was an extremely brutal and very successful pirate. He is reputed to have had 14 wives and to have scattered buried treasure from the Isles of Shoals off the coast of New Hampshire to Trinidad off the coast of Brazil.

No real pirate has been credited with burying more treasure than Blackbeard. The reputed locations of Blackbeard treasures range from the Isles of Shoals off the coast of New Hampshire, to Trinidad off the coast of Brazil.

The search for Blackbeard's hoards in many localities has been undertaken with increased zeal since Christmas Day, 1928, when it was discovered that a treasure chest buried by Black-beard about the year 1716 had been dug up and carried away.

Plum Point is a narrow neck of land in Beaufort county, North Carolina, where Bath Creek flows into the Pamlico River. The end of the Point, low and sandy, is cut off from the mainland by a marsh, so that it is practically an island.

For more than two hundred years the story of a treasure chest, buried on that point at night by Blackbeard and his men persisted. The low ground had been dug over many times during those two centuries. Never a month passed without some digging there by treasure-seekers, or by idlers and trappers of the vicinity who just thought they'd like to get rich if the getting wasn't too difficult.

Many earnest diggers had heard the story in detail, and had given much time to their searching for that treasure chest. They had dug deeply and widely. But it was impossible for any one digger to cover the whole surface of the Point in a reasonably active lifetime, so the diggers, one by one, became discouraged or disillusioned and went away.

On the Christmas Day just mentioned, two trappers were crossing the Point to examine some traps they had set in the marsh. They stumbled over large brickbats scattered on the sand, and at once were awake to the fact that something had happened on the Point.

The broken bricks were scattered near a freshly dug hole. They had been taken out of the hole. About eight feet down was a brick vault that had been broken open on top and at one end. In a minute or two the trappers had forgotten their traps in the excitement brought on by realization of a tremendously sensational fact.

Blackbeard's treasure chest had been found and carried away!

The bricks were very old, larger than bricks now commonly used in building, and hand-made, with rounded edges. The portion of the vault remaining told the story eloquently.

The top of the vault had been rounded, somewhat in the shape of a roof, and the bottom, still intact, was a flat floor made of three courses of bricks. The sides were mostly intact. Only enough of the vault had been broken away to make possible the extraction of the treasure chest, which had been raised out of the hole, apparently by tackle rigged on a tripod of poles.

The floor of the vault had been laid by the hiders of the treasure, the chest lowered upon the floor, and the walls and top then built up with bricks and plenty of mortar, around and over the chest. The chest had been a little more than three feet long, possibly forty inches. It was about thirty-two inches wide and about the same depth. Mortar had been smeared freely in the hasty laying up of the bricks, and had been squeezed into the inside walls of the vault. This mortar retained a perfect imprint of the chest, with its handforged iron straps criss-crossing one another and the large round rivet-heads studded thickly.

There were foot-tracks of three men who had unearthed the chest. There was a trail indicating that the heavy chest had been dragged, mounted upon a plank, from the hole to the river bank, where it evidently had been loaded into a boat.

So the long-sought treasure of Blackbeard had been dug up and carried away! The news caused a sensation in Bath and vicinity that has not yet subsided.

Who got the treasure? How did they know exactly where to dig for it? Why had all the other searchers missed it all these years? The lucky ones had dug straight down, at a spot close to a very old tree. They had had to cut some of the roots of the tree to get down to their treasure trove. The signs indicated that these treasure hunters had known exactly where to dig, for there had been no fresh spade marks anywhere on the Point except where the chest had been dug up.

And what did the treasure chest of Blackbeard contain? There is much speculation on this point in North Carolina. Some say the chest undoubtedly contained thousands and thousands of doubloons and pieces of eight, diamonds and golden goblets. But others repeat a story of Blackbeard that is told by the oldsters of Bath.

Blackbeard was known in the records of the courts as Edward Teach and Edward Thatch. In Bristol, England, where he was observed growing up "for the gallows," as many of the neighbors said, his name was Drummond. Most of the court records I have perused, in following the maturer career of this gentleman, called him Teach, and by that name he was known ashore in Bath Town and neighboring settlements. There are numerous families named Tinch still living along the shores of Pamlico Sound, and some of these claim to be descended from Blackbeard. Considering the known facts of the pirate's history, it would seem probable that he must have a great many descendants somewhere, and the very numerousness of the Tinches would appear to lend color to their claim.

Much of Blackbeard's reputation in song and story is due to his consummate showmanship. He had a fine sense for drama, and he made up for his part better than any other pirate who ever lived.

Most of the successful pirates liked to dramatize themselves. They were fancy dressers. In an age when other seafaring folk went about in rather sober garb, the more dashing pirates wore scarlet and green and yellow silk, romantically tailored, and affected large earrings, heavy gold rings on their fingers, and cocked hats in many colors. This fanciful style of dress had much to do with getting recruits for pirate fleets, just as the shining trappings and plumes provide long waiting lists for the various companies of guards that add so much to the royal pageantry for the remaining monarchs of Europe.

Blackbeard made up for his roles just as meticulously as Edwin Booth ever did. He wanted to be known as the Terror of the Seas, and he tried to live up to that characterization. At sea he let his black whiskers grow. He let his black hair grow. He was abundantly supplied with coarse hair and beard, and when the shaggy growth was flourishing, in the midst of a piratical voyage, the pirate was rather a fearsome looking fellow. Indeed, according to some of the passengers of ships boarded by him, he looked much more terrible than any conventional impersonator of the devil.

He was tall. Some accounts of his depredations describe him as six and a half feet tall, but this may have been a natural exaggeration, due to terror. He was very broad-shouldered and his arms were long, like an ape's, so that his hands hung down below his knees when he was seated. His long reach with a cutlass and dagger had much to do with his remarkable success as a pirate.

Captain Teach was at his best in a charge, leading a boarding party of cutthroats down the deck of an unfortunate merchant ship that had resisted his command to surrender.

On these occasions he was a terror to write letters to the papers about, if ever you should live through the scene. Many survivors of captured crews did write such letters, some of which were published as warnings against ocean travel.

Before climbing aboard the recalcitrant vessel, Blackbeard was wont to don a long sash of scarlet silk, wrapped once or twice around his waist, and passing over one shoulder, somewhat like a glorified Sam Browne belt. In the waistband were stuck three pistols. Three more were slung in the shoulder sash. Another usually was in the giant's left hand. Two or three short knives were in the belt, close to the right hand, and sometimes an extra cutlass was in a scabbard slung from the left side of the belt. The Terror carried a naked cutlass in his right hand, and generally appeared on the enemy's deck carrying a knife about two feet long between his teeth. The plenitude of knives was a part of the Terror's technique. He could throw a knife of almost any size or design very accurately, so as to bury it in the heart of a person across the deck from him.

Blackbeard made the most of his whiskers on these occasions. He made them up for the show according to his whim and according to their length. If they were very long (and they sometimes reached below his waist) he was wont to plait them with black ribbons and stick burning slow matches into the plaits, just for the infernal effect upon the terrified beholders. The slow matches of those days, used to light the priming charges of the cannon, were somewhat equivalent to the punk sticks used by American children on the Fourth of July in places not yet cognizant of the safe and sane Independence Day.

The Terror of the Seas often stuck slow matches under his hat, so that the burning ends were dangling about his face, when his whiskers did not provide suitable nesting places for these little ornaments. The whiskers were really more effective when grown out to about a foot in length, for then they were very bristling and terrible, sticking out in all directions and presenting a peculiarly fiendish appearance. The whiskers grew high on the pirate's face, so that his fiery eyes seemed to gleam out from the midst of them, especially when the coarse hair from the head straggled down around the face.

While he held the knife between his teeth, the Terror looked formidable enough, but when he had thrown it he was ready for his best act—the charge down the deck. Captain Teach was almost brokenhearted when he captured a prize if he could not put on this act.

He led the charge. He did not permit any of his men to go before him, but the villains did not keep many paces to the rear. If there was a crew making a desperate last stand on the deck with a few armed passengers to reinforce the defenders, Blackbeard was pleased. A few weeping and praying women, with children at their sides, added just the touch of melodrama that this superb actor demanded for the exhibition of his best histrionic art.

He bellowed; he roared; he let out infernal yells. Towering above every human being on the deck, he advanced with long strides, swinging his cutlass in his right hand, shooting with his left, or striking with a clubbed pistol. Was there a sturdy group of defenders in the waist of the ship? Blackbeard was upon them with a horrible yell, his great mouth wide open, his eyes flashing hatred and murder, his cutlass dripping hot blood. Left he struck; right he slashed, ahead he kicked with his great feet or butted with his head.

Stout-hearted, indeed, was the group that did not break and run for cover before the swinging cutlass of the monster reached its outskirts.

When up to his best form, Captain Teach used to like to dispose of the women and children who chanced to be on deck, just to make the scene complete. If the fight did not demand all of the leader's immediate attention, he loved to make quick excursions to the sidelines, pick up a woman or a child in his great left paw, and stab repeatedly into the yielding flesh with a dagger, then quickly throwing the murdered person over the side and rushing back to the main business of the moment. This sort of thing always had an effect upon the opposing fighters. When the defenders of the ship saw their women and children thus wantonly butchered, they often desired to surrender, hoping to prevent further slaughter of this kind.

Sometimes Captain Teach would call off his murderous crew the moment the boarded ship struck her flag in token of surrender. If he was so minded, he would become all at once the soul of polite gentility. With his great form soaked in blood and his hands dripping gore, the Terror would salute the ranking officer of the prize, and remark lightly upon the weather or upon the outstanding features of the fight, as a victorious captain of a football team might exchange gossip about the game with his defeated rival.

"By my soul, Captain," he would say, " 'twas a hot bit of a scrimmage, was it not? I hope we have not put you out with our uncouth ways, this hot day! My men are country fellows, mostly, and 'tis little they know of courtesy or of respect for a fine fighting man like yourself. Will you join me on my sloop yonder for a cool pot of ale or a noggin of rum? Faith, we'll drink to the ladies, if there be any of them left alive after this little misunderstanding we've had! Come, Captain; your hand!"

If the humor was strong upon him, he would forbid his men to shed another drop of blood, and would force the captured officers, and often some of the women passengers, to go to his cabin and drink with him.

On other occasions, he would give no quarter, and would not cease butchering or call off his men until every captured person had been slain and thrown overboard. He was a fellow of violent moods, and loved to observe the effect of these moods upon his own men and his victims.

He ruled his men with an iron hand. He was feared by all of them. He took advantage of every opportunity to keep that fear alive.

One of Blackbeard's most confidential lieutenants was Basilica Hands, generally set down as Israel Hands by chroniclers of Blackbeard's exploits. Stevenson's coxswain in Treasure Island took his name from this villain. Hands was faithful to Teach, and a valuable fighter. But the boisterous Captain went too far with Hands just once.

Blackbeard was drinking in his cabin with Hands and Richards, his first mate. Two loaded and primed pistols lay on the table in front of the Captain. Hands and Richards were across the table. Suddenly,

Teach blew out the candle, crossed the pistols under the table, and pulled both triggers. Richards was uninjured, but Hands was shot through the left knee. When Hands complained bitterly over such wanton deviltry, Blackbeard shouted: "Aha, you bellyache over a little thing like that? Well, if I didn't kill or maim one of you fellows once in a while, we'd never know who is Captain here!"

Teach was Captain, all right, but that little demonstration was to cost him more than he could have suspected. Hands nursed his wound and his grievance long. He was a cripple for the rest of his life.

One of the classic stories of Blackbeard, told many years later by Basilica Hands in a London tavern, concerns Captain Teach's demonstration of hell. There had been some little talk about hell among the group of favorites in the Captain's cabin. Eternal damnation was a thing much argued about in those days before hell went out of style in the pulpits.

"Come, my bullies," said Blackbeard, "we'll make a little hell of our own, right here in my cabin. Since we all must go to the brimstone country soon, it's no harm to get the smell of the stuff in our nostrils now. I tell you, I'm not afraid of hell. Brimstone is like incense to me."

So he ordered a pot of sulphur (then generally called brimstone) brought in and lighted under the table. The window and the door were closed tight, and a jolly endurance contest was on. The four men who were the Captain's guests in the little cabin hell sputtered, choked and coughed. But whenever one of them staggered toward the door, Captain Teach was there to bar the way and to fling the suffering villain back into his chair. It seemed to be great fun for the Captain. He roared with mighty laughter when one of the victims declared they would all die unless the door were opened at once.

"If we die, we'll never know it, boys!" he shouted. "We'll be in hell anyhow, with our lungs full of brimstone. Why, Richards, I believe we're dead already, and smoking in hell! Don't you remember, bully, that you were hanged at Execution Dock for a bloody pirate, and you and I have just met here in hell? Don't cough so, my brave lad, you have only a million years to spend in this room, and then we move on to the broiling cage!"

When the door finally was flung open by Blackbeard, his victims were nearly asphyxiated, but he was in a hilarious mood, laughing and slapping his long thighs with glee, and drinking great beakers of hot rum to clear his throat.

Captain Teach had, besides great physical strength and size, a supply of sagacity and a knowledge of a certain type of human character that might have made him, had he been born two hundred years later, a great captain of industry or a successful Secretary of the Interior. He knew his men. He was not far wrong when he said that he had to shoot one of the boys now and again to demonstrate his leadership.

A tale that was told by Teach's men ashore after a certain long cruise concerned the presence of Satan aboard ship. The men swore that they had been out two weeks and had become thoroughly acquainted with one another, when a stranger made his appearance on the ship, from nowhere. They had not had contact with any other vessel. But here was this stranger, dressed handsomely, in red silk, some said, walking about the vessel, looking her over, as though appraising a piece of property. The tall, courtly stranger did not mix with the men, and he was not seen speaking to any of the officers except the Captain, with whom he seemed always to be on familiar terms. The men put their heads together and decided immediately that this was none other than the Devil himself. Sometimes they saw him aloft in the cross-trees, looking off toward a little dark cloud and making peculiar motions with his hands. In such cases, they said, the wind invariably rose, and there was, at least figuratively, the devil to pay. It was the opinion of the hands that there was the devil to pay quite literally, for the handsome stranger, smiling mysteriously, was seen to betake himself to Blackbeard's side in the height of one such storm, and the two went below together. When they returned to the deck, an hour and a half later, the storm began to abate. The pirates thoroughly believed that Blackbeard's infernal partner had forced a settlement from the "old man," and they chuckled to think that somebody could make old Blackbeard himself come to terms.

What planning and stage-setting that little scenario of the devil aboard ship must have cost the redoubtable Blackbeard! You see the dramatic genius of the fellow.

Captain Teach kept a log, just as legitimate captains always have done. One little fragment of that log has survived:

> Such a day! Rum all out. . . . Our company somewhat sober. . . . A damned confusion amongst us . . . rogues a-plotting . . . great talk of separation . . . so I looked sharp for a Prize . . . took one with a great deal of Liquor aboard . . . so kept company hot, damned hot . . . things went well again.

The story of the treasure of the Isles of Shoals is associated with Blackbeard. It can be told here, before we go into the recital of the main facts of the pirate's career, since there is much variation in the stories told by different chroniclers as to the period in Blackbeard's life in which the incidents relating to the Isles of Shoals occurred.

Captain Teach, according to those who attempt to explain certain traditions of the Isles, was operating off the coast of Scotland during one of his brief absences from American waters. Lying off the west coast of Scotland, awaiting the scheduled passage of a richly laden East Indiaman, Teach's pirate sloop was hailed by a lone man in a rowboat.

The little boat came alongside, and a Scotch seafaring man came up the rope that was tossed to him, hand over hand. The visitor had no difficulty in finding Captain Teach, who seemed to be expecting him. The two conferred in Blackbeard's cabin for three or four hours. Then they appeared on deck, very friendly, and Blackbeard called his officers together and introduced the stranger:

"Boys, here's Sandy Gordon, a pirate that can show a lot of you tricks in spilling blood.

"He's going to be with us for a while and we're going to work together, even after he gets a ship of his own.

"You know my rule on this ship against women. We want no women aboard, except in the Captain's cabin, and we don't want them there often or long. But I'm making a little exception to the rule. Captain Gordon is going to bring a lady aboard as his guest for a little while. She'll have the cabin next to mine, and all hands are to keep clear of that cabin until Gordon and his lady go aboard their own ship."

The officers and men aboard Blackbeard's vessel were not much pleased with this news, but they managed to hide their dissatisfaction from their boss. Women caused trouble aboard ship. That was part of every pirate's creed. Nearly all articles signed by captains and crews of piratical vessels in those days forbade the presence of women on the ship. Blackbeard maintained the same rules, except as to his own personal women. When it suited him to keep a captured woman aboard for a few days, he did so, usually throwing her overboard with his own hands when he thought the time appropriate. It was observed that the men were always harder to handle during or after one of these romances, for they were plainly and wickedly jealous of their Captain, and would not suffer him to violate the rule against women were it not that they were afraid to oppose him in anything. They had seen too many men choked to death by the powerful hands of Blackbeard.

So there was talk, but not loud talk, among the men of Blackbeard's crew when, the night after the arrival of Sandy Gordon aboard, the vessel put close in toward shore, and Sandy, with one of Blackbeard's men, rowed up the little inlet toward a quiet farmhouse. Before daylight the boat returned. The third passenger was a fair-haired Scotch girl, whose feet and hands were bound.

The fair passenger seemed to be unconscious. She was carried to her cabin.

She was Martha Herring, and she had been in custody of Pirate Sandy Gordon for several weeks, afloat and ashore.

Sandy had been a mariner from earliest boyhood. He had served as ship's carpenter on many peaceful voyages. Sailing to and from the Guinea coast aboard slavers, he had observed with satisfaction the large profits made by his employers. Sandy was pleased because he had no intention of remaining a ship's carpenter all his life. He, too, would make profits.

But he was in his late twenties, and still a ship's carpenter, when he sailed aboard the *Porpoise*, under Captain John Herring, to capture some of the Algerine corsairs who were doing great damage to English shipping. The *Porpoise* was an armed merchantman, privately outfitted on a private business venture. There were profits in capturing Barbary corsairs sometimes.

Now, as in the case of the memorable schooner *Hesperus*, the Captain had taken his little daughter, to bear him company. But in this case, the Captain's little daughter was quite eighteen years of age, and Captain John Herring soon learned to his sorrow that one does not take one's beautiful daughter along on pirate hunting expeditions. Captain Herring never did it again.

Sandy was young himself, and the good ship *Porpoise* was not more than four days out of the port of London when Sandy Gordon was seized with a great fancy for the Captain's daughter. Neither history nor legend tells us how the beautiful Martha responded to the attentions of the amorous young Scot. But this we know: Captain Herring was indignant, furious. He gave Sandy warning. And just then Sandy began to realize that he was a very fearless young man.

Sandy sought out the beautiful Martha in the Captain's cabin. The Captain entered.

There followed some rather trying hours for Sandy.

Suffering from the effects of seventy-two lashes on his bare back, Sandy lay in irons in the ship's hold and meditated. In thirty days one may do a lot of meditating, especially if one be alone and in irons.

When our young hero was permitted to resume his duties aboard the *Porpoise*, he was very quiet and orderly in his demeanor. Also, he was very friendly with certain of his shipmates. Sandy was plotting mutiny.

Before the first Algerine corsair came in sight, the mutiny broke.

It was a dark night, and Sandy had the mid-watch. A shot from his pistol was the signal. The mutineers, constituting an active minority of the crew, rushed to their bloody work.

The Captain was dragged from his cabin, bound, and lashed to a gun. The mate, who attempted to protect the Captain's daughter, was shot through the head, his blood streaming over the unconscious girl.

The Captain was wounded more than twenty times by handspikes wielded by his mutinous men. But Sandy saved him from death.

"Belay that, lads!" cried Sandy, "I've a bonnie score to settle with this mon, ye ken!"

Most of the sailors were spared at Sandy's command. They could be used with profit in the business just ahead.

Sandy himself wielded the lash upon the back of the helpless Captain. Seventy-two!

"Now," said Sandy, "ye may rest a wee bit."

At the end of an hour, Sandy laid on seventy-two more lashes. And so it was continued at intervals of one hour until there was no life left in the body of the unfortunate Captain.

Sandy took charge of Martha and did not permit any member of the crew to approach her. He kept her locked and guarded in her cabin while her father was being whipped to death.

When Sandy called his crew together in council, he was all dressed in red. He had appropriated the full dress uniform of Lieutenant Meeks of the Royal Marines, who had been in charge of the fighting force aboard the *Porpoise* that was to overcome the Algerines.

Sandy liked himself in the red uniform. He had suddenly become a striking figure. He proclaimed himself Captain of the ship, and announced that all nations were his enemies.

Those of the crew who did not instantly agree with everything the Captain said were thrown overboard without ceremony. And then the Captain posted an astonishing set of rules that he had been writing ever since he had been released from solitary confinement. The rules set forth that on this pirate ship there was to be no division of plunder, share and share alike, as was the custom among all other pirates.

The expedition was the property of Captain Gordon. It was his private business venture. The profits were to be all his. The expedition was a closed corporation, and Sandy owned all the stock. The men were to be paid wages, twenty-five per cent more than wages paid on merchantmen. Wounded men were to be compensated according to a prudent scale of insurance. Dissenters were to be thrown overboard.

When the men read the new regulations, there was quite a bit of throwing overboard to be done. But Sandy attended to it, efficiently and promptly. He pointed out to his mate that this was the most economical method of disposing of undesirable persons, since there was no wear and tear on tackle, and no expenditure of powder. Thereafter drowning was made the official form of execution, for enemies as well as for shipmates.

This first piratical cruise of Captain Gordon's was brought to a close off the Scottish coast, after several prizes had been taken. The men mutinied against Sandy's parsimonious policy. They wanted to share in the profits of the business, and Sandy held that such an arrangement was contrary to sound business principles.

The men won the argument, and Sandy, his lady, and his efficiency program were bundled over the side into a rowboat. They had landed and set up a very restricted form of house-keeping in an old farmhouse. Sandy had had some difficulty in keeping Martha from deserting him. He had solved the problem by knocking her unconscious and tying her up from time to time.

Captain Teach and a small party of his men had come upon the distressed pirate and his unwilling consort while ashore one night, seeking water and Scotch liquor. Blackbeard had been affected by the brawny Scotsman's tale of adventure, enterprise and maltreatment.

"Come aboard me, and we'll see how good a pirate you are," said Teach. "If you prove as good as your boasting, I'll see you outfitted, and maybe we can do business together."

That was the beginning of a profitable partnership.

A week later, Blackbeard fought a jolly battle with a tall East Indiaman, homeward bound for London. She was a rich prize, and well worth fighting for. But she was well defended too. It was a fine opportunity for Sandy Gordon. He recognized the situation as one that might make possible a prosperous career for him. He fought like a wild beast, and when the two vessels were lashed together, Gordon and Blackbeard were side by side in leading the boarding party that swept the Indiaman's deck clear of defenders.

Out of the survivors of the crew, Blackbeard picked a few, and inquired of them whether they would like to sail this ship under Captain Gordon, under the black flag, and under strict agreement concerning an equitable distribution of the spoils.

None of the men refused. Articles were drawn up, and Blackbeard forced Sandy to consent to the usual clauses concerning a share of the loot for every man.

"A muckle waste, I call it," said Sandy, "but do as ye will."

A rendezvous was appointed for the Isles of Shoals, and an approximate date set down for a grand celebration there. The men of Sandy's new crew were promised that no woman would be permitted aboard ship after the rendezvous. Until that time, Captain Gordon should enjoy the unusual privilege of retaining his fair companion.

The two pirate vessels parted company, each going its own way.

Gordon's first impressive prize was a great Spanish galleon. As soon as she was sighted, explicit instructions were given out to every member of the crew of the *Flying Scot*, as the great ship had been named by Sandy. Each man knew exactly what was expected of him.

But Sandy's men behaved themselves better than their master had hoped. Their lives were not so precious to them as the average reader, comfortably perusing these lines, might suppose.

Some months at sea as a common sailor, under the conditions prevailing in the early years of the eighteenth century, had a tendency to make life seem of no great importance. If a man could die fighting, he generally did so with great gusto. A good fight was likely to end forever the spiritless ennui that pervaded the life of the sailing ship.

The galleon fired a broadside when she was in position to do so, but she tried her best to run away. She was quickly overhauled.

The *Flying Scot* was lashed to the side of the galleon and a boarding party fought its way to the broad deck that was half filled with panic-stricken Spaniards, hopeless of victory but determined to sell their lives dearly. Most of the Spaniards were tossed overboard, after the first rush of the boarders had caused the defenders of the galleon to throw down their arms.

Captain Gordon, prodigious in his scarlet trappings, prudently boarded the galleon some fifteen minutes after the first of his men had started the battle. He was in time to save the Captain, the chaplain, and half a dozen sailors, from immediate death. These unfortunates were tortured until they revealed the amount of treasure on board and the secret places in which most of it was stored. Then they too were thrown overboard.

Careful check of the treasure showed that Captain Gordon was indeed a wealthy man. He had more than a million dollars' worth of gold and silver out of this vessel.

Other good captures were made, and Sandy's crew soon was recruited to full strength by the simple expedient of giving captured seamen their choice of piracy or instant death.

It was six weeks after the capture of the galleon that Sandy Gordon was called upon to exercise his genius for thrifty administration in an extraordinary crisis. There was a fearful storm. The pirate vessel was heavily laden with the Spanish treasure. She was making no headway against the tremendous seas that poured over her deck and threatened to send her to the bottom.

Sandy called the entire crew to prayer. While the service of supplication was in progress, a picked squad of ruffians rushed upon the kneeling sailors, bound twenty of them fast, and threw them overside.

Thus lightened, the *Flying Scot* weathered the storm.

Martha accommodated herself to her new station in life, when she gave up hope of altering her condition materially by rebellion. She appeared on deck during a fight one day, and bound up most tenderly the wounds of her lord and master. From that day forward she had the run of the ship, and the men, without too much politeness, suffered her to go where she would without molestation.

The *Flying Scot* arrived at the Isles of Shoals some weeks ahead of Blackbeard and his crew. She carried a heavy cargo of treasure. On Star Island, the day after arrival, division of the treasure was made. The crew separated into groups, and many burial parties were organized. Each group swore its members to secrecy, and in each little treasure company there was an understanding that the survivor or survivors were to take all, in case of the death of some members.

Captain Gordon and his fair companion betook themselves to White Island, and there, according to the surviving legend, their treasure was buried. They had a small house constructed for themselves here, and during the remainder of the stay of the pirates at the Isles of Shoals these two enjoyed a honeymoon. Although the partnership had started off badly and bloodily enough, the remarkable adaptive powers of the young woman were such as to make a honeymoon on the Isles a romantic and almost idyllic interlude.

When Blackbeard and his crew arrived, there was more burying of treasure, and some other burials too, for Captain Teach took it upon himself to kill three of his men in a little academic argument about the disposal of certain valuable pieces of plate that had been taken from a Spanish ship.

There were long business conferences between Gordon and Teach, and the general belief of the men was that these conferences resulted in further enrichment of the Captains at the expense of the crews, but no one ever was able to make any proofs of any such collusion.

Blackbeard did not tarry long at the Isles of Shoals. He had no honeymoon on his hands, and did not shave off his whiskers. He was soon off to sea again.

A week or two later, a lookout sighted a sail. Sandy Gordon assembled his crew and lifted his anchor. The men were eager to take a prize, loot her, and return to the Isles to finish their holiday. When Martha was about to embark, Captain Gordon was reminded of his promise, in his contract with his men, to have no women aboard after reaching the Shoals. Reluctantly Sandy led Martha back to their little house on the hill on White Island. According to the legend of the Shoals, he made her swear a terrible oath that she would stay there and guard the treasure until his return, however long that period of waiting might be.

The strange sail proved to be a British warship, looking for pirates.

The battle was long and bloody, and when it was over the *Flying Scot* was a sinking hulk, drifting in toward the Isles of Shoals. So far as known, the only pirates who escaped death in the battle were hanged at the yardarm of the victorious man-of-war.

Old frequenters of the Isles of Shoals tell the story of a wraith-like figure in white with streaming blonde hair that may be seen on stormy nights on a low point of White Island, looking off to sea.

Treasure hunters should put a large cross on the Isles of Shoals. But those who are afraid of ghosts had better keep away from White Island.

For a time the careers of Blackbeard and Stede Bonnet were inter-mingled. Near the mouth of the Cape Fear river, close to the tip of the peninsula formed by New Hanover county, North Carolina, as it dips toward New Inlet, is a spot marked with a cross by many treasure-hunters, for here Bonnet, near the end of his career, is said to have buried large quantities of treasure. And Bonnet, unwillingly enough, was associated with Blackbeard in the latter's most prosperous days of treasure gathering.

Major Stede Bonnet went pirating because he couldn't stand his wife.

In movies one goes down to the sea in pirate ships only because one's king has abused one, made a slave of one, and deserted one in trouble.

Stede Bonnet's King had used him well. He had given him a life job in the Royal Colonial Army in Barbadoes, and, when Bonnet had reached middle age and the rank of major, His Majesty had been pleased to retire him with honor and half pay.

No, Major Bonnet hadn't anything against his King. But if the King had known the Major's wife, Bonnet might have had royal clemency when he needed it sorely.

Major Bonnet, after retiring from the army, became a professional prominent citizen of the city of Bridgetown, Barbadoes. He was rated a wealthy man. Probably he had taken a flyer now and again in colonial shipping enterprises while serving his time in the army. He was a dignified personage; a man of property and education. I can imagine him a vestryman of the quality church of the city, a position which, in that place and at that time, was equivalent in glory to the post of Grand Exalted Ruler of the Elks in our own epoch.

But Stede Bonnet couldn't stand his wife. She is set down in the annals of Bridgetown as a harridan most horrible. Poor Bonnet had managed to maintain appearances and uphold his social standing as an army officer and a man of substance as long as he was busy bossing troops. If he heard foul language at home in the morning, he could take it out on the men during the day. He could order extra maneuvers in the hot Barbadoes sunshine, and his temper could thus be kept under.

But when he retired from the army and the affairs of war, he wanted peace and quiet—and he had to go pirating to get them.

We have no detailed record of the domestic battles that so racked his morale, but it is recorded by the historians of those troubled days that his neighbors and associates pitied him, and did not blame him, concluding that his reason must have been unsettled by his wife's appalling nagging.

In the spring of 1717, he began looking about for a vessel. Having plenty of money and being of unquestioned standing, he found no difficulty in buying a fine sloop and arming her with ten guns. No one questioned his purpose. Nobody in Bridgetown knew Mrs. Bonnet quite so well as her husband knew her, so nobody suspected that he was preparing to sail forth to slay hundreds of surprised Christians, inwardly gloating because each victim of his cutlass was a vicarious sacrifice, standing for the revolting Mrs. Bonnet.

On a dark night that spring Major Bonnet sailed out of the harbor of Bridgetown as owner and captain of the pirate sloop *Revenge*. Commentators have been puzzled that a clever and well-educated man of quality should show no more originality in naming his ship. There were more than a dozen *Revenges* sailing the seas under black flags at that time. Every second pirate felt it necessary to pretend that he had a score to settle with the nations of the world. If you were going pirating and had no imagination or originality, you called your ship the *Revenge* to indicate that you had been put upon and were going to get even.

But Stede Bonnet had imagination. He was going out for revenge. He could imagine how his querulous wife would feel when all the neighbors crowded about to sympathize with her because her husband hadn't been able to stand her any longer and had gone off to sea under the skull and cross-bones! Oh, the Major had his revenge!

Unluckily, he did not know port from starboard. He had never been to sea, except as a dignified passenger, uncurious about the gear that made the ship proceed from point of departure to destination. Now he found himself captain of a fine sloop, and the only order he knew how to shout to his seventy salty ruffians was: "Forward! March!"

When the crew discovered that their captain was ignorant of the uses of a belaying pin and thought that aft was the name of a cabin, mutiny was narrowly averted. The spectacle of the commander, very seasick and altogether at sea, consulting with the first mate as to the best method of getting from south to north when the wind was south-southeast, was one to wring the heart of any respectable mariner. That any man with ambition to become a real pirate should serve docilely under such direction was beyond the scope of the imagination of every cutthroat aboard the *Revenge*.

Major Bonnet won his first and most praiseworthy victory at sea when he demonstrated to his men that he was really captain of the ship and knew how to enforce obedience, even if he didn't know a pennant from a pinnace. He had his men soundly flogged, flogged again, served with a double ration of rum, and again flogged.

That was language a good sailor could understand. The Major had failed for lack of a firm hand in managing one establishment. But he wasn't married to the crew of the *Revenge,* and he didn't have to be a gentleman any more unless he wanted to be one.

One of the first captures made by him was the ship *Turbet,* from Barbadoes. He put the crew into boats and, after taking out most of the merchandise, set fire to the ship. One may well fancy that this rough conduct was indulged in to give the wife a good scare. When the sailors from the *Turbet* got back to Barbadoes, how they must have regaled Madame Bonnet with tales of the fierce pirate she had nourished unawares! No doubt the good woman's blood ran cold when she remembered how often and how dangerously she had tempted this raging monster, supposing him to be hopelessly domestic and thoroughly harmless.

Stede Bonnet is the patron saint of all henpecked husbands. Suppressed homelovers should call upon his name before they go forth to roister.

Standing off the Virginia capes for a short cruise, he took half a dozen vessels, mostly from Scotch ports. In most cases he detained the prize only long enough to transfer the loot. Then he let her proceed, after taking a few precautions to make her progress slow and uncertain. But occasionally, no doubt to celebrate his freedom from matrimonial bondage, he would stage a party. He gets credit for inventing the game known as walking the plank. In fact, it is the opinion of many learned historians that he was the only pirate who ever actually indulged in it.

According to tales told by survivors, Bonnet did, upon occasion, rig a wide plank sticking straight out to sea at the port gangway. But this was done only when the captured vessel carried a large passenger list.

When an ordinary crew was to be dispatched to its reward, Bonnet's trusty men, who had learned to obey cheerfully that they might be long-lived upon the earth, waded in with heavy cutlasses, and the job was accomplished as expeditiously as is the laying low of a half-acre of sunflowers by a Kansas farmer armed with a sharp and heavy corn-knife. But passengers required more delicate attentions. Passengers were apt to be finicky. The ladies, sadly overdressed and undernourished, used to faint below decks at the sound of hacking cutlasses making contact with sturdy frames. Stede Bonnet's men looked decidedly foolish, lugging unconscious ladies up the ladders to toss them ungracefully overside.

So the plank was rigged, and it proved a blessing. Timid passengers were blindfolded and marched in single file to the plank, and then permitted to continue marching just as far as the limited accommodations would allow. That surprised step into space, followed quickly by a splash into salt water below, furnished unrivalled entertainment for the bully boys of the good ship *Revenge*. Major Bonnet, they swore, was a jolly tar, despite his limited knowledge of the art of navigation.

Favorite survivors of the first cruise off the Virginia capes were taken to New York, whither Bonnet shaped his course so as to dispose of his handsome load of mixed merchandise. All these survivors were men. No women had been spared. Major Bonnet's experience in life had not made him partial to the dainty sex. The happy prisoners were landed quietly at Gardiner's Island and the word was sent around that a bloody pirate was in port, awaiting customers. New York was then an excellent market for pirated goods, and well-behaved pirates who were not unreasonable in their relations with public officials and public-spirited merchants were made to feel that it was a friendly port of call.

Bonnet sold his cargo and bought provisions, gave his men a bit of shore-leave, and sailed away. He next appeared off the bar at Charleston, where he instituted a sort of benevolent blockade. He took an inbound brigantine from New England, under command of Thomas Porter, and another Barbadoes vessel, a sloop laden with rum and commanded by Joseph Palmer. The sloop was burned after the crew had been set adrift, as in the case of the previous Barbadoes capture. Bonnet was bound to have the good news travel back to the home folk that there had been a real he-man once in charge at the home of Mrs. Bonnet.

After cleaning his sloop and taking on water at an inlet on the North Carolina coast, he sailed southward, and dropped anchor in the Bay of Honduras, which was then a favorite meeting place for pirates.

Here the redoubtable Major fell in with Blackbeard.

Major Bonnet had acquired a great respect for his own executive ability during the months since he had escaped from his fair commander-in-chief in Bridgetown. He called upon Blackbeard on board the latter's ship, and suggested that the two of them, being the best pirates afloat, should join company and effect a merger. He pointed out that the *Revenge* was an uncommonly graceful sloop, for which he had paid a fancy sum of money.

When Blackbeard heard that Bonnet had paid for his ship, he was desolated by gales of merriment. Continuing the conversation but a little way, the gay old dog discovered his guest's regrettable ignorance of nautical affairs. Although he had spilled a goodly measure of blood and sailed north and south with his own planks under his feet, Major Bonnet was still a major, and not a captain in very truth. Also, he still called a ship's ladder a stairway.

Blackbeard called his trusted mate, Richards. He ordered him to take command of the *Revenge*, and informed Major Bonnet that he was to act in a clerical capacity aboard Blackbeard's own ship. The two vessels would sail in company, but both must be in command of pirates who knew their salt water. If Bonnet should behave well and make no disturbance, he might live—and learn.

The proud army man made the best of a humiliating situation. He became chief bookkeeper for the piratical enterprise of Ed Teach. He ranked as a sort of apprentice pirate. And he learned the trade under a master.

Stede Bonnet learned much from Blackbeard. The two vessels sailed north along the coast, and were joined by others, attracted by the marvelous name of the bewhiskered terror. Soon there was a fleet of three sloops and a full-rigged ship, the latter carrying forty guns. The fleet was manned by four hundred husky blood-letters. Major Bonnet was studying piracy in no mean academy.

He made several cruises under Blackbeard, and was permitted to take part in the fun whenever he showed any progress in his work. After a few months of this training, he was competent, in the opinion of Professor Blackbeard, to take out a ship under his own command.

Blackbeard disbanded his fleet at Topsail Inlet, in North Carolina, and took a sabbatical year ashore. After all, time was passing, the jolly old throat-slitter was as rich as a king, and there were no ladies to speak of at sea. So the master gave his apprentice permission to take his own sloop, the *Revenge*, and go out on his own account.

Now, George the First, by the grace of God, King, had recently issued a grandiose pardon to all pirates who would surrender to authorized pardoners and obtain a certificate of good character. George was getting into another war, and wanted pirates in his royal navy, or at least in the privateering business. Most pirates were only privateersmen devoid of a good and official war, and they were always eager to sign any sort of document that would add the King's license to their own determination to live by blood-letting.

Bonnet left the *Revenge* at Topsail Inlet and journeyed to Bath. He surrendered to Governor Eden, expressed his unwavering loyalty to the King who had given him his lifetime job in the army, and begged to be permitted to serve His Majesty as a legalized privateer against the Spaniards. This permission was readily given, and Stede Bonnet became once more, for a short time, officially a patriot. He obtained clearance papers for St. Thomas.

He had no crew, but he knew how to get a good one. Blackbeard, just before disbanding his fleet and going in for respectability, had marooned a shipload of men on a barren island, not far from the Inlet, so as to avoid having to pay them for their services. Bonnet picked up these poor devils and gave them jobs, on condition that they would serve him forever, particularly in punishing their ungrateful master, Blackbeard.

He had determined to go out after Blackbeard, if he could find him afloat, and prove how well he had learned piracy from the master. He had many a score to settle with the baleful old ogre, and he had all of the rescued seamen as stout partisans in his desire. The most able and intelligent of these men was David Herriot, who had had a vessel of his own in honest trade, and had been captured by Blackbeard in the Bay of Honduras. He had become a pirate, and a good one, when there seemed no way out of it. He had served under Blackbeard, but he had become attached to Bonnet, and had secretly commiserated with the latter during his enforced clerkship.

The Major made Herriot sailing master of the *Revenge,* which he now named the *Royal James,* in honor of the current pretender to the English throne. These jolly pirates were pretty good politicians in their way, and several of their captives testified that Bonnet and his men were wont to drink damnation to the King and a health to James, the Pretender, whenever they started out to loot a cargo of rum.

The first cruise of the revivified *Royal James* was up the coast of Ocracoke Inlet, where, gossip said, Blackbeard and his favorite henchmen might be found aboard a small vessel, holding council concerning the division of their spoil.

Bonnet declared he could not go to sea as an honorable pirate until he had settled scores with Blackbeard and punished the bewhiskered old fakir for his sins. This got a great hand with the crew, and for weeks the *Royal James* scoured the sea and the inlets in search of the old boss. Had the two forces joined battle, a lot of trouble later on would have been avoided, for undoubtedly they would have wiped each other out. Stede Bonnet, by that time, was a match for any pirate who sailed the seas; even for his devoted instructor.

But weeks were wasted, and Blackbeard, like Evangeline's lover was always about a day's sail ahead of his pursuer, without knowing that he was being pursued. Bonnet finally gave over the wild goose chase, and went into ordinary commercial pirating.

On this cruise he called himself Captain Thomas, and compelled his men to address him so. He put an antic disposition on in other respects also. Whenever he robbed a ship of her cargo, he insisted upon giving something for the goods taken. He carried a good many barrels of rice of no great value, and usually he made the captain of the captured boat a present of several of them after transferring his cargo to the *Royal James.* On one occasion Bonnet gave his prize an old rusty cable, and when he took twenty barrels of pork out of a Virginia sloop, he traded two barrels of rice and a hogshead of molasses for the goods, without asking consent. He took another Virginia vessel that had nothing aboard but a few combs and needles and such-like accessories of the toilet. Bonnet gravely transferred some pins and needles to the *Royal James,* and ordered two barrels of bread and a barrel of pork hoisted over the side and transferred to the captured ship, which was then told to go on her way.

Back and forth between Cape Fear River and St. Thomas he cruised, taking plenty of vessels and demonstrating to the world that a hen-pecked army officer, given a fair chance, could rehabilitate and assert himself. He became, in the absence of Blackbeard from the sea, the most talked-about pirate afloat.

In August, 1718, he arrived in Cape Fear River aboard the *Royal James,* and accompanied by two sloops recently taken in action. The *James* was leaking badly, and she was careened. The men were set to work at the repairing and cleaning job, and when timbers were needed they stole a shallop and tore it up to supply the necessary materials.

During this time Bonnet is reputed to have gone ashore with a small squad of men and buried three chests of treasure.

It was very hot weather, and the job lagged. Meantime the report had spread to Charleston that Bonnet was in the river, preparing for a descent upon the city. Charleston had suffered much at the hands of pirates, and the authorities there were quite generally unfriendly to the rovers, although in New York pirates were able to live in the style to which they had become accustomed and were seldom molested.

Fortunately for Charleston, there were public-spirited rich men in the town. Most noteworthy of these citizens was Colonel William Rhett, receiver-general of the province. Colonel Rhett's descendants are still prominent in Charleston, and they have accumulated a family tradition that is worthy of their pride. They have not forgotten the example set by their ancestor in 1718, when their fine old city was threatened by Bonnet and his pirates.

Colonel Rhett went to Governor Johnson and asked permission to fit out an expedition against Bonnet at his own expense. The Governor was happy to comply, since the province itself was helpless, and there were no warships along the coast. Rhett had learned that Bonnet was ready, or would soon be ready, with his three vessels, well armed. He was given a commission, and presently fitted out and manned with fighting Carolinians two sloops, the *Henry,* of eight guns and seventy men, and the *Sea Nymph,* of eight guns and sixty men. Rhett went aboard the *Henry,* and on September 10 sailed across the harbor to Sullivan's Island, to complete his preparations. Sullivan's Island (miscalled Swillivant's Island by an early pirate historian and his later paraphrasers) plays a further part in Charleston's history, for it was on it that Fort Moultrie was built years later.

Rhett took supplies aboard, and on September 15 crossed the bar of Charleston and set out to capture his pirates. He wasted several days in the pursuit of rumors, but finally arrived at Cape Fear on the evening of September 26.

As soon as he entered the river, he went aground on the sandbar with both his sloops. The Carolinians could see the topmasts of the pirate fleet, beyond a bend in the river bank. Simultaneously, Bonnet's watchers brought him word of the hostile-looking vessels at the mouth of the river, and the pirates prepared for action.

At dawn Bonnet hoisted his anchors and sailed down the river to meet his enemy, all sails set. Rhett had got off the sandbars, and, weighing anchor, went to meet the pirates. Their two sloops took positions upon either quarter of the *Royal James*, and forced her aground. The Carolina sloops themselves grounded only a few minutes later. The *Sea Nymph* was out of range, but the *Henry* was within pistol shot.

At the outset of this extraordinary struggle, it appeared that the god of battles was with the pirates. Both the pirate ship and the *Henry* careened on their sandy beds, both leaning in the same direction, and in such manner that the deck of the Carolinian was wholly exposed to the pointblank fire of the pirate, while the latter's deck was sheltered from the fire of Rhett's guns by the tipped-up hull.

Nevertheless, Rhett began pounding away with all the guns he could bring to bear on the pirate.

For five hours the combatants awaited the tide that would float them, meantime using both large and small arms as well as they could. Rhett's deck was swept by merciless musket fire, and his men had to be satisfied with inflicting what damage they could on the pirate's hull.

Whoever got first afloat would win the battle. That was understood by everybody on both sides. So Bonnet and Rhett watched the tide flow in for five hours, and never has a tide meant more to men than did that tide in the Cape Fear River to all those gallant lads, pirates and pirate-chasers, on that September day in 1718.

There was a good deal of droll mockery back and forth between the two ships. The pirates waved a red flag at the Carolinians, and kept asking Rhett to come aboard. This the stout Colonel from Charleston was fully resolved to do, if he could get afloat before being destroyed.

The *Henry* began to float first! The pirates were sorely alarmed, and some of them demanded that their chief surrender at once. But Bonnet wasn't that kind of a pirate. He had surrendered too often in the great house at Bridgetown. He told his men that he would fire the magazine himself if any man attempted to surrender.

But the debate continued among the pirates, although Bonnet took his stand on the deck, two pistols in his hands, and tried to shoot all the defeatists.

The *Henry*, now altogether afloat, made for the *Royal James*, and Rhett gave the order to board.

Bonnet was beaten. His men prevailed. They ran up a white flag in spite of their chief, and the defeated freebooter received Colonel Rhett on board the *James* and gave up his sword like a genuine Major of His Majesty's forces in distress.

Rhett lost twelve men killed and eighteen badly wounded. The pirates suffered rather fewer casualties.

Colonel Rhett sailed into Charleston harbor amid public excitement comparable to that of Armistice Day. He brought with him not only his own two sloops, but also the *Royal James* and the two Bonnet sloops that had remained out of the fight. He brought Stede Bonnet, the most redoubtable pirate afloat, and thirty of his men.

Bonnet and his pirates were delivered to Provost-Marshal Nathaniel Partridge, who was obliged to turn the rank and file of the men over to the military for safekeeping in an army guardhouse, since there was no adequate prison. Major Bonnet at once made an impression upon his captors. It was evident that he was a fellow of quality, and the South Carolinians could never be guilty of confining such a personage along with the rag-tag of the piratical world. So Major Bonnet was invited to be the guest of the marshal at his home, but with the formality of two guards at his door.

David Herriot, loyal sailing master for Bonnet, also managed to get himself transferred to the marshal's home, and Ignatius Pell, one of the pirates who had agreed to turn King's evidence, was lodged there to keep him from being killed by the other pirates. Thus the marshal had a full house.

Major Bonnet had behaved himself in such magnificent fashion that he quite captured the imagination of many good residents of Charleston. He was a good-looking man, dignified and gracious, and it was known that he was not understood at home. What wonder that the town was soon divided into pro-Bonnets and anti-Bonnets! There were some major disturbances in the city while preparations for the trial were under way, and there was a considerable demand that this gentleman pirate be permitted to go his way in such peace as he could muster.

The pro-Bonnet movement finally settled down to a plot for the pirate's delivery, and this was effected, apparently by bribing the guards. Herriot, the faithful, went along, and a party of Bonnetites was waiting with a boat. This was on October 25, three days before the trial of the pirates was scheduled to begin.

Governor Johnson immediately offered a reward of £700 for the recapture of Bonnet and Herriot. He sent out the hue and cry, replaced the provost-marshal with a person who was thought to be less susceptible to the blandishments of gentle manners, and called Colonel Rhett into conference.

Rhett was never found wanting in time of need. He set out at once with a small party, and trailed the fugitives to Sullivan's Island, where they had been forced by rough weather and shortage of supplies to land.

Bonnet and his little band of faithful followers were hiding in the brush among the sandhills. They were surrounded and fired upon, but made no effort to defend themselves. When Herriot fell beside his master, Bonnet seemed to lose all his fighting ardor. He surrendered and was taken back to Charleston. This time he was put in close confinement.

Meantime, the trial of the other pirates was under way before a special admiralty court, presided over by the notable Nicholas Trott, one of the most picturesque tyrants who ever graced the bench.

The pirates had a grand trial, with an imposing bench crowded with twelve prominent citizens who acted as judges under the presidency of Trott. The defendants were not allowed counsel. Trott frequently interrupted the proceedings to denounce them, and he spoke to the prisoners as one might to so many very naughty dogs. All but four of them were found guilty, and sentenced to be hanged.

Bonnet was captured before the trial of his men was completed, but he was not brought to trial until two days after his old companions in arms had been hanged at White Point, near Charleston. The bodies of the pirates were buried between high and low water, in a marsh.

The hanging of his men transformed poor Bonnet. Once the most swaggering and daring of the sea rogues, he now became a shaking, shuddering coward, abjectly pleading for his life. Facing death in a bloody fight at sea, he had been invincible. Bullying his crew of brawling brutes, he had shone as a master whom the worst of men feared to cross. But now, as his merry men swung lightly in the soft November breezes, and he himself faced judgment, he became even more craven than the Major Bonnet who had suffered quietly so long under the lash of a shrewish wife.

The same court that had tried his men tried Bonnet, and Tyrant Trott again presided. He was not so rough with the chief as he had been with the common seamen; not for a moment, indeed, did anybody forget that Bonnet was a rich man and a gentleman.

But the pirate chief was not allowed counsel. Occasionally he ventured to speak in his own defense, and when he did so he spoke humbly and as a broken reed.

"May it please Your Honors," he said, "and the rest of the gentlemen, though I must confess myself a sinner, and the greatest of sinners, yet I am not guilty of what I am charged with."

Trott interrupted to ask him what he had to say in answer to the witnesses who had testified to having been captured by him.

Bonnet, with the straightest face in the world, replied that he had never taken any part in the seizure of a vessel, except when he was acting as Blackbeard's clerk. He explained that when piracies were committed by the men under his charge, when he was sailing in his own ship, it happened because he was asleep in his cabin, and had no knowledge of what the men were doing.

Trott's charge to the jury was a much better speech for the prosecution than either of the prosecuting attorneys had made. He wound it up with this cynical play:

"So I think the evidence have proved the fact upon him: but I shall leave this to your consideration."

The verdict was guilty, and the sentence was that Bonnet be hanged.

Trott, in passing sentence, read a long document in which he quoted Holy Scripture for more than an hour to prove that the prisoner would go direct from the scaffold to Hell, to take his "part in the lake which burneth with fire and brimstone, which is the second death."

December 10 was named for the execution of the sentence. Bonnet spent the time until then pleading for his life and planning for a reprieve. He sent a message to Colonel Rhett, who had twice captured him, begging the gallant Colonel to do something for him.

Rhett admired and pitied the fallen pirate. He admired him as a gallant fighter and a pleasant gentleman, and he pitied him in his present plight, because he had heard the story of the scolding wife in Barbadoes who had driven this estimable fellow to destruction.

Rhett comes very near being the hero of the story. He actually came forward and tried to persuade Governor Johnson to permit him to take Bonnet to England for another trial. He offered to be surety for the prisoner (and this after Bonnet had once escaped!) and likewise offered to furnish the ship to take him to the other side.

Rhett worked for nothing and always turned up when needed, but he is one hero whose city hasn't forgotten. In one of the old churchyards in Charleston, within a few feet of one of the principal streets of the town, I found his grave, covered by a great granite block on which is carved:

> In Hopes of a Joyful Resurrection
> Here rests the body of
> Col. William Rhett,
> late of this Parish,
> Principall officer of His Majesties Customs in
> this Province.
> He was a person that on all occasions promoted the
> Publick good of this Colony and severall times gener-
> ously and successfully ventured his life in defence of
> the same
> He was a kind Husband, a tender Father, a faithfull
> Friend, a Charitable Neighbour, a religious and con-
> stant worshipper of God
> He was borne in London 4th Sept. 1666
> Arrived and settled in this country 19th Novemr. 1694
> And dyed suddenly but not unprepared 12th Janry.
> 1722 in the fifty-seventh year of his age.

Good old Rhett! He would have taken Bonnet for a ride to the motherland in the hope of saving a fine pirate and a noble swasher of buck-
lers, of whom he knew the world had all too few! But Governor
Johnson would have none of it. Someone produced an insulting letter
to the Governor, which, it was claimed, Bonnet had written the night
before the battle on the sandbars at Cape Fear. In this bit of bravado,
Bonnet boasted that if he should win the fight he would take up his
station off Charleston and burn every vessel coming in or going out.
Bonnet must hang, declared Johnson.

Now Bonnet reached the depths. He wrote to Governor Johnson an
abject letter, in which he humiliated himself far below the level to
which a brave man commonly is supposed to descend, even in the
gravest emergencies. He said, among other things:

> . . . I intreat you not to let me fall a Sacrifice to the Envy
> and ungodly Rage of some few Men, who, not being yet

satisfied with Blood, feign to believe that if I had the Happiness of a longer life in this world, I should still employ it in a wicked Manner, which to remove that, and all other Doubts with your Honour, I heartily beseech you'll permit me to live, and I'll voluntarily put it ever out of my Power by separating all my Limbs from my Body, only reserving the use of my Tongue to call continually on, and pray to the Lord my God, and mourn all my days in Sackcloth and Ashes to work out confident Hopes of my Salvation, at that great and dreadful Day when all righteous Souls shall receive their just rewards.

This crawling in ashes went even further. The fearsome pirate begged that he might be permitted, after severing his arms and legs from his body, to go far inland, out of sight of the sea, and there serve the Governor in some menial capacity for the rest of his life. His parting benediction to the Governor was:

Now the God of Peace, that brought again from the dead our Lord Jesus, the great Shepherd of the Sheep, thro the blood of the everlasting Covenant, make you perfect in every good work to do his Will, working in you that which is well pleasing in his Sight, through Jesus Christ, to whom be Glory forever and ever, is the hearty prayer of

Your Honour's
Most Miserable, and
Afflicted Servant,
Stede Bonnet.

But the Governor was not impressed. Perhaps he suspected that the jolly freebooter did but jest, and that respite would but increase his chances for escape and further depredations.

So on the appointed day Stede Bonnet was hanged at White Point, and buried in the sand, between the rising and falling of the tide. When he was brought to the gallows, he was but semiconscious. Fear had practically killed him before the noose was about his neck.

Blackbeard's most important vessel was the *Queen Anne's Revenge,* a large ship mounting forty guns. At various times he commanded other vessels that he had taken at sea and thought too good to sink, burn, or turn back to their owners.

He was at the height of his sea power when he cruised northward from Honduras after adding Bonnet's sloop, the *Revenge,* to his force. He captured several vessels along the way. Some of these he sank, after looting them. Others he added to his fleet.

The pirates established a blockade of Charleston harbor, standing off the bar for a week and capturing the harbor's pilot boat and every incoming ship. There was an outbound ship, too, commanded by one Robert Clark, bound for London with mixed cargo and some passengers. Among the passengers taken was Samuel Wragg, member of the Council of the Province.

Blackbeard's surgeon had reported a shortage of medicines and bandages. So the swaggering pirate, who was now slightly intoxicated with his power and importance, sent ashore a party in charge of Richards, commanding the *Revenge,* to demand a full case of medical and surgical supplies from the authorities of Charleston.

Richards took several of his own men and one of the captured passengers, who is known to history simply as a Mr. Marks. Strangely enough, it is not known that Mr. Marks has any descendants in Charleston to-day, or any tombstones in the ancient Charleston churchyards bearing his name. He was simply a Mr. Marks who won brief notoriety because he was compelled to deliver a message from the pirate chief to Governor Johnson of the Province of South Carolina. The message was, in effect:

"Blackbeard is just off the bar with an overwhelming force. He has many Charlestonians as prisoners. Fill a large ship's medicine chest with all things needful, and the prisoners will be released. Refuse or delay, and the prisoners will be murdered, beginning with Councilman Wragg."

The Governor put the ultimatum up to the Council in special session, and both Governor and Council were shocked and humiliated that a notorious pirate should be able to deliver such a demand so insolently at the seat of a government.

But the relatives of the prisoners aboard Blackbeard's ships carried the day. The Province of South Carolina would accede to the pirate's demands. The medicines, bandages and instruments were bought in Charleston at the expense of the government, and turned over to the pirates.

Marks and the shore party had been given by Teach two days in which to make the trip and return with the medicines. The Charlestonians aboard the *Queen Anne's Revenge* were informed that, if the boat did not return with the chest of medicines by the second sunset, they were to prepare for death.

When the second sunset arrived, there was no boat in sight. Blackbeard was in a temper. Just as the sun was dipping to the horizon he had all prisoners summoned on deck. He stormed up and down in front of the frightened company of helpless men, women, and children. He cursed Charleston and its people, and swung his mighty cutlass menacingly. He called out Samuel Wragg. He informed that worthy that he had better enjoy the fine sunset, as it was the next to the last thing he would ever enjoy, the last being the experience of losing his head right where he stood.

Wragg was not a bad advocate. In this emergency he pleaded a hopeless cause before a somewhat prejudiced judge, who was also, by appointment of the court, executioner. Advocate Wragg represented to Judge Captain Blackbeard Teach that the authorities in the city were not crazy, and would not be permitted to cause the deaths of so many citizens merely for lack of a few hundred pounds' worth of drugs and bandages. There had been some mishap, and if the Court please, it was not beyond the bounds of the probable that Captain Richards or some of his men had become slightly intoxicated, or even bewitched by some fair Charleston damsels, thereby and thus delaying the return of the medicines by some few hours.

Blackbeard pondered. He liked the humor of this lawyer who could plead so well in such annoying circumstances. He granted a stay of sentence.

It was as Wragg had suspected. While the Governor and Council were conferring and shopping for balsams and bandages, Richards and his merry men were striding up Meeting Street, taking both sides and the middle of that thoroughfare. They were met with hostile stares at first, but presently the traditional hospitality of the Charleston people was aroused by the genial and swaggering manner of the strange guests. The pirates spent their gold freely, and had plenty of it to spend. They drank enormous quantities of rum, and bought rum for whomsoever would partake. They sang pirate songs for the delectation of the children in the streets, and delighted the young women who had been saving all their thrill capacity for the day when real pirates, with gold ear-rings and red silk sashes, should chuck them under the chin and call them beautiful.

So Richards and his men were in no condition to get back to the *Queen Anne's Revenge* by the second sundown. Marks led the citizens' movement to find ways and means to have the agreement and Blackbeard's orders kept to the letter, and it was he who went out in a row-boat to carry to Blackbeard the news that the shore party was unavoidably detained "by some slight mishap" in the town.

When this message reached the pirate flagship, it was dawn, and Blackbeard was summoning all the prisoners on deck a second time to receive notice that they must die at once. Samuel Wragg was spared the necessity for making another plea by arrival of the message from shore.

Eventually the slightly sobered shore party of pirates arrived with a handsome box of medicines, and Blackbeard made good his promise. He sent all the prisoners ashore, but not until he had robbed them of all their money, jewelry and desirable items of clothing. Samuel

Wragg's eloquence did not avail to save the six thousand dollars he had in his money belt.

Captain Teach felt the shore a-calling. For, while he was a great villain and a picturesque pirate afloat, he was quite a personage ashore too. He was a different person, quite, when he had shed the mantle of sea authority. On land, he was a ladies' man. He always shaved off his fearsome whiskers as soon as he had come ashore, and donned respectability as one might put on a garment for a festival. Thenceforward, as long as his residence ashore lasted, Captain Teach was a Don Juan, courting the women assiduously, astounding the countryside by his generosity and lavish spending, and delighting polite companies with his witty tales of the sea.

Usually Captain Teach stayed ashore on one of these long leaves for several months. Always he married while ashore. It was said by his detractors, at the close of his career, that he had actually been married sixteen times. I do not think this charge can be proved by the scanty records now extant, but it is certain that the gay Captain was a great one for marrying. The mortality rate among his wives was comparable to that prevailing among Chicago racketeers.

When Blackbeard reached Topsail Inlet, North Carolina, as heretofore related, he abandoned his piratical career for a while, and permitted Bonnet to sail away with the *Revenge* on his own account.

While Bonnet was wasting valuable time looking for Captain Teach, that he might show him how good a pirate he had become under the teaching of the master, the redoubtable Terror of the Seas was transforming himself into a Beau Brummel landsman in and about the town of Bath.

But first Captain Teach made friends with the reigning politicians, as all wise pirates have ever done. Charles Eden was Governor of North Carolina, with headquarters at Bath, and Tobias Knight, a finished politician, was the Governor's secretary. Blackbeard approached the Governor through the secretary, and very soon an *entente cordiale* was established all around. Blackbeard became a Prominent Citizen of the community, and Governor Eden and Secretary Knight became very prosperous.

After an understanding had been reached, Blackbeard and twenty of his rogues went before the Governor and formally renounced piracy, whereupon they were handed His Majesty's Most Gracious Pardon for all past crimes, and were certified to all and sundry as good and worthy citizens.

Blackbeard at once began the erection of a suitable home for himself at Plum Point. The site chosen was ideal. It was conveniently distant from the town of Bath. It was isolated, and close enough to deep water to permit the anchoring of a pirate ship close to the land that constituted Blackbeard's front yard. The house, constructed of hand-made bricks, was large and gloomy. Its shuttered windows looked out toward the sea. Its great cellars were well stocked with wines and rum. Its broad verandas were covered by cowl-like roofs that shut out the sun and the gaze of the curious.

When the house was finished, Blackbeard, who was now Captain Teach, the wealthy mariner, dressed up more luridly than ever, and went a-courting. He had had no wife since the beginning of his long cruise that had ended at Topsail Inlet.

The Captain's fancy picked Prudence Lutrelle, a girl of sixteen, only daughter of Marie Lutrelle, widow of a small planter.

And this is the story of Captain Teach and his last love affair, as told by the oldsters of Bath.

The wealthy Captain called at the humble home of the Widow Lutrelle with a fine swagger, all dressed in red and blue silk, and carrying a sword. He paid his compliments to the widow, while with great coolness and deliberation he appraised the pretty daughter.

Prudence was dark and fragile, and her deep brown eyes were wells of innocence. From the first, she disliked the haughty Captain.

Teach made half a dozen calls. Finally he proposed marriage, addressing the mother while looking at the daughter.

Marie Lutrelle plainly considered this a good match, but she asked the Captain to call later for his answer.

Prudence sat on a low stool beside her mother on the evening appointed for the Captain's coming. She was pale and she could not keep back the tears.

"I am afraid of him, Mother," said the frightened girl. Her mother felt the trembling of the child's frail body as Prudence looked up into the older woman's eyes, a very picture of helplessness. "I have heard much about his piracies and his many wives that have all disappeared. Why should I have aught to do with this man?"

"You are young and full of notions, girl," said the stout Marie. "You are afraid of a husband, and that is the measure of your worry. This day next year you will laugh at yourself. Here is a fine man, this captain, and could he be a friend of the governor's if he were a pirate?"

"I know naught of that, Mother. You have heard the talk and that Governor Eden and Knight, his secretary, do share the loot that this same captain brings in from sea. I fear I shall laugh but little if I become his wife. And, Mother, why should I marry now? I want to wait for—yes, Mother, for love!"

"You are full of notions, I tell you——"

A loud knocking at the door and in stepped Captain Teach, arrayed in his finest, and beside him the Governor of North Carolina himself. Mrs. Lutrelle was in a frenzy of excitement and embarrassment because of the presence of these mighty men in her humble home. She poured wine and the great ones talked loudly.

"So here's the bride you'll be taking with you, my Captain!" shouted the Governor, catching Prudence by the shoulders and holding her up to examine her by the light of the candles on the mantel, "Oho, a right pretty morsel, by my faith! Luck will go with you this time, Captain!"

Prudence was frightened. She tore herself from the Governor's grasp and started for the door. Captain Teach crossed the room in three strides, intercepted her, folded her in his arms and, despite her struggles, kissed her upon the mouth.

The impetuous lover was angry because of the resistance, but the Governor was in great good humor. He roared with laughter, and while

Teach still held the fighting maid he stepped to the front door and called in two pages who attended him.

Then there was a marriage. The pages were witnesses. The Governor read the service from a prayer book drawn from an inside pocket.

Prudence wept, but said nothing. The Governor repeated the responses she was supposed to make, and she did not resist, for she saw that resistance was useless.

Marie Lutrelle was worried by the highhanded manner of the marrying, but she was afraid to lift her voice in protest lest there be no marriage at all. And to have a daughter married to a wealthy man by the Governor himself was something in Marie's life.

"You understand, Madam," said the Governor after the brief ceremony, "there is need for haste. The Captain sails upon a long cruise in the morning. Everything is shipshape aboard the *Revenge* and it needed only this one knot to be tied. Now we all go to the Captain's house, for the wedding supper and the guests are waiting."

There was a brief assurance by Captain Teach that everything necessary to his bride's comfort already had been provided. Conveyances were waiting outside. The Governor was conversing loudly with the mother.

Prudence, still white and trembling, stepped into her bedroom to get her wraps. The bridegroom followed her. Immediately there was a sound of struggle, a muffled oath, an overturning chair. The captain emerged smiling, but with blood outlining a long scratch across his left cheek.

"Stormy voyage ahead, Governor!" said the pirate chief. "The jade is wild. I think I have tamed wilder." He spoke in even tones and did not cease to smile, but in his eyes there was fire.

There was a great wedding feast that night in the long banquet room of Captain Teach's new mansion by the sea. Governor Eden was there, at Captain Teach's right hand, and Tobias Knight was on the Governor's right. The place at the foot of the long table was occupied by the white-faced little bride, whose excited mother was beside her, too bewildered to eat. Seventy guests, including Blackbeard's officers for the cruise that was about to begin, drank copious toasts to the bride and bridegroom, and cried loud and tipsy good wishes for the voyage.

Basilica Hands did not sit down. He was not going upon this voyage. His crippled knee was bothering him, and probably would keep him a landlubber the rest of his life, he explained to friends. He wandered disconsolately about the great house, drinking ever and anon a great draught of rum, and occasionally peering through, a half-opened door upon the gay wedding feast.

Blackbeard was in good form. He seldom slept on one of these noisy nights preceding the beginning of a new voyage, or on the eve of a good battle. To-night he was gloriously drunk. He shouted, sang, and exhorted his guests to greater feats of hilarious drinking. He totally ignored the existence of his shrinking bride.

It was nearly daylight when six seamen carried in a great iron chest and heaved it upon the center of the table. Now Blackbeard rose, strode to the center and raised the heavy iron lid. The wedding cake was inside. Otherwise the chest was empty.

"Bride ahoy!" shouted the master of the feast, smashing a bottle of wine on the upraised lid, "This is the bride's chest and it's coming back full of treasure! The greatest treasure that's ever filled a sea chest! Sink me forty fathoms if not!"

There was a roar of appreciation from the crowd as Blackbeard continued:

"What comes home in that chest is not for you, Governor! It's the bride's chest! Pipe up, Mrs. Blackbeard! Fair weather, is it? Hoist a signal to your captain!"

The pale girl sat as if unhearing, or as if hypnotized into silence and immobility.

Captain Teach jumped upon the table and, making a megaphone of his hands, roared: "Mate ahoy! Up anchors! Set sail! To sea we go!"

The guests were struck dumb by the raging of the Terror of the Sea. The gigantic pirate, roaring great sea-curses upon and against everybody, smashed dishes right and left, felled guests with unreasoning blows, and shouted orders to his officers.

While the guests were making the best of their way out of the banquet hall, sailors were busy aboard the *Queen Anne's Revenge*, a few paces from the veranda, carrying out orders for immediate departure. In the midst of the confusion, six men picked up the sea-chest and carried it aboard. Blackbeard himself, roaring a bloody pirate chantey, strode to the end of the room, tucked the little bride under one arm as though she had been a bag of meal, and went aboard the *Revenge*, just as the sails were being spread for the new voyage.

It was a great cruise and a hard one, members of the crew reported to their friends when the *Queen Anne's Revenge* cast anchor at Bath Town thirteen months later. Forty prizes had been taken, looted and burned, with never a hand from any one of them spared. Blackbeard had been himself at his worst. The *Revenge* returned well laden with silver and gold.

The bride? Little was spoken of her by the men unless they were pressed for details. The first day out she had been imprisoned in irons in a little cabin beside the Captain's. Through many months she lay shackled to her bed through storm and calm and battle. She had never come on deck.

After the first month's discipline Blackbeard had visited her. He came away with a bad knife cut which reached from his left shoulder to a point just over his heart. Prudence had remained shackled from that time on until the day before making port at Bath Town.

Certain members of the crew had been detailed at the beginning of the voyage to carry food to the pale prisoner and to minister to her wants under the Captain's supervision. They were told to cease their ministrations on the last day out of home port. Blackbeard again visited his wife and she was not seen any more by any of the crew.

The first night in port the *Revenge* was anchored off the end of Plum Point. Toward midnight, a working party with shovels went ashore, headed by Blackbeard, grim and silent, and carrying the great iron chest. Six men bore the weight of the big box and found it heavy going.

They dug a pit by the light of lanterns and buried the chest. Blackbeard stood by. They laid a floor of bricks, plentifully mortared, set the heavy chest upon the floor and built up a brick wall around the sides and ends, finishing all with a vaulted roof of bricks and mortar. Then they shoveled in the soil, and nothing at all was said as the party returned at dawn to the vessel.

Every one of those six men of the burial party disappeared during the first week of the *Revenge's* stay in the home port. Blackbeard was known to have killed two of them with his own hands with no apparent provocation. But he was immune from arrest, for he had not forgotten Governor Eden on the occasion of this homecoming.

The division of spoils by Blackbeard after this last voyage became notorious scandal in North Carolina. It was known that Eden and Knight had received, over and above such gold as the pirate was willing to disgorge for them, most of a cargo of rum and sugar brought in by Blackbeard aboard a French vessel that he had taken.

Knight, who was collector of the port of Bath, sat as Vice Admiralty Judge upon this prize, and condemned her as lawfully taken, although Great Britain and France were at peace. Knight formally declared the vessel to be Spanish. Then he and the Governor divided the cargo between them, and Blackbeard took the captured vessel out into the river and burned her to the water's edge and sank her bottom, so as to destroy the evidence.

Meantime, Blackbeard, according to a witness who survived these events for many years, was burying boxes and cases of treasure at various places along Pamlico Sound.

But the evil-doers were over-reaching themselves.

The planters of North Carolina, outraged by the scandalous behavior of the pirates and politicians, sent a delegation to complain to Governor Spotswood, of Virginia, known as an honorable and law-enforcing officer of the Crown. Governor William Keith of Pennsylvania already had issued a warrant for Blackbeard's arrest, hoping to catch him upon one of his visits to Philadelphia, where he had mercantile connections.

Governor Spotswood was indignant when he learned the story of corruption and piracy from the planters of North Carolina. He took the matter before the assembly, and the following proclamation was issued:

> *By his Majestys Lieutenant Governor, and Commander in Chief, of the Colony and Dominion of Virginia,*
>
> A PROCLAMATION
>
> Publishing the Rewards given for apprehending, or killing Pyrates. *Whereas,* by an Act of Assembly, made at a Session of Assembly, begun at the Capital in Williamsburgh, the eleventh Day of November, in the fifth Year of his Majesty's Reign, entitled, An Act to encourage the apprehending & destroying of Pyrates: It is, amongst other Things enacted, that all and every Person, or Persons, who, from & after the fourteenth Day of November, in the Year of our Lord one thousand seven hundred & eighteen, & before the fourteenth Day of November, which shall be in the Year of our Lord one thousand seven hundred & nineteen, shall take any Pyrate, or Pyrates, on the Sea or Land, or in case of Resistance, shall kill any such Pyrate, or Pyrates, between the Degrees of thirty four, and thirty nine, of Northern Latitude, and within one hundred Leagues of the Continent of Virginia, or within the Provinces of Virginia, or North-Carolina, upon the Conviction, or making due Proof of the killing of all, and every such Pyrate, and Pyrates, before the Governor & Council, shall be entitled to have, & receive out of the publick Money, in the Hands of the Treasurer of this Colony, the several Rewards following; that is to say, for Edward Teach, commonly called Captain Teach, or BlackBeard, one hundred Pounds, for every other Commander of a Pyrate Ship, Sloop, or Vessel, forty Pounds, for every Lieutenant, Master, or Quarter-Master, Boatswain, or Carpenter, twenty Pounds; for every other inferior

Officer, fifteen Pounds, and for every private Man taken
on Board such Ship, Sloop, or Vessel, ten Pounds; and
that for every Pyrate, which shall be taken by any Ship,
Sloop, or Vessel, belonging to this Colony, or North-
Carolina, within the Time aforesaid, in any Place whatsoever, the like Rewards shall be paid according to the
Quality and Condition of such Pyrates. Wherefore, for
the Encouragement of all such Persons as shall be
willing to serve his Majesty, and their Country, in so
just & honourable an Undertaking, as the suppressing a
Sort of People, who may be truly called Enemies to
Mankind: I have thought fit, with the Advice & Consent
of his Majesty's Council, to issue this Proclamation,
hereby declaring, the said rewards shall be punctually &
justly paid, in current money of Virginia, according to
the directions of the said Act. And, I do order &
appoint this Proclamation, to be published by the
Sheriffs, at their respective County-Houses, & by all
Ministers & Readers, in the several Churches & Chap-
pels, throughout this Colony.

Given at our Council Chamber at Williams, this
24th. Day of November, 1718, in the fifth Year of his
Majesty's Reign.

GOD SAVE THE KING.

A. SPOTSWOOD

The Governor consulted with the captains of two of His Majesty's
men of war that lay in the James River, but it was known that these
deep-draught vessels could not be used in an attack upon Blackbeard
in his retreats along the North Carolina coast, for the pirate used vessels of light draught and kept well inside the little islands and shoals
that made navigation dangerous for larger vessels.

It was agreed that Governor Spotswood should hire two small
sloops, and the navy would man them. Captain Brand and Lieutenant

Maynard were given the commands. They were told to go and get Blackbeard, dead or alive, and to take such other measures for the restoration of law and order in the neighboring colony of North Carolina as might seem good in the premises.

No cannon were mounted aboard the sloops, because of the weight such armament would add, and the increased draught that would result. The Virginians would carry small arms only, although they knew that Blackbeard was supplied with cannon.

The commanders of the sloops were confident that their trained men could beat the pirates in hand-to-hand conflict, if once they could get aboard the pirate vessels.

On the evening of Nov. 21, 1718, the punitive expedition stood off Ocracoke Inlet, where, confidential information said, Blackbeard was preparing to set sail on a minor expedition.

The confidential information, which proved correct in every detail, was supplied, we have every reason to believe, by no less a pirate than Basilica Hands himself. Captain Teach did himself no great favor when he fired that pistol ball through his worthy servant's knee!

Teach had warning that the Virginians were coming up the river on the morning of November 22. Either he did not take the warning seriously, or he thought little of the prowess of the boys who were seeking him. He spent that last night in uproarious revelry. He drank himself into a state of hilarious helplessness. Of course, most of his men drank heavily too.

The battle, next morning, was as bloody an affair as even a pirate of Blackbeard's proclivities might wish for.

There was some shouting of defiance between Lieutenant Maynard and Blackbeard, whose sloop ran aground after giving Maynard two broadsides that sadly racked the Virginians and covered their deck with dead and dying. Brand's vessel was out of the battle most of the time, on account of winds and shoals.

Maynard's men plied their oars in an effort to come aboard the pirate. The Virginians were exposed to wicked cannon fire, and were able to reply with small arms only. But they were waiting for the boarding.

As they came close aboard, Maynard ordered all his men to lie low, some on the deck and some below, only himself and the helmsman appearing in upright postures. The pirates threw bottles of explosives upon the attacking sloop, and then, led by Blackbeard himself, jumped to the smoking deck. They had saved the Virginians the trouble of boarding! Blackbeard, as usual, took the offensive.

This time, as the giant charged down the deck, he met no yielding line of merchantmen, women, children and common sailors. He met, in fact, Lieutenant Maynard in person. Maynard was calm and collected. He was also quite determined. And he was no amateur with the pistol and cutlass.

Blackbeard roared and came at the Lieutenant as if to eat him up. He was met by a pistol ball from Maynard's left-hand weapon, squarely in the chest. As the monster paused ever so little upon receiving this surprise, Maynard dodged his cutlass and inflicted a deep gash across the pirate's body.

The fight was on, and gave promise of developing into something really interesting. The two crews were fairly well matched in numbers, but the King's men had all the better of the battle.

Maynard was handling the long-armed Terror very well, but it must be confessed that he had a little help from his men occasionally. Blackbeard was fair game for any passing naval man who could spare a shot or a sword-thrust from his own engagements.

Maynard suffered the loss of his cutlass at a critical moment. The giant struck it out of the Lieutenant's hand with a great slash, and then, although almost blinded with blood which streamed from a wound in his head, he advanced to finish his gallant foe.

Maynard jumped backward, drew a pistol, and cocked it.

But he would never have had time to fire that pistol, had not one of his men seen his plight, and, leaping to Blackbeard's side, slit the giant's throat from ear to ear.

Blackbeard fell dying to the deck. His body bore five pistol balls and twenty cuts and stab wounds.

The battle was over. The surviving men of Blackbeard's boarding party jumped overboard and begged for quarter. This favor was granted. The pirates remaining aboard Blackbeard's vessel were rounded up and ironed. Counting losses, Maynard found he had lost twelve men killed, while twenty-two were wounded. The Lieutenant himself escaped with a slash across the knuckles.

Blackbeard's head was severed and stuck up on the bowsprit of the victorious ship.

Search of the pirate vessel disclosed correspondence and papers indubitably implicating Governor Eden and Secretary Knight as accomplices of the pirate. Maynard, under his instructions to do what was necessary in the premises, sailed to Bath, where the sight of Blackbeard's head must have struck the Governor and Collector of the Port with chills. In fact, Knight took to his bed that night, and died some weeks later. It was fright that killed him, the doctors said, although meantime he had been whitewashed by a board of inquiry.

Maynard sent a shore party to search the premises of the Governor and Knight, and recovered the cargo stolen from the French boat.

Basilica Hands also went aboard Maynard's vessel at Bath, and delivered evidence against Knight and Eden. Hands was taken back as a prisoner, but turned King's evidence against the other pirates at the trials that followed in Virginia. There were fifteen prisoners. All were hanged except Hands, who was released for the assistance he had given the prosecution, and one Sam Odell who, although badly wounded in the fight, proved that he had been forced by Blackbeard to join his crew only the night before the battle, while the orgy was in progress on the pirate's ship.

Hands lived many years in London, a cripple and a beggar. Much of the substance of the preceding narrative, and much that is known of Blackbeard, was gleaned from the conversations of Basilica Hands in London taverns during those drab days toward the close of this unfortunate pirate's life. So I do not say that all the story is true in detail. I hazard the opinion that it is about as true as the histories of pirates are ever likely to be.

But what was in the treasure chest that the three strangers took from Plum Point at Christmas, in 1928?

I challenge the finders to tell the world!

The Uneasy Ghost of Lafitte

by Julia Beazley

This legend, published in a 1924 compilation by the Texas
Folklore Society, tells the story of pirate ghosts and buried
treasure in La Porte, Texas.

"Or if thou hast uphoarded in thy life
Extorted treasure in the womb of earth,
For which, they say, you spirits oft walk in death,
Speak of it."

"It faded on the crowing of the cock."—*Hamlet.*

Within the memory of men still living, Texas coast dwellers used to
gather around firesides on northery winter nights, and while the rich
juice of sweet potatoes roasting among the ashes oozed through the
jackets, tell tales of "the Pirate of the Gulf." Not a few of these tales cen-
tered about an ancient and dilapidated house at Bayshore Park, La
Porte, in Harris County. Under it, so they say, is the blood marked

booty of Lafitte; and though old tales and old times and old houses pass, anyone hardy enough to spend the night in this deserted building may yet, according to report, receive a visit from the guilt-harried spirit that sometimes in distress and sometimes in anger is still trying to win absolution for his earthly sins.

The legend runs that upon a certain occasion Lafitte and his buccaneering crew sailed up to what is now Bay Ridge (which is opposite the haunted house of La Porte). He anchored his schooner offshore, and rowed to the beach with two trusted lieutenants and the heavy chest which none dared touch except at his orders. When the skiff grounded, the watchers on the schooner saw their chief blindfold his helpers; then they saw the three disappear with the chest behind a screen of grapevine-laden trees. Two hours later Lafitte returned alone. He was in a black mood and no one had the temerity to question him. It was supposed that he had caught one of his helpers trying to mark the location of his cache, and had killed them both. Some say that he led them back to the pit they had dug and filled up, made them reopen and enlarge it, and while they were bent down digging, shot them dead. Soon afterwards Lafitte and his followers went down together in a West India hurricane, and his crime-stained treasure still lies buried in its secret hiding place.

Yet to many, as I have intimated, that place has not been secret. It is under the old house. As faithfully as I can follow the tale, I shall relate an experience connected with that old house as it was told me by a Confederate veteran who has now passed on. For personal reasons I shall call him Major Walcart, though that was not his real name. The tale, however, is a genuine legend in that it has long been current in the vicinity of La Porte.

"It was on a February night back in the eighties," the Major used to say. "The early darkness of a murky day had overtaken me, and I was dead tired. I do not think mud ever lay deeper along the shore of Galveston Bay, or that an east wind ever blew more bleakly. When I came to a small stream I rode out into the open water, as the custom then was, to find shallow passage. A full moon was rising out of the bay. Heavy clouds stretched just above it, and I remember the unearthly aspect of the blustering breakers in its cheerless light. The immensity and unfriendliness of the scene made me feel lonesome, and I think the horse shared my mood. By common consent we turned across before we had gone far enough from shore, and fell into the trench cut by the stream in the bottom of the bay.

"We were wretchedly wet as we scrambled up a clayey slope and gained the top of the bluff. A thin cry which I had not been sure was real when I first heard it now became insistent. It was like the wail of a child in mortal pain, and I confess that it reminded me of tales I had heard of the werewolf, which lures unwary travelers to their doom by imitating the cry of a human infant. By the uncertain light of the moon, which the next moment was cut off entirely, I saw that I had reached a kind of stable that crowned the bluff, and from this structure the uncanny summons seemed to come.

"The sounds were growing fainter, and I hesitated but a moment. Dismounting, I led my horse through the doorless entrance, and now the mystery was explained. Huddled together for warmth lay a flock of sleeping goats. A kid had rashly squeezed itself into the middle of the heap, and the insensate brutes were crushing its life out. I found the perishing little creature, and its flattened body came back to the full tide of life in my arms. Its warmth was grateful to my cold fingers, and I fondled it a moment before setting it down on the dry dirt floor.

"I tied my horse to a post that upheld the roof of the stable, and with saddle and blanket on my arm started toward the house, which I could make out in its quadrangle of oaks, not many yards distant. The horse whinnied protestingly as I left him, and when the moaning of the wind in the eaves smote my ears I was half in mind to turn back and bunk with the goats. It was a more forbidding sound than the hostile roar of the breakers had been in the bay.

"I called, but only the muddy waves incessantly tearing at the bluff made answer. I had scarcely hoped really to hear the sound of a human voice. The great double doors leading in from the front porch were barred, but the first window I tried yielded entrance. Striking a match,

I found myself in a room that gave promise of comfort. Fat pine kindling lay beside the big fireplace, and dry chunks of solid oak were waiting to glow for me the whole night through.

"I was vaguely conscious that the brave fire I soon had going did not drive the chill from the air so promptly as it should, but my head was too heavy with sleep to be bothered. I spread my horse blanket quite close to the cheerful blaze, and with saddle for pillow and slicker for cover I abandoned myself to the luxury of rest.

"I do not know how long I had slept when I became aware of a steady gaze fixed on my face. The man was looking down on me, and no living creature ever stood so still. There was imperious command in the unblinking eyes, and yet I saw a sort of profound entreaty also.

"It was plain that the visitant had business with me. I arose, and together we left the room, passed its neighbor, and entered a third, a barren little apartment through whose cracks the wind came mercilessly. I think it was I who had opened the doors. My companion did not seem to move. He was merely present all the time.

" 'It is here,' he said, as I halted in the middle of the bare floor, 'that more gold lies buried than is good for any man. You have but to dig, and it is yours. You can use it; I cannot. However, it must be applied only to purposes of highest beneficence. Not one penny may be evilly or selfishly spent. On this point you must keep faith and beware of any failing. Do you accept?'

"I answered, 'Yes,' and the visitant was gone, and I was shivering with cold. I groped my way back to my fire, bumping into obstructions I had not found in my journey away from it. I piled on wood with a generous hand, and the flames leaped high. I watched the unaccountable shadows dance on the whitewashed walls, and marked how firebeams flickered across the warpings of the boards in the floor. Then I dozed off.

"I do not know how long I had been asleep when I felt the presence of the visitant again. The still reproach of his fixed eyes was worse than wrath. 'I need your help more than you can know,' he said, 'and you would fail me. The treasure is mine to give. I paid for it with the substance of my soul. I want you to have it. With it you can balance somewhat the burden of guilt I carry for its sake.'

"Again we made the journey to the spot where the treasure was buried, and this time he showed it to me. There were yellow coins, jeweled watches, women's bracelets, diamond rings, and strings of pearls. It was just such a trove as I had dreamed of when as a boy I had planned to dig for Lafitte's treasure, except that the quantity of it was greater. With the admonition, 'Do not force me to come again,' my companion was gone, and once more I made my way back to the fire.

"This time I took up my saddle and blanket and went out to the company of my horse. The wind and the waves were wailing together, but I thought I saw a promise of light across the chilly bay, and never was the prospect of dawn more welcome. As I saddled up and rode off, the doleful boom of the muddy water at the foot of the bluff came to me like an echoed anguish."

But Lafitte does not appear to every one who spends a night in the house, and any person seeking the treasure from purely selfish motives is likely to rue his pains. A story is told of an acquisitive and enterprising man who came hundreds of miles with the purpose of helping himself to the chance of finding pirate gold, but who abruptly changed his mind after spending a night in the house. As Lafitte steadily pursues his object of finding a fit recipient for his dangerous gift, never succeeding, his disappointment is sometimes terrible, so they say, and some simple folk believe that when there is a particularly dolorous moan in the wash of the waves, it is the despair of the pirate finding voice in the wail of the waters.

Lafitte:
Privateer, Pirate, and Terror of the Gulf of Mexico (1780–1826)

by Charles H. L. Johnston (1877–1943)

from *Famous Privateersmen and Adventurers of the Sea*

Charles H.L. Johnston wrote a handful of juvenile adventure books in the early 1900's. Here he gives a rousing and colorful account of Jean Lafitte, the New Orleans blacksmith-turned-pirate who was a major smuggler in the Gulf of Mexico during the early 19th century.

"He was the mildest mannered man,
That ever scuttled ship or cut a throat;
With such true breeding of a gentleman,
That you could ne'er discern his proper thought.
Pity he loved an adventurous life's variety,
He was *so* great a loss to good society."
                                        —*Old Ballad.*—1810.

"Captain, we can't live much longer unless we have food. We've got enough to last us for two weeks' time, and then—if we do not get fresh provisions—we'll have to eat the sails."

The fellow who spoke was a rough-looking sea-dog, with a yellow face—parched and wrinkled by many years of exposure—a square figure; a red handkerchief tied about his black hair; a sash about his waist in which was stuck a brace of evil-barrelled pistols. He looked grimly at the big-boned man before him.

"Yes. You are right, as usual, Gascon. We've got to strike a foreign sail before the week is out, and capture her. And I, Lafitte, must turn from privateer to pirate. May my good mother at St. Malo have mercy on my soul."

And, so saying, he turned to pace restlessly upon the sloping deck of the two-hundred-ton barque which boiled along under a spread of bellying canvas, and was guided by the keen eye of this youthful mariner. He came from the same little town in France which sheltered the good mother of Du Guay Trouin, the great French "blue." His name was Jean Lafitte.

This sea-rover had been born in 1781, and had taken to the ocean at the age of thirteen, when most boys are going to boarding-school. After several voyages in Europe, and to the coast of Africa, he was appointed mate of a French East Indiaman, bound to Madras in India. But things did not go any too well with the sturdy ship; a heavy gale struck her off the Cape of Good Hope; she sprung her mainmast, and—flopping along like a huge sea-turtle—staggered into the port of St. Thomas in the island of Mauritius, off the east coast of Africa.

"Here," said young Lafitte to his Captain, "is where I leave you, for you are a bully, a braggart, and a knave."

And, so saying, he cut for shore in the jolly-boat, but—if the truth must be known—Lafitte and the Captain were too much alike to get on together. They both wished to "be boss." Like magnets do not attract, but repel.

Luck was with the young deserter. Several privateers were being fitted out at the safe port of St. Thomas and he was appointed Captain of one of them. Letters of Marque were granted by the Governor of the Mauritius.

"Ah ha!" cried the youthful adventurer. "Now I can run things to suit myself. And I'll grow rich."

This he speedily succeeded in doing, for, in the course of his cruise, he robbed several vessels which came in his path, and, stopping at the Seychelles (Islands off the eastern coast of Africa), took on a load of slaves for the port of St. Thomas. Thus he had descended—not only to piracy—but also to slave catching; the lowest depths to which a seaman could come down.

When four days out from the curiously named islands, a cry went up from the watch,

"Sail ho! Off the port bow! A British frigate, by much that's good, and she's after us with all speed!"

To which bold Lafitte answered, "Then, we must run for it!" But he hoisted every bit of canvas which he had about and headed for the Bay of Bengal. "And," said he, "if she does not catch us and we get away, we'll take an English merchantman and burn her." Then he laughed satirically.

The British frigate plodded along after the lighter vessel of Lafitte's until the Equator was reached, and then she disappeared,—disgruntled at not being able to catch the saucy tartar. But the privateersman headed for the blue Bay of Bengal; there fell in with an English armed schooner with a numerous crew; and—although he only had two guns and twenty-six men aboard his own vessel—he tackled the sailors from the chilly isle like a terrier shaking a rat. There was a stiff little fight upon the shimmering waves of the Indian Ocean. When night descended the Britisher had struck and nineteen blood-stained ruffians from the privateer took possession of the battered hulk, singing a song which ran:

> For it's fourteen men on a dead man's chest,
> Yo-Ho-Ho- and a bottle of rum.

Lafitte was now feeling better; his men had been fed; he had good plunder; and he possessed two staunch, little craft.

"Let's bear away for India, my Hearties," cried he, "and we'll hit another Englishman and take her."

What he had said soon came to pass, for, when off the hazy, low-lying coast of Bengal, a rakish East Indiaman came lolling by, armed with twenty-six twelve-pounders and manned with one hundred and fifty men. A bright boarding upon her stern-posts flaunted the truly Eastern name: the *Pagoda.*

The dull-witted Britishers had no suspicions of the weak, Puritan-looking, little two-'undred tonner of Lafitte's, as she glided in close; luffed; and bobbed about, as a voice came:

"Sa-a-y! Want a pilot fer the Ganges?"

There was no reply for a while. Then a voice shrilled back,

"Come up on th' port quarter. That's just what we've been lookin' for."

The fat *Pagoda* ploughed listlessly onward, as the unsuspicious-looking pilot plodded up on the port side; in fact, most of the crew were dozing comfortably under awnings on the deck, when a shot rang out. Another and another followed, and, with a wild, ear-splitting whoop, the followers of Lafitte clambered across the rail; dirks in their mouths; pistols in their right hands, and cutlasses in their left.

Now was a short and bloodless fight. Taken completely by surprise, the Englishmen threw up their hands and gave in only too willingly. With smiles of satisfaction upon their faces, the seamen of the bad man from St. Malo soon hauled two kegs of spirits upon the decks, and held high revel upon the clean boarding of the rich and valuable prize. The *Pagoda* was re-christened *The Pride of St. Malo,* and soon went off privateering upon her own hook; while Lafitte headed back for St. Thomas: well-fed—even sleek with good living—and loaded down with the treasure which he had taken. "Ah-ha!" cried the black-haired navigator. "I am going to be King of the Indian waters."

Now came the most bloody and successful of his battles upon the broad highway of the gleaming, southern ocean.

Taking command of the *La Confidence* of twenty-six guns and two hundred and fifty men, whom he found at the port of St. Thomas, he again headed for the coast of British India; keen in the expectation of striking a valuable prize. And his expectations were well fulfilled.

In October, 1807, the welcome cry of "Sail Ho!" sounded from the forward watch, when off the Sand Heads, and there upon the starboard bow was a spot of white, which proved to be a Queen's East Indiaman, with a crew of near four hundred. She carried forty guns.

There were double the number of cannon, there were double the number of men, but Lafitte cried out:

"I came out to fight and I'm going to do it, comrades! You see before you a vessel which is stronger than our own, but, with courage and nerve, we can beat her. I will run our own ship close to the enemy. You must lie down behind the protecting sides of our vessel until we touch the stranger. Then—when I give the signal to board—let each man seize a cutlass, a dirk, and two pistols, and strike down all that oppose him. We *must* and *can* win!"

These stirring words were greeted by a wild and hilarious cheer.

Now, running upon the port tack, the *La Confidence* bore down upon the Britisher with the water boiling under her bows; while the stranger luffed, and prepared for action. Shrill cries sounded from her huge carcass as her guns were loaded and trained upon the oncoming foe, while her masts began to swarm with sharpshooters eager to pick off the ravenous sea-dogs from the Mauritius.

Suddenly a terrific roar sounded above the rattle of ropes and creak of hawsers—and a broadside cut into the *La Confidence* with keen accuracy.

"Lie flat upon the deck," cried Lafitte, "and dodge the iron boys if you can see 'em."

His men obeyed, and, as the missiles pounded into the broad sides of their ship, the steersman ran her afoul of the Queen's East Indiaman. When he did so, many sailors swarmed into the rigging, and from the yards and tops threw bombs and grenades into the forecastle of the enemy, so that death and terror made the Britishers abandon the portion of their vessel near the mizzen-mast.

"Forty of the crew will now board," cried Lafitte. "And let every mother's son strike home!"

With pistols in their hands and daggers held between their teeth, the wild sea-rovers rollicked across the gun-whales like a swarm of rats. Dancing up the deck of the Britisher they beat back all who opposed them, driving them below into the steerage. Shots rang out like spitting cats; dirks gleamed; and cutlasses did awful execution.

But the Captain of the Indiaman was rallying his men about him on the poop, and, with a wild cheer, these precipitated themselves upon the victorious privateers.

"Board! Board!" cried Lafitte, at this propitious moment, and, cutlass in hand, he leaped from his own vessel upon the deck of the East Indiaman. His crew followed with a yelp of defiant hatred, and beat the Captain's party back again upon the poop, where they stood stolidly, cursing at the rough sea-riders from St. Thomas.

But Lafitte was a general not to be outdone by such a show of force. He ordered a gun to be loaded with grape-shot; had it pointed towards the place where the crowd was assembled; and cried—

"If you don't give in now, I'll exterminate all of you at one discharge of my piece."

It was the last blow. Seeing that it was useless to continue the unequal struggle, the British Captain held up his long cutlass, to which was bound a white handkerchief, and the great sea battle was over. Lafitte and his terrible crew had captured a boat of double the size of his own, and with twice his numbers.

Says an old chronicler of the period: "This exploit, hitherto unparalleled, resounded through India, and the name of Lafitte became the terror of English commerce in these latitudes. The British vessels now traversed the Indian Ocean under strong convoys, in order to beat off this harpy of South Africa."

"Egad," said Lafitte about this time, "these fellows are too smart for me. I'll have to look for other pickings. I'm off for France."

So he doubled the Cape of Good Hope, coasted up the Gulf of Guinea, and, in the Bight of Benin, took two valuable prizes loaded down with gold dust, ivory, and palm oil. With these he ran to St. Malo, where the people said:

"Tenez! Here is a brave fellow, but would you care to have his reputation, Monsieur?" And they shook their heads, shrugged their shoulders, and looked the other way when they saw him coming.

The privateersman, slaver, and pirate was not going to be long with them, however, for he soon fitted out a brigantine, mounted twenty guns on her, and with one hundred and fifty men, sailed for Guadaloupe, among the West Indies. He took several valuable prizes, but, during his absence upon a cruise, the island was captured by the British, so he started for a more congenial clime. He roved about for some months, to settle at last at Barrataria, near New Orleans, Louisiana. He was rich; he had amassed great quantities of booty; and he was a man of property. Lafitte, in fact, was a potentate.

"Now," said the privateer and pirate, "I will settle down and found a colony."

But can a man of action keep still?

It is true that Lafitte was not as bold and audacious as before, for he was now obliged to have dealings with merchants of the United States and the West Indies who frequently owed him large sums of money, and the cautious transactions necessary to found and to conduct a colony of pirates and smugglers in the very teeth of civilization, made the black-haired Frenchman cloak his real character under a veneer of supposed gentility. Hundreds of privateers, pirates, and smugglers gathered around the banner of this robber of the high seas.

But what is Barrataria?

Part of the coast of Louisiana is called by that name: that part lying between Bastien Bay on the east, and the mouth of the wide river, or bayou of La Fourche, on the west. Not far from the rolling, sun-baked Atlantic are the lakes of Barrataria, connecting with one another by several large bayous and a great number of branches. In one of these is the Island of Barrataria, while this sweet-sounding name is also given to a large basin which extends the entire length of the cypress swamps, from the Gulf of Mexico, to a point three miles above New Orleans. The waters from this lake slowly empty into the Gulf by two passages through the Bayou Barrataria, between which lies an island called Grand Terre: six miles in length, and three in breadth, running parallel with the coast. To the West of this is the great pass of Barrataria, where is about nine to ten feet of water: enough to float the ordinary pirate or privateersman's vessel. Within this pass—about two miles from the open sea—lies the only safe harbor upon the coast, and this is where the cut-throats, pirates, and smugglers gathered under Lafitte. They called themselves *Barratar-ians,* and they were a godless crew.

At a place called Grand Terre, the privateers would often make public sale of their cargoes and prizes by auction. And the most respectable inhabitants of the State were accustomed to journey there in order to purchase the goods which the *Barratarians* had to offer. They would smile, and say,

"We are going to get some of the treasure of Captain Kidd."

But the Government of the United States did not take so kindly to the idea of a privateer and pirate colony within its borders. And—with malice aforethought—one Commodore Patterson was sent to disperse these marauders at Barrataria, who, confident of their strength and fighting ability, defiantly flaunted their flag in the faces of the officers of the Government. "We can lick the whole earth," chuckled the piratical followers of Lafitte.

Patterson was a good fighter. On June the eleventh he departed from New Orleans with seventy members of the 44th regiment of infantry. On the sixteenth he made for the Island of Barrataria, with some six gun-boats, a launch mounting one twelve pound carronade; the *Sea Horse* (a tender carrying one six-pounder) and the schooner *Carolina.*

"We must fight, Boys," cried Lafitte to his ill-assorted mates. "Come, take to our schooners and show these officers that the followers of Lafitte can battle like Trojans."

A cheer greeted these noble sentiments.

"Lead on!" yelled his cut-throats. "Lead on and we'll sink these cocky soldiers as we've done to many an East Indiaman!"

So, about two o'clock in the afternoon, the privateers and pirates formed their vessels, ten in number (including their prizes) near the entrance of the harbor.

Crash!

A shell from the forward gun of the leading gunboat spun across the bows of Lafitte's flagship and buried itself in the gray water with a dull sob.

Up went a huge white flag upon the foremost masthead of the king pirate and these words could be plainly seen:

"Pardon for all Deserters."

"Ah, ha," chuckled Patterson. "The arch ruffian has heard that some of my men are ashore and this is the way he would hire them."

Crash!

Another shell ricochetted across the still surface of the harbor and sunk itself in the side of a piratical brig.

"Hello!" cried a Lieutenant, running up to the United States Commander. "They're giving up already. See! The beggars are hastening ashore in order to skip into the woods."

"I'm afraid so," answered the disappointed Commodore. "All my pains for nothing. The fellows are getting away."

Sure enough—afraid to remain and fight it out—the craven followers of Lafitte now turned their schooners to the shore—ran their bows into the sand, and, leaping overboard, made into the forest as fast as their legs could carry them. Thus—without firing a shot—the cowardly pirates of Barrataria "took to the bush."

"The enemy had mounted on their vessels, twenty pieces of cannon of different calibre," wrote Patterson, after this tame affair. "And, as I have since learnt, they had from eight hundred to one thousand men of all nations and colors. When I perceived the pirates forming their vessels into a line of battle I felt confident, from their fleet and very advantageous position, and their number of men, that they would have fought me. Their not doing so I regret; for had they, I should have been enabled more effectually to destroy or make prisoners of them and their leaders; but it is a subject of great satisfaction to me, to have effected the object of my enterprise, without the loss of a man. On the afternoon of the 23rd, I got under way with my whole squadron, in all seventeen vessels, but during the night one escaped and the next day I arrived at New Orleans with my entire command."

Thus ended the magnificent (?) attempt of the vainglorious Lafitte to stem the advance of the Government of the United States. In the parlance of the camp, "He was a fust-class quitter."

But he did not show himself to be a "quitter" in the battle of New Orleans.

The English and Americans, in fact, were soon at each other's throats in the ungentle game of war. At different times the British had sought to attack the pirates of Barrataria, in the hope of taking their prizes and armed vessels. On June 23rd, 1813, while two of Lafitte's privateers were lying to off of Cat Island, an English sloop-of-war came to anchor at the entrance of the pass, and sent out two boats in the endeavor to capture the rakish sea-robbers. But they were repulsed with severe and galling loss.

On the 2nd of September, 1814, an armed brig appeared on the coast, opposite the famous pass to the home of the rangers of the sea. She fired a gun at a smuggler, about to enter, and forced her to poke her nose into a sand-bar; she then jibed over and came to anchor at the entrance to the shallows.

"That vessel means business, sure," said one of the pirates to Lafitte. "She has spouted one gun, but now she's lyin' to. Better see what's up."

"You're right," answered the famous sea-rover. "We'll go off in a boat and look out for what's going to happen."

So, starting from the shore, he was soon on his way to the brig, from which a pinnace was lowered, in which could be seen two officers, one of whom had a flag of truce. The two boats rapidly neared each other.

"Where is Mr. Lafitte?" cried one of the Britishers, as the pinnace neared the shore. "I would speak with the Laird of Barrataria."

But Lafitte was not anxious to make himself known.

"He's ashore," said he. "But, if you have communications for him, these I can deliver."

"Pray, give him these packages, my good man," spoke the English tar, handing him a bundle of letters, tied up in tarpaulin.

Lafitte smiled.

"I would be delighted to do so," he replied. "But, pray come ashore and there I will return you your answer after I have seen the great Captain, who is camping about a league inland."

The Britishers readily assented, and both rowed towards the sandy beach, where a great number of pirates of Barrataria had collected.

As soon as the boats were in shallow water, Lafitte made himself known to the English, saying:

"Do not let my men know upon what business you come, for it will go ill with you. My followers know that war is now on between Great Britain and the United States, and, if they hear you are making overtures with me, they will wish to hang you."

It was as he had said. When the Englishmen landed, a great cry went up amongst the privateers, pirates and smugglers:

"Hang the spies! Kill the dirty dogs! To the yardarm with the rascally Englishmen! Send the hounds to New Orleans and to jail!"

But Lafitte dissuaded the multitude from their intent and led the officers in safety to his dwelling, where he opened the package, finding a proclamation addressed to the inhabitants of Louisiana, by Col. Edward Nichalls—British commander of the land forces in this state— requesting them to come under the sheltering arm of the British Government. There were also two letters to himself, asking him to join and fight with the English.

"If you will but battle with us," said Captain Lockyer—one of the British officers—"we will give you command of a forty-four gun frigate, and will make you a Post Captain. You will also receive thirty thousand dollars,—payable at Pensacola."

Lafitte looked dubiously at him.

"I will give answer in a few days," he replied, with courtesy.

"You are a Frenchman," continued the British Captain. "You are not in the service of the United States, nor likely to be. Come—man—give us a reply at once."

Captain Lafitte was obdurate, for—strange as it may seem—he wished to inform the officers of the State Government of this project of the English. So he withdrew to his own hut.

As he did this, the pirates seized the British officers, dragged them to a cabin, and thrust them inside. A guard was stationed at the door, while cries went up from every quarter:

"To New Orleans with the scoundrels! A yard-arm for the butchers! A rope's end for the scurvy tars!"

Lafitte was furious when he learned of this, and, after haranguing the crowd, had the Britishers released.

"If you treat men under a flag of truce as prisoners," he cried, "you break one of the first rules of warfare. You will get the same treatment if you, yourselves, are captured, and you will lose the opportunity of discovering what are the projects of the British upon Louisiana."

His men saw the good sense of these words of advice, and acted accordingly.

Early the next morning the officers were escorted to their pinnace with many apologies from Lafitte, who now wrote a letter to Captain Lockyer, which shows him to have been a man of considerable cultivation, and not a mere "rough and tumble" pirate—without education or refinement. He said:

> Barrataria, 4th Sept., 1814.
>
> To CAPTAIN LOCKYER,
>
> SIR:—The confusion which prevailed in our camp yesterday and this morning, and of which you have a complete knowledge, has prevented me from answering in a precise manner to the object of your mission; nor even at this moment can I give you all the satisfaction that you desire. However, if you could grant me a fortnight, I would be entirely at your disposal at the end of that time.
>
> This delay is indispensable to enable me to put my affairs in order. You may communicate with me by sending a boat to the Eastern point of the pass, where I will be found. You have inspired me with more confidence than the Admiral—your superior officer—could have done, himself. With you alone I wish to deal, and from you, also, I will claim in due time, the reward of the services which I may render you.
>
> Your very respectful servant,
>
> J. Lafitte.

His object in writing this letter—you see—was, by appearing to accede to the proposals, to give time to communicate the affair to the officers of the State Government of Louisiana and to receive from them instructions how to act, under circumstances so critical and important to his own country: that is, the country of his adoption.

He, therefore, addressed the following epistle to the Governor of Louisiana. Do you think that you, yourself, could write as well as did this pirate?

Barrataria, Sept. 4th, 1814.

To GOVERNOR CLAIBORNE:

SIR:—In the firm persuasion that the choice made of you to fill the office of first magistrate of this State, was dictated by the esteem of your fellow citizens, and was conferred on merit, I confidently address you on an affair on which may depend the safety of this country.

I offer to you to restore to this State several citizens, who perhaps, in your eyes, have lost that sacred title. I offer you them, however, such as you could wish to find them, ready to exert their utmost efforts in the defence of the country.

This point of Louisiana, which I occupy, is of great importance in the present crisis. I tender my services to defend it; and the only reward I ask is that a stop be put to the proscription against me and my adherents, by an act of oblivion, for all that has been done heretofore.

I am the stray sheep wishing to return to the fold.

If you are thoroughly acquainted with the nature of my offences, I should appear to you much less guilty, and still worthy to discharge the duties of a good citizen. I have never sailed under any flag but the republic of Carthagena, and my vessels were perfectly regular in that respect.

If I could have brought my lawful prizes into the ports of this State, I should not have employed illicit means that have caused me to be proscribed (hounded by the State authorities).

I decline to say more upon this subject until I have your Excellency's answer, which I am persuaded can be dictated only by wisdom. Should your answer not be favorable to my ardent desire, I declare to you that I will instantly leave the country, to avoid the imputation of having cooperated towards an invasion on this point, which cannot fail to take place, and to rest secure in the acquittal of my conscience.

I have the honor to be,

Your Excellency's Most Humble Servant.

J. LAFITTE.

Now how is that for a swashbuckling privateer? Anyone would be proud of such a letter and it does honor to the judgment of this sand-spit king, giving clear evidence of a strange but sincere attachment to the American cause. Hurrah for the Frenchman!

This missive, in fact, made such an impression upon the Governor that he had an interview with Lafitte, who was ushered into his presence only to find General Andrew Jackson (Old Hickory) closeted with the chief executive.

"My dear sir," said the effusive Governor. "Your praiseworthy wishes shall be laid before the council of the State, and I will confer with my august friend, here present, upon this important affair, and send you an answer."

Bowing low, the courteous privateersman withdrew.

"Farewell," cried Old Hickory after his retreating form. "When we meet again I trust that it will be in the ranks of the American Army."

And in two days' time appeared the following proclamation:

"The Governor of Louisiana, informed that many individuals implicated in the offences hitherto committed against the United States at Barrataria, express a willingness at the present crisis to enroll themselves and march against the enemy.

"He does hereby invite them to join the standard of the United States, and is authorized to say, should their conduct in the field meet the approbation of the Major General, that that officer will unite with the Governor in a request to the President of the United States, to extend to each and every individual, so marching and acting, a free and full pardon."

When Lafitte saw these words, he fairly yelled with delight, and it is said that he jumped into the air, cracking his heels three times together before he struck the ground.

The orders were circulated among his followers and most of them readily embraced the pardon which they held out. Thus—in a few days—many brave men and skillful artillerists flocked to the red-white-and-blue standard of the United States. And when—a few months afterwards—Old Hickory and his men were crouched behind a line of cotton bales, awaiting the attack of a British army (heroes, in fact, of Sargossa), there, upon the left flank, was the sand-spit King and his evil crew. Lafitte's eyes were sparkling like an electric bulb, and the language of his followers does not bear repetition.

It was the morning of January eighth. The British were about to attack the American Army defending New Orleans, which—under the leadership of stout Andrew Jackson—now crouched behind the earthworks and cotton bales, some miles from the city. Rockets shot into the air with a sizzling snap. The roar of cannon shook the thin palmettos, and wild British cheers came from the lusty throats of the British veterans of Spain, as they advanced to the assault in close order—sixty men in front—with fascines and ladders for scaling the defences. Now a veritable storm of rockets hissed and sizzed into the American lines, while a light battery of artillery pom-pomed and growled upon the left flank. All was silence in the dun-colored embankments.

But look! Suddenly a sheet of flame burst from the earthworks where lay the buck-skin-clad rangers from Tennessee and Kentucky: men who had fought Indians; had cleared the forest for their rude log huts, and were able to hit the eye of a squirrel at one hundred yards. *Crash! Crash! Crash!* A flame of fire burst through the pall of sulphurous smoke, a storm of leaden missiles swept into the red coats of the advancing

British, and down they fell in wind-rows, like wheat before the reaper. *Boom! Boom! Boom!* The cannon growled and spat from the cotton hales, and one of these—a twenty-four pounder—placed upon the third embrasure from the river, from the fatal skill and activity with which it was managed (even in the best of battle),—drew the admiration of both Americans and British. It became one of the points most dreaded by the advancing foe. *Boom! Boom!* It grumbled and roared its thunder, while Lafitte and his corsairs of Barrataria rammed home the iron charges, and—stripped to the waist—fought like wolves at bay.

Two other batteries were manned by the Barratarians, who served their pieces with the steadiness and precision of veteran gunners. The enemy crept closer, ever closer, and a column pushed forward between the levee and the river so precipitously that the outposts were forced to retire, closely pressed by the coats of red. On, on, they came, and, clearing the ditch before the earthworks, gained the redoubt through the embrasures, leaped over the parapet and quickly bayonetted the small force of backwoodsmen who held this point.

"To the rescue, men," cried Lafitte, at this juncture. "Out and at 'em!"

Cutlass in hand, the privateer called a few of his best followers to his side; men who had often boarded the decks of an East Indiaman and were well used to hand-to-hand engagements. With a wild cheer they leaped over the breastworks and rushed upon the enemy.

The British were absolutely astonished at the intrepidity of this advance. Pistols spat, cutlasses swung, and one after another, the English officers fell before the snapping blade of the King of Barrataria, as they bravely cheered on their men. The practiced boarders struck the red-coated columns with the same fierceness with which they had often bounded upon the deck of an enemy, and cheer after cheer welled above the rattle of arms as the advancing guardsmen were beaten back. All the energies of the British were concentrated upon scaling the breastworks, which one daring officer had already mounted. But Lafitte and his followers, seconding a gallant band of volunteer riflemen, formed a phalanx which it was impossible to penetrate. They fought desperately.

It was now late in the day. The field was strewn with the dead and dying. Still spat the unerring rifles of the pioneers and still crashed the unswerving volleys from their practiced rifles. "We cannot take the works," cried the British. "We must give up." And—turning about—they beat a sad and solemn retreat to their vessels. The great battle of New Orleans was over, and Lafitte had done a Trojan's share.

In a few days peace was declared between the United States and Great Britain, and General Jackson—in his correspondence with the Secretary of War—did not fail to speak in the most flattering terms of the conduct of the "Corsairs of Barrataria." They had fought like tigers, and they had been sadly misjudged by the English, who wished to enlist them in their own cause. Their zeal, their courage, and their skill, were noticed by the whole American Army, who could no longer stigmatize such desperate fighters as "criminals." Many had been sabred and wounded in defence of New Orleans, and many had given up their lives before the sluggish bayous of the Mississippi. And now, Mr. Lafitte, it is high time that you led a decent life, for are you not a hero?

But "murder will out," and once a privateer always a privateer,—and sometimes a pirate.

Securing some fast sailing vessels, the King of Barrataria sailed to Galveston Bay, in 1819, where he received a commission from General Long as a "privateer." Not content with living an honest and peaceful life, he proceeded to do a little smuggling and illicit trading upon his own account, so it was not long before a United States cruiser was at anchor off the port to watch his movements. He was now Governor of Galveston, and considered himself to be a personage of great moment. Five vessels were generally cruising under his orders, while three hundred men obeyed his word. Texas was then a Republic.

Sir—[wrote Lafitte to the Commander of the American cruiser off the port of Galveston] I am convinced that you are a cruiser of the navy, ordered here by your Government. I have, therefore, deemed it proper to inquire into the cause of your lying before this port without communicating your intention. I wish to inform you that the port of Galveston belongs to and is in the possession of the Republic of Texas, and was made a port of entry the 9th day of October, last. And, whereas the Supreme Congress of the said Republic have thought proper to appoint me as Governor of this place, in consequence of which, if you have any demands on said Government, you will please to send an officer with such demands, who will be treated with the greatest politeness. But, if you are ordered, or should attempt, to enter this port in a hostile manner, my oath and duty to the Government compel me to rebut your intentions at the expense of my life.

Yours very respectfully,

J. Lafitte.

But to this the American officer paid no attention. Instead, he attacked a band of Lafitte's followers, who had stationed themselves on an island near Barrataria with several cannon,—swearing that they would perish rather than surrender to any man. As they had committed piracy,—they were open to assault. Twenty were taken, tried at New Orleans, and hung,—the rest escaped into the cypress swamps, where it was impossible to arrest them.

When Lafitte heard of this, he said with much feeling:

"A war of extermination is to be waged against me. I, who have fought and bled for the United States. I who helped them to win the battle of New Orleans. My cruisers are to be swept from the sea. I must turn from Governor of Galveston, and privateer to pirate. Then— away—and let them catch me if they can."

Now comes the last phase of his career. Too bad that he could not have died honestly!

Procuring a large and fast-sailing brigantine, mounting sixteen guns, and having selected a crew of one hundred and sixty men, the desperate and dangerous Governor of Galveston set sail upon the sparkling waters of the Gulf, determined to rob all nations and neither to give quarter nor to receive it.

But luck was against him. A British sloop-of-war was cruising in the Mexican Gulf, and, hearing that Lafitte, himself, was at sea, kept a sharp lookout at the masthead for the sails of the pirate.

One morning as an officer was sweeping the horizon with his glass he discovered a long, dark-looking vessel, low in the water: her sails as white as snow.

"Sail off the port bow," cried he. "It's the Pirate, or else I'm a land-lubber."

As the sloop-of-war could out-sail the corsair, before the wind, she set her studding-sails and crowded every inch of canvas in chase. Lafitte soon ascertained the character of his pursuer, and, ordering the awnings to be furled, set his big square-sail and shot rapidly through the water. But the breeze freshened and the sloop-of-war rapidly overhauled the scudding brigantine. In an hour's time she was within hailing distance and Lafitte was in a fight for his very life.

Crash!

A cannon belched from the stern of the pirate and a ball came dangerously near the bow-sprit of the Englishman.

Crash! Crash!

Other guns roared out their challenge and the iron fairly hailed upon the decks of the sloop-of-war; killing and wounding many of the crew. But—silently and surely—she kept on until within twenty yards of the racing outlaw.

Now was a deafening roar. A broadside howled above the dancing spray—it rumbled from the portholes of the Englishman—cutting the fore-mast of the pirate in two; severing the jaws of the main-gaff; and sending great clods of rigging to the deck. Ten followers of Lafitte fell prostrate, but the great Frenchman was uninjured.

A crash, a rattle, a rush, and the Englishman ran afoul of the foe—while—with a wild cheer, her sailors clambered across the starboard rails; cutlasses in the right hand, pistols in the left, dirks between their teeth.

"Never give in, men!" cried the King of Barrataria. "You are now with Lafitte, who, as you have learned, does not know how to surrender."

But the Britishers were in far superior numbers. Backwards—ever backwards—they drove the desperate crew of the pirate ship. Two pistol balls struck Lafitte in the side which knocked him to the planking; a grape-shot broke the bone of his right leg; he was desperate, dying, and fighting like a tiger. He groaned in the agony of despair.

The deck was slippery with blood as the Captain of the boarders rushed upon the prostrate corsair to put him forever out of his way. While he aimed a blow a musket struck him in the temple, stretching him beside the bleeding Lafitte, who, raising himself upon one elbow, thrust a dagger at the throat of his assailant.

But the tide of his existence was ebbing like a torrent; his brain was giddy; his aim faltered; the point of the weapon descended upon the right thigh of the bleeding Englishman. Again the reeking steel was upheld; again the weakened French sea-dog plunged a stroke at this half-fainting assailant.

The dizziness of death spread over the sight of the Monarch of the Gulf of Mexico. Down came the dagger into the left thigh of the Captain; listlessly; helplessly; aimlessly; and Lafitte—the robber of St. Malo—fell lifeless upon the rocking deck. His spirit went out amidst the hoarse and hollow cheers of the victorious Jack-tars of the clinging sloop-of-war.

> The palmetto leaves are whispering, while the gentle trade-winds blow,
> And the soothing, Southern zephyrs, are sighing soft and low,
> As a silvery moonlight glistens, and the droning fire-flies glow,
> Comes a voice from out the Cypress,
> 'Lights out! Lafitte! Heave ho!'

Sea Horror:
Blackbeard

by Arthur M. Harris
from *Pirate Tales from the Law*

By most accounts, Edward Teach—known as Blackbeard the Pirate—was a ruthless and wicked man. In this account published in 1923 we learn about his unlikely partnership with Stede Bonnet, a wealthy and respected merchant who—legend claims—turned to piracy to escape his shrewish wife.

I f you want to know a real pirate—a true terror of the seas—meet Mr. Blackbeard; called, in what could scarcely have been an innocent childhood, Edward Thatch, or Teach. Little Edward must have been suckled on brass filings and have cut his teeth on iron hails, for he grew up to be consistently and completely evil. Perhaps he fell when an infant and injured his head, or more probably was born with a twist to the bad; for no sane, normal man could have been so wild and wicked.

He, not Kidd, is the fellow you have in mind when you think of a pirate. He was the genuine, plank-walking, marooning, swashbuckling boy of the seven seas; Bill Kidd and Jack Quelch, so far from being in his class, would barely have been tolerated by him as ordinary seamen under the "black flagg with a humane skelleton" which terrified the old-time mariners. To win his yellow-fanged grin of approval one would have to be absolutely, unreservedly inhuman.

Blackbeard! Folks got along with him best who addressed him with that pretty name. He had no use at all for "Mister Thatch." Plain Blackbeard to high and low, fore and aft; for his pride, his pleasure, his life were in his beard; an enormous bush, unusually, weirdly, wonderfully black; a huge mat of hair, really beginning at his ears, arching across his nose, and ending with his knees,—a regular jungle from behind which his veined and boozy eyes peeped like those of a beast spotting its prey, the while the long, leathery lips slavered with the thirst for blood. Nice-looking chap—very.

He might not take time to wash his nose—the only island of skin in that sea of hair—but no hour was too long or too tedious which was spent in curling, preening, pulling and twisting that beard into the most fantastic shapes and effects. One day he would swagger out on deck with his chin the axle for a half-dozen spokes of tightly rolled whiskers; another, it might be one great spike, thrust outward and upward in a unicorn symbol. Practically he had a fashion for every mood, especially for the belligerent.

People had to keep out of his cabin when the skipper was trimming up his beard for a fight. Really he was the first patentee of frightfulness. That was his specialty. When action threatened, those whiskers were wrought into an appearance of ferocity beyond depicting.

Nor was that all; he had other artistic touches in the nightmare line. For instance, there were those long, thin, slow-burning matches which he stuck all around his head, beneath his hat—alight they looked as if the inferno had vomited forth a demon; there were the three braces of pistols over his shoulders; the two dirks in his brilliant Caribbean sash, and the cutlass that never stammered. A gulp of raw Jamaica rum and he was ready to eat 'em alive.

How amiable an apparition to behold oozing up over your bulwarks some fine morning! No wonder the Altantic, where it slaps the West Indian beaches on the one side and the shores of the Carolinas on the other, whispered his name with fear.

It was going to be a big job for the forces of law and order to snare this bird.

January, 1718, was the happy month for the Carolinas. Then it was that Blackbeard, coming from the West Indies by way of New England and the North Atlantic provinces, chose to make his hole at Ocracoke Inlet, on Pamlico Sound, North Carolina.

Not that Blackbeard came with his hat-matches lit and his beard glorious for strife, and his cutlass speaking sudden, certain death. Oh, my, no! Far indeed would this supposition be from the fact, for Blackbeard had come to Carolina to turn over a new leaf; to leave the wicked practices which had made him king of the wicked Indies; to forswear the black flag; generally to amend his way; particularly to take the Act.

"Taking the Act" was a joke beloved by all the best pirates. It was specially good after a profitable plunder cruise; useful, too, in a way, for it gave one a chance to spend one's salt-water money without having to fight somebody every five minutes. To take the Act was the only way a hard-working pirate could get a vacation.

The thing worked something like this: George the First, of England, at about this time was having trouble with the Swedes, and in consequence the British fleet was all tucked away up in the Baltic; he was troubled, too, by the merchants of London and the colonies, who were getting rather pert about this matter of pirate depredations.

Being completely at sea in more ways than one, the British Admiralty fell back to the old pardon business that they had tried in Captain Kidd's time, and which had been so successful that less than twenty years later the sorry scheme was dragged forth again.

Taking the technical peelings off, the meat of the matter was that if within a year from the date of the proclamation any pirate should surrender himself to any one of the king's colonial governors and swear to renounce his criminal courses, all the past should be forgiven and forgotten. The weakness of the plan, of course, was that a man you could not catch would not care much about your pardon. And still another,—that the word of a pirate could poorly compare with a bond.

But the boys liked this Act of Grace as it was called, and some had even been known to abide quite consistently with its terms. The leading men of the business, of course, could not be expected to take it too seriously.

Blackbeard wanted a little lay-off from years of steady grind. Then, too, it was January, with its season of new resolutions; why not start the year right?

They all talked it over, coming along the Virginia coast—near where they had heard of the proclamation—and it rather appealed to everybody. They grew solemn, serious, not a little drunk, and decided to break up. Here was a chance to wipe the slate clean and start all over again.

They anchored in Ocracoke Inlet and marched off to take the Act. Let us go with them.

Lithe chaps, aren't they? See how the muscles ripple and play under those bright silk shirts; how column-like the brown necks groove into the bulging shoulders; in the fine, perfect pink of condition every one; strong, you can easily see; strong everywhere, that is, except in the head. Weak, there, lamentably weak.

In the heart, too, for they are really bad, capable of all evil, for which their environment and early associations can extenuate but not exculpate them. In truth, these are the creatures of a dark age; these men believe in witches and fear to whistle aboard ship lest they blow up a tempest. Most of these fellows are Englishmen, with some Spaniards and Frenchmen, all caring little for international animosities, enfranchised in the Commonwealth of Crime. You can hear the outlandish burring of the Yorkshiremen, the hissing z's of the West Englander, the pitch, too, of what is to become the Cockney whine of a little later day, tussling with a jargon made up of many languages, founded on English.

Notice, too, these negroes from Barbados and other islands of the Indies, children of slaves brought but lately from Africa for the plantations. These don't rate as seamen on even the pirate ships, but are menials whose big job is to keep continually at the pumps. Still, it seems all a great lark to them; see how they laugh, joke, leap around in unequalled vigor, till the great gold rings in their ears, the gold chains about their necks and the heavy metal bangles on their wrists jingle and rattle with their motions. This thing of jewelry is affected by white and black alike; and how they like those wide, many-hued sashes, and the silk stockings under their knee-length breeches!

So they roll, seaman fashion, singing and romping to the small frame house where reigns the servant of the Proprietors and the master of the colonists, his Excellency, Governor Eden. At their head goes that strangest of all the strange creatures of the sea, that powerful, apelike figure swathed hideously in hair—to-day all curled in hundreds of ringlets smeared with pomatum—looking like a thing from a bad dream.

They bulge unafraid into the mansion; full weaponed and together, they fear nothing at sea or ashore. But nobody is of a mind to trifle with them; the folk here are used to seeing everything that is grotesque washed up by the sea; nay, these men have many acquaintances among the inhabitants, for not a few have shipped from these parts.

Governor Eden enters, portly in a London flowered-silk waistcoat, stylish French shoes and peruke, high-pointed and white-powdered. He gasps a little at the gang jammed into the room and glances sharply over at Tobias Knight, Secretary of the Province, who a moment ago was scratching with his quill pen an encouraging story of graft to the Proprietors at home, but who now is nervously pulling his sword more accessibly across his round fat knees. Neither he nor the governor had even seen anything quite like that in old Pall Mall, you know.

"Takin' the Act, y'honor," growled Blackbeard, leering at constituted authority.

"Aye," chorus, froglike, his bully boys.

The job is soon done. With upraised right hands one and all swear to leave off piracy. They come in children of the rope; they depart free and law-abiding men. It is very easy.

All leave, that is, save Blackbeard.

"I salvages ships, your honors," thunders this gentleman, spreading himself out on a chair so that his beard should flow in its glory like a blanket over his person, while all its fancy little curly-cues, ringlets and twists dance with every movement of his chin. "My real trade, your honors—ship salvager. Mebbe I'll have business here. Lost ships is what I go for and lost ships I finds.

"No need for a good ship to be lost while Blackbeard's around to take 'em home again. No occasion to leave a lost ship to drift around till them dirty seadogs of pirates mauls 'em over. Law says lost ships must be reported to the governor, and now I abide the law."

"How d'ye mean, Captain?" says the governor. "D'ye pull 'em off the rocks?"

The audience chamber—if it may be so called—shakes with the visitor's laughing.

"Ye don't know rocks, your honor, beggin' pardon; rocks don't let nothing go oncet they get aholt. Deserted ships I picks up; ships with a little water in 'em don't always go down as fast as the master fears.

"There's where I comes in. I get a ship like that; I comes in to you. Says I, 'Your honor, I have salvaged a ship.' Says your honor, 'Accordin' to law, I declares you to have salvage of her.' I sell her for a good price. Says I to me, 'The governor, his honor, works hard; he ought to have his wages.' Says I to you, 'Your honor will perhaps accept a little present.' 'Captain Blackbeard,' says you, 'have a jog of rum.' We all stands up and drinks the king's 'ealth."

Governor Eden claps his hands smartly, and the black servitor jumps in.

"Boy, bring the Madeira and glasses for three."

Governor Eden, in his corrupt connivance with Blackbeard, was not representative of the public opinion of the Carolinas in 1718. The proprietary provinces—for these things were shortly before the revolution which placed them directly under the Crown—had become tired of pirates.

It's a long story, but of powerful interest. The short of the matter is that the Carolinas had fostered pirates for her own interest until in time they became a menace. From the middle of the sixteen-hundreds the Southern provinces had been the outfitting grounds of a shoal of privateers who under royal commissions threshed the waters of the Spanish Main for Monsieur le Roy, as the French were called, or the Dons of Spain.

These letters-of-marque lads really protected the baby colonies from those two voracious wolves for quite a while, but naturally if business in the legitimate line of their letters slacked up, they were prone to mistake the ensign of St. George for that of the Fleur-de-lys, and thus kept their hands in practice by despoiling friends as well as foes. Far too often they crossed too easily the thin line which separated a privateer from a pirate, so that in something less than half a century Charles Town, which had trembled at the French and Spanish invasions, now was equally fearful of the guns of the erstwhile protectors, the pirates.

English navigation laws, which had delivered the provinces, bound hand and foot, into the hard fists of the English merchants, did not a little to promote piracy, for the sea robbers came to town with holds crammed full of all sorts of merchandise and peddled it to the colonists less the duties and imposts, and so made one of the cheapest markets in the world. Their customers all along the coast met them gladly and made no bones of the traffic, until the black flag threatened to monopolize the whole commerce, when the community awoke to the circumstance that there was a price in the cheap bazaar after all.

Consider that Blackbeard, a month or so before he took the Act of Grace, had "salvaged" no less than twenty-seven ships—nearly a ship a day—and you have a measure of the situation; add, too, this, that Blackbeard was but one of many, and you will understand why Jamaica, for instance, wailed to the home Government that it was ruined.

North and South Carolina had not formally divided at that time, though the distinction of names was used; Governor Eden ruled wickedly in the North; Governor Johnson ruled justly and wisely in the South.

The vicinity where Blackbeard made his establishment was well chosen for his job. When one knew the channels between the low, sandy islands which lay all about the inlet one could run in and careen the ship, lay by and swagger alongshore, and when one got ready to abjure his oath and swing off on the plundering account again, one could intercept two lines of commerce,—the coastwise from New England to the West Indies and the provinces, and that from the provinces to the north, to the West Indies and to the mother country. Blackbeard knew his business.

It should be explained that our whiskery hero was a sort of admiral, for he commanded not only his own ship, but he was attended by three auxiliary sloops, one of which—the *Revenge*—belonged to the peculiar and picturesque Major Stede Bonnet.

What did these ships look like? Well, the old British Navy had five classes of men-of-war, rated on the number of guns; Blackbeard's own ship, the attorney general on a later occasion said, was equal to a fifth-class man-of-war; that is, he mounted forty guns, ranged on two decks, carrying a complement of some one hundred and forty or fifty men when his articles were full. She was about twenty feet in the beam and a little more than a hundred feet long; rigged with square sails and capable of good speed.

The sloops, a general term for a variety of small ships, fought only ten guns, though the man-power was not proportionate, fifty or sixty men sometimes being crowded aboard. Shipbuilding was to wait generations for the start of the impetus which carried it to its culmination in the early nineteenth century.

Nobody knows just what turned Major Bonnet to pirating. Some say he had so much domestic misery that he simply felt he would have to chaw up something or somebody; others, that the works in his brains had slipped a little out of gear.

It could hardly have been money, for Bonnet was a well-to-do planter of Barbados, where his civic spirit had been so keen that he had earned the military title of major in service against the enemies of that colony. Perhaps he had been reading the *Diamond Dick* stories of that era, and was so fired by them as to forget his middle years, his decorous manners, his respectable standing, and craved for a taste of real life.

However that may have been, he bought a sloop, christened her romantically the *Revenge*, and, under the usual pretense of going privateering, picked up the right gang and put to sea in the late summer of 1717. He knew nothing about the sea except that under certain circumstances it would drown one.

His crew were quick to see that their commander was no sailorman. His pretense at seamanship provoked their great-mouthed grins and deriding whispers and nods. He was driven to hide behind his mate, who really worked the ship; and to the end of his career, which lasted just about one year, he employed usually a sailing master. But his courage, his hard temper, his resolution kept his feet on the quarter-deck and forced a respect that his landlubberliness denied him.

That is, he wrung a deference from all but old Blackbeard. Bonnet fell in with him in August, 1717, and they made it up to sail together.

The bearded bear, however, soon saw that his partner was no skipper, and, growling and contemptuous, he summarily removed Bonnet from his own deck and articled him in an inferior position on Blackbeard's craft, putting one Richards, a bad egg but a good sailor, in Bonnet's place. This was a collar that galled the neck of Bonnet.

All the ships came in to Ocracoke about the same time; but Bonnet and a large number of men disdained to palter with the Act of Grace, and lay about the settlement waiting for Blackbeard to get over his whim and down to business.

The days ashore passed in debauch. Here the softer side of Blackbeard's character is shown in his affectionate devotion to fourteen wives,—as he called them. With them he was most playful and kittenish.

He loved to make these ladies laugh by blowing out the candles with his pistols; or sometimes, crossing his arms, a weapon in each hand, he would fire promiscuously about the room, whereupon the most merry play of hide-and-seek was enjoyed by all the company, wives and visitors alike, when those who could not get under the table quickly enough would catch bullets in the funniest places,—like behind the ear or just above the heart. Everybody looked forward to these evenings.

Spring came on Ocracoke, and the adventure sap stirred in Blackbeard's veins. He stood it until the end of May, then tore his oath in two, kicked the Act of Grace in the face, flung the skull and crossbones to his masthead and sailed off for Charles Town, his minion sloops dancing and bobbing on the waves beside him. He was going shopping, if you please, for medical supplies, a great necessity by reason of his fleet's method of living and working. He was going to honor Charles Town with his patronage.

While this happy surprise for the little colonial seaport was coming around the sea-washed bulk of Cape Fear, a Mr. Wragg and a Mr. Marks, on board a merchantman, were slipping across the Charles Town bar, bound for England. Both were prominent local gentlemen, Mr. Wragg being nothing less than an assemblyman. There were several other passengers on the list, while in the ship's chest were seven thousand five hundred dollars in broad gold coins and pieces-of-eight.

Mr. Marks stood at the stern of the ship and looked a long time at the old town as it dropped away behind them.

"Neighbor Wragg," said he with a gently melancholic sigh, "it will be many a day before we tread the streets of Charles Town again."

Mr. Wragg squeezed his friend's hand sympathetically.

"Only a twelvemonth perhaps," he suggested. "Take courage, Marks."

They were both poor guessers. Instead of twelve months it was less than twelve days a good deal when Mr. Marks again looked his fellow citizens in the eye and face-to-face. If somebody had told his fortune at cards that night he might have truthfully said that a dark man was coming across the water to see him.

"Do you see what I see?" asked the captain of the mate next day, as the gray light of morning was turning all the waters to the look of molten slate. The mate gazed northward.

"I count four of 'em," he said slowly. "Looks like they're coming right for us."

They were. Very soon a shot whistled over the nightcap of Mr. Marks, who had thrust his head from his cabin with that sense of something amiss peculiar to shipboard.

"Heave back the tops'ls," growled the master.

The sails flatted down, and the ship came to. She was quickly circled by Blackbeard's fleet. The skull grinned amiably at them as the black flag stood out tautly in the wind. Somebody shouted something from the pirate ships; and the merchant captain ordered the boat lowered, and with two of the crew to row him set off for the marauding flagship.

"I've been pirated in these waters twenty times," grumbled the captain, steering with an oar, "so I know what they want."

The pirates wanted everything. They put a prize crew over on the captured brig. Mr. Marks was paged.

"Mistah Blackbeard's compliments, suh," grinned a big black fellow, looking coy in a hat made of a twisted red silk handkerchief, "and if you be Mistah Marks, suh, will you be so 'bliging as to step over to his ship."

Mr. Marks, with pallid face, looked pathetically at Mr. Wragg, whose sympathy was again subjected to a heavy sight draft.

"Why didn't he send for you, Wragg?" he complained unheroically. "You're a councilor—you've got the precedence."

Mr. Wragg patted him on the shoulder encouragingly.

"I'll advise your family, Marks, if anything happens," he said kindly; "but I'm sure it won't."

He felt pretty sure it would.

All stood in for Charles Town. Mr. Wragg once or twice thought he saw Mark's hand waving at him from Blackbeard's ship, where he and the merchant captain were detained. Or was it poor Mark's nightcap tossed in a dreadful struggle with the villains? Who could tell?

Captors and captives lay at the bar; and Blackbeard sent the long-boat off to town, carrying Mr. Marks under guard of Richards and half a dozen nasty rascals. The astonishment of the town was unwordable when it saw the respectable Marks in company so dreadful.

But when they heard what Mr. Marks had to tell them their astonishment turned to fighting wrath. For Blackbeard ordered four hundred pounds' worth of medical supplies delivered to Richards or, first, Mr. Marks would be shot on the spot; second, Mr. Wragg's head and those of all the other passengers would arrive by the next boat; third, the pride of the province, Charles Town itself, would be blown from its foundations.

Governor Johnson was a strong man, and his council were strong men; but here was a puzzle for them. Sixteen years before this they had beaten off the French invaders with a courage that is notable in the history of municipalities; but now the gun was right straight at them, and it looked like hands up.

Things were stirring about in Blackbeard's fleet as well as in the town. Especially when two days went by and no word came over to the bar from Richards or Marks. On the evening of that day, Blackbeard, steeped in rum, lined his hostages along the deck and raved and thrust his awful beard into their faces and generally behaved in a most ungenteel manner.

"Shake your heads, my pretty landlubbers," he bellowed; "shake 'em while they're on your necks, for if Richards don't come back in the mornin' your heads will go to town at noon."

The wretched part of it was that the ruffian meant what he said.

A messenger carne from Richards, however, in the morning, and so reprieved Mr. Wragg and his fellows for a few hours more. The messenger stated that in going from the bar to town the boat in which Marks was being taken capsized and there had been no end of trouble and delay in getting ashore. Further that the provincial council had been called together and were debating Blackbeard's proposition.

Another day or so of strain and another silence from the town. Again Blackbeard stamped about and waved his cutlass and carried on as any obstreperous and brutal drunk might be apt to do. Oh, for a king's ship to happen along as chucker-out! But king's ships, like the night watch, are generally anywhere but where they're needed.

Blackbeard filed the frightened hostages forth again. This time he had the machinery of their destruction ready,—a huge black, his great-muscled right arm bare to the shoulder, his hand hefting a bright cutlass. Blackbeard, perched on a keg of powder, beckoned to his captives in mocking solicitude.

"Step up, pretties," he leered, "and get your hair cut."

This was no opera, comic or otherwise. It was a situation to be met, and immediately. One whom history does not remember spoke up. "Cap'n Blackbeard," said he, talking for his life, "we've decided if you'll be so good as to let us, to join with you if you're going to take the town. We'll help you. They've betrayed us for a few pills and powders, so we owe them nothing."

"Spoke like a man," said Blackbeard. "You're proper men; you'll be real cocks of the old game. Heave the anchor and shot the guns— the tide will be right in an hour."

Perhaps this was not a heroic subterfuge; but let those judge who have been hostages, helpless in the hands of such a desperado. It saved the lives of a number of folk. For ere the tide lifted them over the bar the longboat returned with Richards, the pirate boatmen and great piles of all sorts of medicines. The town had capitulated. There would come another day, it properly figured, and its wisdom was justified by the event.

Blackbeard left the merchant brig and its passengers rocking at the bar, but by an unfortunate oversight he sailed off with the ship's chest containing the gold coins and the pieces-of-eight.

Partnership was dissolved soon after leaving Charles Town. Blackbeard had already apparently decided to abdicate the cocked hat of an admiral and assume the subordinate rank of a captain. He planned to concentrate his power in his one vessel.

So without concern he returned the dissatisfied Bonnet to the *Revenge* and recalled Richards and the hardiest members of the *Revenge*'s personnel, leaving Bonnet with half a dozen hands of indifferent expertness to work the sloop.

That accounted for one of his three tenders. The second he resolved to abandon at Topsail Inlet, on his way to Ocracoke. This he effected in the regular Blackbeard fashion by ordering it driven ashore at Topsail Inlet and wrecked. Her crew might make what escape they could from the mess. They could not argue with the forty muzzles of his guns, so crack went the sloop's hull upon the rocks, while Blackbeard lay by and laughed at the men struggling in the surf.

These unfortunates at once went to work saving the sloop's food and powder, which hard labor was no sooner ended than Blackbeard stood in and came ashore in the boat. He took all the salvaged stores and every first-class seaman among the men and left, leaving nearly a score of his late followers destitute and marooned on a wild and isolated beach. In this way Blackbeard paid for faithfulness.

The castaways had nothing to do but huddle about the sand and hope for help. It did not occur to them to go back into the wilderness behind them, perhaps because, as sailors, they would not trust themselves to any but their wonted environment, perhaps also for the reason that the unsettled interior promised them even scantier succor than the wide sea before them, on which a coastwise ship might possibly be attracted by their signals. So they lay around listening to the *creak-creak-creak* of the occasional sea gull, the thumping and swirling of the inrushing waves and the cracking of the ship's gear and planking.

Before serious privation befell them, however, the hoped-for sail fluttered out of the horizon. They took the shirts form their backs and hopped vehemently up and down the beach and flew to the headlands in a frenzy of inarticulate appeal.

Joy unspeakable; they saw the topsails heaved back and the ship come to! Saved! The men massed at the very edge of the water and stared hard at the boat which now put off and came swinging in toward them.

"If it ain't Major Bonnet!"

There was a kind of pleasure in the way they said this as the boat's crew could be identified. They had never expected that the commander of the old *Revenge* could ever have looked so good to them. A dozen welcoming hands pulled at the bow of his boat when it grated on the sand.

"A dirty deal, boys," said the major; "a dirty deal to leave ye all like this—all governors of a maroon island."

That was a loved witticism of the major; marooning with him was always to be invested with the dignity of governor of the maroon sandspit. He had quite a turn for pleasantry. He chuckled, and then got down to business.

"Getting to the point, my lads," he continued, "let us leave this outlaw life which has brought us nothing but grief. Come with me to St. Thomas in the Indies, and we'll get a privateering commission there against the Spanish dogs, and show 'em the kind of metal that is in a British cutlass."

He put a punch into his proposition by explaining, sympathetically but firmly, that if they refused his offer he would be quite obliged to sail away and leave them still in the governorship of Topsail Inlet.

Nobody wanted that distinction, and the marooned left in boatloads for Bonnet's ship. As they came under her bows they marked that the name *Revenge* had been painted out, and in its place were the words, *Royal James*, being the major's compliment to the Pretender and a vivid indication of the major's politics.

The tide crept in and washed the last heel mold out of the sands of Topsail Inlet, where the gulls were left to peck speculatively at the protruding nails and tangled cordage of the battered ship, the while they wondered at the ways of that queer creature, Man.

Commons were lean on the *Royal James*. When the rescued pirates found that there was not very much to eat on the ship, the first gush of joy at their deliverance sloughed off quickly.

"Ye see, men," Bonnet explained, "the pantry is pretty low. The first job of a sailorman is to eat, so we may have to stop somebody on our way to St. Thomas and beg a bite."

A very reasonable suggestion.

"Somebody" appeared before the cruise was very old. He showed no concern, however, to answer their hail but jammed up into the wind and sped away. That was certainly no proper sea courtesy.

To teach the rude fellows a lesson in manners, the *Royal James* swung behind and followed fast, and as pursuit was quite in her line she soon pulled down the fleeing traveler and with a shot across his bow brought him to with a bang. Bonnet shoved alongside and soon stuffed his hold and his men with quarters of beef and barrels of rum.

That was a fair start. All waist belts were comfortably tight; drooping corners of lips went up and the old zest for piracy swelled and rippled like a flood tide in the veins of the men of the *Royal James*. So when with a grin the captain sped the black flag up the lines the general contentment was not grievously shaken.

Two Bermuda-bound ships were pulled in the day following the first capture, and the day after that they picked up a fourth. The tally of takes now began to run up smartly. Inside of a week five ships were looted, from which a number of recruits were made, including negroes who were delegated to the pumps and the menial jobs with the status of slaves, and whose signs to the sloop's articles were not invited.

Here is a typical haul from one craft: Twenty-six hogsheads and three barrels of rum, valued at fifteen hundred dollars; twenty-five hogsheads of molasses, worth seven or eight hundred dollars; three barrels of sugar, value one hundred and fifty dollars; cotton, indigo, wire cable of varying values, a small amount of French and Spanish coins, one pair of silver buckles and one silver watch. Thus, you see, the boys cleaned up systematically from the hold to the captain's waistcoat pocket.

They peddled their merchandise alongshore, where the business, though more risky than in a happier day, was still keen. They grabbed vessels on the high seas or at anchor in way ports. One captured in the latter situation was the *Francis*, and here is her mate, Mr. Killing, who is anxious to tell us himself just how it all happened. Proceed, Mr. Killing.

The 31st of July (1718) between nine and ten of the clock, we came to an anchor about fourteen fathom of water. . . . In about half an hour's time I perceived something like a canoo: So they came nearer. I said, here is a canoo a-coming; I wish they be friends. I haled them and asked them whence they came? They said captain Thomas Richards from St. Thomas's. . . .

"They asked me from whence we came? I told them from Antegoa. They said we were welcome." (Pirates certainly loved their little joke!) "I said they were welcome, as far as I knew." (Which you observe was not very far. A man of careful statement, this Mr. Killing.) "So I ordered the men to hand down a rope to them. So soon as they came on board they clapped their hands to their cutlasses; and I said we are taken. So they cursed and swore for a light. I ordered our people to get a light as soon as possible. . . .

"When they came into the cabin the first thing they begun with was the pineapples, which they cut down with their cutlasses. They asked me if I would not come and eat along with them? I told them I had but little stomach to eat. They asked me why I looked so melancholy? I told them I looked as well as I could—" (Before we smile at the worthy mate let us wonder a moment how we would have looked in the same fix.)

"They asked me what liquor I had on board. I told them some rum and sugar. So they made bowls of punch and went to drinking the Pretender's health, and hoped to see him king of the English nation—" (This was doubtless the result of Major Bonnet's treasonable propaganda. Here was an incipient navy for the Pretender had he only known it.) "They then sung a song or two. The next morning . . . they hoisted out several hogsheads of molasses and several hogsheads of rum.

290 Arthur M. Harris

In the after part of the day two of Bonnet's men were ordered to the mast to be whipt. . . .

"Then Robert Tucker came to me, and told me I must go along with them. I told him I was not fit for their turn, neither were my inclinations that way. After that Major Bonnet himself came to me, and told me I must either go on a maroon shore" (no doubt with his usual little jest about the governorship) "or go along with them, for he designed to take the sloop *(Francis)* with him.

"That evening between eight and nine we were ordered to set sail, but whither I knew not. So we sailed out that night, and I being weary with fatigue, went to sleep; and whether it was with a design or not I can not tell, but we fell to leeward of the *Revenge (Royal James)*; and in the morning Major Bonnet took the speaking trumpet, and told us if we did not keep closer he would fire in upon us and sink us. So then we proceeded on our voyage till we came to Cape Fear.

Thank you, Mr. Mate; you have given us an interesting and living picture of just how these wretches went about their dirty work.

Cape Fear! When a "naval historian" tells us that the battle at Cape Fear was merely a matter of a few shots and a surrender, he not only understates the fact, but beclouds the due glory of a company of heroic men. Mr. S. C. Hughson, whose patient accuracy has given the complete story to the world, not only describes a serious engagement but shows that the result was so open a question that the pirates, during the fight, beckoned with their hats to their opponents in mock invitation to board and take them, in full confidence of victory.

Cape Fear is on Smith Island, at the mouth of the Cape Fear River, on the coast of North Carolina, and between Charleston and Ocracoke Inlet. At New Inlet, where the river swims into the sea, it divides what are now called Brunswick and Hanover Counties. Shoal waters and sandy islets make the work of navigation here uncertain.

Major Bonnet had made his sea-nest in this region, his knowledge of the channels and depths protecting his comings and goings. In this place he could repair and refit his ship as well as set up a sort of market for the purveying to the local folk his varied plunder. For the coastwise pirate, as distinguished from the pirate of the Kidd and Quelch school, was simply a smuggler who stole his wares, and if you hyphenate him thus, smuggler-pirate, you can separate him from the typical smuggler who acquires his contraband lawfully in a cheaper market to run it past the customs to a dearer market.

It was to Cape Fear, then, that Bonnet came in the beginning of August with his ship and two captive sloops, one of them being the *Francis*, and it was here that toward the end of the next month Justice presented her bill to him at the point of a cannon.

Colonel Rhett, of Charlestown, was the agent of Justice in this instance. Not long after Blackbeard had held up Charles Town for a quantity of pills and plasters, as we have noticed, another rascal tried the same trick but could not make it work. This fellow's name was Vane, sometimes called Vaughan, and quite a bad actor in his own way.

Of all the citizens who sharply resented these piratical impertinences, Colonel Rhett, a noted colonist, took it most to heart. On his own initiative he fitted out as sloops-of-war two ships, the *Henry*, on which he himself sailed, and the *Sea Nymph*, which he manned with many "gentlemen of the town, animated with the same principle of zeal and honor for our public safety, and the preservation of our trade."

Heartily seconded by Governor Johnson of South Carolina, who unlike Governor Eden of North Carolina was a terror to pirates, Rhett's little fleet put out in pursuit of Vane; for Vane, seeing that his plans had slipped, decided that he had better also slip. He slipped so effectively that Rhett never came up with him.

Since leaving Topsail Inlet with his recruits Bonnet had taken no less than thirteen vessels, and word of this pirate had come to Charles Town while Rhett was outfitting. Missing Vane, Rhett "and the rest of the gentlemen were resolved not to return without doing some service to their country, and therefore went in quest of a pirate they had heard lay at Cape Fear." There they certainly found their opportunity of doing a public service and most commendably appropriated that opportunity.

At evening on September 26 the *Henry* and the *Sea Nymph* came to Smith Island while daylight enough was left to show them the topmasts of the pirate above a spit of land behind which the *Royal James* lay. They threw their anchors into the mud of the inlet and waited for morning. At dusk three boatloads of armed men came out of the river and coolly reconnoitered. Major Bonnet had spotted Colonel Rhett.

All that night of late summer the Charles Town gentlemen could make out the threats and persuasions of Bonnet and his officers driving on the efforts of their crew in making ready for the morrow's deadly debate, which Bonnet, rather than surrendering, evidently chose to maintain. The tide brimmed up the river from the Atlantic and was sucked back again to those vast waters, yet it lulled no one to sleep on any of the ships.

All night the wind-blown torches and lanterns lit the work of the pirates; all night the glare of them flickered and jumped beyond the bump of land which separated the besiegers and the besieged. The pirate sloop was like a warrior unbuckled and relaxing in his tent, expecting no hostile surprise. Her deck was disorderly with bits of cargo; barrels of rum, quarters of beef, hogsheads of molasses, all to be cleared off for the free action of the guns. Her gear, too, was probably at odds and ends in course of repair.

The work of weeks had now to be punched up into the fleet hours of one night, for when the dawn should come the *Royal James* must be a warrior harnessed and prepared. All night the men of the *Henry* and the *Sea Nymph* lay at watch.

Sun-up began the day of fate. Beyond the headlands which sheer above the river, the east was bannered with yellow and purple and rose-pink; a strong breeze blew directly from the land. The sails of the *Royal James* went up with the sun, the blocks and tackle creaking like a flock of hungry gulls; the chains rattled with the hoisting of the anchor.

Bonnet had to fight two to one. His chance—and it was an approved method of pirate strategy—was to get to open water and battle on the run, broadsiding one or the other of his enemies but never permitting both to get at him at once.

The major had become quite a sailor now. He gathered all his men on the *Royal James* and left the two captured sloops with only Mr. Killing and the other prisoners on board of them. The refusal of these latter to aid him in his fight with Rhett was allowed to pass without punishment.

"Here they come!"

Beyond the hummock the Charles Town men could see the masts of the pirate, fully freighted with sail, running swiftly toward the point. Bonnet was making a break for the sea.

Rhett's ships quivered with action. As the *Royal James* thrust her bowsprit into sight, the *Henry* and the *Sea Nymph* crowded down on either of her quarters.

They made it in time; Bonnet, dodging, was elbowed into the shore. If the channel had been deep there, he might still have made it; but the channel was shallow, and his ship thudded into the sandy bottom, and there she lay, with her full suit of canvas tugging at the sticks until they promised to snap.

Rhett grinned and swung about, but he could not make it sharply enough, and his satisfaction waned with the bump of his ship into the same bottom that gripped his enemy. The *Sea Nymph,* also turning, likewise found herself hard and fast ashore.

Here then was the situation. The *Henry* was grounded on the pirate's bow within pistol shot; the *Sea Nymph* struck the sand out of range, and there she stayed for the greater part of the fight, a spectator of the struggle, unable to bear a part or give any help to the *Henry.*

And Rhett's flagship needed help. When she hit she slanted, but in the same direction as the pirate had tilted, with the result, of course, that she presented her unprotected deck squarely to Bonnet's broadsides, while the latter's position offered more of his hull and less of his deck to Rhett's ordnance.

For all of that, the South Carolinians gave the Barbados gentleman all their ten guns at once with a smart peppering of small-arm fire. Bonnet roared back with all of his pieces, smashing the *Henry*'s deckwork and reddening her scuppers. The Charles Town boys who stood by the guns on that open, inclined deck of that Saturday morning, never letting the fight flag for a moment, certainly passed the supreme physical test one hundred per cent, to the good.

But there was to be another deciding element of the contest than cannon balls, musketry or cutlasses. The tide, which was now turning and flooding in, would award the victory. For whichever ship righted herself first must have the critical advantage.

The opponents must have known this from the first, and, of course, the benefit of the tide being uncertain, each desperately strove to finish the other and thus leave no chance to the arbitrament of Nature. The mud flats disappeared beneath the oncoming waters; the lower islands sank from sight; the battling ships jerked now and then with the powerful tug of the stream at their hulls, and with the rising of the river crammed more shot into the hot guns till the smoke burned the eyelids of the fighters red, and ten good men lay in the shocked attitudes of death on the *Henry*'s decks, and eighteen wounded groaned in her hold. Seven of Bonnet's crew had signed on with the real skull-and-bones flag.

The tide came swirling in. High noon gave place to afternoon; the moment of decision was at hand. One or other of the ships would gain her keel in a few minutes. Which would it be?

It was the *Henry*. Bonnet, who had fought supremely, saw with vehement despair the yards of his enemy tilting up, while he himself lay in the sand inert and helpless. He rushed with his pistol cocked to the magazine of powder thus to make the grand finish, but his men threw themselves upon him to restrain his rash and horrible act, while one of them jumped in the shrouds and waved the white flag of the conquered.

Rhett boarded and chained up some thirty men, including their leader, and after repairing the *Henry* set out for home. The public service had been rendered—by the tide.

Charles Town went wild with excitement, though not exactly in the way they mean who keep this tired phrase in currency. When Rhett came in laden with pirate prisoners and convoying the *Royal James* and the two sloops captured by that ship, the *Fortune* and the *Francis*, he was the hero of one faction in town and the villain of the other.

Friends of piracy in general and the personal acquaintances of the enchained pirates in particular shared a common indignation. They must have been numerous, for they promised to liberate the prisoners or burn the city to the foundation blocks. Bonnet, as was fitting for a gentleman who happened to be a criminal, was locked up in the residence of the marshal, while the baser fellows were thrown into the watch-house, there being no jail in the town at that time.

The fashion of the port went out to look at the ships. The *Henry* was all knocked about, while the *Royal James*—whose name had been immediately changed back to *Revenge* by a proper patriotic gesture— had not much more than a chipped hull.

If the ships had not grounded as they did Bonnet would have been against overwhelming odds. The *Henry* had eight guns and seventy men; the *Sea Nymph* had the same number of cannon and sixty men. Bonnet fought with ten guns and about fifty men.

But the sticking of the ships had made his chance more even, for in that situation he commanded two more guns than did Rhett, and the latter's slight excess of men was more than canceled by the bad slant of his deck, with its consequent openness to the enemy's cannonade.

Before the trouble in town could blaze into tumult, the pirates were put to trial in the Vice-Admiralty Court, presided over by Judge Trott. Bonnet, however, did not stand among them; by bribing with a free palm he had escaped and was at that moment fleeing up the coast in a small boat, to the great scandal of all lovers of good government.

The trial was brief and characteristic of the times. The defendants, without counsel as was usual, feebly pleaded that Bonnet had deceived them at Topsail Inlet into sailing with him. Ignatius Pell, boatswain of the *Royal James*, turned state's evidence, and other witnesses were Mr. Killing, whom we have quoted, and the captain of the *Francis* and the captain of the *Fortune*.

There could not be a doubt of their guilt and in that age not a doubt of their fate; they were sentenced to be hanged by a judge who preached at and denounced them in the vigorous fashion of the Elizabethan courts. In less than one week all but three or four who had proved compulsory service were executed at old White Point, near the present beautiful promenade.

One cheerful ray lightened the black misery of their situation: Stede Bonnet was recaptured. "He was the great ringleader of them," said the prosecuting attorney, "who had seduced many poor, ignorant men to follow his course of living, and ruined many poor wretches; some of whom lately suffered, who with their last breath expressed a great satisfaction at the prisoner's (Bonnet) being apprehended, and charged the ruin of themselves and loss of their lives entirely upon him."

Colonel Rhett had again been the fate of Major Bonnet. After Bonnet's flight from the marshal's home, Rhett went after him and ran him down on a little island near the city. Heriot, sometime shipmaster for the major, was shot in the short scrimmage, and his employer again brought to Charles Town in manacles.

They tried Stede Bonnet in the same court and the same fashion and with the same evidence as they had his crew. He was tried on two indictments, one for taking the *Francis* and the other for taking the *Fortune*.

To both he pleaded not guilty and was first tried on the affair of the *Francis*. He stood up for himself in good shape; but the facts, as well as the court, crushed him. He claimed, as Captain Kidd had claimed some years before in a similar fix, that a mutinous crew drove him protesting into these criminal courses. He explained that the only piracy he had ever been in was when with Captain Thatch. One wonders how much the mutinous crew, as alleged, had to exert themselves to persuade an old Blackbeard man to steal a fat ship or two.

A curious little circumstance comes up in this trial. Pell, the boatswain, in answer to a question, said Bonnet was in command of the ship, "but the quartermaster had more power than he," adding that the quartermaster took charge of the loot and sometimes divided it. One wonders if the crew did not have a great deal more to say about things than would be supposed, tolerating Bonnet as a business manager.

Bonnet might have come down as a somewhat romantic person, but the nerve he had always shown, even in his trial, broke at the last; and when on December 18 he was hanged in the same place as his followers had been, he was almost senseless from fear. Thus in a miserable huddle he left a stage on which he had not been too modest, on which he had even swaggered.

This is all the story of one summer. The blockade of Charles Town by Blackbeard had happened in May of 1718, and December of the same year saw the end of Stede Bonnet. And to Bonnet, as to his men, there came a spark of joy before he went to the rope—and that was the news that his old superior, Blackbeard, had died upon the cutlass on November 22.

Abdicating the high estate of admiral and breaking up his fleet, leaving a part of it, as we have seen, to roll as wreckage on the tides of Topsail Inlet, Blackbeard came back to Ocracoke and a lazy summer.

Perhaps it was during these thoughtful, meditative days that he persuaded a young lady to become his fourteenth wife for there is record of a merry marriage at which Governor Eden himself condescended to appear as a well-wishing guest and give the occasion the suitable air to promote the new Mrs. Blackbeard's social fortunes. At the feast a good deal of somebody else's rum, somebody else's victuals and somebody else's money were laid under contribution. Governor Eden, however, had a peculiarly happy detachment to the minor questions of somebody else's property. That phase of his disposition doubly endeared him to his pirate friend.

But the gold pieces that he sent spinning dwindled anon; little Toby

Knight began to bore him and even the Governor commenced to get on his nerves. Respectable shore life was entirely too much for him, so Blackbeard again yearned for the reeling decks and the roar of his bully boys. With a laudable regard for the proprieties, he gave out that he was putting to sea again on a "commercial venture," and even registered his ship at the local custom's house.

"Salvage," he murmured, looking intently into little Toby's honest face; pressing the secretary's round, fat hand in farewell.

"Salvage," grinned Toby, glad to get even the friendly grip of the sea monster released, and instinctively rubbing his hand slyly on the tails of his flaring coat.

Still delicate, Blackbeard waited until the land faded into the sea line behind him ere, with the feeling that he had had a pleasant vacation and was glad to get back to work again, he threw out his sinister ensign,—the flag of skull and bones. Blackbeard was himself again.

And now there happened that which many of the crew had often fearfully predicted,—the Devil came aboard Blackbeard's ship.

The weather had been threatening for some time, and now, on a late afternoon, the great ocean heaved murmurously beneath the bows. In the rigging the wind fretted and complained, shrilly and more shrilly as though the white-green tumult of the waters was disturbing it; in the cabin below the dark horror of delirium tremens was falling upon the bearded master. On the decks, the mate—doubtless the effective Mr. Richards—stripped his ship for the approaching combat and drove his men aloft into the swaying yards. Now and then Blackbeard, still the sailor, reeled on his cabin threshold and blurted insane orders to the gale. Whereat Mr. Richards, well accustomed to the storms of wind and waves and delirious masters, slammed the door in his face and laughingly went about his work.

Palely the day expired in the west, and as though they had only been waiting for the night, wind and water strengthened to the struggle and now persuaded a third element, the rain, to join them in the conspiracy of destruction. These three witches began to make the cauldron boil.

Mr. Richards still laughed; his sails were in and he was with the helmsman, sweating to keep the vessel from a fatal lurch.

"What's that sound?" gasped the steersman to his officer, leaning full weight to his work. Forward they could see nothing but the black void and a white wash of sea where their decks and bowsprit should ordinarily be, nor could look in that direction long for the whips of rain with which the screaming winds lashed them.

"The wind," hollered Richards, bending close to be heard.

The steersman shook his head. "No—that!" he shouted.

The gale paused in one of those lulls by which it seems to recover for a effort of fresh fury. And in the second of quietness there rose and fell a long, horrible scream of inhuman defiance. Richards grinned and pointed with his finger below. Blackbeard was wrestling with the principalities and powers of darkness.

"Who's that?" bellowed the steersman, his momentary reassurance flown. His face was turned with a gaze of inexpressible fear at the gleaming, plunging masts. "There—there—"

Richards peered in the rain-whipped night; peered and shrank back, his mouth open wide and his eyes protruding. He rallied, pulled out a heavy wooden pin from the ship's side and started forward. Within ten paces of the mainmast he stopped, and gathering his strength, hurled the pin with all his force crashingly against the mast. The pin fell into an invading sea and was whirled overboard. But the Thing stood, dark and sinister.

Richards felt the ship getting beyond control of the cowering helmsman. He rushed back in time to save them from ruin; the man had dropped to the deck, a bundle of abject fright. While the mate was still calling for help, the boatswain crawled up on hands and knees and turned an ashen face to his superior.

"There's a strange man," he shouted as loudly as a quavering voice would permit, indicating with a backward jerk of his thumb. "Aloft—"

The Thing was moving about the yards; there was a sort of solid blackness to It that somehow made It visible even against its somber background.

Turning the helm over to the boatswain, the mate rushed below for his pistol, but when he came back to the deck the Thing was gone.

Richards laughed thinly. "The Devil's signed on with us, boys!"

"Then that's the end o' us," groaned the boatswain.

But the fact that a New Hand was on the ship if not on her articles was not immediately disastrous. For very shortly after that vivid night, Blackbeard, recovered now of his bout, met and took a very fine French ship, which was in so excellent a condition that to call it "salvage" was indeed the very subtlest of piratical jokes.

And the joke was made good, too, when, taking her at once into Ocracoke, His Excellency, with little hesitation, gave her captor a certificate of salvage, accepting as his fee for the certificate some sixty hogsheads of sugar. What the Governor did not use, Toby Knight obligingly allowed to be stored in the Knight barn.

This was the final straw that caused the proverbial fatal accident to the camel. North Carolina, at the end of patience, now flared up, and, ignoring her own corrupt authorities, appealed to the capable Alexander Spotswood, Governor of Virginia, for the extermination of the pest of Ocracoke Inlet.

Virginia heard and responded and dispatched Captain Brand and Lieutenant Maynard, each in command of a small ship of war, to the Carolina coast in quest of Blackbeard.

Brand and Maynard appreciated the size of their job, so they gathered into their crews picked men who were volunteering for the duty, and who would be likely to keep the same zestful lookout for the oncoming terror as does a whaler in fat and profitable fishing grounds for the dark bulk which shall fill all his barrels with oil.

They reached Pamlico Sound, of which Ocracoke Inlet is a part, toward the evening of November 21, and with jumping pulses spotted the masts of the black beast as he lay in wait for prey. Blackbeard was surprised just as Bonnet had been, and like Bonnet spent the night in getting ready for battle.

The Virginians had to lie outside the inlet all night and wait for the morning to light them through the risky channels. When next day they sailed in, Blackbeard, knowing the soundings, was able to make the running-fight pirate tactics prescribed for such emergencies, and blasted Brand and Maynard with his broadsides; and though steeped to the eyebrows in rum, he was at all times the adept and finished sailor.

But the enemy were getting at him, too, and his decks were cluttered with the slain. He was undermanned, having only some twenty men at the time, so that his losses from the attackers' fire left him but a sparse crew to work his ship and man eight guns, as well as keep going an effective musketry volleying. There was left but one resource, and that was hand-to-hand conflict.

He got within grappling distance of Maynard's ship, and with his usual ferocity of appearance and manner threw himself and his surviving men into the Virginia's rigging, and plunged, demoniacally fighting, to the decks. For a second the pirates shook their enemy with the shock of the impact, but not long; with that roaring vigor which gave the English-speaking sailors their dominion of the oceans of the world, Maynard's men rallied and an indescribable butchering ensued.

Blackbeard made for the commander, and Maynard met him with equal courage and the added strength which the moral side of the matter always lends a warrior's arm. The arch-pirate's body was open at more than twenty places; but on those heaving, blood-wet decks he fought the lieutenant with the verve of an athlete fresh for the field. A sudden chance and he thrust a cocked pistol straight into his opponent's chest, but before the finger could pull the trigger back, Maynard laid the cutlass squarely across the pirate's throat. He sank to the deck like a slaughtered bull.

It was all over. Those pirates who could, leaped over the bulwarks and swam to the shore, leaving a red trail in the water behind them.

Twilight came down on the sea. Beneath the shallow waters the bodies of the slain quivered with the motion of the waves as if they were still alive and still struggling, and among them was the headless corpse of Blackbeard.

For that terrible head was hung at the bowsprit of Maynard's ship. All the way back to Virginia the gruesome figurehead swung and dipped and ducked with the movements of the vessel the ocean pounded and played with it and twisted that strange beard into more fantastic shapes than Blackbeard had ever dreamed of, weaving into it the weeds and slime-flora of the sea, and for a last touch washed from their sockets the baleful eyes which glared in the fixed glassiness of death.

from

Thomas the Lambkin:
Gentleman of Fortune

by Claude Farrère (1876–1957)

In this excerpt from Claude Farrère's seagoing adventure
novel, French corsair Captain Thomas Trublet teams up
with British filibuster Captain Edward Bonney "Redbeard"
to sail against the Spanish.

From the crow's-nest perched high above the cross-
pieces of the topgallant, the lookout man scrutinized the horizon.
Then hands to mouth, funnel-wise, he leaned forward, and called out
to the deck below:

"Land ho! Three points to larboard! Land!"

As he caught the words on the forecastle, the steersman sprang, axe
in hand, to the main-hatch where with all his might he repeated the
cry, so that do one on board, whether in galley or on spardeck, could
fail to hear the news.

"Land ho! Three points to larboard! Land!"

Whereupon every man took to his legs, rushing to the deck; and
many a lad of the crew climbed the shrouds, the better to see.

Sixty days, just, it made since setting sail in Mer Bonne. Sixty days to cover the fifteen hundred great sea-leagues that stretch between the Tortoise and St. Malo—that is nothing at all! A swift-sailing craft, the *Belle Hermine* must have been to do it.

All the more so since Thomas Trublet, duly instructed by his owner and by certain old Malouins, well-practiced in those waters, had been at great pains to take the best course, which was by no means the shortest.

No sooner had he cleared the Brittany isles than he put his helm hard to southward, skirting the Spanish coast and Portugal, and sighting one after another, the island clusters off the African coast—Madeira, the Fortunees, and the Cape Verde archipelago. Then only, the trade wind now swelling his sails on the right side of the canvas, did he change his tack and set helm on the Americas, sailing due west across the Atlantic, and leaving the detestable Sargossa seas far to northward; and finally, the forty-fifth day, he landed on one of the Windward Islands—which one it matters little to know. Fifteen days more, and the *Belle Hermme*, taking her dose of alternating squalls and dead calms, beat northward the whole length of the Virgin Islands, thence to Porto Rico and San Domingo. The sixtieth day dawned. And the land sighted this time could be none other than the desired Tortoise, object and goal of the long voyage.

The rear door of the poop-castle opened, and Captain Thomas Trublet, with Louis Guénolé, his lieutenant, issued therefrom. Arm in arm they walked the length of the deck, and mounting the starboard ladder, climbed to the forecastle. There each raised a hand to his eyes (the better to see), and looked intently for the land announced. Roundabout the crew stood attentive, ears pricked for orders. Neither Trublet nor Guénolé were of that breed of commanders that their men can ignore.

"That's our island," pronounced Thomas, after a steady scrutiny.

"So it appears to me," said Louis Guénolé. "Such it is as old Kersaint described, he who had spent four years hereabouts."

The object sighted did, indeed, appear to be land, still a great distance away, and barely emerging from the horizon, for it also was blue, and nearly transparent. But those sharp sailor eyes, in spite of the distance, already descried the arched outline of a mountain range, steep on the north, but sloping gently to the southward.

"In these seas," observed Louis Guénolé, "sight can reach so far that it's a marvel. Devil take me if ever, approaching land in our home waters, the sharpest-eyed mate on board could guess, at this distance, that there was land out yonder."

"*Parguienne!*" approved Thomas Trublet.

Whereupon he grew silent and continued to gaze.

The *Belle Hermine* was sailing large, all sails set save the topgallants that are often difficult to reef quickly enough in regions subject to squalls. Thus rigged, the *Belle Hermine* was making a good eight knots an hour, duly recorded by the log, and the Tortoise began slowly to rise out of the sea.

The bluish land was turning green, a green many shaded and soft to the sense, such as one finds nowhere in the world save in the Antilles. In this rare and perfect verdure, veritably enchanting the eye, there now appeared little white dots, widely scattered. The mountain was covered with them; and against the soft velvet of woods and meadows, the white dots made a lace of that delicate kind worn by noble lords over the silk of their doublets by way of ornament and gewgaws.

"*Ma Doué!*" said Louis Guénolé then, pointing towards the island, "it strikes me that yonder land is a land of the rich. What we see there can be none else than fine country houses and chateaux, most agreeably situated in healthful air of the hills, and pleasant to inhabit."

"Yes," said Thomas Trublet. "And the town itself lies below, on the very brim of the sea. There it comes in sight now, and the port too, by the same token!"

But a cup-handle it was, a slim semi-circlet running off at the shore, where thirty or forty buildings grouped around it, all of surpassing ugliness and more like warehouses than dwellings. But, on the left, the solid stonework of a battery made a good showing, planned no doubt so that the balls from its great cannon of green bronze should cross the range of a solid gun-turret distinguishable on the left. So that, although lying too wide open on the seaside, the port of Tortoise Island had little to fear from hostile attacks which it could so vigourously repulse.

"To our purposes, all this," Thomas pronounced, after his long inspection. "Louis, give orders for casting anchor, and have some of this canvas laid by. I am going back to the cabin for that which you wot of."

Guénolé nodded. "As you command," he replied.

Arm in arm they returned to the poop, and the captain went back to his quarters, while his lieutenant climbed to the taffrail, where manœuvres can best be watched, for from there the eye can take in with one glance the ten yard-arms of all four masts.

In his cabin, sitting in front of his captain's coffer, Thomas Trublet, having upraised the heavy double-padocked lid, was searching in his papers for the most important of them all, the one which in a few hours he counted on presenting to My Lord Ogéron, the Governor. For, at the last news received from Versailles by the Chevalier Danycan, it appeared that in 1666, and even in 1664, the Sieur Ogéron governed the Tortoise and the San Domingan coast for the King, and my lords of the Compagnie Occidentale.

"Save I mistake, here it is," murmured Thomas at last, and unfolded the document, a parchment stamped with green wax, bearing the double tracings of the royal seal. Thomas, though little lettered, knew how to read, and thus he spelled out:

LETTER OF MARQUE

Louis de Bourbon, Count of Vermandois, Admiral of France, to all those who may view these presents, Greeting. The orders which we have received from the King to provide for the just defence of his subjects, and the safety of commerce on the high seas . . .

He skipped several lines; then:

For these reasons, we give leave, power and full permission to the Sieur Thomas Trublet, captain of the frigate, the Belle Hermine by name, of one hundred and sixty tons or thereabouts, with such crew, cannon, cannon-balls, powder, lead, and other munitions and supplies as she may require for glutting to sea, to attack Pirates, Corsairs, or folk of No Professed Calling, and even the subjects of the United Provinces and other Enemies of the State, and to take them prisoner, and dispose of them, their ships, arms, and other things of which he may make seizure, in whatever place encountered. . . .

He interrupted his reading to look up for a moment:

"That is well put!" said he.

Again he skipped a paragraph, and read:

. . . Enjoining said Thomas to hoist no flag but his own—to wit; that of San Malo, blue, bearing a white cross, with quarterings scarlet, bearing the silver ermine, passante; enjoining him also to observe and cause to be observed by his crew the ordinances of the navy and the regulations issued by His Majesty in the year of grace, 1669. . . .

The parchment crackled as it was folded.

"For sure," concluded Thomas, well pleased, "we are Corsairs in good standing."

By the taffrail, Louis Guénolé, standing near the helm, was giving the orders:

"Reef the lower sails! Topmen, aloft."

His Breton voice, dry and singsong, carried well, and could be heard even as far as the topgallant.

"Loose anchors!"

The gunners of the watch loosened the cables in their chocks, while the men in the rigging galloped up the footropes of the lower yards.

"Aloft! Clew sails! 'Ware loose ends!"

On the *Belle Hermine* every manœuvre was executed with that promptness and precision which are the glory of the royal navy.

"Crew below!"

The sheets now reefed, the topmen slid down the length of the shrouds. Then the master-gunner ran to the ladder of the poop-castle, and with bared head reported:

"Ready to cast anchor, sir!"

To which the lieutenant answered with a nod.

To larboard of the taffrail he stood stretched to his full height, an imperious figure. Neither tall nor heavily built was Louis Guénolé, and his smooth white cheeks and longish black hair were like the cheeks and hair of a girl. But, in spite of his delicate features, his steady glance and piercing eyes, where flames were ever smouldering, divested his young face of all girlish gentleness.

A while later, as the *Belle Hermine* was rounding the east point of the Grand Port, Thomas Trublet joined his lieutenant near the poop-castle. And as they stood side by side, one seemed but a slender boy, the other a heavy bluff warrior. Yet, in truth, the boy was no less redoubtable than his captain, and the men of the forecastle, who obeyed the lad almost as though they feared him, knew in what esteem to hold their lieutenant.

"Ça!" said Trublet, "it appears to me that we'll soon reach good anchorage. Louis, tell them to heave the lead!"

The helmsman unwound twelve fathom of plummet. "No bottom!" he sang out.

"Small matter," said Trublet. "There's a brigantine at anchor not far from here. Louis, luff a bit!"

And Louis promptly luffed.

"Reef astern! Soundings astern! Helm to leeward, gently!"

The frigate, obeying, ran closer to land. Soon the sails flapped empty of wind; and the helmsman, casting his lead hand over hand, sang out:

"Bottom! Ten fathom on larboard side, ten fathom!"

"Clear both anchors!" commanded Thomas Trublet. And, turning to his lieutenant:

"You'd best go forward; we cast anchor in a moment," said he.

For, according to rule, the second officer should be in the bow when the anchor is cast, and the moment for casting had come.

Trublet, standing alone, inspected the trim of the sheets. The frigate now carried none but her topsails, and mizzen, and made but little headway. Trublet spat into the water, the better to judge of it and reached a decision.

"Attention! Clew sails!"

Simultaneously, the three tops'ls fell back like three pairs of wings.

"Reef! strike! Reef starboard and larboard!"

The sheets fell in place, and above the tops, braces and lifts suddenly tautened. Thomas, satisfied, looked at his bare masts. Then, raising his voice, so as to be clearly heard by the gunners clustering round the cables of the bow:

"Stand by to cast anchor; starboard! . . . Cast anchor starboard!"

Whereupon the anchor plunged, amid a great noise of splashing waters.

A moment later the helmsman on duty called to Thomas Trublet:

"Captain! hé! Captain! The brigantine lying-t there, she's sending the like of a skiff this way!"

"Ho! Boat ahoy!"

The watch, spike in hand, uttered the regulation "Ahoy" as the skiff approached. But from the craft, a four-oared longboat, there came no reply. A figure stood up in the boat however, and by way of peaceable signal, began to wave a leathern hat, its ribbons streaming in the breeze.

And now the boat was already scraping the frigate's side. The man of the hat called out, "Hollo! . . . Send down a rope!"

A hoarse voice and foreign. The crew from their posts looked at their captain, standing on the taffrail ladder. Thomas gave a nod, and while the sailors, prompt to obey, were lowering the rope asked for, he climbed down to the deck, and stood at the gangway to receive his visitor. The latter, grasping the cordage end, scrambled up the length of it, quick as a monkey. As he sprang aboard Thomas approached and, cordial as becomes one welcoming a stranger, held out his hand, not neglecting, however, to keep his left palm on the butt of one of the pistols stuck in his belt.

"Hurrah!" cried the stranger.

He too wore a brace of pistols, and these he grasped by their butt end, first the one and then the other, offering them to Thomas in token of friendship and alliance. Then, "Hurrah!" he cried once more. Whereupon explanations.

Edward Bonny, known as Redbeard—for through a barbarous, indeed savage-like vanity much resembling that of certain Redskins who paint their bodies, he had stained his beard a vivid crimson—was captain in his own right of the brigantine at anchor in the waters where the *Belle Hermine* had come to anchor. The brigantine, a slight enough craft known as the *Flying King*, carried eight small guns. But to this weakness Redbeard gave small heed, being wont to say to his crew that it was with but four guns and twenty-eight Filibusters that the celebrated Pierre Legrand some fifty years earlier had boarded and seized the galleon of the vice-admiral of the Spanish fleet—a ship with a crew of 396 men, and fifty-four artillery pieces, nearly every one of them cast in bronze. The more numerous the enemy, the larger the booty; in short, "the fewer the lads of the crew the richer each share." Such were the maxims of Edward Bonny, native of Bristol, England. To these he added one other: that, as a man dies but once, and lives but once, he must be a dullard, indeed, who fails to live a merry life for fear of an ill death.

Tall, and heavily built, though far from approaching Thomas Trublet's vast girth, he was surpassed by no one in courage, resolution, and fierce pride. And from the twenty battles he had already fought, on land and sea, all the Americas had learned what manner of man was this Edward Bonny.

Thomas Trublet had, naturally, no inkling of these events. Nevertheless, he did not mistake his man and promptly esteemed the Filibuster at his full value. In the visitor's honour, the oldest wine of the store-room was brought up and served, freshly-drawn, in the largest tankards of the *Belle Hermine's* cupboards. Not a quarter of an hour had passed before the two captains were fast friends, and in token thereof giving one another resounding smacks on the buttocks.

"Hollo!" said Edward Bonny at last, fixing his sharp eyes, as black as his beard was red, on Thomas Trublet, "Hollo! old pal, a fellow like you, with a beard like that of yours there, never came to these parts in search of cocoa, tobacco, or Campeachy wood, save when such supplies are to be had for the picking off the Spaniards just setting sail from New Spain. Do I mistake? May the Grand Cric crunch me alive, if your name's not Corsair, as mine is Filibuster! And such folk as we were made to understand one another, and belike cruise together. Your hand here, mate, and I'll teach you a stroke that'll make us rich, and that we'll try together, good Coast Brothers that we be!"

"Of a truth!" replied Thomas, wisely. "Mate, my boy, that suits me! But what's this of Spaniards and New Spain? *Pardieu*, yes, Corsair I am, and ready to take a run with you, our ships supporting one another as consorts; but only against the Hollanders, who are enemies of the King of France, and not at all against other folk, neutrals, allies, or friends. In proof whereof, here is my letter of marque. Pirate I'd be, truly, if I failed its commands. Read the parchment."

"Hollo!" cried Redbeard. "Do you think that *I* can read? Not I! But, what matter? Hollanders, Spaniards, worm-eaten Papists, and filthy bastards, between sheep's wool, and bull's hide, where the difference? You're mad, matey! And are you, of all the French and English here, going to be the only one to turn tail on that monkey crew from Castille, that, without mercy or truce, is forever burning our houses, hanging our men—every time, that is, we fail to do the hanging and burning first? By their accursed *Mère de Dieu!* Thomas Trublet, Malouin and captain that you are, you're either for us or against us. If for us, your hand, here! If against us, the Grand Cric eat me alive! I'm off to my ship and it's a fight to the death we'll have and presently!"

Thomas took a step back, but did not answer. Redbeard, after this bluster, began again, less roughly:

"What now? Is it this rag from a donkey's hide that's troubling you? Come, mate, when you've lived among us awhile, you'll not be bothering your head any more about the friends and enemies of your goodman King. Your own friends and enemies will suffice. But run free meanwhile! For the present there's no harm. Monsieur d'Ogéron, the Governor, is a clever man, and I doubt not he will know how to find you another letter of marque, better than this one, and one commanding you to attack the Spanish as well as the Dutch. If I speak truth, are you with me?"

Thomas gave him a long look, taking his measure and gauging him:

"Yes," said he; then in his ringing, decided voice. "With Monsieur Ogéron's license, whom I wish to-day to visit, I'll go with you willingly. But what is this arrangement of which you speak, and what letter of marque can they give me beyond this one?"

Edward Bonny burst into a resounding laugh, then plunged into detailed explanations.

Not in those days alone had the inextinguishable war raging between the Filibusters and the Spanish colonies of the New Indies arisen. A long while before—fifty years, or more mayhap, no one was left to remember, exactly—the *Boucaniers*, or hunters of wild bulls, themselves were hunted and right cruelly on their own hunting grounds by the Spaniards. Taking vengeance by attacking in turn, they wrought frightful butchery. At this time, which came long before the period of real Filibustering, the Buccaneers, rustic folk, and simple-minded, being driven to warfare by brutal aggression, had at first bothered no more about diplomacy than about politics. Little did they care whether their enemies were those of His Most Catholic Majesty or not. They scarcely knew that they themselves were subjects of the Most Christian King. When they were molested, they gave blow for blow! "Eye for eye, and tooth for tooth. When you strike, I kill!" What did the rest matter?

Nevertheless, things changed somewhat. Having fought long years on land and sea, and growing accustomed to meeting the same enemy—the Spaniard—at every turn, the Filibusters, heirs and successors to the Buccaneers, had on sundry occasions, solicited and obtained the aid of those diverse nations of Europe, who became successively the enemies of Spain, Portugese, Dutch, and English, in turn, and especially, almost always in fact, the French, who for many years had been fighting their Spanish neighbors. Besides, the Filibusters still remembered that they had, themselves, most of them, been French before being of their present condition. There were even some of them who counted on returning—when they had made their fortunes—to their former motherland. And thus it came about that after numerous adventures of one sort and another, they resolved to ask that a French Governor be appointed for that favorite lair of theirs, Tortuga. And this they besought of Monsieur le Chevalier de Poincy, then ruling in the island of St. Christopher as General in the name of the Order of Malta.

Filibustering then had reached this point in its career at the time of Thomas Trublet's arrival at La Tortue. Less independent than, of yore, and even, nominally at least, subject to the commands of the French King, it yet preserved much real independence, and many of its original rights. Of these the most precious was by all odds that of carrying on warfare at all times against its own enemies even after they had ceased being the enemies of the King of France, a right upheld by a peace treaty that had been signed somewhere in Europe.

In cases of this sort, however, it was for the Governor to find such basis for the Filibusters, acts as would clothe them with a semblance of regularity. The Sieur d'Ogéron, following numerous predecessors, had perfected many methods of procedure already very ingenious. One high in his favour, and of great usefulness in this year, 1672, was that of giving to the Corsairs letters of marque bearing the signature of His Majesty, the King of Portugal—quite authentic letters they were too, and he possessed an inexhaustible supply of them, though by what means obtained it would have been hard to say.

"Thus will he do for you, Thomas Trublet," said the English Filibuster Redbeard, concluding his discourse. "Have no doubts on, that score, and go to see him as soon as may be. By way of beginning, salute him with the seven salvos that are his due. As for me, I'm off to my *Flying King*, and agree herewith to set out with you tomorrow at sunrise. Why waste time? A day will suffice you to lay in water, and victuals, for our journey will take no more than a fortnight."

As the long-boat from the English ship shoved off from the *Belle Hermine's* flank, the first salvo thundered across the bay. Edward Bonny, at the tiller, joyfully shook his red beard. Not much time did it take that damn Malouin to load and fire a cannon!

Thomas Trublet meanwhile, and Louis Guénolé beside him, were looking landward. Already the folk of the town were running out of their houses and gathering on the shore, to see what manner of ship this might be, thus saluting their Governor. And now a man more richly dressed than the others, and wearing a plumed hat, left the crowd and came down the beach, to the water's edge. As the last shot rang out, he bared his head in greeting. And the crew of the *Belle Hermine* did not for a moment doubt that this personage was the Sieur d'Ogéron, as such indeed he was—Governor in the name of the King and the West India Company, of the Ile de la Tortue, and the Dominican coast.

"Know you then," Captain Edward Bonny was saying to Thomas Trublet, and his lieutenant Louis Guénolé, "that less than four hundred marine leagues west-southwest of here, beyond the windward passage and the island of Jamaica, there is a gulf in a great spread of land. All dotted with islands it is, and known as the Gulf of Honduras. Not far from there is the region known as Campeachy, which forms a part of the rich kingdom of New Spain, full of gold, and silver it is, and cochineal, precious woods, excellent tobacco, and that cocoa of which they make chocolate, a salutary beverage. Chief among its flourishing cities and well-fortified ports is Vera Cruz. (In spite of its fortifications, however, eleven years after Redbeard thus described it, Vera Cruz was taken by assault and pillaged by the Filibusters in 1683.) And certainly, it would be a hard and perilous adventure, with but two ships between us, and barely sixty men, to attack any one of these ports. Nevertheless, this is what I would propose to you, for lack of a better enterprise, and I know well enough that you would accept it, like the men you are, worthy of being numbered among the Filibusters. But, thanks be to God, there is no need of running such risks in order to enrich ourselves properly! Listen to me now, both of you! In the very heart of this curving gulf, a river empties out that we Adventurers call the Rivière des Moustiques. Now, in this river, which is easily navigable, the Spaniards yearly equip and arm a *hourque* of seven or eight hundred tons, for use as a transport, and a *patache,* to protect her, and carry in her own hold the more precious and less cumbersome merchandise, that could not well be placed on the *hourque,* such as metals for striking into coin. You know, doubtless, that a *hourque* is a large ship with rounded prow and stern, often well-armed—when it needs to be—and that a *patache* is merely a manner of coast-guard frigate. Now as to this matter we speak of, I am informed that the *hourque* from Honduras carries fifty-six cannon, and the *patache* only forty, but of the largest calibre. Ninety-six pieces in all, against which we have twenty-eight. The contest— that is to say, will be even. It will have odds in our favour if, as I hope, we can capture the *hourque* first and then the frigate, attacking each sep- arately, with our two ships. Such is my plan."

"We favour it," answered Thomas Trublet without a moment's hes- itation, speaking for himself and for Louis Guénolé.

Whereupon Redbeard, leaving the *Belle Hermine,* returned to his *Flying King,* and the two ships, consorts now, set sail from the Tortoise.

They were by this lying at anchor in the lee of Roatan island, one of the Bahias, to take on water and also to keep watch for the *patache* and the *hourque* which could not fail to emerge from the river mouth, and take their bearings from Roatan before sailing northward to round Cape Catoche, for such is the best course to Europe. Thomas and Louis, alone in the main cabin, were ending their noon repast of salted meat— tough it was too—dried beans, or *favots* as the sailors call them, and hardtack, tougher still than the meat. Having ended his meal, Thomas, good Catholic that he was, intoned the chant of Zachary, which he followed with the *Magnificat*. And Louis, after joining in the chorus, then recited the *Miserere*. This they did, as was custom on board all Christian Corsairs, to sanctify each meal. And having thus prayed together, they looked upon one another in friendly fashion.

"A good practice, that," said the Captain. "With these songs in our throats, like to those they sing at church, home seems less far away."

"Yes," Louis Guénolé agreed.

He said not a word more, but sat wrinkling his forehead.

"What now?" asked Trublet, watching him.

"Nothing."

"Of a truth! . . . I say there is something troubling you."

"Nothing, I tell you!"

"Yes! and, *sangbleu!* it strikes me a secret is not fair play between us two!"

"Well then," said Guénolé, "since you take it thus, I'll speak. Be angry if you choose at what I have to say. This is what's troubling me. This enterprise of ours has no very Catholic color to my eye, Thomas Trublet, but hear me out . . . and having listened, think well, before replying! We two, good and true Christians, as we are, what, I ask you, are we doing here in the company of yonder Englishman, who's a heretic by all odds, and a Huguenot, if no worse? And so allied we are going to pursue and fight the Spanish, good true Christians like ourselves, and subjects of a King, who, for the present at least, is the friend of our own King! Is that a good enterprise, think you? Who besides are the usual enemies of us Malouins? Who are those who have sworn, if ever they take our city, to leave not a stone standing, and to have vengeance for all the defeats they have suffered every time they have attacked us? Well you know, my Thomas! They are the English, not the Spaniards! And since you exact this of me, I tell you frankly: I am ill-pleased to see this English ship that's athwart us here become our friend."

"Patience!" said Thomas Trublet.

He had poured out for his lieutenant and for himself two full bowls of that cane sugar rhum that is sold in all the Americas, and of which he had found good provision at La Tortue.

"Patience!" he repeated. "And first, drink that up!"

He emptied his own bowl.

"*Mon Louis,*" he began thereupon, "you do not make me angry, and I think as do you. The English, you say? Do you believe I bear them more love than you do yourself? Their turn will come, rest assured, to serve as targets for our guns. But at present what duty have we, save, above all, to make our bourgeois rich, and ourselves to boot? Our present expedition will take care of that. What matter that some folk be Huguenots, and some Catholics, some neutrals, and some friends, provided we have letters of marque against them all, made out in good and due form? By my faith, let come what will! And may what comes be the blessed day which shall find us bourgeois in our turn, and owners of our ships, free to do with them as we like, and fight whom we please!"

At once he filled the bowls again. But Louis Guénolé did not drink. "What is it now?" Trublet asked again. "Speak, comrade, pour out what lies heavy on your heart!"

Then said the lieutenant, lowering his voice:

"Thomas"—he cast a hesitating, an anxious look even to right and left—"Thomas, you speak well and bravely. But are you mindful that the Cunning One knows well how to spread for us gilded springes? And this, is it not such a springe? St. Anne d'Auray! Hear me, my Thomas."

He lowered his voice yet more; and Thomas brusquely straightened, his own eyes anxious now, and with both hands he fingered the blessed medals that hung from his neck.

"Listen to me, my Thomas. When I was but a shaver, my mother took me to the pardon of Plouguenast. Twelve long years agone that was, in the autumn, and I remember how already the air was growing dark. Plouguenast, if you know it, is high on the mountain and deep in the woods. There are rivers there, a-plenty. But they can scarce be seen, so narrow are they, squeezed between the oaks of the banks, and the fern that grows at the feet of the great trees, and the moss below the thick fern. All this I mention so you can understand what those rivers are like. Well might one fall into one of them without suspecting that a stream was flowing there!

"Well, my mother was pulling me along by the arm, all the length of a rough path, in the very depth of the wood. And it isn't the Korrigans that are lacking in that forest . . . but I felt no fear, not a bit of fear, my word on it . . . not so much fear as now, Thomas, to speak truth . . . and all this because of my mother, who was a fine woman. Hanging on to the end of her arm, I would have walked into the very middle of a witches' ring, St. Yves and St. Louis forgive me!

"But . . . hark a moment! Suddenly my mother stops short and doesn't move, changed, as our priest would say, into a pillar of salt. I look, and see that she is listening. I listen too and I hear . . . plouf! plouf! plouf! . . . Yes. The sound of wet clothes slapping against the washboards."

Thomas with a jerk crossed himself.

"The Washingwomen of the Streams?" he asked, his cheeks blanching.

"Eh!" said Guénolé. "Did I know anything about them, in those days? The Washingwomen it was, though! And this is how I learned that it was they: the next moment my mother let go my hand, and took a step forward, one, two, three, as though to see as far as she could. Then she jumped back, caught me by the hand, and ran as fast as ever woman ran that had a child to drag after her. Away we rushed from the place where we were going, not daring to proceed further, not daring either to look back, even once. And the rest followed as it must."

"She died within the year?" asked Trublet.

"Within the month," said Guénolé. "You see it really was they, busy no doubt washing her winding sheet by moonlight. And now, let me tell you this, for your remembering, Thomas Trublet, captain as you are! I was but a ship's boy then, the least knowing probably, on our street. Just the same, when I heard that plouf! plouf! plouf! of the Washingwomen, I remember feeling, clear as a torch . . . here, between my shoulders, and gliding down to the end of my spine, a freezing cold that gripped my marrow, and twisted my entrails, a cold such as makes the frosts of winter seem warm as coals in comparison . . . yes! Now, the other morning, the day we arrived at the Tortoise, the moment I laid eyes on Bonny Redbeard, whom God and the Saints confound! . . . and every time since that accursed morning, that this same Bonny Redbeard fellow has set foot on our deck . . . well, clear as a torch I tell you, I felt the same frightful cold, that I have never forgotten since that night when I heard the Washingwomen—the cold of mortal sin and death, the cold of a soul in pain of damnation. Thomas! Thomas! Great misfortune will come out of all of this!"

Once more Thomas Trublet crossed himself, and yet again; and he sat pondering.

"Bah!" said he at last. "Let come what will! There's surely a big difference between the Washingwomen, terrible though they are, as every man knows, for no one has yet seen one of them without dying for it, and this Redbeard you speak of, who's of flesh and blood, and who sees many folk daily without any one of them being the worse."

"Who knows?" said Louis Guénolé. "Supposing he did bring bad luck, and sowed the seed of maledictions wherever he goes; that seed would not germinate right away,"

"Louis," said Thomas, "you are a devout lad, and for that I love you. But here, we are not as at home. Save on our moorlands, where sorcerers, and werewolf shepherds are ever wandering, no one has ever found anywhere people of ill-omen living like other men; still less in the form of honest Corsair captains, with ships, and cannon, and crews, and coming, mark you, to seek succour and alliance for enterprises too great for their powers."

"So be it!" said Louis Guénolé. "God grant I am wrong, and may the Redbeard bring us nothing but pieces of eight, by the dozen gross."

As he spoke, a shot, distant and muffled, shook, ever so slightly, the *Belle Hermine's* keel. Captain and lieutenant made quick work of getting on deck. For a single shot was the signal, agreed upon between them and Redbeard, which should announce the appearance at the river mouth, of *patache* or *hourque*.

In the rigging, the sailors were already climbing to the shrouds, each eager to be the first to eight the still invisible enemy. But Thomas Trublet soon checked this incipient disorder by one single command roared out with the full strength of his great lungs:

"Clear decks for action!"

• • •

It wasn't much of a fight, nor at any time hotly contested. True, the *hourque* and the *patache* between them had three times the number of cannon that the *Belle Hermine* and the *Flying King* could muster together. And, even separately, each of them was still far superior to the two Corsairs united. But there's fighting and fighting. The Spaniards, peaceable folk, burghers, merchants, or merchant-mariners, had small knowledge of warfare, and depended on the contingent of soldiers embarked with them. Of these latter there were not many. Moreover, the heaving deck of a ship was less familiar to them than the solid ground on which they had learnt their trade. To this the aim of their cannon bore witness. That of the Corsairs on the other hand was accurate beyond an admiral's dream. The *hourque*, rudely raked by the cross-fire of two adversaries, surrendered in no time. The *patache*, at this juncture, was for escaping to the open. But the *Belle Hermine*, trimmed for speed, overtook her while the *Flying King* was manning her prize. And then it was that Trublet's crew first learned to estimate their captain's skill at its true worth. Thomas, carefully keeping under the Spaniard's stern, caught none but her rear shots; then luffing, and bearing down on her, he riddled her with two broadsides. Caught in this wise, and fearful of imitating the Corsair's manœuvre, lest he should grapple her, the *patache* quickly resigned herself to her fate. Scarce twenty minutes had passed when the flag of Castille and Leon came tumbling in great haste from her poop. The *Belle Hermine* then came alongside the surrendered enemy, and boarded her bow to bow, out of extreme precaution. Thomas, leaping on the bridge of the capture, duly received the sword of the vanquished captain; on the deck fifty or sixty bodies lay scattered about, and entrails littered the gangways.

The victors then proceeded to the division of the booty.

On board the *hourque*, the captors found that their winnings consisted of twenty thousand reams of paper, and a quantity of linen, serge, cloth, ribbons, and other stuffs, all worth money. But the Corsairs could scarce derive any profit therefrom. Those on *the Flying King* without further ado threw into the sea everything they had just won at the cost of good red blood, for several of them were wounded, and some dead. The *patache*, on the other hand, was laden with pure silver, hammered into bars. And while there was not as much of this in the hold as had been expected, the prize was a better one than the *hourque*, and far easier to turn to profit.

But among the Malouin crew dispute was arising; the English too, some of the men contended, should have their share of the silver ingots, for the *Flying King* and her captain had been parties to the hunting compact. The others, arguing that the *Belle Hermine* had alone attacked and taken the *patache*, denied that the *Flying King* should have any share save in what was found on the *hourque*, the latter having surrendered to the united efforts of both Corsairs.

From argument to argument, the dispute grew quarrelsome, and might have become worse. Threats began to fly. Thomas Trublet and Louis Guénolé meantime were both on board the *patache*, busying themselves with setting the prize in good order, and locking up the prisoners in a safe place.

Suddenly, at the moment when they least expected it, a pistol shot rang out on the deck of the *Belle Hermine*. Louis Guénolé, who was attending to the secure closing of the hatch below which the horde of those Spaniards who were still sound and whole had been thrust, raised his head and stood listening. Thomas Trublet, quicker to act, rushed from the hold where he was calculating the exact worth of the silver his prize carried, and scrambled from, ladder to ladder to the forecastle of the *patache*, in order to see, at one glance, what was taking place on his frigate.

And see he did: divided into two camps, his crew was about to begin a hand-to-hand tussle. The man who had fired—narrowly missing a comrade—stood in the middle of the deck, his still smoking weapon at his feet, where he had thrown it down to have a free hand for his sword.

"*Hola!*" cried Thomas Trublet.

Bounding from forecastle to bowsprit, from bowsprit to spritsail, and swinging himself up by the help of a lift that had been cut in two by a bullet, he leapt from rigging to rigging and in less than four seconds was on board his own ship, and in the very midst of the tumult. And good need he had of being thus skilful on the ropes, for the two ships, still bound together by a few grappling hooks, though floating close to one another, were not exactly alongside. The crew therefore, seeing its captain suddenly much nearer at hand than it might have wished, stood, every man of it, stock-still with amazement and as if turned to stone. The fellow with the pistol, who had been shouting and gesticulating a moment before, was the very first to drop his arm, and stand silent, though his mouth remained open.

"What's this?" demanded Thomas, and he was white with cold anger. Nevertheless, he contained himself. In the three months and more that had elapsed since the *Belle Hermine* had set sail from Mer Bonne up to the time of the fight just ended, not a sign of mutiny had there been on board. As a result the men, although they knew their Trublet, and divined that he would be severe enough to punish when there was need, had never until that day experienced his severity. Expecting the worst, therefore, they were about to take comfort at seeing him so calm; he had not even raised his voice.

"What's this?" repeated Thomas Trublet, in the same measured tone.

One of the crew, reassured by this calmness, ventured a step forward to explain matters. The fellow was of those who wanted to share the whole of the prize with the English. The man with the pistol was of the opposite camp, and listening to the explanations being offered by the first spokesman, he too pressed forward without a thought to putting up his naked sabre, and began to offer his own contrary views.

Thomas Trublet, listening with both ears, gave small sign of displeasure. He vouchsafed no answer, however, to either one of the disputants. And both of them, dismayed by this silence, began first to stammer and then grew silent.

Then Trublet, with a look at them, inquired,

"Is that all you have to say?"

They nodded "yes"; and more and more uneasy they grew—not without cause.

Not without cause! For Thomas, without taking a single step to right or left, had placed a hand on each butt end of the brace of pistols in his belt. And suddenly, pulling them out at a stroke, and extending both arms simultaneously in opposite directions, he shot twice, so rapidly that it sounded like one shot, and with so accurate an aim that both men, their heads shattered in like manner, fell in the same instant.

Then Thomas Trublet, arms crossed, stepped back, to the barricading, and faced his crew. No one save himself had moved, and it was with blank terror they looked at him.

"Boys!" he cried. "I have killed two of you. I'll kill twenty or forty more at need. But understand this well. While I live, there's no room for mutineers on this ship. Those who fail me will have my pistol to reckon with. To your posts, every man of you! And as to the sharing of the booty, I alone am the master of that, and shall do as I please."

The two bodies lay bleeding before their mates.

"As to these carcasses," said Thomas, pointing to them, "let them be hoisted to the yard-arm and hung by the neck. Thus every man shall know my justice, for it is both high, and low, and above all speedy. Obey orders!"

The men were not slow to move.

Thomas Trublet, alone on the bridge, raised his eyes to view that which he called his justice. And it was thus that Louis Guénolé found him when he returned from his inspection of the prize, now duly made fast alongside.

Thomas's anger was like those slow rivers which rise little by little, almost imperceptibly, but whose waters flood the land over a far wider extent, and for a longer time than those of impetuous torrents. Thomas Trublet's anger, on this occasion, was still growing and swelling, even after all shadow of mutiny had vanished. Thinking he was acting for the best, Louis Guénolé, drawing near, greeted, his captain with the words:

"Surely, you did well!"

"Hold your tongue!" replied Thomas, with a savage roar.

Scarce daring to breathe, the lieutenant stood facing his captain.

A long time it took, indeed, for Thomas to master his rage sufficiently to be able to speak.

"What think you?" said he to Louis. "Wouldn't I have done better to hang a dozen of the curs?"

"Eh?" said Louis. "We have but a hundred in all! Moreover, they fought bravely today, and merit some indulgence. Besides, 'twas not against you they mutinied!"

"*Sangdieu!*" cried Thomas, "if it should ever be otherwise, I'll put a match to the magazine!"

"Very well!" approved Guénolé, calmly. "And now what is your will, as to the sharing of the prize? Here comes the Filibuster now, helm hard on us."

And between his teeth he added:

"Didn't I say that this cursed dog would bring us ill-luck?" and crossed himself. Thomas meanwhile stood pondering the problem.

"As to the sharing of the prize," said he, "here's the answer. It belongs to us and no one else, for we alone won it. But, on the other hand, Redbeard was our pilot in this matter, and should have his reward. This, therefore, shall I do. One third of the ingots will be for our bourgeois, and one-third for the provisioner, deducting all that we spent in the Tortoise and elsewhere. The remaining third is for us and our men. I'll keep but your share and mine, Louis, and shall give the rest to the Englishman, and the hull of the *patache* besides, as a reward for him and punishment for our men, who'll see from this what comes of rebellion. If they want to grow rich, they'll have to fight again."

And thus was it done, as Thomas Trublet had decreed. Not a man on the *Belle Hermine* dared so much as murmur against a decision which, on the other ship, caused great astonishment. Edward Bonny, well-pleased with the share allotted to him, was loud in his praises of the Malouins, and above all of their chief. Right soon, indeed, did the whole length and breadth of Filibusterdom know of Redbeard's approval and the causes thereof; and on that very day began Thomas Trublet's fame, destined soon to spread throughout the Antilles.

The Pirate Princess

by Howard Schwartz (b. 1945)

In this retelling of a 19th century Jewish fairy tale from Eastern Europe, a princess takes on the life of a pirate in search of her true love.

O nce upon a time there were two kings, each of whom was childless. And each one set out on a journey to discover a remedy that would make it possible for a child to be born to him. Now fate led both kings to the cave of an old sorcerer on the same day, and the sorcerer met with them at the same time. And after each had explained what it was that he sought, the two kings were amazed to discover that they both were on the same quest—each searching for a remedy so that he might be blessed with a child of his own.

After they had spoken, the sorcerer said to them: "I have read in the stars that each of you is destined to have a child, one a boy and one a girl. And I have also read there that these two are destined to marry. If you permit their marriage to take place, you and your descendants will share a great blessing. But if you keep them apart, for any reason, many will suffer before they are reunited." Then the sorcerer stood up, and the kings left the cave. But before they parted they each vowed that if one had a boy and the other a girl, the children would be betrothed.

It happened that before a year had passed the two kings had each become fathers, one to a beautiful boy, and the other to a lovely girl. But the demands of their kingdoms were very great and the distractions endless, and so it happened that they both forgot about their vows concerning their son and daughter. And when their children came of age, they sent them off to study in a foreign land. And fate caused them both to study under a famous scholar, who was, in fact, the sorcerer who had predicted their birth.

In this way the prince and princess met, and knew from the first that they loved each other, and wanted to be wed. Yet even though the sorcerer saw this, he did not reveal their destiny to them, for he wanted them to stay together solely by the power of their love. So it was that the prince and the princess were together every day for several years. When the studies came to an end, he returned to his kingdom and she to hers. But when they were apart each became dejected, and soon it became plain for all to see that they were unhappy, but no one knew why it was.

At last the king who was the father of the prince asked him what was wrong, and why he had become so sad. Then the prince revealed his love for the foreign princess, and when the king heard this, and learned who she was, he recognized the father of the princess to be the king with whom he had made a vow to betroth their children. Therefore he wrote a letter to the other king, and reminded him of the vow, and suggested that their children should now be wed. And he gave the letter to the prince, and sent him to deliver it in person to the king.

Now when the king who was the father of the princess had received the prince and read the letter, he grew afraid, for he had forgotten about the vow he had made with the prince's father. And he had since made an engagement between the princess and a prince whose father ruled a rich and powerful kingdom. So it was that the king decided to delay the prince for as long as possible, until the princess had been wed to another. He then invited the prince to remain with him in the palace, so that he might observe him, and see if he had been properly prepared to be a ruler. But the king also left orders that the prince was not to be permitted to see the princess, nor was she to be told of his presence there.

In this way the prince and princess remained apart, although they were both living in the same palace. But one day the princess overheard two of the servants whispering about the prince, and learned in which chamber he was staying. Then she made a point of passing in front of that chamber as often as possible. Before long the prince caught a glimpse of her in his mirror, and soon they managed to meet in secret. Then the princess told the prince how her father had betrothed her to another, and they decided to run away together that very night.

So it was that the prince and the princess climbed out of their windows at midnight, and ran together until they reached the ship of the prince. They set sail in the middle of the night, and by the time it was discovered that they were missing, they were already far away. They continued to sail together for a long time, until they were in need of fresh food and water. Soon afterward they spied an island on which fruit trees could be seen growing, and they sailed there, docked the ship, and walked together in the forest. There the princess climbed a fruit tree and tossed the fruit that she picked down to the prince, who filled up a sack with it. But it happened that a wealthy merchant's son was passing near that island in a ship, and he was observing the island with his telescope. In this way he happened to see the princess in the tree, and was astonished at her beauty. He had his ship brought to shore, and he set out with several sailors, armed with weapons, to capture the lovely girl in the tree, and to make her come with him whether she wanted to or not.

Now when the princess, from the vantage point in the tree, saw the men coming in their direction, and saw the long swords they carried, she told the prince to hide and not to reveal himself, no matter what happened. Then she tossed her ring to him, which he caught, and she vowed that even if they were separated, they would still one day be reunited. The prince hid himself in the dense woods, and saw the merchant's son and his men arrive at the foot of the tree, but there was nothing he could do about it, for he was unarmed.

At first the merchant's son spoke sweetly to the princess, but when she refused to reply he ordered his men to cut the tree down. And then, when she saw that she could not escape, the princess descended from the tree and returned with the merchant's son to the ship. But before she climbed on the ship, the princess made the merchant's son vow not to touch her until they were married in his land. And even though she was his prisoner, he agreed to this vow, for he was smitten with love for her, and hoped to win her love as well. Nor would the princess tell him who she was, but she promised him that once they were wed she would reveal the secret, but until then he must not ask to know. And this condition, too, the merchant's son agreed to honor. So it was that the princess entertained him on that voyage by playing various musical instruments, and the time quickly passed.

When the day came that the ship approached the land of the merchant's son, filled with much valuable merchandise, the princess told the merchant that the proper thing to do would be for him to go to his home and inform his family that he was bringing with him the one who would become his bride. The merchant agreed to this, and also to the request of the princess that all of the sailors on the ship should be given wine to drink, so that they would share in their celebration.

In this way the merchant's son left the ship to inform his family, and the sailors began to drink. Before long they were all drunken, and they decided to leave the ship to look around the town. And when she had the ship to herself, the princess untied it from its moorings and unfurled the sails and set sail by herself.

Meanwhile the family of the merchant's son all came down to the harbor to greet his bride-to-be. But when they found the ship gone, including all the merchandise it had carried, the merchant was furious with his son, and asked him what had happened. All the merchant's son could say was "Ask the sailors," and when they searched for the sailors they found them sprawled drunken on the ground, and nei-ther then, nor later, when they were sober again, did they have any idea at all of what had happened to the ship. So it was that the mer-chant, in a great rage, drove his son out of his house, to become a wanderer in the world.

Meanwhile the princess continued to sail the ship intent on searching for her lost love. As it happened, she sailed by the kingdom of a king who had built his palace on the shore of the sea. And that king liked to watch the passing ships with his telescope. So it was that he noticed a ship sailing by that seemed to be empty, and sailing without any guidance. Then he sent his sailors to catch up with it, to bring it into port. This they did and in this way the princess was again captured, and became a prisoner of the king.

But when the king met his lovely prisoner, who had been sailing the ship by herself, he was greatly struck with her beauty and royal bearing, and he desired to marry her. This she agreed to do on three conditions: that the king not touch her until after their wedding; that her ship not be unloaded until the same time, so that all might see how much she had brought the king and so that none would say that she had come empty-handed; and, finally, she asked that she be given eleven ladies-in-waiting, to remain with her in her palace chamber. The king agreed to these conditions, and made plans for a lavish wedding. So too did he sent to her the daughters of eleven lords of his kingdom to serve as her ladies-in-waiting. And before long they had all become good friends, and they all played musical instruments together to amuse themselves.

One day before the wedding the princess invited her ladies-in-waiting to go with her onto the deck of the ship, to see what a ship was like. They all were glad to join her there, for they had never before been on a ship, and greatly enjoyed themselves. Then the princess offered them the good wine that she had found stored there, and they drank the wine and soon became intoxicated and fell asleep. Then the princess went and untied the moorings and raised the sails and once again escaped with the ship.

Now when the king was told that the ship was no longer docked, he became afraid that the princess would be distressed to hear it was missing, for he did not know that it was she who had taken it. But when they looked for her in her chamber they did not find her there, nor did they find her ladies-in-waiting. Finally they realized that the princess and her ladies had disappeared along with the ship, and the lords who were the fathers of the ladies were enraged, and forced the king to give up his throne, and afterward drove him from the land, so that he too became a wanderer in the world.

Now the princess and the eleven ladies were already far away at sea when the ladies awoke. And when they saw that they had sailed far beyond the shore, they were afraid and wanted to turn back, for they had never sailed in a ship. But the princess said to them: "Let us tarry here awhile." So they did, but when the ladies asked her why she had left the harbor, the princess said that a storm had arisen, and she had been afraid that the ship might have been broken in the harbor—therefore she had set out to sea. And soon afterward a storm did arise, and the ladies saw that they could not turn back, but were at the mercy of the currents. And when the storm subsided, they found themselves alone at sea, with no idea of how to seek out the land they had left, so they agreed to sail with the princess until they should reach land somewhere.

So they continued to journey at sea, the princess and the eleven ladies. At last they came to an island, and landed there, hoping to find fresh food and water. But it turned out that this was an island of bloodthirsty pirates, and when their sentries saw the ladies on the island, they approached them with their weapons drawn, and brought them to the chief pirate among them, asking if they might kill them right then and there.

Now when they stood before the pirate chief, the princess spoke for the others and said: "We too are pirates, but while you are pirates who use force, we are pirates who use wisdom. If you were wise the twelve of you"—for there were twelve pirates in all—"would each take one of us for a wife, and make use of our wisdom, which will surely help you to become far richer. And for our part we will each contribute a twelfth of the merchandise we have captured as pirates, which you will find on our ship."

Now the chief among the pirates was taken with the great beauty of the princess, and thought to himself how nice it would be to take her for a wife. So too did he think that what she had said made sense, and when the pirates saw all the wealth in the ship, which the princess had taken from the merchant's son, they agreed that they were indeed fine pirates. Therefore the pirates agreed among themselves that they would each, according to his rank, choose a lady to take for a wife. And after the chief of the pirates had chosen the princess, and the other pirates had made their choices among the ladies, the princess invited them to share the fine wine that they had on their ship.

So the princess poured out twelve goblets of wine for them, and the pirates drank until they all became drunk and fell asleep. Then she spoke to the ladies and said: "Now let us go and each kill her man," and they went and slaughtered them all. And there, on that island, they found such great wealth as is not possessed by any king. There was such an abundance that they resolved to take only the gold and precious gems, and unloaded all the merchandise from the ship, to make room for it. In this way they filled the whole ship with treasures, and prepared to set sail. But before they did, the princess had each of them sew a uniform to wear, so that they would all look like sailors, and then they set out to sea.

Once again they sailed for a long time, until they reached a distant port. There they docked the ship and descended into the city, wearing the sailors' uniforms that they had sewn. They roamed about the city, looking very much like men, and in this way they reached the center of the town, where they heard a great commotion and saw many people all running in one direction. One of the ladies inquired as to what was the matter, and she learned that the king of that country had just died childless, and that in such a case it was the custom of the country to have the queen go up to the roof of the palace and from there to throw down the dead king's crown. And on whomever's head it fell, that person became king.

Now the princess had hardly heard of this custom when she was struck with a heavy object, which landed on her head. She cried out, "Oh, my head!" But immediately she was surrounded by the viziers and wise men of the kingdom, who raised her onto their shoulders and cried out: "Long live our king!" The crown had indeed fallen on her head, and since she was wearing men's clothing, no one knew that she was a woman.

When the funeral of the former king was over, the wedding between the new king and the old king's widow was to take place. But the viziers, seeing that the new king was very young, preferred to marry the new king to the daughter of the chief vizier. The old queen agreed that this could be done, for she no longer wished to rule, and the wedding was set for the very next day.

Now the princess, disguised as a man, was afraid of what would happen when the truth came out, and she did not know what to do. Finally she called in the daughter of the vizier, and after pledging her to secrecy, she confessed that she was a woman, and told her the story of how she had been traveling with the other ladies, and how they had just come into port in that city and reached the center of town when the crown had landed on her head. The girl promised to help her, and together they worked out an excuse for postponing the wedding.

Meanwhile the disguised princess had the sculptors of the city brought into the palace, and ordered them to make many sculptures of the new king's head, and to put these up at every crossroad and at every road leading to and from the city. Soldiers were to be stationed at every spot where a sculpture was placed, and they were commanded to arrest anyone who stopped and showed great emotion at the sight of it.

It happened that three such people came along, and were arrested. The first was the prince who was the true bridegroom of the princess. The second was the son of the merchant whose ship the princess had seized, and who had afterward been banished by his father. And the third to be arrested was the king who had been driven out of his kingdom because the princess had sailed off with the eleven daughters of the high lords. For each had recognized the features of the princess, even though the sculpture represented a man.

Then, on the day of the wedding, the princess had these three brought into her presence, and she asked them what had happened to them since she had last seen them, and they told her their stories. The prince who was her true love had journeyed all over the world in search of her. He had come to the kingdom where she had escaped with the merchant's boat, and had passed through the kingdom where the king had been driven out because the princess had escaped with the eleven ladies. And he had also found the island of the pirates, and found their bodies there, along with the clothes of the princess and the ladies. So it was that he had sailed after them and reached that kingdom, which was the closest to the island of the pirates and he had been searching for her there when he had come upon the sculpture of the king who was about to be crowned and had recognized her face. So too had the merchant's son and the deposed king traveled around the world, seeking only their daily bread, and wondering why such disaster had befallen them.

And when the princess had heard what they had to say she turned first to the king who had lost his kingdom and said: "You, king, were driven out because of the eleven ladies who were lost. Take back your ladies. Return to your country and your kingdom, where you will surely be welcomed." And to the merchant's son she said: "Your father drove you out because of a ship filled with merchandise that was lost. Now you can take back your ship, which is filled with much more valuable treasures, whose worth is many times that which you had in it before." Finally she turned to the prince who was her true bride groom: "It is you to whom I was betrothed before any other. Come, let us be married to each other."

Then the princess called in all the viziers and ministers and revealed that she was not a man, but a beautiful woman. And she showed them the ring the prince carried with him, which she had given him in the forest before she had been captured by the merchant's son, which proved that it was he to whom she was truly betrothed.

And the viziers were so impressed with the character of the prince and princess that they asked them to remain among them as their king and queen, and this they agreed to do. That day the prince and princess were married in a great celebration, and afterward they ruled with an evenhanded mercy that all admired, and they lived happily ever after.

A General History of the Pyrates

by Captain Charles Johnson (1674–1748)

Not much is known about the author of this chronicle of pirate life, which was a best seller in 1724. Some scholars claim he is none other than Daniel Defoe. What is clear is that Mary Read and Anne Bonny disguised themselves as men and sailed as pirates in the company of "Calico Jack"—otherwise known as John Rackam, executed for piracy in 1720.

Now we are to begin a History full of surprizing Turns and Adventures; I mean, that of Mary Read and Anne Bonny, alias Bonn, which were the true Names of these two Pyrates; the odd Incidents of their rambling Lives are such that some may be tempted to think the whole Story no better than a Novel or Romance; but since it is supported by many thousand Witnesses, I mean the People of Jamaica, who were present at their Tryals, and heard the Story of their Lives, upon the first Discovery of their Sex; the Truth of it can be no more contested, than that there were such Men in the World, as Roberts and Blackbeard, who were Pyrates.

Mary Read was born in England, her Mother was married young, to a Man who used the Sea, who going a Voyage soon after their Marriage, left her with Child, which Child proved to be a Boy. As to the Husband, whether he was cast away, or died in the Voyage, Mary Read could not tell; but however, he never returned more; nevertheless, the Mother, who was young and airy, met with an Accident, which has often happened to Women who are young, and do not take a great deal of Care; which was, she soon proved with Child again, without a Husband to Father it, but how, or by whom, none but her self could tell, for she carry'd a pretty good Reputation among her Neighbours. Finding her Burthen grew, in order to conceal her Shame, she takes a formal Leave of her Husband's Relations, giving out, that she went to live with some Friends of her own, in the Country: Accordingly she went away, and carry'd with her her young Son, at this Time, not a Year old: Soon after her Departure her Son died, but Providence in Return, was pleased to give her a Girl in his Room, of which she was safely delivered, in her Retreat, and this was our Mary Read.

Here the Mother liv'd three or four Years, till what Money she had was almost gone; then she thought of returning to London, and considering that her Husband's Mother was in some Circumstances, she did not doubt but to prevail upon her, to provide for the Child, if she could but pass it upon her for the same, but the changing a Girl into a Boy, seem'd a difficult Piece of Work, and how to deceive an experienced old Woman, in such a Point, was altogether as impossible; however, she ventured to dress it up as a Boy, brought it to Town, and presented it to her Mother-in-Law, as her Husband's Son; the old Woman would have taken it, to have bred it up, but the Mother pretended it would break her Heart, to part with it; so it was agreed betwixt them, that the Child should live with the Mother, and the supposed Grandmother should allow a Crown a Week for its Maintainance.

Thus the Mother gained her Point, she bred up her Daughter as a Boy, and when she grew up to some Sense, she thought proper to let her into the Secret of her Birth, to induce her to conceal her Sex. It happen'd that the Grandmother died, by which Means the Subsistance that came from that Quarter, ceas'd, and they were more and more reduced in their Circumstances; wherefore she was obliged to put her Daughter out, to wait on a French Lady, as a, Foot-boy being now thirteen Years of Age: Here she did not live long, for growing bold and strong, and having also a roving Mind, she enter'd herself on board a Man of War, where she served some Time, then quitted it, went over into Flanders, and carry'd Arms in a Regiment of Foot, as a Cadet; and tho' upon all Actions, she behaved herself with a great deal of Bravery, yet she could not get a Commission, they being generally bought and sold; therefore she quitted the Service, and took on in a Regiment of Horse; she behaved so well in several Engagements, that she got the Esteem of all her Officers; but her Comrade, who was a Fleming, happening to be a handsome young Fellow, she falls in Love with him, and from that Time, grew a little more negligent in her Duty, so that, it seems, Mars and Venus could not be served at the same Time; her Arms and Accoutrements which were always kept in the best Order, were quite neglected: 'Tis true, when her Comrade was order'd out upon a Party, she used to go without being commanded, and frequently ran herself into Danger, where she had no Business, only to be near him; the rest of the Troopers little suspecting the secret Cause which moved her to this Behaviour, fancy'd her to be mad, and her Comrade himself could not account for this strange Alteration in her, but Love is ingenious, and as they lay together in the same Tent, and were constantly together, she found a Way of letting him discover her Sex, without appearing that it was done with Design.

He was much surprized at what he found out, and not a little pleased, taking it for granted, that he should have a Mistress solely to himself, which is an unusual Thing in a Camp, since there is scarce one of those Campaign Ladies, that is ever true to a Troop or Company; so that he thought of nothing but gratifying his Passions with very little Ceremony; but he found himself strangely mistaken, for she proved very reserved and modest, and resisted all his Temptations, and at the same Time was so obliging and insinuating in her Carriage, that she quite changed his Purpose, so far from thinking of making her his Mistress, he now courted her for a Wife.

This was the utmost Wish of her Heart, in short, they exchanged Promises, and when the Campaign was over, and the Regiment marched into Winter Quarters, they bought Woman's Apparel for her, with such Money as they could make up betwixt them, and were publickly married.

The Story of two Troopers marrying each other, made a great Noise, so that several Officers were drawn by Curiosity to assist at the Ceremony, and they agreed among themselves that every one of them should make a small Present to the Bride, towards House-keeping, in Consideration of her having been their Fellow-Soldier. Thus being set up, they seemed to have a Desire of quitting the Service, and settling in the World; the Adventure of their Love and Marriage had gained them so much Favour, that they easily obtained their Discharge, and they immediately set up an Eating-House or Ordinary, which was the Sign of the Three Horse-Shoes, near the Castle of Breda, where they soon run into a good Trade, a great many Officers eating with them constantly.

But this Happiness lasted not long, for the Husband soon died, and the Peace of Ryswick being concluded, there was no Resort of Officers to Breda, as usual, so that the Widow having little or no Trade, was forced to give up House-keeping, and her Substance being by Degrees quite spent, she again assumes her Man's Apparel, and going into Holland, there takes on in a Regiment of Foot, quartered in one of the Frontier Towns: Here she did not remain long, there was no Likelihood of Preferment in Time of Peace, therefore she took a Resolution of seeking her Fortune another Way; and withdrawing from the Regiment, ships herself on board of a Vessel bound for the West-Indies.

It happened this Ship was taken by English Pyrates, and Mary Read was the only English Person on board, they kept her amongst them, and having plundered the Ship, let it go again; after following this Trade for some Time, the King's Proclamation came out, and was published in all Parts of the West-Indies, for pardoning such Pyrates, who should voluntarily surrender themselves by a certain Day therein mentioned. The Crew of Mary Read took the Benefit of this Proclamation, and having surrender'd, liv'd quietly on Shore; but Money beginning to grow short, and hearing that Captain Woodes Rogers, Governor of the Island of Providence, was fitting out some Privateers to cruise against the Spaniards, she, with several others, embark'd for that Island, in order to go upon the privateering Account, being resolved to make her Fortune one way or other.

These Privateers were no sooner sail'd out, but the Crews of some of them, who had been pardoned, rose against their Commanders, and turned themselves to their old Trade: In this Number was Mary Read. It is true, she often declared, that the Life of a Pyrate was what she always abhor'd, and went into it only upon Compulsion, both this Time, and before, intending to quit it, whenever a fair Opportunity should offer itself; yet some of the Evidence against her, upon her Tryal, who were forced Men, and had sail'd with her, deposed upon Oath, that in Times of Action, no Person amongst them was more resolute, or ready to board or undertake any Thing that was hazardous, than she and Anne Bonny; and particularly at the time they were attack'd and taken, when they came to close Quarters, none kept the Deck except Mary Read and Anne Bonny, and one more; upon which, she, Mary Read, called to those under Deck, to come up and fight like Men, and finding they did not stir, fired her Arms down the Hold amongst them, killing one, and wounding others.

This was Part of the Evidence against her, which she denied; which, whether true or no, thus much is certain, that she did not want Bravery, nor indeed was she less remarkable for her Modesty, according to the Notions of Virtue: Her Sex was not so much as suspected by any Person on board till Anne Bonny, who was not altogether so reserved in Point of Chastity, took a particular Liking to her; in short, Anne Bonny took her for a handsome young Fellow, and for some Reasons best known to herself, first discovered her Sex to Mary Read; Mary Read knowing what she would be at, and being very sensible of her own Incapacity that Way, was forced to come to a right Understanding with her, and so to the great Disappointment of Anne Bonny, she let her know she was a Woman also; but this Intimacy so disturb'd Captain Rackam, who was the Lover and Gallant of Anne Bonny, that he grew furiously jealous, so that he told Anne Bonny, he would cut her new Lover's Throat, therefore, to quiet him, she let him into the Secret also.

Captain Rackam (as he was enjoined) kept the Thing a Secret from all the Ship's Company, yet, notwithstanding all her Cunning and Reserve, Love found her out in this Disguise, and hinder'd her from forgetting her Sex. In their Cruise they took a great Number of Ships belonging to Jamaica, and other Parts of the West-Indies, bound to and from England; and whenever they met any good Artist, or other Person that might be of any great Use to their Company, if he was not willing to enter, it was their Custom to keep him by Force. Among these was a young Fellow of a most engaging Behaviour, or, at least, he was so in the Eyes of Mary Read, who became so smitten with his Person and Address, that she could neither rest Night or Day; but there is nothing more ingenious than Love, it was no hard Matter for her, who had before been practiced in these Wiles, to find a Way to let him discover her Sex: She first insinuated herself into his Liking, by talking against the Life of a Pyrate, which he was altogether averse to, so they became Mess-Mates and strict Companions: When she found he had a Friendship for her, as a Man, she suffered the Discovery to be made, by carelessly shewing her Breasts, which were very white.

The young Fellow, who was made of Flesh and Blood, had his Curiosity and Desire so rais'd by this Sight, that he never ceas'd importuning her, till she confessed what she was. Now begins the Scene of Love; as he had a Liking and Esteem for her, under her supposed Character, it was now turn'd into Fondness and Desire; her Passion was no less violent than his, and perhaps she express'd it, by one of the most generous Actions that ever Love inspired. It happened this young Fellow had a Quarrel with one of the Pyrates, and their Ship then lying at an Anchor, near one of the Islands, they had appointed to go ashore and fight, according to the Custom of the Pyrates: Mary Read was to the last Degree uneasy and anxious, for the Fate of her Lover; she would not have had him refuse the Challenge, because, she could not bear the Thoughts of his being branded with Cowardice; on the other Side, she dreaded the Event, and apprehended the Fellow might be too hard for him: When Love once enters into the Breast of one who has any Sparks of Generosity, it stirs the Heart up to the most noble Actions; in this

Dilemma, she shew'd, that she fear'd more for his Life than she did for her own; for she took a Resolution of quarrelling with this Fellow her self, and having challenged him ashore, she appointed the Time two Hours sooner than that when he was to meet her Lover, where she fought him at Sword and Pistol, and killed him upon the Spot.

It is true, she had fought before, when she had been insulted by some of those Fellows, but now it was altogether in her Lover's Cause, she stood as it were betwixt him and Death, as if she could not live without him. If he had no regard for her before, this Action would have bound him to her for ever; but there was no Occasion for Ties or Obligation, his Inclination towards her was sufficient; in fine, they plighted their Troth to each other, which Mary Read said, she look'd upon to be as good a Marriage, in Conscience, as if it had been done by a Minister in Church; and to this was owing her great Belly, which she pleaded to save her Life.

She declared she had never committed Adultery or Fornication with any Man, she commended the Justice of the Court, before which she was try'd, for distinguishing the Nature of their Crimes; her Husband, as she call'd him, with several others, being acquitted; and being ask'd, who he was? she would not tell, but, said he was an honest Man, and had no Inclination to such Practices, and that they had both resolved to leave the Pyrates, the first Opportunity, and apply themselves to some honest Livelihood.

It is no doubt, but many had Compassion for her, yet the Court could not avoid finding her Guilty; for among other Things, one of the Evidences against her, deposed, that being taken by Rackam, and detain'd some Time on board, he fell accidentally into Discourse with Mary Read, whom he taking for a young Man, ask'd her, what Pleasure she could have in being concerned in such Enterprizes, where her Life was continually in Danger, by Fire or Sword; and not only so, but she must be sure of dying an ignominious Death, if she should be taken alive?—She answer'd, that as to hanging, she thought it no great Hardship, for, were it not for that, every cowardly Fellow would turn Pyrate, and so infest the Seas, that Men of Courage must starve:— That if it was put to the Choice of the Pyrates, they would not have the Punishment less than Death, the Fear of which kept some dastardly Rogues honest; that many of those who are now cheating the Widows and Orphans, and oppressing their poor Neighbours, who have no Money to obtain Justice, would then rob at Sea, and the Ocean would be crowded with Rogues, like the Land, and no Merchant would venture out; so that the Trade, in a little Time, would not be worth following.

Being found quick with Child, as has been observed, her Execution was respited, and it is possible she would have found Favour, but she was seiz'd with a violent Fever, soon after her Tryal, of which she died in Prison.

The Life of Anne Bonny

As we have been more particular in the Lives of these two Women, than those of other Pyrates, it is incumbent on us, as a faithful Historian, to begin with their Birth. Anne Bonny was born at a Town near Cork, in the Kingdom of Ireland, her Father an Attorney at Law, but Anne was not one of his legitimate Issue, which seems to cross an old Proverb, which says, that Bastards have the best Luck. Her Father was a married Man, and his Wife having been brought to Bed, contracted an Illness in her lying in, and in order to recover her Health, she was advised to remove for Change of Air; the Place she chose, was a few Miles distance from her Dwelling, where her Husband's Mother liv'd. Here she sojourn'd some Time, her Husband staying at Home, to follow his Affairs. The Servant-Maid, whom she left to look after the House, and attend the Family, being a handsome young Woman, was courted by a young Man of the same Town, who was a Tanner; this Tanner used to take his Opportunities, when the Family was out of the Way, of coming to pursue his Courtship; and being with the Maid one Day as she was employed in the Household Business, not having the Fear of God before his Eyes, he takes his Opportunity, when her Back was turned, of whipping three Silver Spoons into his Pocket. The Maid soon miss'd the Spoons, and knowing that no Body had been in the Room, but herself and the young Man, since she saw them last, she charged him with taking them; he very stifly denied it, upon which she grew outragious, and threatned to go to a Constable, in order to carry him before a Justice of Peace: These Menaces frighten'd him out of his Wits, well knowing he could not stand Search; wherefore he endeavoured to pacify her, by desiring her to examine the Drawers and other Places, and perhaps she might find them; in this Time he slips into another Room, where the Maid usually lay, and puts the Spoons betwixt the Sheets, and then makes his Escape by a back Door, concluding she must find them, when she went to Bed, and so next Day he might pretend he did it only to frighten her, and the Thing might be laugh'd off for a Jest.

As soon as she miss'd him, she gave over her Search, concluding he had carry'd them off, and went directly to the Constable, in order to have him apprehended: The young Man was informed, that a Constable had been in Search of him, but he regarded it but little, not doubting but all would be well next Day. Three or four Days passed, and still he was told, the Constable was upon the Hunt for him, this made him lye concealed, he could not comprehend the Meaning of it, he imagined no less, than that the Maid had a Mind to convert the Spoons to her own Use, and put the Robbery upon him.

It happen'd, at this Time, that the Mistress being perfectly recovered of her late Indisposition, was returned Home, in Company with her Mother-in-Law; the first News she heard, was of the Loss of the Spoons, with the Manner how; the Maid telling her, at the same Time, that the young Man was run away. The young Fellow had Intelligence of the Mistress's Arrival, and considering with himself, that he could never appear again in his Business, unless this Matter was got over, and she being a good-natured Woman, he took a Resolution of going directly to her, and of telling her the whole Story, only with this Difference, that he did it for a Jest.

The Mistress could scarce believe it, however, she went directly to the Maid's Room, and turning down the Bed Cloaths, there, to her great Surprize, found the three Spoons; upon this she desired the young Man to go Home and mind his Business, for he should have no Trouble about it.

The Mistress could not imagine the Meaning of this, she never had found the Maid guilty of any pilfering, and therefore it could not enter her Head, that she designed to steal the Spoons her self; upon the whole, she concluded the Maid had not been in her Bed, from the Time the Spoons were miss'd, she grew immediately jealous upon it, and suspected, that the Maid supply'd her Place with her Husband, during her Absence, and this was the Reason why the Spoons were no sooner found.

She call'd to Mind several Actions of Kindness, her Husband had shewed the Maid, Things that pass'd unheeded by, when they happen'd, but now she had got the Tormentor, Jealousy, in her Head, amounted to Proofs of their Intimacy; another Circumstance which strengthen'd the whole, was, that tho' her Husband knew she was to come Home that Day, and had had no Communication with her in four Months, which was before her last lying in, yet he took an Opportunity of going out of Town that Morning, upon some slight Pretence:— All these Things put together, confirm'd her in her Jealousy.

As Women seldom forgive Injuries of this Kind, she thought of discharging her Revenge upon the Maid: In order to this, she leaves the Spoons where she found them, and orders the Maid to put clean Sheets upon the Bed, telling her, she intended to lye there herself that Night, because her Mother-in-Law was to lye in her Bed, and that she (the Maid) must lye in another Part of the House; the Maid in making the Bed, was surprized with the Sight of the Spoons, but there were very good Reasons, why it was not proper for her to tell where she found them, therefore she takes them up, puts them in her Trunk, intending to leave them in some Place, where they might be found by Chance.

The Mistress, that every Thing might look to be done without Design, lyes that Night in the Maid's Bed, little dreaming of what an Adventure it would produce: After she had been a Bed some Time, thinking on what had pass'd, for Jealousy kept her awake, she heard some Body enter the Room; at first she apprehended it to be Thieves, and was so fright'ned, she had not Courage enough to call out; but when she heard these Words, Mary, are you awake? she knew it to be her Husband's Voice; then her Fright was over, yet she made no Answer, least he should find her out, if she spoke, therefore she resolved to counterfeit Sleep, and take what followed.

The Husband came to Bed, and that Night play'd the vigorous Lover; but one Thing spoiled the Diversion on the Wife's Side, which was, the Reflection that it was not design'd for her; however she was very passive, and bore it like a Christian. Early before Day, she stole out of Bed, leaving him asleep, and went to her Mother-in-Law, telling her what had passed, not forgetting how he had used her, as taking her for the Maid; the Husband also stole out, not thinking it convenient to be catched in that Room; in the mean Time, the Revenge of the Mistress was strongly against the Maid, and without considering that to her she owed the Diversion of the Night before, and that one good turn should deserve another; she sent for a Constable, and charged her with stealing the Spoons: The Maid's Trunk was broke open, and the Spoons found, upon which she was carry'd before a Justice of Peace, and by him committed to Gaol.

The Husband loiter'd about till twelve a-Clock at Noon, then comes Home, pretending he was just come to Town; as soon as he heard what had pass'd, in Relation to the Maid, he fell into a great Passion with his Wife; this set the Thing into a greater Flame, the Mother takes the Wife's Part against her own Son, insomuch that the Quarrel encreasing, the Mother and Wife took Horse immediately, and went back to the Mother's House, and the Husband and Wife never bedded together after.

The Maid lay a long Time in the Prison, it being near half a Year to the Assizes; but before it happened, it was discovered she was with Child; when she was arraign'd at the Bar, she was discharged for want of Evidence; the Wife's Conscience touch'd her, and as she did not believe the Maid Guilty of any Theft, except that of Love, she did not appear against her; soon after her Acquittal, she was delivered of a Girl.

But what alarm'd the Husband most, was, that it was discovered the Wife was with Child also, he taking it for granted, he had had no

Intimacy with her, since her last lying in, grew jealous of her, in his Turn, and made this a Handle to justify himself, for his Usage of her, pretending now he had suspected her long, but that here was Proof; she was delivered of Twins, a Boy and a Girl.

The Mother falling ill, sent to her Son to reconcile him to his Wife, but he would not hearken to it; therefore she made a Will, leaving all she had in the Hands of certain Trustees, for the Use of the Wife and two Children lately born, and died a few Days after.

This was an ugly Turn upon him, his greatest Dependance being upon his Mother; however, his Wife was kinder to him than he deserved, for she made him a yearly Allowance out of what was left, tho' they continued to live separate: It lasted near five Years; at this Time having a great Affection for the Girl he had by his Maid, he had a Mind to take it Home, to live with him; but as all the Town knew it to be a Girl, the better to disguise the Matter from them, as well as from his Wife, he had it put into Breeches, as a Boy, pretending it was a Relation's Child he was to breed up to be his Clerk.

The Wife heard he had a little Boy at Home he was very fond of, but as she did not know any Relation of his that had such a Child, she employ'd a Friend to enquire further into it; this Person by talking with the Child, found it to be a Girl, discovered that the Servant-Maid was its Mother, and that the Husband still kept up his Correspondence with her.

Upon this Intelligence, the Wife being unwilling that her Children's Money should go towards the Maintainance of Bastards, stopped the Allowance: The Husband enraged, in a kind of Revenge, takes the Maid home, and lives with her publickly, to the great Scandal of his Neighbours; but he soon found the bad Effect of it, for by Degrees he lost his Practice, so that he saw plainly he could not live there, therefore he thought of removing, and turning what Effects he had into ready Money; he goes to Cork, and there with his Maid and Daughter embarques for Carolina.

At first he followed the Practice of the Law in that Province, but afterwards fell into Merchandize, which proved more successful to him, for he gained by it sufficient to purchase a considerable Plantation: His Maid, who passed for his Wife, happened to die, after which his Daughter, our Anne Bonny, now grown up, kept his House.

She was of a fierce and couragious Temper, wherefore, when she lay under Condemnation, several Stories were reported of her, much to her Disadvantage, as that she had kill'd an English Servant-Maid once in her Passion with a Case-Knife, while she look'd after her Father's House; but upon further Enquiry, I found this Story to be groundless: It was certain she was so robust, that once, when a young Fellow would have lain with her, against her Will, she beat him so, that he lay ill of it a considerable Time.

While she lived with her Father, she was look'd upon as one that would be a good Fortune, wherefore it was thought her Father expected a good Match for her; but she spoil'd all, for without his Consent, she marries a young Fellow, who belong'd to the Sea, and was not worth a Groat; which provoked her Father to such a Degree, that he turn'd her out of Doors, upon which the young Fellow, who married her, finding himself disappointed in his Expectation, shipped himself and Wife, for the Island of Providence, expecting Employment there.

Here she became acquainted with Rackam the Pyrate, who making Courtship to her, soon found Means of withdrawing her Affections from her Husband, so that she consented to elope from him, and go to Sea with Rackam in Men's Cloaths: She was as good as her Word, and after she had been at Sea some Time, she proved with Child, and beginning to grow big, Rackam landed her on the Island of Cuba; and recommending her there to some Friends of his, they took Care of her, till she was brought to Bed: When she was up and well again, he sent for her to bear him Company.

The King's Proclamation being out, for pardoning of Pyrates, he took the Benefit of it, and surrender'd; afterwards being sent upon the privateering Account, he return'd to his old Trade, as has been already hinted in the Story of Mary Read. In all these Expeditions, Anne Bonny bore him Company, and when any Business was to be done in their Way, no Body was more forward or couragious than she, and particularly when they were taken; she and Mary Read, with one more, were all the Persons that durst keep the Deck, as has been before hinted.

Her Father was known to a great many Gentlemen Planters of Jamaica, who had dealt with him, and among whom he had a good Reputation; and some of them, who had been in Carolina, remember'd to have seen her in his House; wherefore they were enclined to show her Favour, but the Action of leaving her Husband was an ugly Circumstance against her. The Day that Rackam was executed, by special Favour, he was admitted to see her; but all the Comfort she gave him, was, that she was sorry to see him there, but if he had fought like a Man, he need not have been hang'd like a Dog.

She was continued in Prison, to the Time of her lying in, and afterwards reprieved from Time to Time; but what is become of her since, we cannot tell; only this we know, that she was not executed.

from

The Count of Monte Cristo

by Alexandre Dumas (1802–1870)

Edmond Dantès, falsely accused as a spy, spends 14 years in the hideous prison known as the Chateau D'if. During his incarceration he is befriended by Faria, an old abbot, who, as he lies dying, tells Edmond of a fabulous fortune buried on the island of Monte Cristo.

N ow that the treasure, which had for so long been the object of Faria's meditations, could assure the future happiness of the young man he truly loved as a son, its value had doubled in his eyes. Every day he spoke of the immensity of the treasure, explaining to Dantès all the good a man could do for his friends in our modern times with such a fortune. At those moments Dantès' face would darken, for he remembered the oath of vengeance he had sworn, and he thought of how much harm a man could do to his enemies in our modern times with such a fortune.

Faria did not know the Isle of Monte Cristo, but Dantès did. He had often passed by that small island, located twenty-five miles from

Pianosa, between Corsica and the Isle of Elba, and once he had landed there. It was, and still is, completely deserted; it is a rock of almost conical form which seems to have been thrust up from the bottom of the sea by some volcanic cataclysm.

As Faria had predicted, his arm and leg remained paralyzed and he lost almost all hope of ever reaching the treasure himself, but he continued to dream of an escape for his young companion. For fear the letter might be lost, he made Dantès learn it by heart, word for word.

Then one night Dantès awoke suddenly with the impression that someone had called him. He opened his eyes and tried to penetrate the darkness. His name, or rather a plaintive voice trying to articulate his name, reached his ears. He leaped out of bed and listened. No doubt of it, the voice was coming from Faria's cell.

"Good God!" murmured Dantès. "Could it be that . . . ?" He shoved back his bed, rushed into the underground passage and was soon at the opposite end of it; the flagstone was raised. By the flickering light of the lamp we have already described, he saw the old man, his face deathly white and contracted by the horrible symptoms which Dantès already knew and which had filled him with such terror the first time he saw them.

"Well, my friend," said Faria resignedly, "you understand, don't you? There's no need for me to explain anything to you. Think only of yourself from now on, of making your captivity bearable and your escape possible. You'll no longer have a half-dead body tied to you, paralyzing all your movements. God is doing something good for you at last, and it's high time for me to die."

Dantès could do nothing except clasp his hands and cry out, "Oh, my friend! My friend!" Then, regaining a little of his courage, he said, "I saved you once and I'll save you again!" He lifted the foot of the bed and took out the small bottle, which was still one-third full of the red liquid.

"There's no hope," said Faria, shaking his head, "but you may try if you wish. I'm growing cold, I feel the blood rushing to my brain, and that horrible trembling is beginning to shake my whole body. In five minutes the attack will begin in earnest; in a quarter of an hour there will be nothing left of me but a corpse."

"Oh!" cried Dantès, his heart breaking.

"Do as you did before, only this time don't wait so long. After you've poured twelve drops down my throat, if you see that I'm not regaining consciousness, pour the rest. Now carry me to my bed, I can't stand up any longer."

Dantès picked up the old man and laid him on his bed.

"And now, my friend," said Faria, "sole consolation of my wretched life, you whom heaven gave me a little late, but gave me nonetheless, at this moment when I am about to be separated from you forever, I wish you all the happiness and all the prosperity that you deserve. My son, I bless you." Dantès dropped to his knees, leaning his head against the bed.

A violent shock interrupted the old man. "Farewell! Farewell!" he murmured, pressing Dantès' hand convulsively.

The attack was terrible. Twisted limbs, swollen eyelids, bloody foam, a motionless body—this was all that remained of the intelligent being who had been there only a moment before. When he believed it to be the right time, Dantès pried Faria's teeth apart with the knife and poured twelve drops of the liquid into his mouth. He waited for ten minutes, a quarter of an hour, half an hour; there was no sign of a movement. Trembling, his forehead streaming with cold sweat, he decided the time had come to try his last resource. He poured the rest of the liquid into Faria's mouth.

The medicine produced a galvanic effect. The old man shook violently in every limb, his eyes opened, frightening to behold, and he heaved a sign which sounded like a shriek. Then his trembling body gradually became rigid again. Finally the last murmur of his heart ceased, his face grew livid and the light faded entirely from his eyes, which remained open.

It was six o'clock in the morning. The first feeble rays of dawn invaded the cell, casting weird reflections over the face of the corpse and giving it an appearance of life from time to time. As long as the struggle between day and night lasted, Dantès was still able to doubt, but as soon as day won out he realized fully that he was alone with a corpse. An overwhelming terror seized him; he no longer dared press that hand hanging over the edge of the bed, nor look at those vacant, staring eyes which he had vainly tried several times to close, but which had always opened again. He blew out the lamp, hid it carefully and fled from the cell, replacing the stone behind him as well as he could.

He left none too soon, for the jailer was coming. This time he began his visit with Dantès' cell. Nothing indicated that he was aware of what had happened. He went out. Burning with impatience to know what would happen in the cell of his unfortunate friend, Dantès crawled back into the underground passage in time to hear the jailer calling for aid. Other jailers soon arrived, then came the heavy, measured footsteps of soldiers. Behind them came the governor.

Dantès heard the bed creaking as they tried to rouse the dead man. The governor ordered them to throw water in his face, then, seeing that this had no effect, he sent for the doctor. The governor left the cell and several words of compassion, mingled with crude jokes and laughter, reached Dantès' ears.

"Well," said one voice, "the old lunatic's gone off to find his treasure. *Bon voyage!*"

"With all his millions he still didn't have enough to pay for his shroud," said another.

"Oh, the shrouds of the Château d'If don't cost much."

"Since he's a priest, maybe they'll go to a little extra expense for him."

"That's right: he'll have the honor of the sack."

Dantès listened without losing a word, but he did not understand much of what was being said. Soon the voices died away and it seemed to him that everyone had left the cell. He was nevertheless afraid to go back in: a jailer might have been left behind to guard the dead man.

After an hour or so the silence was broken by a faint noise which gradually grew louder. It was the governor coming back, followed by the doctor and several officials.

There was a moment of silence; the doctor was evidently examining the body. He declared the prisoner dead and diagnosed the cause of death.

"Not that I doubt your competence, doctor," said the governor, "but we can't be satisfied with a mere examination in such cases. I just ask you to carry out the formalities prescribed by law."

"Very well, then," said the doctor, "heat up the irons."

This order made Dantès shudder. He heard hurried footsteps and the sound of a door being opened. Several moments later a jailer came back into the cell. Then the thick, nauseating odor of burning flesh penetrated the wall behind which Dantès was listening in horror. Beads of sweat burst out on his forehead and for a moment he thought he was going to faint.

"You see: he's really dead," said the doctor. "That burn on the heel is decisive. The poor madman is cured of his madness and delivered from his captivity."

Dantès heard a sound like the rustling of cloth. The bed creaked, there were heavy footsteps like those of a man lifting a burden and the bed creaked once again under the weight which had been placed back on it.

"Will there be a mass?" asked one of the officials.

"Impossible," replied the governor. "The chaplain asked me for a week's leave yesterday and he's already gone. If the poor priest hadn't been in such a hurry he'd have had his requiem."

"That's all right," remarked the doctor, with the impiety common to those of his profession; "God won't give the devil the pleasure of receiving a priest."

There was a burst of laughter. Meanwhile the body had been laid out.

"Tonight," said the governor.

"What time?" asked one of the jailers.

"At around ten or eleven o'clock, as usual."

"Shall we watch over the body?"

"What for? Just lock the door as though he were still alive."

The footsteps went away and the voices died down. Then a silence more mournful than that of solitude—the silence of death—invaded everything and chilled the depths of Dantès' heart. He slowly raised the stone with his head and cast a swift glance around the cell. It was empty. He entered.

Stretched out on the bed, faintly illuminated by the pale ray of daylight coming in through the window, he saw a sack of coarse cloth under whose ample folds he could discern the outlines of a long, stiff form. It was Faria's shroud, that shroud which, according to the jailers, cost so little. It was all over; Dantès was separted forever from his old friend. Faria, his helpful, kind companion, now existed only in his memory. He sat down on the edge of the frightful bed, plunged in deep and bitter melancholy.

Alone! He was alone again! The idea of suicide, which his friend's presence had driven away, now rose up again like a phantom beside his corpse. "If only I could die," he said, "I'd go where he's gone and I'd be with him again. But how can I die?" He thought for a moment, then said, smiling, "It's very easy: I'll stay here and attack the first man who comes in. I'll strangle him and they'll guillotine me."

But then he recoiled from the idea of such an infamous death and swiftly passed from despair to a burning thirst for life and freedom. "Die? Oh, no!" he cried out. "What would be the point of having lived and suffered so much if I were going to die now? No, I want to live, to fight on to the end. I want to win back the happiness that was taken away from me. I must punish my enemies before I die, and I may also have some friends to reward. But they'll forget me here, and the only way I'll ever leave this dungeon is like Faria."

As he spoke these words he sat stock-still, staring into space like a man suddenly struck by a terrifying idea. Then he stood up, put his hand to his forehead as though he were dizzy and murmured, "Who sent me this thought? Was it you, O God? Since only the dead leave here, I'll take the place of a corpse!"

Without giving himself time to reconsider his desperate resolution, he leaned over the hideous sack, slit it open with the knife which Faria had made, took out the corpse, carried it into his own cell, put it on his bed, wrapped around its head the rag which he himself always wore, pulled his blanket over it, kissed the cold forehead one last time, tried once again to close the rebellious eyes, which persisted in remaining open, and turned the head to the wall so that when the jailer brought in his evening meal he would think he was already asleep, as he often was. Then be went back into Faria's cell, took out the needle and thread, threw off his clothes so that the jailers would feel bare flesh under the sackcloth, slipped into the sack, placed himself in the same position as the corpse and sewed up the sack again from the inside. If the jailers had happened to come in at that moment they would have heard the beating of his heart.

His plan was all worked out: if the gravediggers discovered that they were carrying a living man instead of a corpse, he would quickly rip open the sack with his knife and take advantage of their terror to escape; if they tried to stop him, he would use the knife on them. If they carried him all the way to the cemetery and laid him in a grave, he would let himself be covered over, then, since it would be night, as soon as the gravediggers had turned their backs, he would force his way up through the soft earth and escape. He hoped the weight would not be too heavy for him to raise, otherwise he would be smothered to death. But even this possibility did not dismay him: at least everything would be finished.

Toward seven o'clock in the evening his anxiety began in earnest. He trembled in every limb and his heart felt as though it were being gripped in an icy vise. The hours passed without bringing the slightest movement in the prison; so far his ruse had not been dis- covered. Finally he heard footsteps on the stairs. The time had come. He summoned up all his courage, held his breath and tried to repress the pounding of his heart.

The door opened and a dim light reached his eyes. Through the cloth covering him he saw two shadows approach the bed. A third one stood in the doorway holding a lantern. The first two men took hold of the sack from both ends. Dantès made his body rigid.

"He's very heavy for such a skinny old man," said one.

"They say every year adds half a pound to the weight of a man's bones," said the other.

They carried him out on a stretcher and the funeral procession, led by the man with the lantern, went up the stairs. Suddenly Dantès felt the cold, fresh night air and the sharp wind from the sea. The sensation filled him with both joy and anxiety.

They carried him some twenty yards further, then stopped and laid the stretcher on the ground. Dantès heard one of the men walking away. "Where am I?" he wondered.

His first impulse was to try to escape, but fortunately he controlled himself. A few moments later he heard one of the men walk up to him and drop a heavy object on the ground. At the same time he felt a rope tied around his feet with painful tightness.

"Have you made the knot?" asked the man who had remained idle.

"Yes, and it's well made, I'll answer for that."

"All right, then, let's go."

The stretcher was raised again and the procession continued on its way. The sound of the waves breaking against the rocks on which the Château d'If is built reached Dantès more distinctly with every step.

"What miserable weather!" said one of the men. "I wouldn't like to be at sea tonight."

"Yes," said the other, "there's a good chance the priest may get his feet wet!" They both burst out laughing.

Dantès did not understand the joke, but his hair stood on end nevertheless.

"Here we are," said the first man after a while.

"No, further on, further on! You know the last one got smashed on the rocks and the next day the governor called us a couple of lazy rascals."

They went on a few more steps, then Dantès felt them pick him up by the head and feet and swing him back and forth.

"One! Two! Three!"

With the last word he felt himself flung into space. Fear clutched at his heart as he fell like a wounded bird, down, down, down. Finally, after what seemed an eternity, there was a tremendous splash and he plunged like an arrow into the icy sea. He uttered a scream which was immediately choked off as the water closed over his head. He was being swiftly dragged to the bottom by a cannon ball tied to his feet.

The sea is the cemetery of the Château d'If.

Although he was stunned and almost suffocated, Dantès nevertheless had the presence of mind to hold his breath and rip open the sack with the knife which he still held in his right hand. But he was still being dragged downward by the cannon ball tied to his feet. He bent double and cut the rope just as he was about to suffocate. Then he kicked vigorously and rose to the surface of the sea. He paused only long enough to take a deep breath, then dived again to avoid being seen.

When he came up the second time, he was already fifty yards away from the spot where he had plunged into the sea. Above his head he saw a black, stormy sky; before him lay the dark plain of the sea, whose waves were beginning to churn as though before the approach of a storm, while behind him, blacker than either the sky or the sea, the granite giant rose up like a threatening phantom. He decided to head for the Isle of Tiboulen, the nearest uninhabited island, about one league away. But how was he to find it in the thick darkness which surrounded him? Suddenly he saw the Planier lighthouse shining like a star. If he headed straight for this lighthouse, he would pass the Isle of Tiboulen on his left; by heading a little to the left, therefore, he ought to place the island in his path. He noticed with joy that his years of forced inaction had taken away none of his strength and agility and that he was still master of the element in which he had played so often as a boy.

An hour passed, during which Dantès continued to swim in the direction he had chosen. "Unless I'm mistaken," he thought, "I shouldn't be far from the Isle of Tiboulen now. But what if I'm mistaken?" He shuddered and tried to float for a while in order to rest himself, but the sea had become so rough that it was impossible. "Well, then," he said, "I'll go on to the end, till my arms are exhausted, till I'm seized with cramps, and then I'll sink to the bottom." He began to swim with the strength and drive of despair.

Suddenly it seemed to him that the sky, which was already dark, became still darker, and that a thick, heavy cloud was descending on him. At the same time he felt a sharp pain in his knee. His imagination instantly told him that he had been struck by a bullet and that he would soon hear the sound of the shot. But he heard no shot. He put out his hand and felt something solid; he drew up his other leg and felt land. He then saw what it was that he had taken to be a cloud: twenty yards ahead of him rose a mass of strangely shaped rocks which looked like an immense, petrified fire. It was the Isle of Tiboulen.

Dantès stood up, took a few steps forward, then murmured, "Thank God!" and lay down on the jagged rocks, which seemed softer to him than any bed he had ever known. In spite of the wind, the storm, and the rain which was beginning to fall, he went to sleep.

An hour later he was awakened by the roar of a tremendous clap of thunder. He took refuge beneath an overhanging rock just before the storm burst in all its fury. A flash of lightning which seemed to open the heavens to the very throne of God illuminated the space around him and, a quarter of a league away, he saw a small fishing boat appear, carried along by the wind and the waves. It vanished between two waves, then reappeared an instant later on the crest of another wave, approaching with frightful rapidity. Dantès cried out and looked around for something to wave to them and warn them they were approaching their doom, but they were well aware of it themselves. By the light of another flash of lightning he saw four men clinging to the masts and rigging, while a fifth clutched the tiller of the broken rudder. Then he heard a terrible crash, followed by agonized cries. A third flash of lightning showed him the little boat smashed against the rocks and among the wreckage, heads with desperate faces and arms stretched up toward heaven. Then all was dark again. Dantès quickly climbed down the silppery rocks, at the risk of falling into the sea himself. He looked and listened, but he neither saw nor heard anything more: no more cries, no more human efforts; there was nothing left except the storm with its roaring winds and foaming waves.

Little by little, the wind died down. The big gray clouds rolled off westward and soon a long reddish streak appeared on the eastern horizon. Light suddenly touched the waves and turned their foamy crests into golden plumes. Daylight had come.

"In two or three hours," thought Dantès, "the jailer will enter my cell, find the corpse of my poor friend and give the alarm. They'll question the two men who threw me into the sea and who must have heard the cry I uttered. Boats filled with armed soldiers will begin searching the sea for me and the cannon will alert the coast not to give shelter to a naked, hungry fugitive. I'll be at the mercy of the first peasant who wants to earn twenty francs by turning me in. Oh, my God! My God! You know how much I've suffered! Help me now that I can no longer help myself!"

Just as he finished this fervent prayer, he saw on the horizon the lateen sail of a ship which his experienced eye recognized as a Genoese tartan coming from Marseilles. "Oh!" he cried, "to think that I could swim out to that ship in half an hour if I weren't afraid of being recognized as a fugitive and taken back to Marseilles! Those men are all smugglers and semi-pirates; they'd rather sell me than perform an unprofitable good deed. What story could I invent to deceive them? I have it: I'll say I'm one of the sailors from the boat that was smashed on the rocks last night! There won't be anyone to contradict me, because the crew all drowned." So saying, he looked toward the spot where the little vessel had perished. A few planks were still floating there and he saw with a start that the cap of one of the sailors had come to rest on the point of a rock.

Dantès dived into the sea, swam over to the cap, put it on his head, took hold of one of the planks and began kicking toward the spot where he estimated that the ship would pass.

When he was close enough, he made a supreme effort, lunged almost entirely out of the sea, waved his cap and uttered a loud cry. The ship turned toward him and he saw the crew make ready to lower a boat.

Thinking he no longer needed the plank, he let go of it and began to swim vigorously toward the boat. But he was counting on a strength which he no longer had. His legs and arms began to stiffen, his movements became heavy and irregular, and his chest began to heave. The two rowers in the boat redoubled their efforts and one of them called out to him in Italian, "Courage!" Dantès thrashed desperately for a while, then sank below the surface. He felt himself being pulled up by the hair, then he fainted.

When he opened his eyes again he found himself lying on the deck of the tartan. One sailor was rubbing his limbs with a woolen blanket; another, the one who had called out "Courage!" to him, was holding a gourd to his mouth; while a third, the captain of the ship, was looking at him with that selfish pity which most men feel in the presence of a misfortune which they have escaped yesterday and which may strike them tomorrow.

"Who are you?" asked the captain in bad French.

"I'm a Maltese sailor," replied Dantès in equally bad Italian. "We were coming from Syracuse. A storm caught us off Cape Morgiou last night and smashed our ship against those rocks over there. I'm the only one who survived. When I saw you coming I held on to a piece of the wreckage and swam out to meet you, but I'd have drowned if one of your sailors hadn't grabbed me by the hair."

"That was me," said a sailor with a frank, open face. "It was time, too, because you were sinking."

"Yes, I was," said Dantès, holding out his hand to him. "Thank you, my friend."

"I almost hesitated to pull you out, though," said the sailor. "With your six-inch beard and your hair a foot long, you looked more like a bandit than an honest man."

Dantès abruptly recalled that he had cut neither his hair nor his beard the whole time he had been in prison. "Once when I was in danger," he said, "I made a vow to Our Lady of Piedigrotta not to cut my hair or my beard for ten years. The ten years are up today and I almost celebrated it by drowning."

"Now, what are we going to do with you?" asked the captain.

"Whatever you like. I'm a good sailor, so you can leave me at the first port you touch and I'm sure to find work on some merchant ship."

"Do you know the Mediterranean?"

"I've been sailing on it since I was a child. There are few harbors, even the most difficult, that I couldn't take a ship into and out of with my eyes closed."

"Well, then, captain," said Jacopo, the sailor who had saved Dantès' life, "why can't he stay with us?"

"Very well," said the captain to Dantès, "I'll take you on if you're not too unreasonable."

"Just pay me what you pay the others."

"All right," said the captain. "Now, Jacopo, do you have any extra clothes you can lend this man?"

"I have a pair of trousers and a shirt."

"That's all I need," said Dantès. Jacopo slid down a hatchway and came up an instant later with the two garments.

"Do you need anything else?" asked the captain.

"I'd like a piece of bread and another drink of that fine rum I tasted just now." Jacopo handed him the gourd and another sailor brought him a piece of bread.

Dantès asked if he could take over the helm. The helmsman, delighted to be relieved of his duties, looked at the captain, who motioned him to give up his place to his new shipmate. Dantès took over, keeping his eyes fixed on the coast of Marseilles.

"What day of the month is it?" he asked Jacopo, who had sat down beside him.

"The twenty-eighth of February."

"What year?"

"What do you mean? Don't you know what year it is?"

"I was so frightened last night," replied Dantès, laughing, "that I almost lost my mind, and my memory is still confused, so I'll ask you again, what year is it?"

"It's 1829," said Jacopo.

It had been fourteen years, to the day, since Dantès had been arrested. He was nineteen when he entered the Château d'If; he was now thirty-three. A sad smile passed over his lips as he wondered what had become of Mercédès during all that time when she must have believed him to be dead. Then his eyes flashed with hatred as he thought of the three men to whom he owed his long and cruel captivity, and he renewed the oath of vengeance against Danglars, Fernand and Villefort which he had already sworn in prison. And this oath was no longer a vain threat, for at that moment the fastest ship in the Mediterranean could not have overtaken the little tartan as she scudded along under full sail toward Leghorn.

Dantès had been on the *Jeune-Amélie*, the Genoese tartan, for less than a day when he realized that he was dealing with smugglers. He therefore had the advantage of knowing what the captain was without the captain's knowing what he was. He adhered rigidly to his original story, filling it out with all sorts of accurate details about Naples and Malta, which he knew as well as he did Marseilles, and even the shrewd Genoese captain accepted his story completely.

When they reached Leghorn, Dantès was eager to see whether he would recognize himself, for he had not seen his own face for fourteen years. As soon as they landed, he went to a barber to have his hair and beard cut. When the barber had finished, Dantès asked for a mirror and looked at himself.

He was now thirty-three years old, as we have said, and his fourteen years of prison had greatly altered his face. He had entered the Château d'If with the round, smiling face of a happy young man who has made a good beginning in life and who counts on the future to unfold itself as a natural deduction from the past. All that was now changed. His oval face had lengthened; his smiling lips had taken on the firm lines of resolution; his eyebrows had become arched beneath a single thoughtful wrinkle; his eyes wore a look of deep sadness, with occasional flashes of dark hatred; his skin, which had been away from the sunlight for so long, had grown pale; the deep learning he had acquired was reflected in his face by an expression of intelligent self-confidence. Furthermore, although he was naturally rather tall, he had acquired that stocky vigor of a body which constantly concentrates its strength within itself. Furthermore, his eyes, which had been so long in darkness and semi-darkness, had developed the faculty of distinguishing objects in the dark, like those of the hyena and the wolf.

Dantès smiled as he looked at himself. It was impossible that his best friend, if he still had any friends, would recognize him; he did not even recognize himself.

When he returned to the *Jeune-Amélie*, the captain renewed his offer to take him on as permanent member of the crew, but Dantès, who had other plans, would agree only to an engagement of three months.

Within a week after her arrival at Leghorn, the ship was filled with muslin, cotton, English gunpowder and tobacco on which the excise authorities had neglected to affix their seal. It was now a question of getting all this out of Leghorn free of duty and landing on the shore of Corsica, where certain speculators would take over the task of smuggling the goods into France.

They set sail, and Dantès once again found himself moving across that blue sea which he had seen so often in his dreams during his imprisonment.

When the captain came up on deck the next morning, he found Dantès leaning over the bulwarks and gazing, with a strange expression on his face, at a pile of granite rocks which shone pink in the rising sun: it was the Isle of Monte Cristo. The *Jeune-Amélie* passed it about three-quarters of a league to starboard. Fortunately, Dantès had learned to wait. He had waited fourteen years for his freedom; he could certainly wait six months or a year for his wealth. He repeated the cardinal's letter word for word in his mind.

Two and a half months went by, during which Dantès became as skillful a smuggler as he was a sailor. He had become acquainted with all the smugglers along the coast and learned all the masonic signs by which these semi-pirates recognized one another. He had passed his Isle of Monte Cristo at least twenty times, but without a single opportunity to land there.

He therefore decided that as soon as his engagement with the captain of the *Jeune-Amélie* was ended he would rent a small bark and go to the Isle of Monte Cristo on some pretext or other. He would be able to search for his treasure at leisure, but he would no doubt be spied upon by the men who took him there; this was simply a risk he would have to take. Try as he might, he could think of no way to get to the island without being taken there by someone else.

He was still grappling with this problem when one evening the captain, who had great confidence in him and was anxious to keep him in his service, took him to a tavern in the Via del Oglio which was a favorite meeting-place for the smugglers of Leghorn. On this particular evening an undertaking of great importance was being discussed. It concerned a ship laden with Turkish carpets, cashmere and cloth from the Levant. It was necessary to find some neutral ground where the exchange could be made, and then attempt to land the goods on the coast of France. The profit would be enormous if the undertaking succeeded: fifty to sixty piasters per man.

The captain of the *Jeune-Amélie* suggested that the Isle of Monte Cristo, being completely deserted and free of soldiers and customs agents, would be a good place to unload the cargo. When he heard the name of Monte Cristo, Dantès trembled with joy. He stood up to hide his emotion and walked around the smoky tavern. When he returned it had been decided that they would land on Monte Cristo and that they would leave the following night.

At seven o'clock the next evening everything was ready; they rounded the lighthouse at ten minutes past seven, just as the beacon was being lit. The sea was calm and there was a fresh wind blowing from the southeast.

By five o'clock the next evening the Isle of Monte Cristo was clearly visible. They landed at ten o'clock. The *Jeune-Amélie* was the first to arrive at the rendezvous. Despite his usual self-control, Dantès could not restrain himself. He rushed ashore before any of the others and would have kissed the earth if he had dared. But it would have been useless to begin his search at night, so he regretfully put it off until the next day. Besides, a signal from half a league out to sea, which the *Jeune-Amélie* answered by a similar signal, had just indicated that it was time to go to work. The late-comer, reassured by the signal, soon appeared, white and silent as a ghost, and dropped anchor a short distance off shore. Then the work of unloading the cargo began. As he worked, Dantès thought of the shouts of joy he would draw from all those men if he were to tell them of the thought with which his mind was constantly filled.

No one suspected anything, however, and when he took a gun the next morning and announced his intention of going off to shoot one of the wild goats which could be seen leaping from rock to rock, his excursion was attributed only to either a love of hunting or a desire for solitude. Jacopo was the only one who insisted on going with him and Dantès was afraid to oppose him, lest he arouse some suspicion. But he managed to kill a goat before they had gone a quarter of a league and sent Jacopo to carry it back to his companions, inviting them to cook it and signal him when it was done by firing a shot into the air.

Dantès continued on his way, looking back from time to time, until he finally reached the spot where he supposed the caves to be. Examining everything with meticulous attention, he noticed that on several rocks there were notches which had apparently been made by the hand of man. They seemed to have been cut with a certain regularity, probably to indicate a trail. These signs gave Dantès hope. Why could they not have been carved by the cardinal in order to guide his nephew? He followed them until they stopped, but they had taken him to no cave. A large round rock perched on a solid base seemed to be the only goal to which they led. It occurred to him that, instead of being at the end of the trail, he was at the beginning. He turned and retraced his steps.

Meanwhile his companions had finished cooking the goat. Just as they were taking it off the improvised spit they saw Dantès leaping from rock to rock. They fired a shot to signal to him. He changed direction and came running toward them. But as they were all watching him, his foot slipped and they saw him stagger on the edge of a rock and disappear. They all rushed forward at once, for they all loved Dantès despite his superiority.

They found him bleeding and almost unconscious. He had apparently fallen from a height of twelve to fifteen feet. They poured some rum down his throat and he soon opened his eyes, complaining of a sharp pain in his knee, a feeling of heaviness in his head and unbearable twinges of pain in his back. They tried to carry him to the shore, but as soon as they touched him he groaned and said be did not feel strong enough to continue. The captain, who was obliged to leave that same morning, insisted that they try to get him on board the ship, but Dantès declared that he would rather die where he was than suffer the attrocious pain which so much movement would inflict on him. "Just leave me a supply of biscuits, a gun to hunt with and a pickaxe to build some sort of shelter with in case you should be delayed in coming back for me," he said.

"But you'll starve!" said the captain. "We'll be gone at least a week."

"Listen, captain," said Jacopo, "here's the answer to the problem: I'll stay here with him and take care of him."

"Do you mean you'd give up your share of the profit in order to stay with me?" asked Dantès.

"Yes," replied Jacopo, "and without regret."

"You're a good friend, Jacopo," said Dantès, "and God will reward you for your good will, but I don't need anyone. A day or two of rest will put me back on my feet." He shook Jacopo's hand affectionately, but his resolution to stay, and stay alone, remained unshakable. The smugglers finally gave him the things he had requested and left him.

An hour later the little ship was almost out of sight. Then Dantès stood up, as agile and light on his feet as one of the wild goats of the island, took his gun in one hand and his pickaxe in the other, and ran toward the rock at which the trail of notches ended.

"Now," he exclaimed, thinking of the story of the Arabian fisherman which Faria had told him, "open sesame!"

After following the trail of notches in the opposite direction, Dantès found that it led to a little creek which was wide enough at the mouth and deep enough at the center to enable a boat to enter it and remain hidden. He deduced that the cardinal, not wishing to be seen, had landed at that creek, hidden his boat in it, then followed the line marked out by the notches and, at the end of that line, buried his treasure. It was this supposition that led him back to the large circular rock.

But there was one thing which upset his whole theory: The rock must weigh at least two or three tons; how could the cardinal have hoisted it up to the base on which it rested?

Suddenly an idea occurred to him: perhaps, instead of being raised, it had been lowered. He climbed above the rock to search for its original resting place. He soon discovered that a slope had been made; the rock had slid down it to its present position, where it had been fixed in place by another rock about the size of an ordinary building stone, which had been used as a wedge.

Dantès chopped down an olive tree, cut off its branches and tried to pry up the rock with the trunk. But the rock was so heavy and was held so firmly in place by the rock wedge beneath it that no human strength could have budged it. He reflected for a moment and decided that he would have to direct his efforts against the wedge. He looked around him; his eyes fell on the powder horn his friend Jacopo had left him.

With his pickaxe he carved out a long hole between the large rock and the wedge and filled it with gunpowder. He then made a fuse by tearing a strip of cloth from his handkerchief and rolling it up with powder inside it.

He lighted the fuse and ran back. The explosion was not long in coming: the upper rock was lifted from its base for an instant by the tremendous force and the rock wedge beneath it was shattered into a thousand pieces.

Dantès came back to the spot. The upper rock, now almost without support, was hanging over the cliff. He walked around it, chose the loosest spot, placed his tree trunk in a crevice and began to pry with all his might. The rock tottered, then finally gave way completely and tumbled headlong into the sea. In doing so it revealed a square stone with an iron ring set in the middle of it.

Dantès uttered a cry of surprise and joy. His legs trembled so violently and his heart beat so wildly that he was obliged to stop for a moment. Then he put his lever through the iron ring and lifted vigorously, displacing the square stone. Beneath it he saw a steep staircase leading down into the dark depths of a cave.

Anyone else would have rushed forward with a shout of joy; Dantès stopped doubtfully and turned pale. "I mustn't let myself be shattered by disappointment," he said to himself, "or else all my suffering will have been in vain." He then began to climb down into the cave with a smile of doubt on his lips, murmuring that ultimate word of human wisdom: "Perhaps!"

After he had been in the cave for a few seconds, his eyes, accustomed as they were to seeing in the dark, were able to penetrate into every corner. The walls of the cave were of granite. He recalled the words of the cardinal's letter: "In the furthest corner of the second opening." He had found only the first cave; now he must search for the second one. He sounded the wall with his pickaxe. At length he found a spot where the granite gave forth a hollower and deeper sound. He struck it again, more vigorously. This time he noticed something strange: his blow had chipped a sort of plaster off the wall, revealing a softer, grayish stone beneath it. The opening in the granite wall had been sealed up with another kind of stone and then covered over with this plaster, on the surface of which the appearance of granite had been imitated. He struck the stone with the sharp end of his pickaxe: it penetrated to a depth of about one inch.

Dantès went to work. After some time he noticed that the stones had not been cemented together, but simply piled on top of one another and covered with a layer of plaster. He shoved the point of his pickaxe into one of the interstices, pushed down on the handle and, to his great joy, one of the stones fell at his feet. From then on he had only to pull each stone toward him with his pickaxe. Finally, after hesitating once again for several seconds, he entered the second cave.

It was as empty as the first. The treasure, if it existed, was buried in the furthest corner. The hour of anguish had arrived: two feet of earth was all that lay between Dantès and supreme joy or supreme despair. He walked over to the corner and, as though seized by a sudden resolution, energetically attacked the ground. At the fifth or sixth blow his pickaxe struck metal. He struck a little to one side of the spot; he still encountered resistance, but not the same sound. "It's a wooden chest bound with iron," he said to himself.

Just then a passing shadow cut off the daylight for an instant. Dantès dropped his pickaxe, picked up his rifle and rushed out of the cave. A wild goat had leaped over the entrance to the first cave and was grazing a few feet away. Dantès thought for a moment, cut down a small pine tree, lit it from the remaining flames of the fire over which the smugglers had cooked their goat and came back to the cave with this torch. He did not want to lose a single detail of what he was going to see.

He held his torch up to the small excavation he had made and saw that he was not mistaken: his blows had struck wood and metal. He planted the torch in the ground and went on with his work. A short time later he had cleared away a space about three feet long and two feet wide and could clearly see an oaken chest bound with wrought iron. In the middle of the lid on a silver plaque were the arms of the Spada family, which Dantès easily recognized, for Faria had drawn them for him countless times. It was impossible to doubt it now: the treasure was there. No one would have taken such precautions in order to put an empty chest back in place.

Dantès rapidly cleared away the earth around the chest. Soon the center lock appeared, then the handles at each end, all delicately wrought in the manner of that period when art made precious even the basest of metals. He took the chest by the two handles and tried to lift it, but it was impossible. He tried to open it; it was locked. He inserted the sharp end of his pickaxe between the chest and the lid and pushed down on the handle. The lid creaked, then flew open.

Dantès was seized with a sort of giddy fever. He cocked his gun and placed it beside him. Then be closed his eyes like a child, opened them and stood dumbfounded.

The chest was divided into three compartments. In the first were shining gold coins. In the second, unpolished gold ingots packed in orderly stacks. From the third compartment, which was half full, Dantès picked up handfuls of diamonds, pearls and rubies. As they fell through his fingers in a glittering cascade, they gave forth the sound of hail beating against the windowpanes.

After he had touched them, fingered them, and buried his trembling hands in the gold and precious stones, Dantès ran out of the cave with the wild exaltation of a man who has come to the brink of madness. He climbed up on a rock from which he could see the surrounding sea. He was alone, all alone with those incalculable, unheard-of, fabulous riches which belonged to him! But was he dreaming or waking? He needed to see his gold again, yet he felt that, for the moment, he did not have the strength to look at it. He pressed his head between his hands for an instant, as though to prevent his reason from escaping, then he began to run frenziedly around the island, frightening the wild goats and seagulls with his shouts and gesticulations. Then he returned, still doubting his senses, rushed into the cave and found himself once again in the presence of his mine of gold and jewels. This time he fell to his knees, convulsively pressed his hands over his pounding heart and uttered a prayer that was intelligible to God alone.

The next day, Dantès filled his pockets with precious stones, carefully buried the chest again and disguised the entrance to the cave until no trace of it was visible. Then he began to wait impatiently for his companions to return. He had no desire to stay on the island looking at his gold and diamonds, like a dragon guarding a useless treasure. It was time for him to go back among men and take up the rank, influence and power which great wealth gives in this world.

The smugglers returned on the sixth day. Dantès recognized the *Jeune-Amélie* from a distance and dragged himself down to the shore. When his companions landed he told them that, although he was still in pain, he was considerably better. Then he listened to the account of their adventures. Their trip had been successful and all of them, especially Jacopo, regretted that Dantès had been unable to take part in it in order to have his share of the profits, which would have been fifty piasters. Dantès managed not to smile at this. Since the *Jeune-Amélie* had come to Monte Cristo only for him, he boarded her that evening and went on to Leghorn.

In Leghorn he sold four of his smallest diamonds for five thousand francs each. The next day he bought a small ship for Jacopo, adding a hundred piasters to the gift to enable him to hire a crew, on condition that Jacopo go to Marseilles and ask for news of an old man named Louis Dantès and a young woman called Mercédès. Jacopo thought he must be dreaming. Dantès told him that he had become a sailor only on a youthful impulse and that upon arriving in Leghorn he had received an inheritance from his uncle. Dantès' superior education made this story plausible and Jacopo did not doubt its truth for an instant. The next day Jacopo set sail for Marseilles. He was to meet Dantès later at Monte Cristo.

That same day, Dantès took leave of the crew of the *Jeune-Amélie,* giving each of them a handsome present and promising to let the captain hear from him.

Dantès went to Genoa. The day of his arrival, he bought a small yacht which had been ordered by an Englishman who had heard that the Genoese were the best shipbuilders of the Mediterranean. The Englishman had agreed to a price of forty thousand francs; Dantès offered sixty thousand on condition that the yacht be turned over to him immediately. The shipbuilder offered to help Dantès engage a crew, but Dantès replied that he was in the habit of sailing alone and that the only thing he desired was that a secret compartment be built in the cabin. The compartment was finished the next day, and two hours later Dantès sailed out of the harbor of Genoa, headed for the Isle of Monte Cristo.

He arrived toward the end of the second day. His yacht was an excellent sailer and had covered the distance in thirty-five hours. The island was deserted. He went to his treasure and found it exactly as he had left it. By the next day his immense fortune had been transferred to his yacht and locked up in the secret compartment.

Dantès waited for eight days, during which he maneuvered his yacht around the island, studying it as a horseman studies his mount. By the end of that time he had recognized all its good qualities and all its defects; he promised himself to augment the former and remedy the latter.

Jacopo arrived on the eighth day and tied up his small ship alongside Dantès' yacht. He had a sad answer to each of the two questions Dantès had asked: old Louis Dantès was dead and Mercédès had disappeared. Dantès' expression remained calm when he heard this news, but he immediately went ashore and refused to have anyone go with him. He returned two hours later. Two sailors from Jacopo's crew came on board his yacht to help him sail it. He gave orders to head for Marseilles.

The news of his father's death was not unexpected; but what had become of Mercédès? There were also other things he wanted to know which he could trust no one else to find out for him. In Leghorn his mirror had shown him that he ran no risk of being recognized. Furthermore, he had every means of disguise at his disposal. One morning, therefore, the yacht, followed by Jacopo's ship, boldly sailed into the harbor of Marseilles and stopped opposite the very spot where Dantès had set out for the Château d'If.

It was not without a certain anxiety that Dantès saw a gendarme coming out to meet him in the quarantine boat, but, with the perfect self-assurance which he bad acquired, he presented an English passport he had bought in Leghorn and went ashore without difficulty.

from

Sandokan:
The Tigers of Mompracem
by Emilio Salgari (1862–1911)

Not all treasure comes in the form of gold doubloons and jewels. This tale by Italian author Emilio Salgari tells what follows when the fearsome pirate Sandokan—the Tiger of Malaysia—sets his sights on a young woman known as the Pearl of Labuan.

Less than ten minutes later, the two pirates had arrived at the banks of the river. The wind had died down, and the crews had boarded their prahus and were in the process of lowering the sails.

"What's happening?" Sandokan asked, jumping onto the bridge.

"Captain, we're under attack," said Giro-Batol. "A cruiser is blocking the mouth of the river."

"Ah!" said the Tiger. "The British are looking for a fight. Well, my friends, we'll ready our weapons and head for the sea. We'll show those men what the Tigers of Mompracem can do!"

"Long live the Tiger!" yelled the two crews, their voices ringing with frightening enthusiasm. "Attack! Attack!"

Moments later, the two ships began descending the river and soon reached the open sea. Six hundred meters from the coast, a large heavily armed ship, weighing about fifteen hundred tons, was slowly patrolling the waters, barring the way westward. The sounds of officers shouting orders from the bridge intermixed with the pounding of drums summoning the crew to battle.

Sandokan coldly studied that formidable adversary. The ship was enormous. It had a vast range of artillery and its crew was three or four times greater than that of his prahus. But instead of being intimidated, he simply turned to his men and thundered, "Man the oars!"

The pirates rushed to take their positions below deck while the artillerymen aimed the cannons and firelocks.

"Now to business," said Sandokan, as the prahus, driven by the power of their oars, shot forward like two arrows.

A light flashed on the cruiser's deck and seconds later a large cannonball whistled past the prahu's masts.

"Patan!" shouted Sandokan. "Man your cannon!"

The Malay, one of the best cannoneers in all of piratedom, fired. The projectile smashed through the gangway of the enemy bridge, simultaneously snapping the flagpole in two. Instead of returning fire, the warship veered about and displayed its portside gun ports, home to a half dozen cannons.

"Patan, don't waste a single shot," said Sandokan, as a volley of fire thundered through Giro-Batol's prahu, fracturing its masts and smashing its wheel to pieces, "and when your aim starts to falter, get yourself killed."

At that instant the cruiser seemed to catch fire. A hurricane of steel whizzed through the air and struck the two prahus squarely, razing them like pontoons. Terrible cries of anger and rage arose from the decks of the pirate vessels, but were quickly suppressed by a second volley that sent oarsmen and artillerymen flying.

Engulfed in a whirlwind of black and white smoke, the warship suddenly tacked about and sailed to less than four hundred paces from the prahus. However, instead of halting, it continued on for another kilometer, and then began to fire once again. Sandokan had been felled by a yardarm but was unharmed and quickly got back on his feet.

"Wretches!" he thundered, shaking his fist at the enemy vessel. "You cowards may attempt to flee, but I'll catch you!"

He whistled to summon his men on deck.

"Build a quick barricade in front of the cannons and then full speed ahead!"

In a flash, extra masts, barrels full of cannonballs, old cannon parts, and whatever loose wreckage could be found, were stacked up on the bows of both ships, forming solid barricades. When the preparations had been completed, the twenty strongest men went below to man the oars, while the others crowded behind the barricades, arms clutching their carbines, daggers clenched between their teeth.

"Full ahead!" commanded the Tiger.

The cruiser had stopped retreating and now advanced slowly, spewing torrents of black smoke.

"Fire at will!" yelled the Tiger.

The gunfire resumed, each side matching shot for shot, volley for volley, cannonball for cannonball.

The three crews, bent upon victory or death, could hardly see each other, engulfed as they were by the immense clouds of smoke that stubbornly clung to all decks, but they continued to roar with equal furor, as fire was met with fire.

The ship had the advantage of its great bulk and vast artillery, but the two prahus lead by the brave Tiger refused to give up. Riddled with holes, sails shredded, with water in their holds, brimming with the bodies of the dead and wounded, the pirate ships continued to fire, despite being showered with an incessant hail of cannonballs. Delirium had taken hold of those men, and they wanted nothing more than to get on the bridge of that formidable ship. If they could not win, they wanted to die fighting on their enemy's deck.

Patan, true to his word, had had himself killed while stationed at his cannon and another capable artilleryman had taken his place; many men had fallen, and others still, horribly wounded, struggled hopelessly among torrents of blood. Giro-Batol's prahu had not faired much better, its cannon had been disabled and its firelock hardly fired, but it no longer mattered. The decks of the two pirate ships still carried men thirsty for blood and they valiantly performed their duties.

Metal flew about those brave men, streaking the bridges, smashing in bulwarks, tearing through arms and smashing in chests, shattering everything they touched, but no one spoke of retreating. The pirates hurled insults at the enemy and continued with their challenge, and when a gust of wind would momentarily blow away the clouds of smoke that covered the three ships, from behind the barricades would emerge faces twisted and darkened with rage. In the middle of that pack of Tigers, their captain, the invincible Sandokan, clutching his scimitar in his right hand, a fiery look on his face, his long hair flying in the wind, encouraged his warriors with a voice that thundered above the roar of the cannons. The terrible battle lasted twenty minutes. Then the cruiser retreated a further six hundred meters, in order to avoid being boarded.

A cry of fury erupted from the two prahus in response to that new retreat, for it was now no longer possible to do battle against their enemy. Taking advantage of their superior ship, the British could easily avoid all attempts at boarding.

Sandokan, however, refused to give up.

Cutting through the men about him, with one quick movement he reloaded a still smoking cannon, corrected the aim, and fired. Seconds later the cruiser's mainmast, severed at its base, fell into the sea, dragging with it the marksmen that had been stationed on the tops of the crosslets. The vessel stopped firing and came to a halt so that an attempt could be made to rescue the men before they drowned. Sandokan took advantage of the lull and had Giro-Batol and his crew gather their weapons and climb aboard his prahu.

"Let's head for the coast," he thundered.

Giro-Batol's prahu, which up until then had been kept afloat by pure miracle, was quickly evacuated and abandoned to the waves. Taking advantage of the warship's inaction, the pirates immediately manned the oars and quickly rowed away, taking shelter in the nearby river.

And just in time. Despite the hasty patchwork attempt to seal the most serious damage caused by cannon fire, the poor ship, riddled with holes, was drawing water from all sides and slowly sinking. It groaned like a dying man, beneath the weight of the invading liquid, listing towards its starboard side as it moved forward. Sandokan, who had taken the wheel, pointed it towards the nearest shore and grounded it on a sandbar.

As soon as the pirates realized that the prahu was no longer in any danger of sinking, they jumped on deck like a pack of famished tigers, weapons in hand, ready to resume the struggle with equal ferocity and determination. Sandokan stopped them with a single gesture; then after consulting the watch he had attached to his belt, issued his orders.

"It is now six o'clock. The sun will set in two hours. I want every man to get to work so that the prahu will be ready to sail by midnight."

"Are we going to attack the cruiser?" asked the pirates excitedly.

"I can't promise that, but I swear to you that we'll avenge our losses soon enough. We'll shower the enemy with cannon fire, and hoist our flag over the ramparts of Victoria."

"Long live the Tiger!" howled the pirates.

"Silence!" thundered Sandokan. "I need two men to go to the mouth of the river and keep an eye on the cruiser and another two to go into the jungle to eliminate all possibility of an ambush. Once we've tended to the injured, we'll start our repairs."

While the pirates quickly tended to the wounded, Sandokan went to the stern of his ship. He could make out the surface of the bay through a rift in the trees and he quickly scanned the waters. He was undoubtedly looking for the cruiser, but it had not dared to run the risk of getting too close to the shore, perhaps out of fear of getting stranded on one of the numerous sandbars hidden beneath the waters.

"They know they have us," murmured the formidable pirate. "They're waiting for us to come out into the open so they can destroy us, but if they think I'll lead my men on an attack, they are sadly mistaken. I can exercise caution."

He sat on a cannon and called for Sabau. The pirate, one of his bravest men, having earned the rank of commander after risking his life more than twenty times, rushed to his side.

"Patan and Giro-Batol are dead," Sandokan sighed. "They were killed aboard their prahus, while leading their brave crews in an attempt to board that wretched ship. As of now that command belongs to you."

"Thank you, Tiger of Malaysia."

"You will fight as bravely as they have."

"When my captain orders me to die, I will be ready to obey."

"Now help me."

They gathered their strength, pushed the cannon and the firelocks to the stern and pointed them toward the small bay, so as to be ready to spray it with machine gun fire, in the event the commander of the cruiser decide to send a launch down the river.

"We'll be safe now," said Sandokan. "Have you sent two men to keep an eye on the mouth of the river?"

"Yes, Tiger of Malaysia. They are hiding among the reeds."

"Excellent."

"Are we going to wait until nightfall before we cast off?"

"Yes, Sabau."

"You plan to sneak past the cruiser's crew?"

"The moon is going to rise very late this evening and there are clouds rolling in from the south that will help keep us hidden."

"Are we going back to Mompracem, Captain?"

"Directly."

"With our dead unavenged?"

"There are too few of us left to challenge the cruiser once again. Besides, Sabau, they are too well armed and our ship is in no condition to take on a second fight."

"True, Captain."

"Patience for now. The day for revenge will come soon enough."

While the two captains were talking, their men continued to work feverishly. They were all capable seamen and several skilled carpenters and ship builders were numbered among their ranks. It took them only four hours to raise two new masts, reinforce the bulwarks, seal all the holes and repair the rigging, having had an abundance of cables, fibers, chains and ropes on board. By ten o'clock, not only could the ship set sail, it could also engage in battle once again, for new barricades made of tree trunks had been erected to protect the cannons and firelocks.

During those four hours, not one of the cruiser's launches had dared to appear in the waters of the bay. The British commander, knowing full well with whom he was dealing, had not deemed it wise to have his men engage in a battle on land. Besides, he was certain he could force the pirates to surrender or push them back towards the coast if they tried to attack or attempted to flee. Towards eleven, Sandokan, determined to set sail, summoned the men that had been ordered to stand guard at the mouth of the river.

"Is the bay safe?" he asked.

"Yes," replied one of the two.

"And the cruiser?"

"Still in front of the bay."

"How far?"

"About a half-mile."

"Then we have enough room to pass," Sandokan murmured. "The darkness will hide our escape." Then, he turned to Sabau and said, "Time to raise anchor."

Fifteen men immediately jumped onto the sandbar and with one rapid movement, pushed the prahu into the river.

"I want complete silence. No one is to speak for any reason whatsoever," said Sandokan imperiously. "Keep your eyes open and your weapons ready. We are about to play a deadly game."

He sat down near the tiller, Sabau at his side, and began to steer the ship towards the mouth of the river.

The darkness favored their escape. The moon had not yet risen and not a single star was visible. Massive storm clouds had invaded the heavens, completely blocking out all light. Unfortunately, the shadows projected by the durian trees, palm trees and giant banana leaves, made it difficult for Sandokan to scan the riverbanks.

A deep silence, broken only by the gurgling of the river, reigned over that small stretch of water. The leaves did not rustle, for the colossal trees did not allow so much as a trace of wind to pass through the forest. Nor could a single sound be heard from the deck of the ship. It seemed as if the entire crew, spread out from bow to stern, had for the moment refrained from breathing for fear of disrupting the silence. The prahu had almost reached the mouth of the river, when it started to slow and came to an abrupt stop.

"Stuck?" asked Sandokan.

Sabau looked over the bulwark and studied the waters. "Yes," he replied. "We've hit a sandbar."

"Can we pass?"

"The tide is rising rapidly and I think we'll be able to resume our descent in a few minutes."

"Let's wait then."

Though unaware of the cause of the delay, the crew remained silent. Sandokan, however, had heard the familiar clack of carbines being loaded and he motioned his men to silently man the cannons and the two firelocks.

Several anxious moments passed for all. Then a creaking sound emanated from beneath the keel. The prahu, elevated by the fast rising tide, was sliding off the sandbar. Rocking lightly, it had suddenly managed to free itself from the tenacious seabed.

"Hoist the sail," Sandokan ordered the men in charge of the rigging.

"Will one sail be enough, Captain?" asked Sabau.

"Yes, for now."

A few minutes later a lateen sail was hoisted up the foremast. It had been painted black in order to have it blend in with the darkness of the night. The prahu began to pick up speed, as it followed the bends in the river. It sped along easily, passing over sandbars and reefs, crossed the small bay and headed silently for the open sea.

"The ship?" asked Sandokan, jumping to his feet.

"There, a half mile from us," Sabau replied.

A dark mass was visible; from time to time, several small bright points circled above it, undoubtedly cinders escaping from its smokestack. Listening carefully, one could hear the slightly muffled sounds of its boilers.

"Its fires are still burning," murmured Sandokan. "It's waiting for us."

"Let's hope it doesn't detect us," said Sabau.

"Can you see any launches?"

"None, Captain."

"We'll stay close to the shore for a while, we'll try to blend in with the trees and vines for as long as we can, then we'll make a run for it."

The wind was rather weak and the sea was calm. Sandokan ordered a sail hoisted on the mainmast, then pointed the ship towards the south, following the outline of the shore. Since the jungle's large trees were projecting their dark shadows onto the waters, there was little chance that the pirate ship would be detected.

Always at the wheel, Sandokan did not once lose sight of the adversary that at any moment could awaken and unleash a barrage of iron and lead. Despite his efforts to determine the best way of outsmarting his enemy, deep down at the bottom of his soul that proud man terribly regretted the idea of fleeing without so much as an attempt at revenge. Part of him desired to be on Mompracem, but part of him also longed for another battle. The formidable Tiger of Malaysia, the invincible leader of the pirates of Mompracem, felt almost ashamed to leave in this way: quietly, stealthily, like a thief in the night. The very idea made his blood boil. Oh how he would have greeted a cannon blast with joy, even if it were a harbinger of a new and more disastrous defeat.

The prahu had already gone five or six hundred meters from the bay and was preparing to flee, when a strange light appeared in the wake of its stern. It seemed as if a myriad of tiny flames were rising from the murky depths of the sea.

"We're about to be discovered," said Sabau.

"Just as well," Sandokan replied with a fierce smile. "This retreat was beneath us."

"You're right, Captain," replied the Malay. "Better to die fighting than to flee like jackals."

The sea grew more and more phosphorescent. The bright points continued to multiply about the prahu, as its wake sparkled with light. The ship would not pass unnoticed by the men standing watch aboard the cruiser. Cannons could begin firing at any moment.

Even the pirates, lying on deck, had noticed that phosphorescence; however, no one had moved or uttered a single word that betrayed the slightest bit of apprehension. They too could not resign themselves to leaving without firing a single shot. A volley of grapeshot would have been greeted with a cry of joy. Two or three minutes had passed, when Sandokan, who had been keeping his eyes on the cruiser, saw the position lights brighten.

"Have they noticed us?" he wondered.

"I think so, Captain," Sabau replied. "Look!"

"Yes, there are more sparks coming out of the smokestack. They're stoking the engines."

Sandokan jumped to his feet and drew his scimitar. A cry had emanated from the warship: "Battle stations!"

The pirates immediately got to their feet and the artillerymen rushed to man the cannons and the two firelocks. All were ready to undertake the crowning struggle. After that first cry, a brief silence reigned aboard the cruiser, but then the wind carried the same voice, all the way to the prahu once again.

"Battle stations! Battle stations! The pirates are escaping!"

A few seconds later, a drum roll emanated from the cruiser's bridge. The men were being summoned to action. The pirates, assembled on the bulwarks and crowded behind their tree trunk barricades, held their breath, but their ferocious expressions betrayed their state of mind. They clutched their weapons, fingering the triggers of their carbines.

The drum continued to sound on the enemy bridge. They could hear the anchor's chain creak as it was hoisted aboard. The vessel was preparing to attack.

"Stand ready, Sabau!" commanded the Tiger of Malaysia. "Eight men to the firelocks."

Almost immediately after he had given that command, there was a flash on the cruiser's bow, just above the forecastle, lighting up the foremast and the bowsprit. It was followed by a sharp detonating roar and the metallic sound of a projectile whistling through the air. The cannonball severed the tip of the mainmast and landed in the sea with a large splash. Cries of rage echoed throughout the pirate ship. There was no escaping a fight now, much to the delight of those bold adventurers.

Reddish smoke was now spewing out of the warship's smokestack. The buzz of the crew preparing for battle, the shouted commands of the officers and of men running to their stations, the dull grumbling of the boilers and the sounds of the wheels powerfully churning the waters all carried across the surface of the sea. The two lanterns had changed position. The vessel was advancing rapidly towards the small pirate ship determined at all costs to thwart its attempt at escape.

"Prepare to die a glorious death!" yelled Sandokan, who harbored no illusions as to the outcome of the impending battle.

The crew responded with a loud cry, "Long live the Tiger of Malaysia!"

Sandokan gave the wheel a vigorous turn and tacked about as his men quickly trimmed the sails. He was pushing the ship towards the vessel in order to attempt to board it and lead his men onto the enemy deck. Both sides soon began to fire. Cannonballs and volleys of grapeshot whizzed through the air.

"Prepare to board!" Sandokan thundered. "The odds are against us, but we are the Tigers of Mompracem."

Its sharp ram pointed forward, the cruiser advanced rapidly, shattering the silence with furious rounds of cannon fire. Flashes of light ripped through the darkness. The prahu, a toy in comparison with the giant before it, would have split in two and sunk in a direct collision. Nevertheless, it attacked daringly, vigorously firing at the ship.

However, as Sandokan had said, the odds were against them, excessively so. Their small wooden ship could do little against that well armed, mighty vessel of iron. Despite the desperate bravery of the Tigers of Mompracem, it was not difficult to predict the final outcome of the battle.

Regardless, the pirates refused to give up and continued to fire shots in rapid succession, exterminating the artillerymen on the deck and cutting down the sailors on the rigging. They blanketed the quarter-deck, forecastle and mast tops with bullets. Two minutes later, however, their ship, hit repeatedly by enemy fire, was a total wreck. The masts had fallen, the bulwarks had caved in and the makeshift tree trunk barricades no longer provided shelter from that barrage of projectiles. Water gushed in from all sides, flooding the hold. Still, no one spoke of surrendering. They were all prepared to die, but it had to be on the deck of the enemy vessel.

Meanwhile, the volleys continued to increase in intensity. Sabau's weapon had been blown apart, and half the crew lay dead on the deck, massacred by the grapeshot. Sandokan could feel that the final bell was about to toll for the Tigers of Mompracem. Defeat was imminent. It was no longer possible to hold their ground against that giant and its incessant rain of bullets. Their sole option now was to try and board the cruiser, pure madness, for victory would not smile upon those valorous men once aboard that enemy ship.

Only twelve men remained, but they were twelve tigers, led by a captain whose bravery was legendary.

"Stand ready, my brave ones!" he shouted.

Seething with rage, eyes blazing, fists tightly clutching their weapons, the twelve pirates regrouped, shielding themselves with the bodies of their slain shipmates.

The vessel was running at full steam towards the prahu, planning to sink it with its ram, but when the cruiser was but a few meters away, Sandokan gave his wheel a violent turn, and avoided the crash. He then launched his ship towards the cruiser's port side wheel. The collision was violent. The pirate ship listed to starboard and filled with water, spilling its dead and wounded into the sea.

"Launch the grappling irons!" Sandokan bellowed.

Two grappling hooks were immediately imbedded in the cruiser's ratlines. Thirsty for vengeance and almost insane with rage, the thirteen pirates moved as one to the attack. Clinging to the portals of the gun battery deck and to any cables or rope they could find, they scrambled up the cylinder box onto the parapet, and jumped onto the cruiser's deck, before the British, surprised at such audacity, could move to block them.

With the Tiger of Malaysia leading the way, his men rushed against the artillerymen, slaughtering them where they stood, routing the marksmen that had run to block their path; then with their scimitars flailing tempestuously in all directions, they headed towards the stern.

The men of the battery had gathered there at the officers' command. There were sixty or seventy of them, but the pirates, indifferent to their number, threw themselves furiously at the points of their bayonets and engaged them in a titanic struggle.

Retreating and advancing, swinging desperately, lopping off arms and breaking heads, all the while screaming terrible war cries to instill terror in their foes, for a few precious minutes they held their own against their numerous enemies, but dwarfed by that large crew, cut off at the rear, sandwiched among bayonets, those brave men soon fell.

Sandokan and four others, covered in wounds, their weapons bloodied to the hilt, with one final mighty effort managed to open a path and made an attempt to get to the bow, planning to use the ships own cannons to stop that avalanche of men.

Halfway along the deck Sandokan fell, struck in the chest by a bullet, but he immediately got up again howling, "Kill! Kill!"

The British advanced with every shot they fired, bayonets lowered, determined to end the battle once and for all. The shots proved fatal. The four pirates had thrown themselves in front of their captain in order to shield him, but they all fell to the ground, a volley of rifle fire putting a final end to their adventure. The Tiger of Malaysia, however, proved to be more fortunate.

Though his wounds spewed forth torrents of blood, that formidable man gathered his remaining strength and with a last great effort

reached the port bulwark, knocked over a topman, who had attempted
to block his path, and dove into the sea, disappearing beneath the dark
black waves.

Despite the terrible ordeal he had just gone through, such a man,
blessed with such prodigious strength, such extraordinary energy and
such vast amounts of courage, could not die. While the cruiser continued on its course, driven forward by the last turns of its wheels, the
pirate, with a vigorous kick, resurfaced and swam away, in order to
avoid being shot at or cut in two by the enemy's ram. Ignoring the pain
of his wounds and suppressing his rage, he dove beneath the water,
keeping himself almost completely submerged, waiting for the oppor-
tune moment to attempt to reach the island's shore.

The warship was still less than three hundred meters away and had
begun to tack to starboard. It returned to the place where the pirate had
jumped into the water, its captain attempting perhaps to dismember
him with its wheels, but after several minutes, it tacked about once
again. It stopped for a moment, as if wanting to examine that tract of
water that the wheel had churned up so voraciously, then resumed its
course, slicing through that section of the sea, while sailors stationed at
the gun ports and others lowered in fishing nets, shone their lanterns
over the waters. Once convinced of the futility of the search, it headed
off in the direction of Labuan.

The Tiger let out a cry of rage, "Go, wretched ship!" he exclaimed.
"Go, but take heed, I will take my revenge!"

He tied some cloth around his wound; trying to arrest the hemor-
rhaging that could have killed him, then summoned all his strength
and began to swim in an attempt to reach the island. Several times
during his exertions the formidable man stopped to look at the warship, still faintly visible in the distance, and shouted terrible imprecations. There were moments when the pirate, who was perhaps fatally
injured, and still far from the island, tried to follow that ship which

had made him experience the bitterness of defeat, challenging its crew with frightening howls.

Reason soon won out, and with great difficulty Sandokan began to swim once again, all the while scanning the darkness that cloaked the shores of Labuan. He swam for quite a while, stopping from time to time to catch his breath and rid himself of the clothing that was slowing him down, but he soon discovered that his strength was rapidly diminishing. His limbs were becoming stiff, his breathing more and more difficult and his wound continued to bleed, aggravating the situation even further by causing him sharp pain each time it came in contact with the salt water. In order to rest and regain his strength, he curled himself up into a ball, and let himself be carried by the waves.

Suddenly, he felt something against his back. Something had touched him. The very idea that it could have been a shark made Sandokan shiver. Instinctively, he reached out and grabbed a coarse object that was floating just beneath the surface of the water. He pulled it towards him and discovered that it was a piece of wreckage. It was part of his prahu's deck; several cables and part of the yardarm were still attached to it.

"Thank God," murmured Sandokan. "My strength was almost gone."

He slowly pulled himself onto the planks and examined his wound. It had become red and bloated from the effects of the salt water and blood continued to spew out of it in streams. For another hour, that man, who was not yet ready to die, who did not want to admit defeat, fought against the waves that attempted to submerge him. Then his strength gave way and he weakened, and all he could do was clutch the yardarm.

Dawn was breaking, when a violent knock tore him from his melancholy state. It could not have come at a better time for Sandokan had almost fainted. He slowly pulled himself up and looked around. The writhing, foaming waves were now breaking violently around his makeshift raft. He appeared to be rolling on a shoal. Through a red mist, the injured man could make out the coast a short distance away.

"Labuan," he murmured.

He paused for a minute, gathered all his strength, and abandoned that bit of debris that had saved him from an almost certain death. He felt the gritty sandbar beneath his feet as he cautiously advanced towards the shore. Waves attacked from all sides, pushing him back and forth, trying to knock him down, almost as if they wished to prevent him from reaching that accursed island.

He advanced slowly, tottering over the sandbars. Then after battling against a last group of waves, he reached the tree-lined shore, and let himself fall heavily to the ground. Despite his great loss of blood and his exhaustion after such a long struggle, he unwrapped his wound and examined it at length. He had been struck by a bullet, most likely from some pistol, just below the fifth rib on his right side. That bit of lead, after having slipped in between his bones, had gotten lost somewhere inside him, but did not appear to have damaged any vital organs. It was not a serious wound, but it could quickly become so if not promptly tended to, and Sandokan, having been injured several times, was well aware of this.

Hearing the gurgle of a nearby brook, he dragged himself to its bank, and once there, reopened the wound. The prolonged contact with the salt water had bloated it; he washed it carefully, squeezed out a few drops of blood, then carefully resealed it and wrapped it up with a portion of his shirt, which along with his belt and kris were all that remained him.

"I'll heal," he murmured when he had finished, and he pronounced those two words with such energy, that anyone listening would have assumed that this man was indeed the unquestioned master of his fate.

Though alone on an island where he could count nothing but enemies, bleeding, without shelter or resources, without so much as a friend, the pirate was still certain of emerging victorious. He drank some water to calm the fever that was beginning to overpower him, then dragged himself under an areca tree whose gigantic leaves, no less than fifteen feet long and five or six feet wide, would provide him with excellent shade. He had just reached the foot of the tree when he felt his strength give way again. He became terribly dizzy, closed his eyes and after having tried, but in vain, to stand up, he fell to the ground unconscious. He did not come to until several hours later, just as the sun was slowly beginning its descent towards the west.

He awoke wracked with thirst. Though no longer throbbing incessantly, his wound was still the source of sharp unbearable pain. He tried to get up and drag himself to the brook, but he fell back down almost immediately. Then that man, who so wanted to be as strong as the wild animal whose name he bore, with a mighty effort, got up onto his knees and started to yell with all the power of his voice.

"I am the Tiger! I will not fall!"

He grabbed the tree trunk, pulled himself up, and with prodigious strength, managed to maintain his equilibrium, as he slowly made his way to the small brook, collapsing only when he reached its bank. He quenched his thirst, wet his wound, then rested his head in his hands and watched the waves as they noisily, almost deafeningly crashed upon the shore.

"Ah!" he exclaimed, talking aloud as delirium began to attack his reason. "Whoever would have guessed that the day would come when the Lions of Labuan would have beaten the Tigers of Mompracem? Who would have thought that I, the invincible Tiger of Malaysia, would have landed here, on this shore, beaten and injured? When will I get my revenge? Revenge! All my prahus, my islands, my men, my very riches to destroy these odious men that dare dispute my sea!

"What does it matter if they've beaten me? In a month or two I'll return here with my ships and unleash my indomitable men upon these shores! Who can withstand a legion of my men thirsting for blood and revenge? What does it matter if today the British Lions gloat over this victory? They will all fall dying at my feet! Let all the British of Labuan tremble, for they'll see my flag flying proudly in battle once again!"

The pirate had gotten to his feet, his eyes blazing madly, his right hand menacingly slashing at the air as if it still clutched his terrible scimitar. Despite his injuries, he was still the indomitable Tiger of Malaysia.

"Patience for now, Sandokan," he said, as he fell to the ground once more. "I'll heal, even if I have to live in this forest for one or two months, eating nothing but fruit and oysters; and when I've regained my strength, I'll return to Mompracem; I'll build myself a raft or steal a canoe, I'll subdue an entire crew with my kris if I have to."

He remained lying beneath the large leaves of the areca tree for several hours, gloomily looking at the waves as they came to die near his feet. He seemed to be scanning the waters for the remnants of his ships, so recently sunk along with the remains of his slain crew. The fever grew stronger and he could feel waves of blood rushing to his brain. The wound throbbed incessantly, but not a single groan escaped the lips of that formidable man.

At eight, the sun descended towards the horizon and, after a brief twilight, darkness fell over the sea and invaded the forest. Inexplicably, Sandokan, who had never feared death, and who had faced the dangers and ravages of war with desperate courage, grew pale.

"Nightfall!" he exclaimed, clawing at the earth with his fingernails, "I don't want the darkness! I don't want to die!"

He pressed his wound with both hands, and quickly got to his feet. He scanned the sea but saw only an inky black surface; he peered beneath the trees, and carefully searched through their dark shadows; then taken perhaps by a sudden delirium, he began to run through the forest like a madman.

He had fallen prey to an incredible, inexplicable terror. In his delirium, he thought he heard dogs barking in the distance, men shouting, and the roars of wild animals. His mind leapt to a single conclusion: they had discovered him and they were now hunting him down.

The run became dizzying. Completely overcome with fear, Sandokan began to rush into the grip of insanity, flinging himself into the middle of bushes, jumping over fallen tree trunks, leaping over brooks and ponds, all the while cursing, howling, and menacingly waving his kris. Its diamond inlaid handle flashed in the moonlight. He ran for ten or fifteen minutes, advancing ever further into the forest, his cries echoing among the dark trees. Suddenly, he stopped, breathless and panting.

His lips were covered with bloody foam; his eyes were bloodshot. He shook his arms crazily then crashed noisily to the ground. He was delirious; his temples were pulsating violently and his head felt like it was about to explode. His wound had started to burn and his heart pounded powerfully, almost as if it wanted to escape.

He thought he saw enemies everywhere: beneath the trees, among the bushes, behind mounds of dirt, between the roots that meandered along the ground. His eyes detected men hiding in ambush, while the air before him filled with phantoms grinning angrily among the large leaves of the surrounding trees. Beings sprang forth from the soil, howling, their heads bleeding, their limbs severed, their bodies impaled. All were laughing, snickering, mocking the impotence of the terrible Tiger of Malaysia. Sandokan, in the clutches of this terrifying delirium, rolled along the ground, got up, fell, clenched his fists and waved them threateningly at his visions.

"Away you dogs!" he howled. "What do you want of me? I am the Tiger of Malaysia, I fear no one! Attack me if you dare! Ah! You laugh? You think the Lions have injured and beaten the Tiger? I'm not afraid! Why do you look at me with those eyes of fire? Why do you dance about me?

"So, Patan, you've come to mock me? And Pagkon . . . you as well? . . . Damn you both, I'll send you back to hell! And you, Kimperlain, what do you want? My scimitar was not enough to send you to your death? . . . Away from here all of you, back to the bottom of the sea . . . back to the kingdom of darkness . . . or I will slay you once again!

"And you, Giro-Batol, what do you want? Revenge? Yes, you shall have it; the Tiger will heal. He will return to Mompracem . . . arm his prahus . . . and he'll return here to destroy the British Lions . . . all of them, to the very last man!"

The pirate stopped, wide eyed, features frighteningly twisted, his hands clutching his hair. Then, with one rapid movement, he resumed his wild run, howling, "Blood! Give me blood to quench my thirst. I am the Tiger of Malaysia."

He ran for a long time, howling and cursing continuously. He left the forest, crossed a small field at the end of which he thought he saw a building, then stopped again and fell to his knees. He was exhausted, breathless. He rolled himself up into a ball and remained that way for several minutes, then tried once again to get up, but this time his strength failed him, a stream of blood flowed into his eyes, and he fell heavily to the ground, uttering a last cry that faded into the darkness.

To his immense surprise, when he came to, he was no longer in the little field he had crossed during the night, but in a spacious room papered with a Fung floral print, lying on a comfortable, soft bed. At first, he thought himself in a dream and he rubbed his eyes repeatedly, trying to awaken, but he soon realized that everything was real, and promptly sat up wondering where he was.

He looked around but did not see anyone. He turned his attention to the room and began to examine its contents in detail; it was a vast room, elegantly decorated and lit by two large windows that looked out onto a garden.

He spotted a piano in one end of the room, on which were scattered some pages of music. An easel stood in the opposite corner, proudly displaying a drawing of a seascape. A mahogany table took up the middle of the room. It was covered by an embroidered silk cloth, undoubtedly the work of talented female hands. There was a richly decorated ottoman by his bed, inlayed with ebony and ivory, on which Sandokan saw, to his surprise and pleasure, his beloved kris and right next to it a book, partially opened, with a dried flower between its pages.

He strained his ears, but could not hear a single voice; only a few soft delicate sounds could be heard, sounds that seemed to be made by someone playing a mandolin or guitar.

"Where am I?" wondered Sandokan. "In the home of friends or enemies? Who bandaged and tended my wound?"

At one point, his eyes rested once again upon the book that lay on the ottoman. Driven by an irresistible curiosity, he reached out and drew it towards him. The cover bore a name imprinted in letters of gold: Marianna. He reread the name and felt himself overcome by an unknown feeling. An unfamiliar sweetness invaded that heart of steel that usually remained closed to the strongest emotions. He opened the book and found that it was full of beautiful calligraphy, elegant and neat, but though the language resembled the Portuguese of his friend Yanez, he could not understand its meaning.

As if driven by a mysterious force, he took the delicate flower that he had seen among the pages and examined it at length. He smelled it several times, being careful not to damage it with those fingers more accustomed to the hilt of his scimitar. Once again he felt a strange sensation, a mysterious thrill. Then that bloodthirsty man, that warrior, was overcome by a strong desire to bring the flower to his lips!

He put it back between the pages, almost with displeasure, closed the book and set it back on the ottoman. It was just in time. The handle of the door rattled and turned and a man quietly entered the room.

He was about fifty years of age, rather tall and vigorous, with deep blue eyes and a face framed by a ginger beard that was beginning to show traces of gray. One could see immediately that he was a man accustomed to command.

"I'm happy to see you resting; your delirium made you toss and turn for three days."

"Three days!" Sandokan exclaimed surprised. "I've been here for three days? This isn't a dream then?"

"No, my friend, I can assure you, this is not a dream. You are in the hands of good people, who nursed you with the greatest of care, and who will continue to do all that is possible to cure you."

"And who have I the pleasure of addressing?"

"Lord James Guillonk, Captain in the service of Her Majesty, the gracious Empress Victoria."

Sandokan started and his brow darkened; but he quickly recovered himself, and with a supreme effort to hide the hatred he felt for all that was British said, "I thank you, Milord, for all that you have done for me, a stranger, who, for all you knew, could have been a mortal enemy."

"It was my duty to take a man wounded as you were, into my house.

Your injuries could have been fatal," replied his lordship. "How are you feeling now?"

"Strong enough I suppose, I no longer feel any pain."

"I'm glad to hear it. I've been wondering what happened to you. I extracted a few bullets from your chest and your body was covered with wounds that could only have been caused by European weapons. I'd be interested in hearing your story, unless of course, the memory is still too painful."

Despite expecting this question, Sandokan could not help but give a strong start. But he did not give himself away, nor did he lose spirit.

"In truth, I do not know," he replied. "One night several men attacked my ship, boarded it and slaughtered my crew. I am unaware of their identities . . . I did not recognize them . . . I fell into the sea after the first blows, covered in cuts and bruises."

"You were undoubtedly attacked by the Tiger of Malaysia's men," said Lord James.

"Pirates!" exclaimed Sandokan.

"Yes, the Tigers of Mompracem. Three days ago they were conducting raids in the vicinity of this island, but their ship was destroyed by one of our cruisers. Tell me, where were you attacked?"

"Near the Romades."

"You managed to swim all the way here?"

"I grabbed on to some debris. Where did you find me?"

"Laying on the grass, you were delirious. Where were you heading, when you fell under attack?"

"I was on my way to deliver gifts to the Sultan of Varauni, on behalf of my brother."

"Your brother?"

"The Sultan of Shaja."

"You are a Malay prince then!" exclaimed his lordship extending his hand.

After a brief hesitation, Sandokan shook it, masking his feelings of horror.

"Yes, Milord."

"I'm very glad that I have the honour of having you as my guest, and I will do my best to see that you are not bored once your health returns. Then, if you find it agreeable, we can visit the Sultan of Varauni together."

"Certainly, and . . ."

He stopped and cocked his head, as if trying to focus on a sound that was still far off in the distance. The sweet sounds of a mandolin could be heard coming from outside, perhaps the same sweet sounds that he had heard earlier.

"Milord!" he exclaimed excitedly, overcome by a feeling he could not explain. "Who is playing that music?"

"Does it matter, my good prince?" asked his lordship with a smile.

"I do not know . . . but I have a strong desire to see the person that is playing so divinely. You could say that the music is touching my heart. It's inexplicable."

"Wait a few minutes."

He gestured for Sandokan to lie down and went out. The pirate lay back on his pillow, but sprang back up almost immediately. The inexplicable emotion that had gripped him at first had now taken hold of him with even greater intensity. Blood raced furiously through his veins, and his heart beat rapidly.

"What am I feeling?" he wondered. "Is the delirium coming back?"

He had just uttered these words, when his lordship reentered, but this time he was not alone. Behind him there advanced, it seemed barely touching the carpet, a splendid young woman, at whose appearance Sandokan could not hold back an exclamation of surprise and admiration.

She was a young woman of about seventeen; short, slender and elegant, with a waist so thin that one arm would have sufficed to surround it. She had a beautiful face, with cool fresh skin and eyes as blue as the sea. Her blonde hair fell to her shoulders like a shower of gold.

Upon seeing that young woman, the pirate felt himself shaken to the very depths of his soul. His heart, which had previously been beating quickly, now burned. It felt like fire was flowing in his veins.

"Well, my dear prince, what do you think of this attractive young woman?" asked his lordship.

Sandokan did not reply. He remained frozen, like a statue, staring fixedly at the young woman, appearing not to breathe.

"Do you feel ill?" asked his lordship, observing him.

"No! . . . No! . . ." exclaimed the pirate eagerly, trembling.

"Then allow me to present you to my niece, Lady Marianna Guillonk."

"Marianna Guillonk! . . . Marianna Guillonk! . . ." repeated Sandokan excitedly.

"What do you find so strange in my name?" asked the young woman with a smile. "It seems to have given you quite a shock."

Upon hearing that voice, Sandokan started strongly. Never had such a sweet sound caressed his ears, ears that were accustomed only to cannon fire and the death cries of battle.

"Strange? Nothing . . ." he said, his voice slightly altered. "It's just that your name is not new to me."

"Oh!" exclaimed his lordship. "And where have you heard it?"

"I read it a little while ago on the cover of that book over there, and I imagined that the owner had to be a delightful young woman."

"You are joking," said the young lady, blushing. Then changing tone, she asked, "Is it true that pirates gravely injured you?"

"Yes, it's true," replied Sandokan hoarsely. "They beat and injured me, but I'll heal and then woe to those that reduced me to such a state."

"Are you in much pain?"

"No, Milady, and now even less so."

"I hope you get better soon."

"Our prince is quite sturdy," said his lordship, "and I would not be surprised to see him on his feet in ten days or so."

"I hope so," replied Sandokan.

Sandokan, who throughout the discussion had never taken his eyes from the young woman's face, noting that her cheeks, from time to time, would blush ever so slightly, suddenly bolted upright.

"Milady!" he exclaimed.

"Are you all right?" asked the young woman as she drew a little closer to him.

"Tell me, do you bare another name, infinitely sweeter than that of Marianna Guillonk?"

"What?" asked his lordship and the young woman in unison.

"Yes, yes!" exclaimed Sandokan forcefully. "You must be the one the natives call the Pearl of Labuan!"

His lordship jumped back in surprise, a deep frown forming on his face.

"My friend," he said gravely, "How do you know of this, if as you have just told me, you come from a far off Malay peninsula?"

"It can't be possible that this nickname has reached all the way to your far shores," added Lady Marianna.

"I didn't hear it in Shaja," replied Sandokan, knowing full well he had almost given himself away, "but in the Romades, where I disembarked a few days ago. There they spoke of a young woman of incomparable beauty, with eyes of blue, and hair that smelled like the jasmine of Borneo; of a skilled hunter that rode like an Amazon; of a young woman that often at sunset would appear on the shores of Labuan, charming the fishermen of the coasts with a voice that was sweeter than the murmur of a stream. Ah, Milady, I too one day hoped to hear that voice!"

"They attribute such talent to me!" replied the young lady with a laugh.

"Yes, and I see that the men who told me about you were telling the truth!" exclaimed the pirate passionately.

"Flatterer," she said.

"My dear niece," added his lordship, "You will end up bewitching our prince as well."

"I'm sure of it!" exclaimed Sandokan. "And when I return home, I shall tell my compatriots that a young woman has conquered the heart of a man who thought himself invulnerable."

The conversation lasted a little while longer, touching on Sandokan's homeland, on the pirates of Mompracem, on Labuan. Then, night having fallen, his lordship and the young woman retired to their rooms.

When the pirate was finally alone he remained still for a long time, his eyes fixed on the door where the lovely young woman had exited. He seemed anxious and absorbed in deep thought. Perhaps in that heart of his, unaccustomed to feeling tender emotions, there raged a terrible storm.

At one point, Sandokan trembled. A dull moan formed at the bottom of his throat, ready to burst, but his teeth remained tightly clenched, and his lips would not break their seal. He remained that way for several minutes, his brow covered in perspiration, his hands clutching his thick long hair. Then his lips parted and he uttered a name.

"Marianna!"

The pirate could no longer control himself.

"Ah!" he exclaimed almost angrily, wringing his hands. "I think I'm going crazy . . . I think I'm falling in love."

Short Glossary of Nautical Terms

aft—At, in, toward, or close to the stern of a ship.

Barbary Coast—The Mediterranean coastline of North Africa, from Egypt to the Atlantic coastline.

boatswain (also bosun)—A warrant officer or petty officer on a merchant ship who is in charge of the ship's rigging, anchors, cables, and deck crew.

Brethren of the Coast—A self-given title of the Caribbean buccaneers between 1640-1680 who made a pact to discontinue plundering amongst themselves.

brigantine—A small vessel equipped for sailing and rowing often used for piracy, spying and landing. A two-masted sailing ship, square-rigged on both masts.

broadside—The side of a ship above the water between the bow and the quarter.

buccaneer—A pirate, especially one of the freebooters who preyed on Spanish shipping in the West Indies during the 17th century. The buccaneers or " boucaniers" were originally hunters of pigs and cattle on the islands of Hispanola and Tortuga who turned to piracy after having been driven off by the Spanish.

come about—To bring the ship full way around in the wind. Used in general while sailing into the wind, but also used to indicate a swing back into the enemy in combat.

colors—The national flag and or other flags.

Corsair—A privateer: chiefly applied to the authorized cruisers of the Barbary coast. Also a pirate-ship sanctioned by the country to which it belongs.

doubloon—A Spanish gold coin.

filibuster—A pirate, generally English or French, who pillaged the Spanish colonies in the West Indies in the 17th century.

fo'c's'le (or Forecastle)—(1) The section of the upper deck of a ship located at the bow forward of the foremast. (2) A superstructure at the bow of a merchant ship where the crew is housed.

galleon—A large three-masted sailing ship with a square rig and usually two or more decks, used from the 15th to the 17th century especially by Spain as a merchant ship or warship.

galley—A low, flat vessel propelled partly or wholly by oars.

jib—A triangular sail stretching from the foretopmast head to the jib boom and in small craft to the bowsprit or the bow.

jolly boat—A light boat carried at the stern of a larger sailing ship.

Jolly Roger—A pirate flag depicting a skull-and-crossbones. It was an invitation to surrender, with the implication that those who surrendered would be treated well. A red flag indicated "no quarter."

lee—The side away from the direction from which the wind blows.

letter of marque—A letter from a sovereign government granting immunity from piracy laws.

long boat—The largest boat carried by a ship that is used to move heavy or cumbersome loads such as anchors, chains, or ropes.

mainsheet—The rope that controls the angle at which a mainsail is trimmed and set.

man-of-war—A vessel designed and outfitted for battle.

mizzen—A fore-and-aft sail set on the mizzenmast.

mizzenmast—The largest mast located in the mizzen; the third mast or the mast aft of a mainmast on a ship having three or more masts.

pirate—One who robs at sea or plunders the land from the sea without commission from a sovereign nation.

poop deck—The highest deck at the stern of a large ship, usually above the captain's quarters.

port—When facing forward, the left side of the vessel.

privateer—A privateer is a sailor with a letter of marque from a sovereign government granting him immunity from piracy laws.

quarterdeck—The after part of the upper deck of a ship.

schooner—A fore-and-aft rigged sailing vessel having at least two masts, with a foremast that is usually smaller than the other masts.

sheet—A line running from the bottom aft corner of a sail by which it can be adjusted to the wind.

ship of the line—A warship big enough to take her place in the line of battle. A large, square-rigged warship, carrying from 50 to 100 guns on two or more completely armed gun decks.

six pounders—Cannons that throw shot weighing six pounds.

sloop—A single-masted, fore-and-aft-rigged sailing boat with a short standing bowsprit or none at all and a single headsail set from the forestay. This boat was much favored by pirates because of its shallow draught and maneuverability.

Spanish Main—Lands taken by Spain from Mexico to Peru including the Caribbean islands.

square-rigged—Fitted with square sails as the principal sails.

starboard—The right side of the ship when facing the prow.

stern—The rear part of a ship.

strike colors—To lower a ship's flag as a signal of surrender.

topgallant—Of, relating to, or being the mast above the topmast, its sails, or its rigging.

topmast—The mast below the topgallant mast in a square-rigged ship and highest in a fore-and-aft-rigged ship.

topsail—A square sail set above the lowest sail on the mast of a square-rigged ship or a triangular or square sail set above the gaff of a lower sail on a fore-and-aft-rigged ship.

transom—Any of several transverse beams affixed to the sternpost of a wooden ship and forming part of the stern.

yardarm—The main arm across the mast that holds up the sail; either end of a yard of a square sail.

Acknowledgments

Many people made this anthology.

At Thunder's Mouth Press and Avalon Publishing Group:
Thanks to Will Balliett, Nate Knaebel, Linda Kosarin, John Oakes, Michael O'Connor, Susan Reich, David Riedy, Cole Wheeler, and Mike Walters for their support, dedication and hard work. Special thanks to the patient and meticulous Maria Fernandez.

Thanks to Carol Pickering and Taylor Smith for securing permissions for the selections in this book.

At the Portland Public and Thomas Memorial Libraries:
Thanks to the librarians for their assistance in finding and borrowing books from around the country.

Finally, I am grateful to the writers whose work appears in this book.

Permissions

Bibliography

Ballantyne, R. M. *The Coral Island.* New York: Puffin Books, 1994.

Barrie, J. M. *Peter Pan.* New York: Henry Holt and Company, 1987.

Beazley, Julia. "The Uneasy Ghost of Lafitte." Edited by J. Frank Dobie. First appeared in *Legends of Texas,* no. 3. Dallas, TX: Southern Methodist University Press, 1976.

Defoe, Daniel. *The King of Pirates.* New York: Tudor Publishing, 1943.

Driscoll, Charles B. *Doubloons: The Story of Buried Treasure.* New York: Farrar and Rinehart, 1930.

Dumas, Alexandre. *The Count of Monte Cristo.* Mattituck, NY: Amereon, 1976.

Farrère, Claude. *Thomas the Lambkin: Gentleman of Fortune.* Translated by Leo Ongley. New York: E.P. Dutton and Company, 1924.

Harris, Arthur M. *Pirate Tales from the Law.* Boston: Little, Brown and Company, 1923.

Hawes, Charles Boardman. *The Dark Frigate.* New York: Little, Brown and Company, 1971.

Johnson, Charles [Daniel Defoe]. *A General History of the Pyrates.* Mineola, NY: Dover Publications, 1999.

Johnston, Charles H.L. *Famous Privateersmen and Adventurers of the Sea.* Boston: L. C. Page and Company, 1911.

The Marine Research Society. *The Pirates Own Book or Authentic Narratives of the Lives, Exploits, and Executions of the Most Celebrated Sea Robbers,* no. 4. Salem, MA: The Marine Research Society, 1924.

Meader, Stephen W. *The Black Buccaneer.* New York: Harcourt, Brace and Company, 1920.

Pyle, Howard. *Howard Pyle's Book of Pirates.* Compiled by Merle Johnson. New York: Harper and Row Publishers, 1949.

Ransome, Arthur. *Peter Duck: A Treasure Hunt in the Caribbees.* Boston: David R. Godine, Publisher, 1987.

Salgari, Emilio. *Sandokan: The Tigers of Mompracem.* Translated by Nico Lorenzutti. Lincoln, NE: iUniverse, 2003.

Schwartz, Howard. *Elijah's Violin and Other Jewish Fairy Tales.* New York: Harper and Row Publishers, 1983.

Stevenson, Robert Louis. *Treasure Island.* Stamford, CT: Longmeadow Press, 1986.

Thompson, Ruth Plumly. *Pirates in Oz.* New York: Ballantine, 1959.